A DATE WITH DEATH

MARK ROBERTS

A DATE WITH DEATH

HEAD
of ZEUS

Linda, Eleanor and Edgar
Locked in a bond eternally

THE PAST

1977

When her father returned from Oxford Street Maternity Hospital, she didn't know if the new baby was a boy or a girl. She asked how the baby was and the answer came as a cold silence she knew so well, and that made her want to be sick.

Following this, she knew not to ask after her mother.

That night, as she lay in her bed wondering about the new baby and thinking about her mother in the hospital, she heard the telephone ring in the hall downstairs.

She got out of bed and crept four paces – one for every year of her life – to her bedroom door and listened to her father answering the telephone.

'Yeah?'

He sounded at his angriest and, in one slurred word, fear overwhelmed her.

There was a silence as her father listened to the person on the other end.

'If you must know, the little bastard's a boy!'

Bastard?

It was a word she didn't know the meaning of, a word her father used frequently but one she had learned never to repeat again after the slap in the face he'd given her the one and only time she'd said it.

Downstairs, he slammed the receiver in its cradle and she scurried back to her bed, burying herself under the blankets and pretending to be fast asleep.

At some point, and she didn't know when, she drifted into a dreamless sleep.

In the morning, nothing unusual happened.

As usual, at a quarter to eight, her father left the house to run his businesses, leaving her alone with Mrs Doyle, the cleaning lady, who'd been given a few pounds to stay with her but who she'd overheard being given strict instructions not to talk to her and, especially, not to answer any questions about *the little shit*.

Shit?

Same as bastard, she guessed, as she watched the scene in the hall between her father and Mrs Doyle unfold through the struts on the staircase, the memory of his open-handed slap when she'd used the 'b' word causing her cheek to sting at the thought of it.

She confined herself to her bedroom and, as the morning rolled on, she wondered if there was something wrong with her baby brother.

At lunchtime, when the antique grandfather clock chimed twelve in the hall downstairs, the phone rang and Mrs Doyle answered it.

'Hello?' Mrs Doyle sounded as plain scared as she felt.

She listened and heard her father's voice leaking from the telephone receiver. Not talking then, shouting.

'Half past the hour it is then, sir?'

Sir. The name Mrs Doyle had been commanded to call her father.

She stood at the bedroom window but couldn't see the whole of the garden and drive at the front of the house. On her knees, she pushed her toy box to the window and, when she managed to get it there, she climbed up and had a perfect view of what lay below.

She waited and heard the quarter hour chime and guessed that something important was going to happen when the clock sounded the half hour.

In the top left-hand corner of her bedroom window, she saw a fly struggling against the stickiness of a spider's web and watched as the arachnid drifted towards its prey. It wrapped a tight thread around the fly and, before long, the captured bug looked like it was entombed in a mini blanket.

The throb of the engine of her father's Bentley as it slowed to turn into the drive at the front of the house brought her back into the moment.

The gravel grated against the tyres of her father's car and, as he pulled up to a sharp halt, she knew that things were not good.

The driver's door swung open and her father got out of the car, slamming the door shut as he did so. His mouth was moving as he fumbled with his house keys, making his way to the front door.

She watched the Bentley as her father opened the door, stomped inside the house and threw the door back after himself.

Slowly, the back door of the car opened and her mother stepped out on to the gravel. Even from the height of her bedroom window, she could tell that her mother had been crying.

Mother was dressed in a fur coat and hat, wearing flat, black shoes and a green skirt; she knew her father had spent a lot of money on the clothes because he often repeated the same phrase to her mother – sometimes in anger, sometimes not – *your outfits are costing me an arm and a fucking leg.*

Mother leaned into the back of the car and, after a few moments, she emerged with a small wicker basket, which she carried towards the front door.

She looked down from her bedroom window into the top end of the basket and saw a ball of pink flesh. The baby's face. Her brother. Her brand-new baby brother. All the uneasiness rose from her and was replaced by a sense of awe and wonder.

In her head, a picture she had seen of Jesus walking on the water flashed through her memory and, as she watched her mother bringing the baby closer to the house, she said to herself in a brittle whisper, 'It's like a miracle...'

The house was filled with the sound of the doorbell as her mother rang to be let in.

'Don't fucking talk to her, Mrs Doyle! Don't say anything nice about the baby or I'll fire you on the spot!'

'Yes, sir.'

She crept at speed to the top of the stairs and watched Mrs Doyle walk to the front door, her stomach dancing as a net of butterflies was unleashed inside her.

Mrs Doyle opened the front door, stood to one side as her mother stepped into the house with her baby brother in the basket, and closed the door.

Her father walked past her mother and the baby towards the door and flung it open again.

'Where are you going?' asked her mother.

'I'm going to register its birth at Brougham Terrace and then I'm going back to work.'

Her mother placed the basket down on the ground and lifted the baby out.

'Look at him. Look... at him! He's the spitting image of you,' said her mother.

'Not looking, not listening!'

On his way out, her father closed the door with the same sour energy that he had opened it.

Her mother looked at Mrs Doyle, who was slipping her arms into the same coat she had worn forever.

'Mrs Doyle...' said her mother.

Mrs Doyle shook her head and opened the front door to leave.

As Mrs Doyle left, her mother placed her baby brother back in the basket and took off her fur coat. The baby started to cry and her mother said, 'All right, all right.'

Her mother pulled up her sweater and, picking up the baby, fastened him to her left breast, walking around the hall and rocking him.

The baby stopped crying and her mother walked out of the hall and deeper into the house.

She listened and through the walls of the house came a sound she knew very well.

As her mother fed the new baby, the grandfather clock ticked, hitting the air with a stern metal finger.

And beneath this there was that other sound.

In the morning room, her mother wept.

DAY ONE

WEDNESDAY, 1ST DECEMBER 2021

CATOPTROPHOBIA

FEAR OF MIRRORS

1
6.44 am

The tide went out and death came in.

Detective Chief Inspector Eve Clay walked along the mudflats of the River Mersey towards the remains of a human being, guiding herself forward in the pre-dawn darkness with a torch that sliced the freezing gloom before her.

Walking further away from the concrete promenade that followed the twisting path of the river, Clay felt her rubber boots being sucked into the thick silt beneath her feet.

Tall and slim with long brunette hair snatched back in a ponytail, Clay looked ahead at the random pattern of jagged black rocks and the dead person beyond them but knew there was no mileage in using them as stepping stones. Being floored on the mud with a broken ankle was simply not an option.

Clay glanced back at Otterspool Promenade.

Beneath a pair of arc lamps, Clay saw the marked police car and the constables who had discovered the body. Beneath the artificial light, rain raged in the wind and into the deluge a black mortuary van pulled up alongside Detective Sergeant Gina Riley, a small, rotund woman with fair hair and a dreamy expression that hid her quicksilver mind. Riley raised an arm, acknowledging Clay.

Three supporting officers climbed down the concrete steps from the railings and on to the riverbed.

She carried on, stepping as lightly as she could and shivering in the ice-cold wind, her eyes fixed on the body washed up on a rock at the centre of a large pool of water.

Female, thought Clay, as she concentrated on the body that was becoming clearer with each step forward. *On your back. Naked.*

A foghorn sounded in the distance, its moan like the dying breath of a mythical beast.

Young. Eyes wide open and startled, the gate to your soul exposed to the elements.

In her head, a clock started ticking, taking her into the recent past and a crime scene outside Liverpool that she hadn't been directly involved in but one she remembered clearly.

Number two, she thought. *But a first time outing in Liverpool for the perpetrator.*

She looked back and saw Detective Sergeant Karl Stone, a tall thin man with prematurely grey hair slicked back, at the head of an advancing human triangle, the base of which consisted of Detective Sergeant Terry Mason and Sergeant Paul Price from Scientific Support.

A seagull landed close to the woman's body, looked it up and down with jet-black eyes.

Clay quickened her pace in the direction of the body, deeper into the freezing mist that masked the Wirral Peninsula on the opposite bank of the River Mersey.

The destruction to the dead woman's face was now clear to see.

Her eyeballs poked out of the sockets and her swollen and bitten tongue jutted out of her mouth.

Definitely number two.

Clay recalled an image from a local television news broadcast that had quickly progressed into the national media.

Sandra O'Day, a slim blonde woman in her mid twenties, slaughtered in the late summer twenty or so miles away in Warrington.

Clay looked down at what was left of the woman in front of her and thought, *yes, the same again.*

Where her shoulder-length hair should have hung down in sorrowful clumps, there was nothing except the side of her head, her left ear missing, leaving a pitiful hole in her face.

Clay stood where the seagull had just flown up from and looked at the body from the feet upwards.

Her feet were blue but there was no apparent damage to them.

'Anything?' called Stone.

'She's not the perpetrator's first. I'm guessing she was a natural blonde,' replied Clay.

'How do you know?'

Her legs were slim and long, just like the other victim she knew of, and her face was a knot of purple muscle.

'He's skinned her face and scalped her.'

In the sky to the east, the first crooked finger of muddy light appeared, pointing down in the direction of the docks at Garston, and reminded her of just how close to home she was.

Clay pictured her son, Philip, asleep in his bed and her husband, Thomas, getting up in their bedroom, ready for the start of another day without her because she had been drawn away by the imperative of work.

She dismissed any notion of home as her eyes paused at the surreal sight of the woman's limp hands, fingers floating strangely in the shallow pool around them, as if there was a semblance of life still in her.

What's he doing with the part of you he removed? she asked herself, taking a series of deep breaths to bottle the sour emotion the question provoked and the bitter taste in her mouth that accompanied it.

Stone arrived just behind Clay.

'Last August in Warrington,' replied Clay. 'Sandra O'Day. She was blonde and in her mid twenties. She was dumped in the River Irwell after being missing for ten or eleven days, scalped and with her face removed.'

They stood in silence over the woman's body, the dark air around them studded with flashes of light as Sergeant Paul Price took a series of photographs.

Clay stooped, pointed her torch at the base of the woman's neck and up to her jawline, and saw the place where the perpetrator had cut away her scalp and face.

She pushed into her memory to recall the name given to the killer by the tabloid press when he'd first struck in Warrington but it eluded her.

'What do you want me to do?' asked Stone.

'Stay right here, Karl. Oversee the APTs and Scientific Support.'

Detective Sergeant Terry Mason walked past the body and looked at the mudflats as Sergeant Paul Price continued taking pictures of the woman's body.

'What are you thinking, Terry?' asked Clay.

'I'm thinking this is the crime scene from Hell,' replied Mason. 'If there was any evidence around the body it's probably been washed away and could be anywhere between the Pier Head and the Irish Sea. Sorry to be so negative, but that's the reality of it.'

Clay stood up and, taking out her mobile phone, dialled Detective Sergeant Gina Riley on the shore.

'I can see you from the promenade, Eve. What's happening?'

'I think the victim may well be from Liverpool.'

'OK?'

Clay heard a sliver of doubt beneath the neutral tone of Riley's voice.

'How do I know? A woman's body was found in water in Warrington earlier this year. If this is what I'm pretty sure it is, our victim's a girl local to *us*. Either on the Wirral or somewhere within a mile of here in the South Liverpool suburbs, Aigburth, Mossley Hill or the Sefton Park district.'

'I know the case you mean. Warrington Police got nothing on the perpetrator. It was like she'd been abducted, murdered and dumped by the Invisible Man.'

With deepening dismay, Clay remembered the same, looked at the pool of water surrounding the body and the rock that propped her up.

'Gina, we need to know who this is. Can you please get in touch with Barney Cole and ask him to trawl through missing persons, Liverpool, recent weeks, female, blonde, twenty to forty years of age.'

'I'll do that right now, Eve.'

'And line up victim liaison. I'm ninety-nine per cent certain we're going to be breaking the worst news possible to her next of kin before today's out. Thank you, Gina.'

Clay closed down the call.

She called, 'Paul?'

Sergeant Price stopped taking pictures and looked at Clay.

'I'm going to lift her head. I want you to take pictures of the back of her head, please.'

Clay slid the fingers of both hands between the muddy rock and the back of the victim's head. The backs of her hands felt grainy and wet as they slid along the mud, and her fingers sensed the contours of the skull beneath the muscle.

'I'm sorry,' said Clay beneath her breath as she lifted the woman's head from the rock. She looked at the back of her skull, at the thin wet muscles covering the bone and the skin at the base of her throat.

'Paul, place a light on the skin beneath her jawline, on her throat.'

As torchlight hit skin, Clay saw the rough smudges around her throat and said, 'Strangulation, same MO as Warrington.'

In a handful of seconds, she went through the killer's logic: *Strangulation, up close and personal, and full of sadistic joy, feeling the life drain out through his fingertips and thumbs.*

Clay lowered the woman's head back into the water and noticed that Detective Sergeant Terry Mason looked like a man seeking for a wafer-thin slice of meaning in a storm of chaos.

'Terry?' she called.

'It's literally and metaphorically a fucking washout, Eve.'

It was only the third time in fifteen years she had heard Mason swear. She looked at the mortuary van on the promenade.

'The Anatomical Pathology Technicians, Terry?'

'They might as well come down and pick her up right now.'

'I'll make that call, Eve,' said Stone.

In the sky, the finger of hazy light was widening, stretching out at either end, and Clay faced a grim conclusion.

'Karl, come on, there's nothing we can do here. I need to talk to the constables who found her.'

She walked back towards the concrete steps that she had just climbed down.

'Terry, as soon as the ATPs leave here, call me. I'll meet them at the mortuary as she arrives there.'

Clay took out her iPhone and dialled Detective Constable Barney Cole. As he connected the call in the incident room at Trinity Road police station, Clay heard his voice but was lost in the woman's dead eyes staring from the raw muscles that once opened her missing lids.

'Eve... Eve? Eve, are you there, Eve?'

'Barney, when you've finished your trawl through missing persons, I need you to contact Warrington Police. Ask them for everything they've got on Sandra O'Day, the River Irwell victim, August, this year. I need to speak to the SIO on that case. Roll the ball as fast as you can, Barney.'

2

7.15 am

From the front of her car, Clay watched two police constables walking past the larger-than-life statue of a bright orange bull looking in the direction of the River Mersey, a huge art installation aptly named Sitting Bull.

I wish you could speak, Sitting Bull, thought Clay. *And those blind and unblinking eyes of yours could see.*

She smiled briefly at the memory of a warm day last spring when she and Thomas had helped Philip to climb up Sitting Bull's back, how intoxicated with happiness her son had been and how bleakly anxious she had felt, fearing in case he fell down on to the concrete below.

Clay heard a tapping at the window and snapped back into the moment. She opened the window and weighed up the constables: PC Wendy White, late thirties, a Teflon veteran, and PC Thomas Ruddock, early twenties, rattled by what he'd seen, gazing at Clay as if she were some mythical creature.

'Get yourselves into the back please. And thank you for what you've done here.'

As they settled into the back of Clay's car, they brought in the coldness of the morning, and Clay hit the overhead light to dispel the bleakness of the new day.

She turned, looking each of them directly in the eyes as she introduced herself.

'I'm DCI Eve Clay...'

'I know, I know you are,' said PC Ruddock. 'And can I just say...'

'All right, Tom,' said PC White. 'Listening time.'

'Thank you, PC White,' said Clay, drinking in the hint of a smile in the female constable's steely eyes. 'I'll begin with you, PC White. And then I'll ask you questions, PC Ruddock. OK?'

'That's good,' said PC White.

'Wendy. Please go right back to the beginning of what happened. Tell me everything.'

'We were patrolling Riverside Drive from midnight onwards. There's been a spate of burglaries on the houses across the way from the Festival Gardens, thieves breaking into houses through the early hours. That was our brief,' said PC White. 'Stop any cars and pedestrians heading away from the estate.

'We were driving back from the tip at the bottom of Jericho Lane for the umpteenth time when a call came through from switchboard. There'd been a call from a man on Otterspool Promenade around the Mersey Road area. He said he thought he'd seen a dead body in the river close to Sitting Bull.

'I turned the car round and high-tailed it to the location. I had to come off road and across the grass and down the straight narrow path leading to the prom.

'We went up and down from the gate at the Cressington Promenade end to the path leading up to the Otterspool pub. There was no sign of anyone. We slowed right down and used the headlights to look for blood but there wasn't a drop on the concrete. I was convinced it was a hoax call and, in my own head, I worked out it had come from the Riverside Drive burglars, pulling us away from their turf.

'I decided we needed to use our headlights to look into the river. The tide was out. That was good. Tom saw something in the mud.'

'Tom?' said Clay.

'We had the headlights full on to the riverbed. From the corner of my eye, I saw something light-coloured against the darkness. I thought it was, like, maybe, an animal, a washed-up animal. The caller got it wrong maybe. I said to Wendy, we need to check this out, there's something in the mud. We got as close as we could to the railings and hit the lights fully on in the direction of... the thing. I got out and walked up to the railings. I saw flesh tones and the shape of a body. It was a naked human body. I called but there was no reply. The victim looked stone dead. There was no way he or she was alive.'

'I asked Tom to climb over the railings and down the concrete steps so he could get a look from ground level,' said White.

Clay saw the rising emotion in the young constable's eyes.

'I still feel emotional when I see a murder victim,' said Clay.

Surprise tripped into his eyes. 'You do?'

'Whatever you've got inside right now, bottle it. Never lose sympathy for the victim. Go on, Tom.'

'I took a torch from the boot of the car and got down to the mud by the steps. I managed to get closer via the rocks in the mud. Wendy called to me not to get any closer. There was something wrong with the head. I could see from the shape of the body that the victim was female.' He looked at his colleague. 'There was no chance of saving her. And Wendy said we didn't want to contaminate any evidence if there was any.'

'That's when we called in for help,' concluded White.

'Have either of you got anything to add?' asked Clay.

'No,' said White as Ruddock shook his head.

'Thank you for this, you've done very well, both of you.' She looked directly at PC Ruddock. 'The tide's due back in within the hour. She could have been lost to us for ever.'

'Yes, Tom,' said White. 'Well done. Deals don't come much bigger than this.'

Clay could feel the glow of PC Ruddock's pride and the maternal affection just beneath PC White's tough exterior.

'You didn't see any sign of anyone else in the vicinity?' checked Clay.

'No,' said White. 'We stayed in place to protect the body.'

Clay got out of the car and opened the back door on PC White's side. As the constables got out, she asked, 'You're based at Admiral Street, right?'

'Right.'

'I'll be in touch with Chief Superintendent Frankins. Great work.'

As they walked away, a spark ignited a flame inside her head and, where memory had recently failed her, she recalled the lazy, summer drama of the tabloid press.

'The killer has a name of sorts. The killer is human but the name isn't.'

It came to her like a curse through the river-bound fog.
'The name of the killer is The Ghoul.'

3

8.44 am

Alone in the incident room on the top floor of Trinity Road police station, Detective Constable Barney Cole, muscular and on the verge of middle age, looked at the landline phone on his desk and saw that half an hour had passed since the duty superintendent in Warrington had told him she'd get back to him within ten to twenty minutes.

Cole looked down at the map of the north-west of England spread across his desk and willed the phone to ring.

He picked up the black marker pen he'd already used to make a dot on the map. Warrington. A black dot on the River Irwell near the Moore Nature Reserve, dated 08/2021.

Cole looked at the map and stopped at the point at Otterspool Promenade where he'd learned a second body had been discovered, deposited on the mud. He dotted the place and dated it 12/2021.

Cole tried to visualize lines between the two highlighted places to establish the beginning of some pattern but he just couldn't see one.

He heard the door to the incident room open, continued gazing at the map, saw the blue of the water, and wondered, with grim certainty that it would happen, where the next body would show up.

'Planning your holidays?' asked Detective Sergeant Karl Stone, heading into the kitchen area in the corner of the open-plan room.

'Something like that, Karl,' replied Cole, taking the marked map to the glass noticeboard and putting it up with Blu-Tack. 'You sound cold, matey.'

'It's bloody freezing down at the prom. Do you want a coffee?'

'Get by the radiator. I'll make it for you.'

Dressed in a black overcoat that looked three sizes too big for him, to Cole's eyes, Stone was the human incarnation of a vulture.

As Stone headed for the warmth and Cole to the kitchen, their paths crossed.

'Any more from Otterspool Promenade?' asked Cole.

'Young female victim. Water. Forensic nightmare. It's a repeat performance.'

'How far from the promenade itself was she discovered?'

Cole spooned coffee into two cups, heard the rising rumble of the kettle.

'It took Eve two and a half minutes to get from the shore to the body but it was like she was walking in quicksand. I'd estimate sixty metres.'

Cole glanced over his shoulder as he poured hot water into the cups. Stone had his back to him and was looking at the map.

'I've got pictures from the scene,' said Cole. 'But what was she like in reality?'

'She looked half-human,' said Stone. 'From the neck up, she looked like someone had grafted an alien head on to a human body. I won't forget it as long as I live.'

As Cole walked over to Stone, his sympathy for his colleague intensified, knowing that he had a wife and two sons to go home to and all that awaited Stone at the end of a bad day was an empty flat and a history of broken relationships to dwell on.

Cole handed Stone a cup of coffee and looked out as daylight oozed over the Mersey Estuary, in the direction of Warrington.

He sat down at his desk, picked up a printed-out image of the Otterspool Promenade victim's skinned face and scalped head and was glad he hadn't been like Stone, an eyewitness to the carnage.

The phone on Cole's desk rang out. He snatched up the receiver, hit speakerphone and turned on record on his iPhone.

'DC Barney Cole speaking, Merseyside Constabulary.'

'Duty Superintendent Kate Johnson, Warrington Constabulary.'

'Thank you for getting back to me, Superintendent Johnson.'

'I'm going to send you everything we've got on our River Irwell victim. I'll send you a test email. Her name was Sandra O'Day. She was reported missing on August 1st and showed up dead on August 11th. The pathologist said she'd been dead for four or five days before she'd been discovered in the river.'

A bell rang in Cole's head as he went on to his emails on his laptop, and watched as Superintendent Johnson's test email came through.

'How are we doing, Barney?'

'All good,' said Cole, replying *Thank you* to the email.

'Who's the SIO at your end?' asked Superintendent Johnson.

'DCI Eve Clay.'

There was a brief silence.

'Oh, that's such bad news for The Ghoul. And good news for us. Tell her I'm calling a meeting of everyone involved in the case. The SIO our end's DCI Dave Ferguson.'

'You've just answered the question I was going to ask you next.' As he spoke, Cole wrote the name Dave Ferguson on his notepad. 'DCI Clay has asked me to ask you if DCI Ferguson can make it over to Trinity Road police station so we can pick his brains.'

'I'll contact him for you right now.'

Cole listened. In Warrington Police Station on Arpley Street, a door opened and a voice spoke with rising urgency.

'I've got to go, Barney. We'll be in touch.'

As Cole opened the first email and the PDF attached to it, he felt Stone's presence at his back, moving over him with slow, steady stealth.

The screen of his laptop was filled with an image from the River Irwell from the tail end of the previous summer, a picture of Sandra O'Day's remains, her bloated body half in the water, the top half caught up on the bank, a dead woman without a face or a scalp.

'What does he do with their faces and scalps?' asked Stone.

'Time will tell,' replied Cole, focusing on the next job Clay had asked him to do as she stood in the mud on the bottom of the River Mersey: finding out if any women from Liverpool in their twenties to forties, blondes to begin with, had been reported missing in the last two weeks.

4

8.51 am

Edgar McKee turned back the left-hand sleeve of his white tunic and saw that it was getting on for nine o'clock. The time was near for two significant arrivals into the Stanley Abattoir.

The smudge of a cheap and ill-advised tattoo chipped into his line of vision and, not for the first time, he regretted having invaded his own flesh with ink and needle.

The noise of the machinery revving up for the day's labour was deadened by the red ear defenders sitting either side of the mesh that kept his hair where it should be and off the flesh of the beasts he had to process that day. He scratched his head, felt the velcro-like hooks of the hairs on his scalp irritate his fingertips.

He looked out of the tall window overlooking Old Swan and saw the cattle truck turning into the abattoir compound from Prescot Road.

Breathing in the disinfectant that the night cleaners had doused the walls and the floors with, and the chemicals used to sanitise the equipment from the beginning to the end of the killing and carving process, he could smell yesterday's butchery beneath the surface, and beneath that the butchery of decades.

As the cattle truck backed in to the reception area, Edgar removed his ear defenders and listened hard to what lay beneath the immediate noises around him.

He closed his eyes and pictured the scene, the job he had first worked on in his early days in the abattoir, the meet and greet role.

The tailgate opened and down the ramp came the first of the dumb cattle, eyes accustomed to open spaces and barns confused by the brick and concrete reception area. They lowed as the procession of flesh was sucked into the abattoir's gaping jaws.

Edgar felt his pulse thicken and his heart beat faster as memory collided with the sound of the present, the cattle's disharmonious voices in the distance beneath the immediate and insistent thrum of the machinery close at hand.

The leading cow moved into a bottleneck from which there was no turning back, the head of the cow behind her nudging her tail. Onwards and with no way back, the confusion in their eyes turned to fear and panic, and the emotion in the herd was contagious, registering in their voices, the lowing translating into blind terror, the sounds of extreme anguish bottled up in the confined space in which there was only one way to go: forward.

Edgar imagined the distant sound and tilted his head to gain a better perspective of the beasts on death row as they realised what was coming next.

Her eyes were wide, nostrils flaring as the stun gun was placed against her forehead. The first one he would always remember, his first one, the beast with no name and even less hope. He gripped the stun gun and pulled the trigger, felt the kick run up his arm like mercury in his veins.

He looked out at the staff car park, picked out his white Ford Transit van positioned between a worn-out Vauxhall and a no-hope Honda, both of them dwarfed by the height and width of his vehicle.

'Edgar?'

The sound of his name melted all other sounds, near and far, into one euphoric blur.

'Yes, Neil?' he replied to his supervisor, eyeing up the tall young man standing alongside him, a lock of white-blond hair poking out from the net on his head, and looking straight ahead with a Christ-like gaze, as if seeing a messianic vision that was uniquely for him and him alone.

Neil clapped a hand on the young man's shoulder, bringing him back from the place he inhabited in his head.

'Introduce yourself to Edgar,' said Neil.

The young man scanned around Edgar's eyes, avoiding looking directly into them.

'My name is Wren but I cannot fly. Robin Wren. My mother had a sense of humour and a passion for ornithology. I dislike being called Robin. Wren will do.'

Edgar felt his heart turn to lead but smiled into Wren's eyes, wishing to impress his supervisor with a gloss of empathy.

'My name is Edgar McKee but I cannot open the door. My mother had no sense of humour to speak of and as for her passions, I've no idea as I didn't know her one little bit. You can call me Edgar.'

Wren nodded and, as if from nowhere, he smiled with his eyes but the rest of his face remained set and calm. He laughed, three steady, robotic beats of distilled amusement.

'I get it now. You are a McKee but you cannot open the door.'

'OK, son,' said Neil. 'Go and stand over there for a minute. I need to talk to Edgar.'

As Wren walked away into space, he mimed turning a key in a lock and Edgar wondered at the child-like behaviour of a late adolescent in the early stages of manhood.

Neil placed his gloved hand on Edgar's shoulder and even though he took it as an infringement of his privacy and his natural instinct was to stiffen, he maintained a relaxed posture.

'I really am grateful to you for taking my son under your wing, Edgar.'

'I'm sure he's just a nice lad in need of a little guidance.'

'He couldn't get an apprenticeship anywhere else. God knows I tried just about everywhere. No one would have him even though he's got an IQ of 143. It's his autism holding him back. I had to fight to get him taken on here as an apprentice but as soon as I managed it you were the first person I thought of to place him with.'

'Thank you.' Edgar looked at Wren and then at his father. 'First impression, Neil. He seems rather talkative for someone with autism,' said Edgar.

'Some autistic kids clam up,' said Neil. 'Some are chatterboxes. Some are in between. Wren's a chatterbox. It's not only that you're head and shoulders the best at your job in the whole abattoir, it's your temperament,' he added. 'There's not many people who've got the patience to look after an autistic kid.'

'I'll teach him as best I can, Neil. I'll protect him from the loudmouths in this shithole. If anyone wants to get at Wren, they'll have to get past me first.'

Neil held out his hand and Edgar shook with him. He read the elongated glance that Neil threw at him as he eyed him up, drank in the silent admiration of his muscular bulk.

'Don't worry about him. He'll learn a trade and I'll build his confidence. Leave him with me. I know you're busy.'

'Thank you, Edgar.'

Edgar watched his supervisor walk away and turned to face Wren's back.

'Are you ready, Wren?'

Wren turned in what felt like slow motion.

'You look tired, Edgar.' Wren's eyeballs shifted left and dithered right at speed, again and again. 'You look tired. Very tired.'

Edgar pictured the scene in the bolting room. The world around him disappeared and, for a moment, all that he could see were cattle queuing up to die.

'Wren, I am as fresh as a meadowlark at dawn.'

Bang. Down she goes. Lights out. Slump.

The reality of the end of all sentient life in a bitter nutshell.

'Follow me,' smiled Edgar. 'I can tell, we're going to be great mates.'

5

9.28 am

Driving past the University of Liverpool's nursery on Grove Street, on the way to the Royal Hospital's mortuary, Clay felt a tangle of nostalgia for the time when she dropped Philip off there, before he went up to big school.

Mothers and fathers walked hand in hand with small boys and girls, and all the children were well dressed against the cold and the rain.

Her mind somersaulted to the woman on the mudflats of the River Mersey and, at the red light at the junction of Grove Street and Myrtle Street, she whispered to herself, 'I bet your parents used to wrap you up warm on cold winter mornings like this.'

On her dashboard, Clay's iPhone rang out and when she saw COLE on display, she connected and went to speakerphone, before heading away from the green light.

'Barney?' She was filled with a mixture of curiosity and trepidation.

'There's only one missing person who fits your description for the woman on the Mersey mudflats.'

'Go on?'

Clay turned left on to Pembroke Place, waiting for Cole to speak as he turned over paper on his desk.

'Her name's Annie Boyd. She's twenty-five years old.'

'Barney, does she live in a two-mile radius of the place she was found?'

'She did. 358 Melbreck Road, not far from West Allerton station.'

'Are you one hundred per cent certain it's her?'

'She's a teacher. One hundred per cent attendance for work. But she hasn't been in to work or heard of since she left the school last Thursday. I looked at the pictures Mason and Price sent me from the River Mersey of the dead woman. She's got a mole on her upper left arm the size of a two pence piece. On her upper right arm there's a tattoo of a bluebird in flight. Her parents supplied us with an image of their daughter on holiday in Crete when they reported her missing. She's wearing a sleeveless white blouse. Annie Boyd's got the exact same mole and the exact same tattoo, both in the right places.'

'Email me close shots of her mole and the tattoo. Close shots that give away absolutely nothing else about the condition of her body.'

'Leave it with me.'

She continued on to London Road, felt swamped in the dense traffic that was slowed down by the rain.

'And Barney, find out who her dentist was. Ask them to drop everything and make it to the mortuary with Annie's dental records. Good job, well done. Thank you.'

As she spoke, Clay worked out in her mind the quickest route back from the mortuary to Melbreck Road.

'Anything else, Eve?'

'Same as ever. Keep me posted of anything that comes in, Barney.'

She disconnected the call and, stuck at the lights, prepared herself to look again at Annie Boyd's disfigured body in the mortuary, just over a hundred metres away. In the well of her recent memory, the young woman looked up at her into torchlight from the mud of the Mersey and the effect of her dead eyes made the soles of Clay's feet tingle with pinpricks of heat.

Your eyes, thought Clay with a sorrowful heart, *are as dead as you and all your dreams of life and love and happiness.*

6

9.44 am

Norma Maguire looked into the round compact mirror sitting in the palm of her hand at her only good facial feature. Her lips. She drew a scarlet lipstick across the surface of her top lip and was glad it was the only part of her face she could see in the glass.

She refreshed the coating of lipstick on her lower lip and checked that her recently whitened teeth were not stained red.

There was only one way to do it. Small but tortuous steps.

Norma looked at herself in tiny but painful sections, tracking down the lifelong hopeless cause: she was vile to look at.

Her face was lopsided, constructed of two halves that clearly didn't make a whole. Her left eye was a centimetre higher than the right, which stared at a distinctly odd angle into space, away from its dull and lifeless partner. Within the frame of her ravaged skin, her nose looked like it had been built by the hand of a malicious child and she recalled for the thousand and thousandth time the overall effect of her despicable face: horrid.

Happy birthday, Norma...

Over a chasm of nearly four decades, she heard her mother's words as she handed her the mirror now in her hand. Mother had wrapped it in gold paper and presented it to her on the morning of her thirteenth birthday.

She watched her mother as she walked out of the large front room, drawn by the ringing of the phone into the cavernous hall outside.

Her mother's voice danced as she spoke, her tone masterful, small words that seemed to fill the whole house as she answered the call.

Norma picked up the only photograph on her desk.

Mother. Aged thirty or thereabouts. Hair tied up in intricate patterns in a fashion from a classical age. Beautiful. Poised and ladylike. Dressed in a white gown, thin straps on her shapely bare shoulders. Smiling easily into the eye of the camera. Norma placed the framed photograph back on her desk.

Tap. Tap. Tap.

She made out the shape of the person outside her office door through the frosted glass.

Slim, exquisitely slim. Model tall. Young as the rosy dawn.

'Come on in, Fran,' said Norma, placing her little mirror and the Christian Dior lipstick back in her Gucci handbag.

The door opened slowly and Francesca Christie stepped into the office. The smile on her face lit up her pretty features but her body language was riddled with nervous tension.

'You wanted to see me, Norma?' asked Francesca as she drifted towards the chair on the other side of Norma's desk.

'Yes, yes, yes, I do want to see you.'

Norma indicated the seat and Francesca sat down.

'Very well done, Fran, on closing down the deal on the Elm Hall Drive property. Every other estate agent on Allerton Road who failed, *failed miserably,* to offload that *nightmare house* will be kicking themselves.'

Norma watched the stiffness in Francesca's shoulders ease and the darkness behind the smile on her face fade.

'Maybe, Fran, we should have called it Nightmare on Elm Hall Drive.'

Norma laughed and Francesca joined in but she knew the young estate agent didn't understand the joke. 'It's a reference to an old American horror movie, Fran. Just as a matter of interest, do you like horror movies?'

'I'm more into romantic comedies.'

'Me too, me too.'

Norma processed the information Francesca had offered and remembered the What's On page in the local free paper that she advertised her properties in.

'Why? Why have you called me in, Norma?'

'So, how's your newly repaired laptop serving you, Fran?'

'It's been great, Norma. No problems at all. The virus that was driving me mad – it's sorted.'

'Glad to hear it, Fran.' She loved the cut-back sound of her employee's name, the music of abbreviation.

'I do have a viewing in half an hour...'

'Yes, yes, yes, I know you're busy. I get that.'

'Then...?'

'I'm worried about you, Fran. You know I don't have children of my own and you know I'm old enough to be your mother...'

'Where? Where's this going, Norma?'

Norma nodded.

'I'm not going to beat around the bush. When your laptop went away for repair, I received a report back from the IT technician who had a good old root through your history in the process.'

'I'm sorry. I didn't know the IT technician had the authority to do that.'

'Fran, please don't tell me you didn't read our IT policy when you joined us.'

'I did. Of course I did...'

'Then you must have forgotten that any company technology we use, laptops, iPhones, whatever, is subject to investigation. I haven't invaded your civil liberties. Ultimately it's *my* property you've been using and I have every right to make sure that my *property* isn't being abused.'

Norma pushed a thin card file towards Francesca.

'Do you want to open it or shall I tell you what's in there?'

As Francesca opened the flap and slid out a small sheaf of papers, Norma watched the colour rise in her throat and chase up the channels of her unblemished skin to her cheeks, saw her face flood with pure embarrassment.

'I'm sorry, Norma.'

She placed the papers back inside the file and closed the cover.

'Fran, you've been going on to internet dating sites during office hours. During my time.'

'It was only during my breaks.'

'The times and dates of your many visits to these sites are listed in that file.'

Norma took a tissue from the box on her desk and handed it to Francesca.

'Don't get upset, Fran. I haven't brought you in here to read the riot act to you.'

Francesca made eye contact with Norma.

'Then why have you brought me in?'

'Come here...'

Norma turned her wheelchair around to gaze out of the window overlooking the junction of Allerton Road and Penny Lane, the curve of her back turned on her employee. As she did so, she recalled a time, over thirty years ago, before the accident, when she had no need of a wheelchair and what wet sand felt like on the soles of her feet and the pure magic of swimming in the Irish Sea off Crosby Beach.

'I'm worried about you,' said Norma. 'These internet dating sites are a menace. Everything the IT specialist told me that you'd posted about yourself was accurate and true. Is everyone else, these men you've been communicating with, are they all above board and honest? I think that's highly unlikely. Don't you?'

'I'm *careful*.'

'I suppose the woman whose body was washed up in Warrington in the summer would have said she was *careful* too... You look puzzled. You didn't hear about it?'

'No.'

'He scalped her and took the skin from her face. According to the police, she met him on an internet dating site, Pebbles On The Beach.'

The tense silence in the room was counterpointed by the hydraulics of a passing double-decker bus beneath the window, and in the sky above, rotating blades chopping the air as the police helicopter travelled in their direction down Church Road.

'I heard a report on Radio Merseyside this morning on my way in to work. There's another body been found closer to home. Otterspool Promenade.'

Norma watched the helicopter as it tracked a stolen car burning a red light and screaming across the junction into Penny Lane and in the direction of Sefton Park, sirens following and a trail of chaos in its wake.

'I can instruct you not to use my IT equipment on my time to go on these sites, but I can't do anything about what you do between the hours of five in the afternoon and nine in the morning when you're at home. Fran, I would hate anything horrible to happen to you. Do not put yourself at risk like this.'

'I'm sorry, Norma. Since Dad died and Patrick walked out on me... I'm OK when I'm selling properties... it's just...'

Francesca looked at Norma, and the words poured from her.

'There's a Dad-shaped hole in one piece of your heart and a Patrick-shaped gap in another part,' said Norma. 'Come over here, Fran.'

Norma felt the side of Francesca's thigh brush against her arm and drank in her sweet natural perfume.

'You're looking for a good man, Fran?'

'There are good men out there, Norma. I just don't seem to meet them.'

'You think you're going to find a quality man on Pebbles On The Beach?'

'I hope so. Pebbles On The Beach is for people who want commitment. It's for men and women who want marriage, children and a future. That's why some people sneer at it. Because it's seen as old-fashioned. Well, I am old-fashioned and I'm not afraid to admit that.'

'Be careful, Fran. There are devils out there masquerading as nice, wholesome men.'

She glanced up at the way Fran's naturally blonde hair hung down on either side of her face and saw great sadness in her eyes.

'What can you see, Fran?' Norma pointed out of the window and down at the pavement.

'People.'

'Men?'

'Yes.'

'If you met a man, say, on the street, you mightn't think it but from the moment you clapped eyes on him, you'd be reading his body language and receiving chemical information about him that would make you either want to get involved with him or run a mile. You don't get that incredibly personal and powerful information from the internet. Promise me you'll stop going on to these dating sites.'

'I promise you.'

'There are other ways to meet men. Nice men. Men who won't hurt or harm you.'

'How though? Nowadays...'

Norma looked out of the window and saw the police helicopter circling the space around Penny Lane.

'Well, would you look at that now? That's it.' Norma clapped her hands together. 'You could always steal a car and get arrested by a strapping police helicopter pilot. Now, wouldn't that make for a zany rom com?'

Norma looked at Francesca, whose eyes were fixed on a point in the distance, and said, 'That's better. You're smiling.

I'm joking with you. Now go wash your face and sell some houses for me.'

At the door of Norma's office, Francesca stopped and turned on hearing, 'Fran? *Make Mine The Moon*. Brad Howard and Elaine Tomeski. It's on at the Odeon in Liverpool One. I think I might treat myself. Are you interested?'

'I've seen it.' Not a beat of hesitation. 'They were better in *The Fourth Wish*.'

'Fair enough.'

'Norma, I really am sorry about using your laptop for non-work-related purposes.'

'Don't apologise. Just don't do it again, Fran.'

There was no sign of blood in Francesca Christie's knuckles as she grasped the handle of Norma Maguire's door to open it.

'Keep safe, Fran. Promise me. Keep safe.'

7

9.46 am

'I called the pathologist in Warrington about the autopsy on Sandra O'Day in the River Irwell,' said Doctor Lamb.

As Clay walked from the gowning room into Autopsy Suite 1, she felt the flickering of a faulty overhead fluorescent light, which induced a tightness beneath the top of her skull.

Doctor Lamb looked at Clay, read her eyes, and glanced up at the faulty light above them. She turned to her ATP and said, 'Harper, please turn that light off or we'll all be going home with migraines.'

'What did the pathologist from Warrington come up with, Doctor Lamb?' asked Detective Sergeant Bill Hendricks from the theatre viewing gallery.

The intensity of light in the autopsy suite dimmed and Clay stood at the foot of the aluminium board on which lay Annie Boyd's disfigured corpse.

Doctor Lamb looked at Hendricks, a tall man with dark cropped hair and eyes full of sharp intelligence, and addressed him.

'First of all, whoever's done this is skilled at what they're doing. In the case of Sandra O'Day, the scalping and removal of facial tissue was done with infinite care and skill.' Doctor Lamb shone torchlight over the dead woman's jawline, at the cleanest of cuts. 'Just like in this case. Cause of death, strangulation. There's a note on Sandra O'Day's autopsy report. An NB. Warrington Police know that she met the man who murdered her through an internet dating site called Pebbles On The Beach. They learned this from a forensic search of her laptop. Her iPhone was never recovered.'

Clay looked at the young woman and despite the faulty light now being off, she felt the sensation in her head tighten up a notch.

This raises the possibility, thought Clay, processing a jet-black thought, *that there are other, undiscovered victims in the north-west of England. And most certainly, there will be more to come.*

'Doctor Lamb, if the person doing these scalpings was a football team, where would you place them?'

'Top of the English Premiership, potential European champions.'

Clay made a mental note to ask DC Cole to trawl through the missing persons of other constabularies in the north-west of England in search of blonde females, in their twenties, who'd gone missing and had not reappeared.

'Have you ever come across anything like this in the past, Doctor Lamb?' asked Hendricks.

Doctor Lamb turned her torch off and looked to the viewing gallery.

'I've seen countless body parts taken for trophies, some taken with care, many taken with savage brutality. But, no. I've never seen scalping and facial tissue removal on this scale.'

Doctor Lamb stooped and placed her face close to the discoloured marks that ran around the flesh on the woman's throat just beneath the red raw muscle where her face had once been. Clay observed her counting down silently from five to one.

Standing to her full height, Doctor Lamb looked directly at Clay.

'Same pattern as Warrington. The two marks that you can see at the centre of her throat are the bruises from his thumbprints. The four marks I'll show you either side of the centre back of her neck just below the place where her hairline was, they're the perpetrator's finger marks. The scalping was performed post-mortem.'

The news came as a crumb of comfort to Clay but she was compelled to ask, 'Are you one hundred per cent sure of that, Doctor Lamb?'

'If she was alive when this was done, the person who did it would have to have had access to extremely powerful anaesthetics, which places the hunt for the killer directly in the NHS or in a pharmaceutical company. I'll be able to tell if she's been given an anaesthetic. In the Warrington case, Sandra O'Day wasn't.'

Harper lifted the woman's head from the table and Clay saw the fingerprints either side of her neck, the bluntness of the dark marks and the comparatively large thumbprints at her throat. In her mind, she made a pair of hands strangling thin air and worked out the position of the killer to his victim.

'Base of her neck,' said Clay, 'is his baby finger. Rising up, next finger's his ring, middle finger next sticking well out of the group and at the top of the line it's his index finger. My hunch is he'd turned her into mental rubble in the days he held her captive and strangled her face to face. Up close and personal and looking right into her eyes as he squeezed the life from her.'

She looked at the network of interconnected muscles where the woman's face should have been and focused on her eyes bulging from their sockets, shocked in death and without the tender mercy of her eyelids to block out the gaze of strangers.

Clay turned back to see Doctor Lamb looking at a colour photograph of Sandra O'Day on the board in another autopsy suite and then at Annie Boyd's body on the board in front of her.

Doctor Lamb looked at Clay and, through over a hundred encounters in the autopsy suite with her, she was pretty certain what was running through the pathologist's mind.

'I know,' said Clay. 'I know. He needs to be caught before he does this again. I'll do everything in my power to do just that, Doctor Lamb.'

Harper combed Annie's torso with torchlight, starting at the top and working his way down. He hummed a tuneless song through clenched lips, his eyes riveted to the illumination on her skin.

'The past. Straight off, can you see any differences this time to the Warrington victim, Doctor Lamb?'

'No.'

Clay pictured Annie's mother and father sitting in the public gallery as this information emerged in court and felt a weight like a paving stone sink to the core of her being.

She imagined the months and years following, their sleepless nights as the information played out in their heads, each time the horror never diminishing, each time falling further down a bottomless pit of grief.

'I'll confirm the cause of death as strangulation by taking out her larynx and hyoid bone. Deep tissue contusion and fracture damage to the laryngeal bone will confirm the external evidence of strangulation. Then, we'll have to open her up and assess the contents of her stomach and internal damage, if any.'

Clay's iPhone vibrated on a nearby aluminium table, rattling the metal with each pulse.

'Better get it, Eve,' said Doctor Lamb.

She saw COLE on display, connected the call.

'Barney?'

'I've had a call from DCI Dave Ferguson, SIO on the Sandra O'Day case in Warrington. He wants to know when you'd like him to travel in to see you?'

'Ask him when he can make it in.'

'I already have done. He can be there in three hours.'

'Tell him I'll be there and thank you very much.'

As she placed her iPhone back on the aluminium table, there was a tentative knock on the door. A middle-aged man in blue scrubs entered the autopsy suite carrying a brown envelope in his hands, trying hard to look anywhere except at the dead woman on the table.

'I'm William Wilson,' he said. 'I'm Annie Boyd's dentist.'

His compulsion to see overwhelmed his instinct to look away. Clay drank in the expression on the dentist's face as he looked at Annie's body with growing horror and disbelief.

'Jesus,' said the dentist. 'Poor woman. Poor Annie. My God.'

'When did you last see her, Mr Wilson?' asked Clay.

'Last week. Tuesday. I whitened her teeth.'

Pearly whites, for the benefit of the man who went on to kill you, thought Clay.

'What's in the envelope, Mr Wilson?' asked Clay, showing him her warrant card.

'My notes on Annie's teeth and her dental X-Rays.'

'Can you send a copy of your notes to Detective Constable Barney Cole at Trinity Road police station, please.'

'Harper,' said Doctor Lamb. 'Show Mr Wilson her teeth.'

As Harper pulled her mouth open, the dentist approached, looked closely at the dead woman's teeth for many moments.

'It's Annie Boyd. She had a V-shaped indentation on her upper left canine.' He turned to Doctor Lamb. 'Do you have access to a mobile X-Ray machine?'

'I'll request one from the Dental Hospital.'

'I'll confirm it beyond any doubt using that.'

'William,' said Clay. 'I'm going to have to communicate this information to family liaison. They're going to have to break it to her parents...'

'In my view, it's definitely her, DCI Clay.'

'How long will you be working on Annie, Doctor Lamb?' asked Clay.

Harper resumed his torchlit inspection of the surface of Annie Boyd's skin.

'I estimate eight hours,' replied Doctor Lamb. 'But I'll flag up anything significant that comes to light directly to you.'

Clay looked around the autopsy suite, saw that there had been changes to the specimen jars. A human brain darkened by syphilis had been replaced by a twenty-week-old foetus floating eternally in formaldehyde. Gone were the lungs lined with asbestos and in was a damaged heart, swollen and diseased by decades of cigarettes.

Babies and lonely hearts, thought Clay. *Life and loneliness,* as she headed for the dressing room to remove her blue scrubs and white rubber boots.

'Eve!'

Clay stopped at the door leading into the dressing room, turned and looked at Doctor Lamb.

'Good luck,' said Doctor Lamb.

Clay felt a cold electricity down her spine, as if someone were standing on the spot where she would one day be buried.

8

10.45 am

In the staff restaurant of the Stanley Abattoir, Edgar McKee watched Wren as he opened his Captain Cyclone lunch box. Across the table from his new charge, Edgar drank coffee from a disposable cup and weighed Wren up.

There was no visible emotion in the teenager's face, no change in colour from the moment they had met and in the hours they had worked together, showing him what to do and what not to do, explaining the hygiene issues and the correct working techniques.

'Captain Cyclone?' asked Edgar. 'That's one superhero I've never heard of.'

'Why should you have heard of him? He only exists here.' Wren touched the side of his head.

'You made him up?'

Wren nodded.

'And painted the lunch box?' The artwork looked professional and polished. 'You're a great artist, Wren.'

Edgar looked into the lunch box and saw two double-finger Kit-Kats sitting neatly in line with two Cheese Straws with two small white triangular ham sandwiches, without crusts, next to two Petits Filous yogurts.

Wren picked out one of the ham sandwiches and, lifting it close to his nose, sniffed it and plunged it whole into his mouth.

'Won't you get hungry this afternoon if you eat your packed lunch now?'

'No,' replied Wren, chewing slowly, the food packed into the left-hand side of his mouth. He swallowed, looked directly at Edgar and then back into his lunch box. Taking the second ham sandwich from the box, Wren sniffed it and stuck it into his mouth, eating on the right-hand side of his mouth. 'I always eat my lunch at a quarter to eleven in the morning.'

'Two of everything, Wren?'

'Pairs. Even numbers. Don't like odd.'

'Fair enough. What you've been learning from me hasn't put you off your food?'

'No. Why should it?'

'You didn't look a bit bothered.'

'I don't like animals, Edgar. A dog bit me when I was five. A horse kicked me when I was seven. Therefore I do not like animals. This is literal. This is logical. The body is a machine, sinew, muscle, bone. Like the animals who walk in here and are carted off in various juicy cuts. There is nothing to be sorry for. There is nothing to fear. I told this to Mr MacArthur, Dad's boss, when he interviewed me for the apprenticeship. He told me I was unlike sentimental people of my own age and shook hands with me immediately on the deal.'

Wren looked around the staff restaurant and asked, 'Why?'

'Why what, Wren?'

'Why does everyone who works here have tattoos?'

'Not everyone who works here has tattoos. You don't have tattoos, do you?'

'Do you have one, Edgar?'

'Just the one. For my mother. She's dead and gone.'

'My mother died also. It was an awful cancerous thing, Edgar McKee. But it doesn't mean I have to tattoo me.'

Edgar saw something melt in Wren. He held up a fist and bumped his knuckles into the flesh and bone of Wren's clenched hand.

He laughed and Wren smiled back at him.

'Are you going to be with me all day, Edgar?'

'I've got to slip off to make a phone call later this morning.' Edgar saw tension flash through Wren's face. 'But I'm going to tell your father just how well you're doing, and just how clever you are.'

Wren beamed with happiness.

'I've got some time off booked this afternoon. I don't think you should be left alone in the abattoir. I've got to go on a message. I'll speak to your father. I'll drop you off at home after I've been on my message. You live in Gateacre, right?'

'Right.'

'Would you like to come with me for the ride? How does that sound?'

'Sounds great. Thanks, Edgar. What car?'

Wren peeled and bent a Cheese Straw, and popped it into his mouth, mashing the food between his teeth on the same side of his mouth as he had chewed the first ham sandwich. Edgar had no doubt the second Cheese Straw would be devoured on the other side.

'Not a car, Wren. A white van. It's nice to sit up high and look down on the tops of people's heads. Eat up, Wren. Soon we have to go back to work.'

Edgar leaned closer into Wren and whispered, 'Wren, I need to know everything there is to know about Captain Cyclone. Who are the good guys?'

'The good guys are the enemies of the enemy agents,' said Wren.

'Damn it to hell, I knew it!' replied Edgar. 'Tell me more. Tell me everything there is to know, Wren!'

Edgar watched a light go on inside Wren and it caused his eyes to shine.

'Wren, start at the beginning and don't leave anything out. I get you. In the name of Captain Cyclone, I get you every single step of the way.'

9

10.48 am

DCI Eve Clay stepped back from the doorstep of 358 Melbreck Road and looked up at the bay window at the front of the house, and the smaller one next to it. She imagined the atmosphere behind the front door.

As she waited for the bell to be answered, she looked over her shoulder at the white Honda Civic parked outside and recognised it as family liaison officer Sergeant Samantha Green's car.

The front door opened and Green spoke in little more than a whisper.

'Hello, Eve.'

'What did you tell them, Samantha?'

'I showed them the images of the mole and the bluebird tattoo on her arms. She had the tattoo done when she just turned eighteen. It caused merry hell when she came home with it. I told them they were from a body discovered in the River Mersey when the tide was out. Her father identified the mole and tattoo as Annie's.'

Clay stepped over the doorstep and closed the front door as quietly as possible.

'When did you have this conversation?'

'Half an hour ago. Her mother's upstairs with their GP. He's given her a sedative. I'm in the living room with her father.'

Clay heard a brief bout of sobbing from behind the closed door of the living room, and felt something merciless spear her heart.

'Are the results back from the dental records, Eve?'

'Her dentist came to the mortuary. Mobile X-Ray. It's Annie. End of.'

On the wall to the right of the living room door were three framed pictures. Annie as a ten-year-old girl in a school photograph. Annie as a proud young woman wearing a black mortar board and gown. Annie at the centre front row of thirty junior school children, smiling and at ease around their young form teacher.

The beginning, middle and end of a brief life in education.

'Her parents worship her, Eve,' said Green.

Clay nodded, knocked on the door.

'Come in...' A voice from the void.

Clay entered the room, saw a thick-set man in his late fifties sitting bolt upright in a black leather armchair.

'Bobby,' said Sergeant Green.

'Yeah?' He stared ahead of himself into the middle of the room.

'This is Detective Chief Inspector Eve Clay. I'm going into the kitchen to make a cup of tea.'

As Sergeant Green closed the door, Clay made her way to the sofa and picked out the best place to get an eyeline with Bobby Boyd. The silence in the house was broken by a sudden hopeless sobbing that leaked down into the room through the ceiling.

'Bobby?'

'I want to go to the mortuary. I want to see my daughter.' He looked directly into Clay's eyes. 'Is there any way another young woman could have the same mole in the same place and the same tattoo. I mean, is it definitely her?'

'The dental records have confirmed for certain that it's her.'

'I want to go to the mortuary and see her body. I need to see my own daughter!'

'That won't be necessary, Bobby. You've got enough stress going on at the moment.' She glanced up at the ceiling and the sorrow pouring through it. 'You need to stay right here to support your wife.'

'I want to go to the mortuary.'

'They won't let you in, Bobby. Please. Let's not go down that route any more. It's not going to happen.'

Clay stood up and walked to a formal framed picture of Annie, aged eighteen and in a sleeveless black prom dress.

She picked out what she estimated was the greatest act of rebellion against her parents, the bluebird tattoo on her arm, and the mole she'd been born with. She engaged Bobby's attention and indicated the picture on the wall.

'You need to remember her like this.'

He pushed himself up on the arms of the chair, hobbled over to the portrait and stood shoulder to shoulder with Clay. She listened to his laboured breathing and her head was filled with a recent memory of Annie's scalped head and face on the bed of the River Mersey.

'Did you see her body?'

'Yes. I was the first officer to go directly to her.'

'Was she wearing clothes?'

'No.'

She watched him wince, heard the quiet inarticulate sound of pain that went with it.

'How did she die?'

For a moment, she juggled in vain with words.

'She was strangled. There was bruising around her neck. Distinctive fingerprints.'

'If you won't let me go to her, then you must describe the condition of Annie's body to me, DCI Clay. I need to know.'

The doorbell rang, a rising and falling scale.

Bobby Boyd walked to the bay window and looked out.

'I'll let her in.'

10

10.54 am

Alone in the living room, Clay scanned the walls and saw an uninspiring watercolour of the River Mersey at sunrise. She checked the signature, *Annie Boyd*, dated 2011, and worked out she must have been fifteen years of age when she painted it.

She painted one of her own destinations en route to her grave, thought Clay, as the sound of a young woman's voice came deeper into the house.

The door opened and a woman in her mid twenties entered the room, her eyes wide with confusion and shock.

'I can't believe it, Bobby!'

The young woman froze and looked at Clay as if she'd just materialised out of thin air. Clay showed the young woman her warrant card and she said, 'Yes. Police. Of course. She's dead? She's definitely dead?'

'This is DCI Eve Clay. DCI Clay, this is Cathy Jones, Annie's best friend. They've been best friends since their first day in the reception class in St Austin's, more than twenty years ago.'

'I'm so sorry,' said Clay as she computed the information about Cathy's relationship to the victim. *And that makes you beyond useful*, she thought. 'When did you last hear from Annie, Cathy?'

'Six days ago. The day she went missing.'

'Six days exactly?' checked Clay as Annie's father and Cathy sat close to each other on the sofa.

'Thursday, 25 November,' replied Cathy.

'What time?'

Cathy glanced at Annie's father, a silent plea for Clay to change direction.

'How about you, Bobby?' asked Clay, pulling him back from the grief that sucked him under. 'When was the last time you saw or heard from Annie?'

'Annie? Six days,' said Bobby. 'The same. The longest silence from her. I – we knew she was dead.'

'You *knew* she was dead?' echoed Clay.

The weak light of a winter's day dissolved into deeper shadow as a cloud swallowed the pale sun.

'We hoped for the best and prepared for the absolute worst...'

Clay pressed record on her iPhone.

'She was the perfect daughter, from the moment she was born until the last time I saw her...'

In the same moment, Clay heard the click of the kettle as it turned itself off in the kitchen at the back of the house, and voices weaving through creaking floorboards above as Annie's mother and her doctor walked towards the stairs.

'We never had a moment's trouble from her, not even when she was supposed to be difficult. There were no terrible twos. No awkward teens. Just that tattoo.'

'That was my fault, Bobby. I got a tattoo and she copied me,' said Cathy.

He appeared not to hear.

'She was just... good, all the time... good as gold.'

'Bobby, tell me about the last time you saw Annie?'

'It was on Thursday morning. She came into the kitchen, running late for work, which wasn't like her. She was carrying a small bag, not one she usually took to school. I asked her what was in the bag. She told me she had a parents' evening after school finished and that she was going out afterwards with her colleagues. She didn't normally go on nights out with her colleagues.'

The darkness of the day crept into his face.

'She didn't normally lie to us. When the head teacher called the next day to ask where Annie was...' He turned to Cathy. 'Do you know what she was up to?'

'I haven't got a clue,' replied Cathy, looking away from the man beside her.

The door opened and Annie's mother walked into the room. She looked directly at Clay. 'Who are you?'

'Mary, this is the detective who found Annie,' said Bobby.

As she advanced towards her, Mary Boyd pointed at the iPhone in Clay's hand.

'Show me the pictures of her. Show me the pictures of her body. You found her. I know you've taken pictures of her. I've seen the pictures of her arms. Why can't you show us the rest of her. Show me. So I know she's definitely dead. You're hiding something.'

'I didn't take pictures of your daughter's body, Mrs Boyd,' said Clay. 'That's not my job. That's the job of our Scientific Support officers. I'm using the iPhone to record what's being said. Mrs Boyd, which school did Annie teach in?'

'St Jerome's in the Dingle.'

As Sergeant Green walked into the room with a tray of mugs, which she placed on the coffee table in front of the sofa, Cathy stood up and said, 'Mary, please come and sit next to Bobby.'

Clay took in the facial similarity between the middle-aged woman sitting next to her husband and the young woman in the framed portrait on the wall, and prepared the couple for the next piece of strangeness to come their way.

'I'm going to be sending my officers round at some point today. They're going to need to go into Annie's room and remove some of her personal belongings.'

'Why?' asked Bobby.

'We'll need to look through her laptop, any phones, diaries and address books Annie may have had.'

Clay felt the buzz of an incoming message on her iPhone. She glanced at the screen and saw COLE.

'I understand,' Bobby replied. 'Most murder victims know the person who killed them.'

She turned off record and, opening the message from Detective Constable Barney Cole, felt a surge of energy.

'What's happening?' asked Mary Boyd. 'Why do you look so troubled?'

'I've just received a message from my colleague. I'm sorry. I have to leave now.'

Clay reached into her pocket and produced two contact cards, which she handed to Annie's father and Cathy.

'Cathy, a word please,' she said. 'Sergeant Green – please keep me posted.'

Clay closed the door of the room and walked towards the front door.

'Walk with me, Cathy.' At the front door, Clay placed a finger against her lips and made a quiet shushing noise. 'I've got to go now, Cathy. Call me on the number on the card you're now holding so I can get back to you, and keep your phone on at all times. I need to talk to you really soon.'

'I'll do everything I can to help you, of course I will.'

'I understand you're in shock right now but you've got to work hard at gathering all your thoughts together. We need to sit down and you must tell me everything about your last conversation with Annie, your last memories of Annie before she disappeared.'

'I understand.'

'Can you just confirm something for me before I go? The internet dating site that Annie was on was Pebbles On The Beach. Right?'

Cathy looked like a woman who had just heard the story of her life told by a complete stranger.

'Pebbles On The Beach?' persisted Clay. 'Is that right?'

'That – that's exactly right. How did you know, DCI Clay?'

Clay grimaced. 'I'm afraid you'll find out soon enough. I'm sorry for your loss, Cathy.'

As Clay closed the front door behind herself and headed towards her car, she called Cole in the incident room in Trinity Road police station.

'You messaged me to call you immediately, Barney. What's happened?'

'You're on speakerphone, Eve. DCI Dave Ferguson, Warrington Constabulary, the SIO on the Sandra O'Day murder. He's arrived at the station. He's sitting next to me.'

'Hello, Dave. Are you really early or have I got the times wrong?'

'I'm early, Eve. I want to know what you know about your victim, your case, before I talk to your team.'

'Not that much, but can you do that for me, Barney? Tell Dave everything we know.'

'Will do.'

For the first time that day, Clay smiled, as she ducked out of the rain and into her car.

'I'm coming back right now.'

She felt relieved as she drove away from Melbreck Road, a relief tinged with a shard of guilt because she was running away from people in their darkest moments.

As she turned on to the roundabout leading on to Heath Road, Annie Boyd's life flashed through her head in a split second in a series of framed pictures on the walls of her parents' house, and came to a crashing halt as her body lay in the mud at the bottom of the River Mersey.

Rain gathered on her windscreen and the wipers squealed as they pushed it away.

Clay put her foot down on the accelerator and felt like the clouds were pressing down on her skull.

11

11.01 am

Francesca Christie opened a brown paper bag and half-filled it with cherries; she took another bag from the greengrocer's hook and selected five plums from the display in front of her – food for lunch and to snack on throughout the day.

As she paid for her fruit, she watched the rain hitting the ground and heard the wind singing through the tarpaulin protecting the produce on display on the pavement outside the shop.

Her iPhone rang out and, looking at the name on the display, she smiled and walked away from the till.

James.

'Hey, your change!' The words followed her but in the moment they meant nothing.

In the open doorway of the greengrocer's, she stepped under the protection of the tarpaulin and connected the call.

'Francesca?' The surface of his voice was like liquid chocolate but beneath that sweetness there was a layer of stone that spoke to her of a unique inner strength. 'Francesca, are you there?' A smile crept into his words.

'Yes, yes, I'm here, James.'

Slow down! Slow down! Slow down! she told herself.

Looking around, she saw a pair of men struggling in the rain to carry a large mirror into the hairdressers two doors down from the greengrocer's.

'I love your new profile picture on Facebook. You've gone from being insanely pretty to downright beautiful.'

She stared directly into the slanting rain and smiled.

'You're a sweet-talker.'

He laughed and the sound was warm and kind.

'Thank you for the picture you sent me. You've got such...'

'Such what, Francesca? Such a nerve to surprise you?'

'A surprise? For me? What is it?'

'If I told you...'

'It wouldn't be a surprise.'

Despite the cold wind that whipped the greengrocer's shop front, Francesca felt her colour rising and something sweet and delicious rising from her core.

'Where? Where are you?' she asked.

'I'm in a meeting room, waiting to go into the next round, Queen Elizabeth Crown Court.'

'Which case is it?'

'I'm fighting the deportation of an asylum-seeking woman and her three-year-old son back to Eritrea. She's genuine. It's pen-pushers versus humanity.'

God, I've never met you but I'm so proud of you, so proud to have anything to do with you. She managed to keep the words from slipping out but felt her heart pound a little faster; and the world around her faded into a different place where a haze of endless dreams could come true.

She heard the sound of a door opening at his end of the line and a woman saying, 'The judge wants to see you in his chambers.' Her voice dropped to conspiratorial. 'I think you're going to be pleased.'

Francesca felt a sudden needle in her happiness. She didn't like the tone of the woman's voice, the familiarity, *her* closeness to *him.*

In the moment before he had the chance to reply to the woman, Francesca analysed her voice more closely. It felt both familiar and strange in the same beat of time, and was filled with the weight of middle-age.

'Thank you, Rhonda.' The door closed behind her with an almost theatrical click, and Francesca dismissed the messenger. It was just a woman he worked with, after all.

'Francesca, remember the deal we made?'

'Of course.'

'We have to make a decision shortly…'

'Friday, 3rd December,' said Francesca. 'Two days to go.' She smiled and tried to sound bright but dreaded some demon stepping out of the shadows and causing the mutual decision to go against her profoundest wishes.

'Maybe we could bring the date closer. Think about it. I've really got to go, Francesca. Francesca? Did you change your profile picture for my benefit?'

'I – I did.'

'Enjoy your surprise, angel.'

Francesca found herself perfectly still on the middle of the pavement, not aware of how she took the four steps to get there. The rain poured down on to her head and she spoke quietly to herself. 'Come on, Francesca, get yourself together.'

She looked right and saw the workmen carrying another mirror into the refurbished hairdressers.

'Fucking hell, it's slipping out of my hands,' said the man at the back.

The man at the front stopped and lowered his end down to the pavement.

'Gently, gently, that's right.' At both ends, the mirror rested safely on the pavement. 'One, two, three, get a grip, up!'

Francesca watched with morbid fascination as the workmen moved slowly through the rain to get the mirror to safety. She saw herself in the rain, a broad smile on her face, and, looking over the shoulder of her own reflection, she saw Norma Maguire on the pavement, an umbrella over her head, a statue in a manual wheelchair – a tiny detail in the background – watching from just outside the door of Maguire Holdings.

Yes, yes, back to work, break time's over… she commanded herself.

As she turned a half-circle on the pavement, Norma was gone and, for a moment, she wondered if seeing her boss was an optical illusion caused by the giddy excitement of talking directly to James.

Francesca walked back to the office through the rain, the ever-present stone in her soul crumbling into dust, and for the first time since she could remember, when she was a young child, she was excited and happy to be alive.

12

11.21 am

As Detective Sergeant Gina Riley placed Annie Boyd's two laptops into evidence bags, she looked around the dead woman's bedroom and imagined the victim's life flashing before her eyes as she died at the hands of The Ghoul.

Riley had gathered two of Annie's old iPhones, a digital camera, a locked diary and an address book.

She opened the wardrobe door and saw a row of neatly ordered clothes hanging from a rail and dozens of pairs of shoes stacked on racks with two empty sections that sang poignantly to Riley. *The sensible shoes you wore for school,* she thought, *and the kind of heels for a date.*

Sliding the wardrobe door over, she stopped, her attention tripped by a dress at the left end of the rail, protected by a zipped plastic cover.

She took the dress out and made a connection.

It was a black dress. She recognised it from the framed photograph downstairs as the one Annie had worn for her prom. Riley looked at the silky fabric and the material was like a flag to blighted hope.

The drawers of the dressing table contained nothing other than underwear. Riley dug her hands beneath the knickers and bras and found nothing hidden there, only the flat base of the drawer. The surface of the dressing table was uncluttered, with only a Jean-Paul Gaultier fragrance and a few less expensive brands of perfume, a hairbrush and a jewellery box that was half-full with a collection of costume jewellery and inexpensive bracelets and necklaces.

She opened the bag on the dressing table and saw a range of mid-market make-up.

Riley picked up the hairbrush and took it to the bed where Annie's other belongings were bagged.

Is Annie on the DNA database? she asked herself. *Almost certainly, no.*

As she bagged the brush for the blonde hairs trapped between the tiny forest of teeth, she reasoned, *If he's got your scalp, your whole head of hair, those hairs may appear on his clothes, in the place he lives or works. This simple hairbrush could be the bridge between you and the fucker who did this to you.*

Riley sat on the stool and looked at herself in the mirror, imagined Annie sitting there and applying make-up as she prepared for a night out, her hopes rising as she wondered if this was going to be *the* night that she met a special man, the elusive Mr Right.

In the mirror, over her right shoulder, Riley caught the reflection of the pillow on Annie's single bed, the intimate sleeping place of a lonely woman with romantic dreams.

She got up from the dressing table, sat on the mattress and ran the flat of her hand over the surface of the cotton pillowslip where Annie's head had once reclined and felt nothing hidden beneath. She turned the pillow over and caressed the back. As her palm crossed the pillowslip, Riley felt a rectangle of paper.

Riley touched the edge of the rectangle and, pinching it as carefully as she could, pulled out a white envelope. She looked at the back of it, the seal carefully pressed down, a letter that had no doubt been another secret from her parents.

In the hall downstairs, the landline rang out and when the receiver was picked up, fresh silence thickened the stony atmosphere.

Riley turned the envelope over and read the name and address carefully printed on the front.

MS ANNIE BOYD
ST JEROME'S RC PRIMARY SCHOOL
DINGLE STREET
LIVERPOOL
L8 3XX

She explored the other information on the front of the envelope, saw the place of postage was Liverpool and the smudged date, 14.11.21.

Riley felt the envelope and the contents were thicker than paper, stiffer, but thinner than card.

Gathering all Annie's bagged possessions together and leaving the bedroom, Riley was hit by the powerful notion that she was somehow leading a funeral procession, taking the young woman's things away not for examination but as material offerings for the grave.

She walked down the stairs into the blighted silence and paused at the living room door.

'Mrs Boyd, I'm taking some of Annie's belongings with me. When we've finished with them we will return them.'

Mrs Boyd didn't look up or appear to hear.

Opening the front door as quietly as she could, Riley was stopped by Mrs Boyd's voice.

'What's the point of bringing them back? Can you bring her back from the dead? Can you? She's not coming back, is she?'

'I'm sorry. No, I can't,' said Riley.

She headed to the front door with the weight of Annie Boyd's possessions in her hands and a wall of indescribable grief at her back.

13

Noon

Norma Maguire wheeled herself towards the lift door outside her office on the first floor of her estate agency, pressed the call button and felt the mechanical action of the lift through the fabric of the building as it rose from the ground. As she waited, she looked at the inverted writing on the window – Maguire Holdings – and wondered if Fran had used her lift when there was only one flight of fourteen steps down to the ground floor.

Wouldn't it be better if you had your office on the ground floor?

Over the years, she had been asked the same question in dozens of ways by as many people and had countered it with the same fudge.

I prefer a room with a view.

The truth was simple. She didn't want to overhear people talking about her when they thought her back was turned, pitying the cripple in one breath, laughing at her funny little ways, then criticising the over-demanding but caring boss in the next.

Norma looked at her blurred reflection in the silver surface of the lift door and was relieved that the image was unclear. She saw the darkness of her curly hair and her face as a pink blob, human but featureless. In the shape of the wheelchair, she saw the dark approximation of the blue trouser suit she wore for work.

As the lift arrived, she pictured the row of trouser suits in her wardrobe at home.

Monday to Friday, one suit, the same suit she always faced the world with; Saturday, suit to the dry cleaners, and then slacks and a jacket as she put in an appearance at the office until lunchtime; Sunday, jeans, a jumper and much solitude.

The lift doors opened and she wheeled herself into the narrow space.

Pressing 'G', she looked down at her legs and was grateful that her fleshy thighs were concealed by the fabric of her trousers.

The doors closed and the short descent began in a confined wood-panelled space that reminded her of the interior of the coffin in which her mother had been laid to rest in their front room in the days between her sudden death and her funeral all those years ago.

The lift sighed to a halt as it reached the ground floor, and the bell that accompanied the end of a short descent announced the arrival of the boss. Beyond the lift, in the open-plan office at the front of the building, there was some laughter in the chorus of animated voices.

Good, she thought. *Happy agents sell houses.*

She wheeled herself out of the lift and into the office at the front of the premises where five people were busily employed on telephones and at laptops, and Francesca Christie was engaged in a meeting with a young couple at her desk near the window.

Norma smiled into the room.

'Norma...' Daniel Ball, the office manager, stood up at his desk. 'I've just finished the sums. We've hit our target for November and we have more on top of it. Twenty per cent, to be precise.'

She threw a smattering of applause into the room and gave a double thumbs up, making eye contact with everyone except Fran, whose back was turned to her. Pleasure pulsed through Norma as she looked at her employees and she felt a strong sense of belonging.

You're like family to me, she thought. *The sons and daughters I never had.* Immediately there was a counter voice inside her head. *Family is pain, Norma.*

'Norma?' Daniel Ball looked and sounded surprised. She quizzed him silently with a look. 'You just said to me *Go away*, Norma!'

She smiled. 'I'm sorry. It wasn't aimed at you, Daniel. I was thinking out loud. Same as usual then. Pick an evening when you're all free, decide where you want to go and as soon as we shut up shop, I'll take you all for a meal. All on me of course. As per usual.'

'Norma,' said the office manager, pointing at Francesca Christie.

She recalled that Fran had closed down a deal on a three-bedroom terraced house in Newcastle Road. 'It's largely been down to her,' said the office manager, quietly.

'Maybe so, but Fran doesn't live or work in a vacuum.'

Norma pointed to the notice she'd had specially made for the office.

IT'S THE TEAM THAT MAKES THINGS HAPPEN

'Thank you,' she said as she wheeled herself to the automated doors at the front of her estate agency. 'You've made my day. Again. Pass it on.'

'Norma?' She heard a well-meaning note in Daniel's voice and guessed what was coming next. He stepped in front of her. 'Wouldn't it be easier, better for you if you had an electric wheelchair?'

'Daniel, I know you're only thinking of me, which is why I'm not going to get cross, but I do recall we had this conversation around twelve months ago. What did I tell you back then? Do you remember?'

'You told me that your arms were fully functional and that you weren't going to give up the right to use the part of yourself that wasn't disabled.'

She smiled at him and tapped her own head. 'Nothing's changed in the past year.'

Norma lifted her hand from the wheel rims and raised her arms.

'This is my independence.'

'Point taken, Norma. I won't mention it again. I'm sorry.'

'Don't be. We're doing just great.'

She turned the wheel rims, the automatic doors opened and winter blasted in her face, making her scrunch her features.

On the pavement, she moved past the glass facade of the trading floor of her business and looked between the photographs of houses for sale in her shop window. She looked directly at Fran, smiling and confident with the young couple on the other side of her desk.

Francesca Christie stood up and, after handing over the keys of 102 Newcastle Road, shook hands with the couple.

I didn't mean to make you cry, Fran, thought Norma as she passed the fruit and vegetables on the pavement outside the greengrocer's next door. *I was trying to protect you. I was trying to warn you. There are predators out there, very bad men...*

Outside the hairdressers, next door but one, at the back of a black van half parked on the narrow kerb, two workmen stepped on to the pavement carrying a large mirror. They stopped in the middle of the pavement, a metre away from Norma, and she froze.

'Don't drop it, Gary, for fuck's sake.'

Norma saw herself reflected perfectly in the surface of the mirror; her limbs, her body, her face.

She closed her eyes tightly, dropped her head and felt the onset of the kind of nausea she knew would inhabit her for hours and a sound in her head like white noise.

'Hey, lady, I'm sorry...' He looked directly at her, fell silent and a look of morbid curiosity crossed his face. '...We're blocking your way.'

She curved the wheels of her chair and, turning an arc that used the whole width of the pavement, her back was completely turned to the mirror and the vile reflection on its surface.

Norma wheeled herself away at speed.

She felt the world fly past her in two continuous streams, either side of her throbbing head, cursed the ill-timing of her journey on to the middle of Allerton Road and knew that if she lived for two hundred years she would never come to terms with the sheer abomination of her face.

14

12.01 pm

Detective Sergeant Gina Riley sat across Poppy Waters' desk in her tiny office on the first floor of Trinity Road police station and placed the bagged evidence from Annie Boyd's bedroom between them.

'What have we got here, Gina?' asked Clay, pulling up a chair and sitting next to Riley.

The wind sobbed at the narrow window overlooking the car park at the back of the police station.

'The dead woman's laptops and two iPhones.'

'What did you make of your visit to her home, Gina?'

'Young adult living at home with her mother and father. I think she had a secretive side to her.'

'How do you make that out?' asked Poppy, a civilian IT expert.

Riley produced a fourth small evidence bag and snapped on a pair of latex gloves. She took out the envelope and pointed out the school address.

'She's had her mail sent to her place of work, which says to me she was secretive around her parents.'

Poppy and Clay slipped their hands into latex gloves.

'Have you seen what's inside yet?' asked Clay.

'No, but I'm about to.'

Clay turned back the flap. 'It's not a letter. It looks like a photograph.'

'Have you noticed anything about the handwriting on the envelope?' asked Riley.

'It's plain block capitals. It's disguised handwriting.'

Riley smiled bitterly as Clay took the top edge of the photograph from the envelope with the tips of her thumb and index finger.

'Annie's friend Cathy confirmed that her best friend had been using Pebbles On The Beach, so I'm guessing this picture came from whoever she's made contact with on the dating website.'

Clay showed the photograph to Riley and Poppy.

'Who or what do you see, girls?' asked Clay.

'I see a young man who couldn't possibly have any need to get a girlfriend from an internet dating site,' said Riley.

Looking at the picture, Clay worked from the top down.

'Mr Handsome. He's standing at an angle, most of his face is visible. He's not looking at the camera but at something or someone, not in the picture, with a great deal of affection. It looks natural and not posed for. It *could* have been taken without his knowledge and presented to him after the event.

'Collar-length black hair, handsome enough for TV, smart white shirt and trousers, well-built, muscular but slim. Designer loafers.'

'See the way his shirt's turned back to the elbow,' said Riley. 'Look at the definition on his forearms. He's a gym-head.'

She examined the overall image, then focused on the empty space into which he smiled.

'Someone or something's been edited out of this image,' said Clay. 'I'm sure of it.'

'What are we going to do with it?' asked Riley.

'We'll send an electronic copy of the picture to Barney Cole. He can work on tracking down Mr Handsome. It's on photographic paper so we'll give the picture itself to Terry Mason and Paul Price, see if they can pull off any prints.'

Poppy indicated the phones and laptops. 'I'll crack on with these then.'

'Before you start, Poppy, do me a favour, please,' said Clay. 'I'd like to see Annie's Pebbles On The Beach profile firstly. And then whatever passed between her and the man hiding behind the identity of the man in the photograph from Annie's pillowslip.'

15
1.31pm

As Clay walked into the incident room at Trinity Road police station, she looked at the people sitting round in a circle and picked out the only stranger to her. Detective Chief Inspector Dave Ferguson from Warrington Constabulary, seated between Hendricks and Riley and facing Cole, Stone and Winters.

Her iPhone buzzed and, seeing Poppy's name on display, she spoke to the group. 'Thank you, can you give me a few seconds? Poppy?'

'Eve, I've just emailed you Annie Boyd's Pebbles On The Beach profile.'

'Anything standing out about it?'

'It's cliché-driven. She likes long walks in the countryside, stadium-level boy bands. Her profile picture's nice but it's static.'

'Thanks for that, Poppy.'

'Are you going to do something with it?'

'I'm working on it. Good work. Let's talk later.'

Clay took her place facing DCI Ferguson.

'Thank you very much indeed, Dave, for coming to see us so quickly. We appreciate your time and support,' said Clay.

'No problem, Eve. You have all our electronic records, right?'

'Your super, Kate Johnson, sent them to me this morning,' replied Cole, handing Clay a set of images printed off from the materials sent from Warrington.

'If it was Kate organising, then you *will* have everything.' Ferguson looked at Clay, sitting directly opposite him in the circle. 'You've got fresh eyes on this, you and your team. Maybe you'll see something we didn't quite see.'

Ferguson took in the whole group with a shift of his eyes.

'Do you want the bad news or the bad news?' he asked. 'When we took in Sandra O'Day's laptop and mobile, and we found out they'd been communicating through Pebbles On The Beach, I thought we had the bastard in a box, through his IP address on her devices. Silly fucking me. He'd downloaded Virtual Private Network software that did him two big favours. One. It disguised his real IP address and generated him a fake one. Two. It bounced his signals into China, Australia and Russia, making it look like he was operating out of those countries. You're going to find the same problem, only he might be more savvy and have used a TOR to bury himself on the dark web.'

'Sly shit hides behind internet technology. I can see the headlines now,' said Clay. The tension in the room dipped and Ferguson looked at Clay with more than a glimmer of thanks in his hangdog eyes. 'How about we look at your pictures, Dave?'

Clay took out the first photograph of Sandra O'Day's body, beginning to look bloated and grey, captured in a bed of reeds at the water's edge, skinned and scalped in exactly the same manner as Annie Boyd.

'The handiwork of the bastard we refer to as The Ghoul. Sandra had been in the water for days before she was discovered by a man out walking in a beauty spot one early morning. It was a very hot day, and although it was in the cool of the morning, he was drawn to the body by the smell. He was on the verge of hysterics when he called emergency services.

'We flooded the area with every available officer and officers were drafted in from Greater Manchester Police. We combed every blade of grass. Nothing.' Colour rose in DCI Ferguson's cheeks and throat.

'How did you identify your victim?' asked Clay.

'We identified her because her mother had reported her as missing. It was a process of elimination. She had a birth mark on the inside of her left thigh. We brought Mrs O'Day into the mortuary, covered the body from the neck upwards. Jesus, I can still hear her screams.'

'Dave,' said Clay. 'What date did she go missing? And when did you find her?'

A look of pure regret passed through Ferguson's eyes.

'Her mother contacted us on August 1st. Our response, unfortunately, was a standard one. We listed it but did nothing about it. What could we do? She was an adult and her mother said she'd been missing for six hours, not picking up her phone, not calling home, which she did religiously. She was discovered on August 11th.'

Clay did a mental sum and asked, 'How long did the coroner say she'd been in the water?'

'At least four days, five even.'

'So Sandra was held captive for five to six days?' said Clay.

'If the coroner's report's worth the shit it's supposed to, yeah. Her injuries and the state of her body. She'd been dead for days.'

'Did you have any suspects?'

'None. No CCTV. No Automatic Number Plate Recognition cameras. One theory went that The Ghoul had dodged CCTV and carried the body to the water. Sandra O'Day wasn't a big woman and we proposed that he was a bodybuilder or someone who dealt with heavy weights in their job, both even.'

'Do you think he was local to the Warrington area?'

Ferguson shook his head.

'We looked at all the local men who had a history of violence towards women and none of them, not one, had a back story that could have reached to the depths of what that lunatic did to Sandra O'Day. They all had drop-dead alibis. We started winding the investigation down after two months. It's still an open case but it's the most frustrating investigation I've been involved in all down the years.'

'Pebbles On The Beach?' asked Clay. 'You posted a note on the coroner's file?'

'Made-up name and bogus address.'

Ferguson's head dropped like a man who'd scored an own goal in a one-nil cup final defeat as the referee blew the final whistle.

'You can't magic evidence out of the air when there simply isn't any, Dave,' said Clay as she looked at the second picture, of Sandra O'Day's body being hauled out of the water, the muscles on her face withered and brown and not resembling anything human.

She passed the top two images on to Hendricks and saw a third picture of Sandra in an unzipped body bag at the water's edge.

She came to an image of two frogmen wading into the water and showed it to Ferguson.

'They found nothing in the water. A team of six searched for two days and nights, Eve.'

Clay saw a picture of a laptop on a bed in a room that was predominantly pink.

'She was on Pebbles On The Beach. That's where she met him. They stopped communicating on the website and went on to mobiles. The Ghoul had her phone and guess fucking what, we came nowhere near his device. No Ghoul. No phone. It was as brutal as it was heartbreaking.'

Ferguson sighed and folded his arms across his chest.

'Time wise,' said Clay. All eyes turned to her. 'The time between his first kill and second kill, we're not going to get that luxury this time. It's going to be weeks if we're lucky, not months, until his next outing. His head's probably swollen to twice its normal size. He thinks he's Mr Undetectable. He's taken on Warrington Police and got away with it. So far. Now he's taken us on. Thank you, Dave. Do you have anything to add?'

'Good luck. You'll need it.' He stood up and stretched the tension out of his limbs. 'I'll keep you posted, Eve, if anything crops up our end.'

'Likewise, Dave.'

Clay watched him walk to the door of the incident room and felt a surge of sympathy for Ferguson.

'Dave!' He stopped, turned. 'Thank you. This can't have been easy for you. I appreciate you turning up in person so quickly.'

'I'm quick to grab the glory when things go well. Got to hold your hands up when it all goes shit-shape. M62 in the rain for me now. Thanks for listening, everyone. And the best of fucking British.'

16

4.03 pm

When Eve Clay stepped outside her house on Mersey Road, she looked down the road in the direction of the river and was sucked into the recent past. She estimated that the place where Annie Boyd's body had been discovered was a seven-minute walk from her front door.

'Mum!' Her son Philip's voice came from the open doorway of their home, snapping her back into the present. 'It's freezing. Brrrhhhh! Come in.'

As she walked up the path, she smiled at Philip, who suddenly appeared much older than the pictures she carried of him in her head when they were apart.

'Are you tired, Mummy?'

You've got a point, Philip, she thought, as she headed in his direction. *Maybe fatigue's playing tricks on my imagination.*

'You've been here before, haven't you, love?' she replied as she followed him into the house, shutting the door after herself.

'How do you mean?' he asked.

'What I mean is for a six-year-old, you're very grown-up in the things you say. Like a much older boy.'

From the kitchen, she heard a kettle whistling and her husband, Thomas, call, 'Tea or coffee, Eve?'

Before she could answer, Philip chipped in, 'Tea, please, Dad.'

'The same for me, Thomas.'

He's drinking tea now? She asked the question in silence and the element of surprise hit her beneath her skin.

Eve Clay followed her son into the living room and sat next to him on the sofa.

'So, how long have you been drinking tea?' she asked.

'I made a cup...'

'*You* made a cup of *tea*?'

'I'm a big boy. I can handle a kettle. I made a cup of tea for Dad. Dad watched me. When his tea was cooler, I asked if I could have a sip. I liked it. So I made another cup for me. We sat and had a cup of tea together.'

Clay smiled but the weight of another missed milestone in her son's journey sank inside her.

'I think I know why you've got such a sad face on you, Mum.'

She smiled at him and said, 'I'm not sad. I'm having a short break at home with you and that dad of yours. I'm not sad, love. Tired, maybe. That's all.'

'Well, OK, you say you're not sad but it was on the radio, Radio Merseyside, about the dead woman found on the river. Are you chasing the baddie?'

'I'm the Senior Investigating Officer, so yes, Philip, I'm very much involved.'

'Is that why you were staring down to the river just now?'

'I was just working something out.'

Just how close to home death had appeared. The dark thought marbled her bones and, as she looked at her son, the words *don't come any closer* dripped through her brain.

'Didn't you want to be a doctor like Dad?' He slid off the sofa, his bottom hitting the floor. 'He gets loads of free time, and helps people get better.'

'Your dad was good at Sciences at school. I wasn't. I was good at Geography, English Literature and History. Places, stories and people interested me. They still do.'

She watched him processing the information, the softness of his brow tightening.

'Last night, when we were talking about you, Dad said, *The world needs different people doing different things, and if it wasn't for your mum and her team there'd be loads more bad people out there doing terrible things. The world needs me to be a doctor and your mum to be a police officer.*'

'You understand that?'

'Of course I do. I'm on Turquoise seven on the Project X reading programme. I've gone up four levels in a year.'

'I know and I'm proud of you and I'm impressed.'

He lay on his side and peered under the sofa.

'There it is.'

Philip stuck his hand and half his arm under the sofa and pulled out a black and red toy truck, which he rolled up and down on the carpet.

'Beep! Beep, Beep!'

'What do you want to do when you grow up, Philip?'

'I'd like to play for Everton.'

Thomas came in and placed two mugs of tea on the coffee table. Clay looked at Thomas, at Philip on the carpet moving his truck around the legs of the coffee table, and back at Thomas.

'Suppose you couldn't be a footie player,' said Thomas. 'What's your next choice?'

'I'd like to be a policeman.' He half-pointed at Clay. 'Just like you, only a man not a woman.'

'Why?' Despite her cast-iron ability not to be shocked by what she saw and heard, she was amazed. In her mind her career flashed before her and, as a mother, she lit a small flame in her heart that this was just a passing phase that he would soon grow out of, and that he would choose something entirely different to the path she had walked.

'Why, Mum? You're famous. All the big kids in the school, the ten- and eleven-year olds, come up to me in the playground and ask me questions about you. They're dead impressed. One lad asked me about that night, years before I was in your tummy. He told me you escaped from a burning building from which you'd arrested a psycho, single-handed.'

The fire that she'd walked through as she arrested The Baptist flashed through her memory.

'Like you say, it was before you were born, Philip. I was much younger, and he seemed to have given up on being a free man. It was like he wanted me to arrest him, like he'd had enough of the terrible things he was doing to people, like he was tired of the life he was living.'

'What...?'

'You know the rule, Philip. What happens out there stays out there. There's no need for us to discuss the details behind our front door. This is our sanctuary. But I will tell you one thing. The building wasn't burning when I entered it. The fire broke out when I was inside, and the only way out was through that fire.'

'You didn't get badly burned?'

'A few scorch marks and some singed hair. The word *miracle* flew around the papers for a few days and then it was all forgotten when the next, bigger, better story came along.'

Anxiety crossed Philip's face.

'Philip,' said Thomas. 'You've nothing to worry about. Your mum wouldn't take an unnecessary risk. She can't. She's got you to think about now.'

'Of course I wouldn't take any big chance.' She squeezed her son tightly. 'So *you* get rid of *your* sad face. OK?'

'Promise?' pressed Philip.

'I promise you.' She changed the subject in a heartbeat. 'Are Everton at home this weekend?'

'Oh, yeah,' replied Philip. 'Me and Dad are going. We'll be in the Lower Bullens, cheering the lads on, like we always do. It's a shame you can't come with us, Mum.'

Inside her coat, Clay felt the vibration of an incoming call on her iPhone. She connected and said, 'Bill, what's up?'

She stood up and walked into the hall, looked at herself in the full-length mirror on the wall.

There was silence at the other end and she rechecked the HENDRICKS on the display.

'Bill, are you there?'

'There's been another body found. Same MO as Annie Boyd. On the public footpath between Allerton Towers and the golf course, off Menlove Avenue.'

'I'll be there in ten minutes.' She disconnected and said, 'Philip, Thomas...'

'I know,' said Thomas, following Philip from the living room into the hall. 'You've got to go.'

As she opened the front door, she felt Philip's hand on her back. She turned and looked at him.

'Don't take any risks. You promised.'

17

4.05 pm

The basement.

The Ghoul.

The Ghoul's eyes opened slowly under a naked red light, and in a room full of shadows, there were only two sounds that mattered. The constant rhythm of the skipping rope hitting the floor and the slap of bare feet that followed the connection of skipping rope to floor.

Eyes closed, The Ghoul blocked out the noises in the room and focused on something superior. The sounds inside, the beat of a huge heart and the blood pumping inside.

Faster. Harder. Faster. Harder. Faster. Harder.

And although the room was fridge cold, beads of sweat poured down from each pore. Face, neck, the entire surface of a body that had been skipping for what felt like well over an hour.

All sense of time was lost.

Under the alluring rouge of the light, memory exploded into life.

The past crashed into the present and next door came alive.

The locked door leading to that other, adjoining space where Annie had waited.

Annie. Her mouth. Her eyes. Annie's body, slack but still alive.

And then there was the other one, more alive because she'd been there for a little less time than Annie. Her voice was trapped inside her throat, her mouth stuffed with a rag. The sound of her chains as she tried... what was she trying to do as the chains smacked the wall at the side of her mattress? Stupid. Not a bit compliant, not a bit like little Annie.

Sitting on the edge of Annie's mattress now, looking at the other one, she turned her head and made eye contact and terror shone there in the faltering red light and flashes as dark as hell itself.

Staring at her but addressing Annie, The Ghoul spoke.

'Annie? Annie...' Her eyes were fixed, dizzying terror now dancing in them. 'You're probably wondering what that table is for, the one between the mattresses, and what those knives and scalpels are for...?

'That's where you're going next, when it's all over for you. I'm going to perform a little cosmetic surgery, post-mortem. Look at the writing on the wall. The writing on the wall says, And, so, off she floats to nowhere.'

Annie made a noise like a newborn baby overwhelmed by her journey into the light from the dark seclusion of the womb.

The Ghoul stood over Annie's roommate.

'And this is the same for you... Look at me... Lurrrammmmeeee...'

The human voice was lost and The Ghoul ascended.

18

4.38 pm

As the world plunged deeper into the darkness of early night, rain tripped over itself as it hurtled to earth from the iron sky.

At the Menlove Avenue entrance to the public footpath leading down to Allerton Road, the rain picked up intensity and stung DCI Eve Clay's cheeks as she dipped under the scene-of-crime tape stretching from the hedge on the edge of Allerton Manor Golf Course to the railings surrounding Allerton Tower Park.

'Who's on the scene?' Clay asked the constable running the log.

'PC Woodrow. We were first here after the call came through from switch. We were on our way to a domestic in Woolton Village...'

'Have you sealed off the Allerton Road end of the footpath?'

'It was too far with the time we had. PC Woodrow sealed it five metres from the body.'

'You did well. Thank you. The caller?'

He pointed down the path. 'On the other side of the tape. Jesus, I've never seen anything like it.'

As Clay hurried down the public footpath, past the sandstone wall to her left and mature shrubs to her right that sheltered the claustrophobic space, rain bounced up from the ground.

Senses raised and razor-sharp, she heard a pair of doors slam on the dual carriageway and recognised a familiar sound: the front doors of the Scientific Support van used by Detective Sergeant Terry Marsh and Sergeant Paul Price.

Twenty metres down the footpath, she saw a pair of feet and lower legs, feminine and slender, resting on the rough ground.

Where's the rest of the body? thought Clay, as she passed a gaping, waterlogged pothole at the side of the path. She looked up, saw rain dripping into the hole from a series of thick branches that acted as a black canopy.

As she passed the next hole in the footpath, Clay slowed down, stopped and tuned in to the piece of her brain that processed her senses and turned their data into hard memory.

'Are you filming this, Terry?' she called to Mason, whose rapid breath she could hear coming up behind her.

'Pricey's doing it, Eve.'

'Sergeant Price, come here alongside me, please.'

Clay focused her whole attention metres away from herself on the knees, legs and feet and the sinkhole in which the rest of the body was hidden.

Two seconds ticked down and she felt the young officer's presence at her side.

'Wait, please, Sergeant Price. PC Woodrow!'

PC Woodrow looked over the scene-of-crime tape. The woman on the other side with him had her back turned on the horror she had uncovered. Dog lead in hand, her black Westie lay on the earth like a discarded puppet, its eyes brimming with sorrow.

'DCI Clay,' said PC Woodrow. 'When we arrived the top half of her body was floating. It sank under two minutes ago.'

'Please take this lady back down the path.' She pointed in the direction of Menlove Avenue. 'Out of sight and sound and away from the scene. Put her in your car and out of the rain. Thank you, madam. I'll need to talk to you very soon.'

The woman turned and looked directly at the victim's feet and lower limbs. She turned back around suddenly and was violently sick on the path.

'Come with me,' said PC Woodrow.

'I'm sorry... I'm sorry... I'm sorry...' she said, free hand acting as a blinker at the side of her face as PC Woodrow led her away from the scene.

'Sergeant Price, focus on the knees, legs and feet, and the hole in the ground.' He nodded. 'Walk with me.' She stepped forward slowly. 'I'm walking towards what appears to be a pair of disembodied feet and legs. Her toenails are painted and there is no sign of hair on her legs. There are dark marks on her knees. Bruising? Maybe.'

The rain's intensity slackened and, as Clay reached the dead woman, it stopped as if some unspoken prayer to an anonymous god had been granted.

'Closer to the hole and the body, I can see water brimming to the top of the hole, and I estimate that the rest of her body, above her knees, is beneath the surface of the water. This time, the MO hasn't altered but the water he's chosen to leave her body in has scaled down from a river in the first and second instance to what amounts to an oversized puddle. Why has he done this? Did he run too much of a risk leaving the body on the mud of the Mersey? Did he run too much of a risk operating in such a wide-open space? Did he throw Annie's body in the water as the tide was going out? Or did he leave her on the mud?'

She looked around at the intimacy of the space and concluded, 'He wanted privacy.' Clay reached the edge of the water.

'Judging by the fact that most of her body's concealed by water, I estimate this pothole is probably at least three-quarters of a metre deep.'

Beneath her feet, Clay felt something vibrating in the ground, subtle but gaining in strength with each passing second.

'I can only make out the shape of her legs and, after that, nothing. To the naked eye, her body ends at the top of her legs.'

Torchlight from DS Mason's hand played over her shoulder, danced on the surface of the water.

'In the water,' said Clay, 'the tops of her thighs are moving up and down under some force or other, and I guess the rest of her corpse is doing likewise but I can't see it.'

A bubble broke on the water's surface and the vibration beneath the ground turned into an anxious growling, as if there was a feral creature buried alive beneath the path.

'How are Doctor Lamb's APTs going to fish her body out of the water?' asked Sergeant Price.

'They'll have to haul her out, plain and simple,' replied Clay.

'Do you want us to do that now, Eve?' said Mason.

'Yes, please. Help her.'

'Eve.' She heard Hendricks approaching quickly and was glad to hear his voice.

Under the water something went crack. A stream of bubbles broke on the water's surface. Crack-crack-crack, louder each time, and the loud noise of air escaping under the water disturbed the surface. Clay watched as air trapped beneath breaking ice escaped, disturbing the hole.

'It's our lady killer, Bill,' said Clay, as she watched the bubbles breaking on the surface. A sound like a window breaking beneath the water was followed by a huge bubble escaping to the surface, bringing up the rest of the body in a sudden gasp, her arms flailing beneath the water as if she were drowning and trying desperately to save her own life. Her skinned face, purple and covered with rotten leaves, burst out of the water, eyeballs bulging, jaws wide and her teeth clenched around a large pebble, gums exposed from the wide-open space where her lips used to be.

The earth exhaled her body from the water and, in the silence that followed, Clay watched as she floated still and defenceless.

Clay turned to Hendricks, Mason and Price, all looking at the victim, and, Clay guessed, bottling their shock just as she was doing.

'Bill, can you organise a door to door on Menlove Avenue and Woolton Village that way, Allerton Road down at the other end of the path.'

'I'll organise it right now, Eve.'

She said, 'Let's get her out of the water and covered up as quickly as we can.'

'What are you thinking, Eve?' asked Hendricks.

'I'm thinking The Ghoul is local to us. His expedition in the summer to Warrington was an out-of-town dress rehearsal. The big time home show is now well and truly on.'

Clay looked at the woman's missing features as she floated on the surface and her rage turned into dark determination.

Two bodies within the same day. The words fell like fork lightning through Clay's head, and when the lightning died down, the thunder spoke.

The Ghoul had held them in captivity at the same time.

19

4.43 pm

In silence, Detective Sergeant Terry Mason and Sergeant Paul Price folded out a sheet of clear plastic with the choreographed telepathy of an old married couple spreading out a bottom sheet to make up the marital bed.

At the Menlove Avenue end of the crime scene, Clay watched Harper and Kline, Doctor Lamb's senior APTs from the mortuary at the Royal Liverpool Hospital, crossing the scene-of-crime tape and carrying a single grey body bag.

She watched the floating woman and, beneath the water, on her submerged wrist, she saw the dark discolorations of a tattoo, the detail of which she couldn't make out.

Detective Sergeant Bill Hendricks closed down a call and said, 'The footpath's sealed off at Allerton Road and Gina Riley's orchestrating the troops on the door to door at that end.'

Mason and Price laid the plastic sheet down on the ground, pinning it down as it flapped in the wind that combed the sodden earth.

'Thanks, Bill.'

'Eve,' said Mason. 'You want us to get her body out of the water?'

She pointed in the direction of the approaching APTs.

'We'll have a word with Harper and Kline. Discuss what we're going to do in a minute.'

Clay made out the bumps and indentations on the side of the woman's head, the scarlet of her facial muscles washed out by the water in which she had been submerged. Her eyes, standing out from their sockets like lumps of blood-flecked putty, looked like they'd been inserted into her face by the hand of a blind and luckless sculptor.

She looked at the woman's chipped and broken teeth and knew that the stone had been placed into her mouth cavity with considerable anger.

The unzipping of a body bag close at hand hauled Clay back into the wider scene. Harper and Kline laid the body bag on the plastic sheet.

'What do you want us to do, Eve?' asked Mason.

'Stay on the plastic sheet, weigh it down.'

She looked at Harper and Kline as they assessed the body.

'You need help getting her into the body bag?' asked Clay.

'If we take her feet, will you and DS Hendricks take her by the hands?'

Hendricks walked towards the top end of the body.

Harper placed two hands on her right foot and Kline on her left.

Getting to her feet from a kneeling position, Clay felt stiffness deep in her muscles and a ripple of electricity like pins and needles danced down her joints.

'One.' She checked Kline, Harper and Hendricks' positioning. 'Two.' She took a breath, prepared for the weight of the lift. 'Three.'

Lifting the woman from the water, Clay matched the lightness of her corpse with the slimness of her body. Water poured from her back and ribs as she was suspended in mid-air.

'Walk backwards, please, Harper, Kline. There are no obstructions on the path between you and the body bag.'

As Clay and Hendricks stepped forwards, past the sides of the hole, the woman's head flopped and bounced, and the stone in her mouth sat caged behind her teeth.

With both hands wrapped around the woman's wrists, Clay felt a wet stiffness in the flesh, and felt her own hands slipping down towards the woman's hands.

'OK, Eve?' asked Hendricks.

She nodded, tightened her grip and said, 'Can we get a move on here, please?'

Clay counted twelve heavy paces before they arrived at the body bag.

'Lower her down,' said Clay.

Her disfigured head was the first part of her to enter the body bag, followed by her back, buttocks and legs.

Oxygen escaped from the flooded pothole and, to Clay's ears, it sounded like the water was sobbing for the woman it had yielded to the earth.

Clay saw the tattoo on her wrist.

MAND-E.

'Get a picture of her tattoo, Paul,' said Clay.

Clay and Hendricks folded her arms at her sides and, as she zipped up the bag covering the woman's dignity, she estimated that she was five feet seven in height.

MAND-E.

Clay wondered if her name was Mandy or Amanda.

Like the others, she thought, rising to her full height, *you'll be blonde. Pretty, no doubt. Lonely. Woefully unlucky.*

She shivered as Harper and Kline lifted her from the ground in the body bag.

'Where's Doctor Lamb?'

'Waiting for us in the mortuary.'

'Bill, will you go with them, watch the autopsy and feed me any information as and when it crops up.'

Hendricks followed the APTs towards Menlove Avenue, the saddest of funeral processions.

Clay took out her iPhone, felt the dead woman's skin on her palms and fingers as if she was still holding on to her flesh.

The rain began again. Ripples formed on the surfaces of flooded potholes and the wind pressed down on the back of Clay's head as she trudged through a tunnel of misery.

20

4.45 pm

The Ghoul opened the door and stepped into the next room.

The basement was red and black.

From the ceiling, the red glow from the faulty fluorescent light was broken up by flashes of stuttering darkness that plunged the space into night.

There was writing on the wall facing the beds, words they could read over and over and trigger wonder as to their meaning.

The bare brick walls that held up the weight of the house were textured with blood and tears, human excrement, sweat and urine, physical outpourings of misery in a space with no window, a space that had never seen the light of day.

Against the left- and right-hand walls, at the furthest point from the wooden steps leading down into the basement, were two narrow beds, their thin mattresses coated in the same cocktail of substances that covered the walls. Attached to the walls alongside the beds were heavy chains, piled up on the mattresses as their former guests no longer had need of the shackles.

The Ghoul's condensed breath looked like a haze of blood in the moments when the red fluorescent light poured into the space and the engines of the coolers that kept the room at freezing point whirred like mythical birds sent down to earth by angry gods to punish womankind for her heinous sins.

Between the beds, at the dead centre of the basement, was a metal table on wheels, loaded with surgical implements, hypodermic needles and clear and coloured chemicals in plastic containers.

Looking directly up at the faltering light, The Ghoul wondered how long it would take the next woman held captive here to show the first signs of despair, to stop screaming for the light to be turned off and demanding absolute darkness. And then, when that happened and the entire basement was flooded with impenetrable darkness, how long it would take before she screamed for the light to be turned back on again.

The Ghoul stepped back into the adjoining room.

Extending across the length of the room was a washing line.

The Ghoul lifted a hand and ran an index finger along the line, listening to memories of their screams, of their silence, of their hysterical sobbing, of their voices straining to appear normal and offering all kinds of wild promises in exchange for mercy.

And the most loved sound of all, after they had delivered on their promises, and they realised mercy was not forthcoming, the animalistic groan deep in their throats, a key note of hopelessness from the centre of their beings.

Finger hovering on the washing line, The Ghoul came to three eyeless faces hanging in the air, their scalps clipped into place by pegs buried in their hair.

The Ghoul pictured them in life, felt the softness of their skins, the silkiness of their hair and the hollowness of their eyes.

Love. Was it real?

Was it real?

Love. Love. Love.

The thing that inspired the things that came to pass for Sandra and Annie and Amanda.

Love that gave The Ghoul the right and the freedom to pursue wild dreams and act on them.

Love... Love... Love.

The writing on the wall came into The Ghoul's heart like divinely inspired poetry.

'And, so, off she floats to nowhere. Love... Love... Look at me!'

Love. The thing that the basement was all about.

21

4.54 pm

In the back of PC Woodrow's marked police car, parked on the grass verge on Menlove Avenue, the caller sat huddled with her Westie now asleep on her knee.

Clay approached the constable and asked, 'Who is she and how is she, PC Woodrow?'

'Her name's Jackie Graham and her dog's called Oscar. She's articulate but shock's setting in fast.'

Clay walked around the police car to the back door and the empty space next to Jackie Graham. She tapped on the window and, as she opened the door, the dog shook from his sleep and whimpered.

She sat next to the witness, closed the door and, seeing how dark it was, was glad that Jackie didn't have to speak in cold light. Outside the car, tall sodium street lights on the grass verge in the middle of the dual carriageway cast down a dull amber glow.

'Jackie?' Clay's voice was filled with kindness but under the surface there was an urgency that made the woman turn her head immediately. 'I'm sorry you had to see what you saw but I thank you for having the presence of mind to call us as soon as you did. The switchboard operator you spoke to stressed how quick and precise you'd been with her.

'This is my warrant card. My name is DCI Eve Clay. I'm going to tape our conversation. Are you OK with that, Jackie?'

'That's fine.'

'Please tell me everything that happened, everything you saw or heard, Jackie.'

Clay saw Jackie flatten the wet fur on the dog's head and Oscar's eyes glinted in what the street lights cast down from the dead sky behind them.

'I walked Oscar down Menlove Avenue from Vale Road and once we'd passed the house where John Lennon lived as a boy we crossed the road at the same point we do every time we go for the walk.'

The smell of wet dog hit Clay and she sensed the witness sinking inside herself.

'Where was that spot, Jackie?'

'By the high-rise flats, at the 76 bus stop, over the road from the footpath that cuts across the golf course. Oscar's a creature of habit. He dictates.'

'Did you see any pedestrians?'

'No. If I did, I didn't notice.'

'Any cars going either way down the dual carriageway?'

'A few. Either way.'

'No one speeding?'

'Not that I'm aware of.'

'Where did you go once you'd crossed the road?'

'Up the wide footpath. There's a gap in the hedge that leads on to the left-hand side of the golf course. Oscar dragged me through it, same as usual. We walked across the golf course towards Allerton Towers.'

'Anyone on the golf course?'

'Oscar saw someone, something. He made this noise in his throat...' She lowered her voice. 'It's a pathetic note. It's the noise he makes when he's really scared. He ran towards it.'

'Jackie, if he was scared, why did he run towards it?'

'It was plain strange. As you say, why run to something he's scared of? But the fact is he did. He pulled on the lead so hard that I let go and he started running at full pelt across the golf course towards the footpath on the other side. He disappeared through the hedge on to the footpath and I thought, *that's it, he's lost*, but when I got through the gap in the hedge, there he was, stock still. I called him but he didn't come. I called him but he didn't so much as make a noise. I walked towards him. He was standing at the side of the pothole. I thought at first it was a mannequin. Some stupid teenage prank. I saw the legs and the feet on the path and the rest of the... her I couldn't see.

'*You're a naughty boy, Oscar,* I said as I came closer. He slinked off a little and flopped himself down on the path.'

Clay heard the sound of staunched tears in Jackie's voice.

'I... I saw her toenails were painted and I thought, *mannequins don't have painted nails*. I touched her ankle with the tip of my little finger, right hand, and I felt bone beneath the skin. And then. And then. It was as if the story on the news about the lady found on the riverbed somersaulted into my mind. Water. Dead body. I don't remember taking out my phone and calling emergency services but the next thing I knew I was talking to some woman on a switchboard. I told her where I was and what I – what he, what Oscar had found, and I waited there. It seemed like hours but it was probably seconds, a minute or more maybe. I heard the siren coming and I thought, *what if the person who's left this woman's body here is still around? What if he takes me next? What if I end up in a ditch? Or a river?*'

She gathered her dog to her body and held on to him as if her life depended on his closeness to her.

'Jackie, did you see anyone at all?' asked Clay.

'I saw a light, a torchlight, a speck of moving light heading down to the houses on old Allerton Road. Then it disappeared as it got too far away.'

'A man?'

'Too far away to tell.'

Clay smiled, wanted her facial expression to register in her voice.

'You're doing very well, Jackie. Come on now, stay with me, keep going.'

As she spoke, Clay knew in her heart that the woman sitting next to her in a marked police car on a dismal day on Menlove Avenue had, by sheer chance, walked over a line that most people would never cross in the course of a lifetime.

'I heard an engine revving up at the Allerton Road end of the footpath. I heard a vehicle driving away.'

Jackie Graham loosened her grip on Oscar.

'Did you have any overall impressions about what you saw, Jackie?'

She was quiet for a moment and said, 'Yes. How can one man carry a dead woman to that spot on his own? Maybe one of them got away with his torch. Maybe the other got away through the golf course. Whoever he was or they were, they were in a hurry to disappear into the dark. I was convinced in my own mind there must be more than one of them. I think that's all I can tell you, DCI Clay.'

Clay handed her a contact card. 'If you think of anything else, call me. Nothing too small, this is a big, big deal, Jackie.'

Jackie reached for the lock.

'It can only be unlocked from the outside,' said Clay. She pointed at PC Woodrow. 'He'll let us both out in a moment.'

Clay stopped recording and listened to Oscar's empty stomach growl in the confined space.

Clay's iPhone buzzed with an incoming call. 'Excuse me, Jackie.' She glanced at the display and connected. 'Barney, what's up?'

'Cathy Jones, Annie Boyd's best mate, she's just showed up in reception. She wants to talk to you.'

'I'll be there in ten to fifteen minutes, Barney.'

22
5.19 pm

'Thank you for stepping forward to talk to me, Cathy,' said DCI Clay.

In Interview Suite 1, DCI Eve Clay turned on the audio recorder on the table between herself and Cathy Jones.

'You were next on my list of people to talk to,' said Clay.

'I've spent all day going over everything,' said Cathy. 'As soon as I had it all straight as I could in my head, I came to speak to you, DCI Clay.'

She turned her wedding ring round and round her finger like she was performing a ritual protecting herself from harm.

'Cathy, you're not a suspect,' said Clay. 'You're assisting us with our enquiries. I know how stressful this must be for you, but please try and relax.'

Cathy nodded, glanced at the digits on the audio recorder, counting down time. Clay poured Cathy a glass of water and pushed it in front of her. She drank it down in one.

'When we first met in Annie's house, I got the distinct impression from your facial expression and body language that you didn't want me to talk about Annie's internet dating activities in front of her father. Is that correct?'

'It's correct.'

'Did her parents know she was doing internet dating?'

'No. They didn't. But I know they'd never have approved in a million years. Annie had a theoretical conversation about it with them after they'd watched a documentary on TV together. They didn't like it because of the risk element and the strange fish the sites attracted. So when Annie joined Pebbles On The Beach, she asked me not to tell anyone in case it got back to her parents.'

'Why did she join?'

'She attracted a lot of unwanted male attention, married creeps, single men who loved themselves. She needed the love of a good man, and was at her wit's end.'

'What do you know about the man she went to meet on the night she disappeared?'

'Nothing much.'

'What about a name?'

'Richard Ezra. That's what he told her he was called. We'd had a falling out. It upset me because we'd always been open with each other about everything since we were little girls. It was like she was going through a sudden massive change. She was becoming more and more distant.'

'Can you tell me about the falling out?'

'I got married to my now husband, Gary, four weeks ago. When we got back from honeymoon, two weeks ago, it was like she was a changed woman. We hadn't spoken while I was away in Dubai but then as soon as I got back she sent me this.'

Cathy looked like a woman whose mouth was running away from her and her brain was sprinting to keep up.

'Go on?' encouraged Clay.

Cathy took out her iPhone and opened the texts.

She slid the phone across the table to Clay.

Cathy – I am genuinely happy for you and am sure that your happiness will increase with time. At least I hope and pray it does. However, things have changed, the goalposts have shifted. You have a husband and home to think about now and the time that we spend together can no longer be the same. We need time apart. Love you, Annie xxx

Annie, wondered Clay, *were you torn between envy and the need to do the right thing by the newlyweds?*

'Have you got other texts from Annie?'

'Very few. We always talked on the phone. But when I did call her, her phone was off or it went to answer machine. I left messages on her phone but she didn't get back to me. We only texted in emergencies or if one or other of us was on the phone to someone else.'

'Mind if I have a scroll, Cathy?'

In three scrolls of the screen, Clay had the entire body of Annie's texts to Cathy and the content could be summed up in a question and an instruction that completely supported Cathy's claim.

Who are you on to, donut?

Call me when you can.

Then she came back to the lengthiest text that Annie had sent to her friend, distancing herself from the woman on the other side of the desk to Clay.

'You've been best friends since you were four or five years old,' said Clay. 'You get married, Cathy, and she pies you off because you're happy.'

Cathy nodded and her eyes glistened in the glare of the lights above her head.

'Tell me,' Clay passed the iPhone back to Cathy. 'Tell me about the last time you spoke.'

'Like I said, she called me to say she was out on a date, a guy she'd met on the internet and spoken to on the phone. She sounded happy and excited. She kept saying that we should meet up and bury the hatchet, and it was her fault the falling out, and that she was sorry.'

'Can I have a look at your incoming calls, please?'

Cathy glanced up at Clay as she pressed the screen and returned the iPhone to her. She scrolled down and found the last incoming call from Annie.

Thursday 7:45. Length of call 3:36.

Clay scrolled and scrolled until she found the previous call from Annie and did the maths. Last call, on or around the wedding of Cathy and Gary.

Clay held the iPhone back across the table.

'Did she tell you where she was meeting this Richard Ezra, Cathy?'

'No, just that she was actually on the way to meet him.'

'Think really hard about this, please. When you were talking to Annie on the phone that last time, was she indoors or outdoors?'

Cathy's face darkened with concentration.

'She was outdoors. I could hear other people's voices as they moved past her.'

'Anything else?'

'No... no, not really...'

'Where did Annie like to go?'

'Restaurants. Some bars, nice ones.'

'More precise than that, Cathy?'

'Liverpool One. The Dock, the Albert Dock. She absolutely loved it there.'

'You asked her, surely, where are you meeting this Richard Ezra? Where are you planning on going?'

'I asked her but she didn't tell me. She just kept saying, *sorry, sorry*. It was like she'd gone into a tailspin because she was going on a date. She said she had to go, that she was running late. And yeah, I could tell she was moving quickly because she was breathy when she was speaking to me and she spoke so quickly.'

'And she was definitely outdoors?'

There was no reaction, no reply. Cathy closed her eyes, her lips moving softly as if she was talking to herself.

'I...' She stared into space and the light inside her played out in her eyes, and Clay watched as Cathy slowly remembered something she'd overlooked. 'I heard the horn of a tug ship blowing. And water lapping against...'

'Was she at the waterfront?'

'Sounded like. That sound you hear when the river hits the concrete wall beneath your feet.'

'Albert Dock, Cathy. If she'd been asked out on a date, where would Annie go to eat, say?'

'Io, the Greek restaurant overlooking Liverpool One.'

Six kilometres downriver, thought Clay, *from where she finally ended up.*

'She didn't forward you a photograph of him?'

'I asked her to. She didn't have one on her phone to send. I thought it was a bit odd. I mean, she didn't say, but you'd think she'd have sent him a picture and he'd have sent one to her. How else would they recognise each other among all those people at the Dock?'

Clay recalled the photograph that Riley had discovered beneath Annie's pillowslip.

'Thank you,' said Clay. 'You've given us some useful things to go on. Unless you can think of anything else to add, that's all for now. Thank you, Cathy.'

Clay turned off the audio recorder and looked at the door of the interview suite but Cathy didn't move, sat stiller than she had throughout the conversation, turning her wedding ring over and over.

'Is there something you want to say, Cathy?'

'There's a lot of muttering on social media that he did something pretty terrible to her. Is it true?'

'Well, yes, for once social media's correct. The detail is going to be released to the media in the next twelve hours.'

'Her parents?'

'Her parents will be the first to be informed. I don't want them finding out what happened to their daughter from social media.'

Tears welled up in Cathy's eyes as she headed for the door.

'Has he done it before to any other women?'

'Yes.'

'Will he do it again?'

They walked towards the glass door leading to reception.

'He already has done. Cathy, you mustn't discuss anything we've talked about with anyone. If you do, what you know will be all over the internet and that's going to help this so-called Richard Ezra character no end.'

'I won't breathe a word. On Annie's memory.'

As Clay watched Cathy leaving, she called Cole.

'Eve, how's it going?'

'Barney, we need all available CCTV footage from the Echo Arena, front, back and sides. Thursday, 25th November. Start before 7pm and go through until after 9pm. We're looking for Annie Boyd's final recorded steps and anyone who was with her.'

23

6.11 pm

Francesca Christie felt a buzz of excitement as she put her key in the lock of her home in Druid's Cross Road. Opening the door, she heard the voice of the newsreader on the BBC six o'clock news.

'Frann-cesca!' She weighed up the tone of her mother's voice. She certainly hadn't had a great day but it wasn't one of her blackest ones either.

'Hi, Mum...'

She walked to the door of the front room and her mother pointed at a large brown box.

'Who's been buying you flowers?'

So this was James' surprise.

'Don't just stand there, Francesca. Open them.'

Francesca's mother got to her feet and headed towards the door. 'Meal'll be on the table soon. Who are they from?'

The most wonderful, caring man, with a kind and warm voice, who makes my heart go faster and fills me with wild hope, she thought.

'Oh, I don't know, Mum…'

'There's a letter for you. Postman brought it this morning.'

Folding back the flaps on the top of the box, Francesca felt a wave of butterflies rise up inside her.

Handle With Care.

She looked inside the box and saw a wall of vivid red.

Fragile.

Francesca plunged both hands either side of the roses, felt and heard the crinkle of the cellophane in which the flowers were wrapped.

Keep upright.

She held the roses up to the light, felt the glory of the multiple shades of red and drank in their sweet fragrance.

Propped up against the box, she saw an envelope. She leaned the flowers against the armchair and opening the envelope, she slid out a colour photograph, taken sideways and at an angle, of a man with dark, collar-length hair and a beautiful, intelligent face. He smiled into the empty space before him and she placed herself in it, absorbing the loving look and wondering how ecstatic she would feel if this was more than a fantasy.

She picked up the remote and pressed mute to silence the police sirens that screamed from the television set and threatened to spoil an almost perfect moment.

In the moment she silenced the television, her iPhone sang from her bag. She fumbled in the bag and, taking the iPhone out, connected.

'Did you like your surprise, Francesca?'

'James, I can't tell you how much I *love* the roses. Thank you so much. I don't know what to say.'

'How about *yes*?'

'Yes? To?'

'Yes you'll meet up with me sooner than Friday.'

Francesca laughed and looked at his picture. 'Yes. I'd love to.' She wanted to press him for a time and place tomorrow, not too early so she had a chance to do her hair and make-up and nails, so she could look her very best. Instead, she said, 'Your picture came in the post.'

'So you can recognise me when we meet for the first time. We have something to celebrate.'

'Go on?'

'My client and her child, they're staying in the country. I won the case.'

Time froze and the world fell away from her.

'Are you OK, Francesca?'

'I'm so happy it went your way in court today.'

'Francesca, I have to go now. I'm meeting with a client. I'll be in touch. Enjoy the flowers.'

Francesca heard him disconnect before she could say goodbye. She looked up at the television at a picture of a blonde teenager in a formal black dress. As she turned the television off, she was struck by her own physical likeness to the girl.

'Francesca! It's coming on to the table now...'

'Coming.'

She picked up the roses by the stems and wanted to embrace them as she headed towards the kitchen sink.

'That's quite a bunch of flowers you've got there, Francesca.'

Steam billowed from the plate as her mother served spaghetti carbonara on to Francesca's plate.

'So you're not going to tell me who they're from.'

'Mum, leave it, please.' She held her free hand up to stop her mother ladling more pasta on to her plate. 'Thank you, that'll do,' said Francesca, looking at the portion of pasta and thinking of what she'd look like in the mirror when she next stepped out of the bath, what he would make of her if things ever went that far.

As her mother carried two plates of pasta to the kitchen table, Francesca placed the roses in the sink.

'This was one of your dad's favourites.'

'I remember.'

Francesca sat across the table from her mother, her appetite gone.

'What's happened to your hand, Francesca?'

She looked at her right hand and saw a spreading pattern of blood from a tiny wound on her index finger.

'Clumsy me,' said Francesca. She looked across the kitchen at the roses in the sink. 'One of the thorns...' She smiled, wrapped a piece of tissue around the wound and pressed down, her normally heavy heart lifting with happiness and excitement at what lay ahead, and she made a big decision that she had been playing with since her earliest days at Maguire Holdings.

It was time to move on and away from Norma Maguire.

24
6.31 pm

For the fifth time, Detective Chief Inspector Eve Clay read Annie Boyd's online dating profile on Pebbles On The Beach and was astonished at what constituted a poor advertisement for self.

In her profile photograph, Annie looked pretty and good-natured and it made Clay feel deeply sorry for her. It was a cropped head and shoulders shot of the picture she'd had taken on holiday, the one from which she had been identified through her mole and the bluebird tattoo on her arm.

The door of the incident room opened and Clay looked up from her laptop.

'You wanted to see me, Eve?' asked Riley, walking towards Clay.

'Grab a seat and sit with me please, Gina.'

As Riley sat next to her, Clay said, 'This is Annie Boyd's dating profile. What do you know about internet dating sites?'

'Quite a bit. When my sister got divorced, she spent half her life online looking for a man and the other half dragging me through the process, each painful step of the way.'

'I'm a novice to this but my instincts are telling me she's really not doing herself any favours. Have a look. See what you think? A second pair of eyes, please.'

Clay pushed her laptop sideways to Riley and watched her face for a reaction.

'What are you plotting, Eve?'

'Just tell me what you think of it, Gina.'

After a couple of minutes, Riley sat back and looked at Clay.

'She's made a pig's ear of it,' said Riley. 'The photograph's nice but it's static. She should have put in an action shot, maybe spinning on the spot or walking towards camera. I don't reckon she's asked her friends for any advice. It's pitted with clichés like *man of my dreams* and *happily ever after*. She's listed her hobbies as reading, listening to music, watching athletics on TV. Hardly the most sociable of hobbies. And she's gone on and on when she should have kept it short and to the point. Negativity. Look.'

Riley pointed at a line in the profile and Clay read, 'I don't like nightclubs where the music is so loud that I can't hear you and you can't hear me, or being around lots of people who look at other people aggressively.' She read on in silence and learned that Annie was frightened of dogs and wary of false people.

'Jesus,' said Riley. 'For a teacher, there are a lot of typos in here. Nightmare profile. Bet she didn't get that many men winking at her.'

'Winking at her?'

'If a man comes on to her profile and likes what he sees, he gives her an electronic wink to show he's interested. She can choose to ignore the wink or wink back. If she winks back, that gives him the OK to open up an online dialogue, which is pretty much akin to corresponding over Messenger. Have we had any feedback from Poppy on who's been shaking her tree?'

'She's working on it,' replied Clay. 'Poppy's got Annie's laptops but I'm certain The Ghoul's got her phone. Guess where we're going next, Gina?'

'Go on?' said Riley.

'Internet dating. I've joined Pebbles On The Beach and set up a fake profile, using all Annie's mistakes and wording them differently. I'll make myself as close as I can to Annie and see if I can draw the killer out. We're all going to do likewise. Desperate, deluded and needy blondes in their mid twenties. Give out the brief and oversee what happens when we go online. We need a spread. We can't assume that the killer goes exclusively on one site. Gina, everyone's to report back directly to you. You report back to me. When Poppy's fished out Annie's exchanges with the killer through the site, I'll have a better idea of how we all play things if any of us get off first base. We'll also know what we're looking for from our killer, how he uses language, his linguistic tics.'

Riley walked to her desk and flipped up the lid of her laptop.

'I'll send everyone an email,' said Riley.

Clay focused on her fake profile picture, plundered from a search of Google Images under the words she'd placed into the search engine: *Pretty blonde woman, mid twenties.*

From a choice of hundreds of images, she had chosen a dead ringer for Annie Boyd. The similarity made Clay hope the effect on The Ghoul would be electrifying, would make it be like looking at a ghost of his victim.

Clay spread out the five pages of Annie Boyd's profile on her desk.

'The thing is, Gina, a lot of men go looking for vulnerable women online and vice versa. The Ghoul isn't going to be looking out for confident, sassy women who come across like they can hold their own. Get that across to the troops, please. Only car-crash dizzy blondes need apply.'

Riley walked over to Clay's desk, looked over her shoulder.

'That's almost uncanny, the likeness. Different enough around the eyes. His mouth will be watering.'

Riley read Clay's fake profile.

Hi boys. My name's Natasha and I love nothing better than curling up in front of a roaring log fire with a glass of red wine and some smooth music in the background. I'm looking for a stand-up guy who knows how to handel a woman like me who loves nothing better than taking care of him and making him very, very happy.

'Handel?' questioned Riley. 'I haven't questioned your spelling so far, Eve, but shouldn't that be *handle?*'

'She's crap at spelling, Natasha. I'm going to make sure she doesn't come across as too clever. A lot of men like that quality in a woman.'

25

11.31 pm

The bedroom was Wren's but the walls belonged to Captain Cyclone.

The wall facing Wren's bed was taken up with a picture of Captain Cyclone in his human incarnation – Captain Benjamin Black, hero of the SAS but not the superhero Captain Cyclone whose powers dwarfed the greatest gifts afforded to mankind. Tall, impossibly handsome and with a body made up from walls of muscle, Captain Benjamin Black's eyes followed their creator when he moved around the room.

Wren watched the rain roll down his window and the sheer darkness behind the glass, the kind of weather that Captain Cyclone loved. He looked at his mobile phone, the one he'd held in the palm of his hand since Edgar McKee had dropped him off at home after they'd finished work early, and wished that Edgar would call him or send a text.

He looked at the hands of his bedside clock, bright green in the darkness, and saw that it was getting too late to call Edgar even if he had been allowed. Which he wasn't. Edgar had been quite firm when he suggested in the van they swap numbers.

I'll call you, Wren. Don't call me unless it's an emergency. I'll reveal the reason when the time is right.

Edgar had said it so firmly but with such kindness that the memory of the whole day filled Wren with a warmth he hadn't felt for many years.

Wren tried to put the journey from the abattoir back home to Gateacre into some sequence but he was totally unfamiliar with most streets and suburbs in the part of South Liverpool that they'd travelled through together.

I can tell we're going to be great mates, Wren. I've only known you a matter of hours and I feel like you're my mate already. I like you. I like you a lot.

Edgar had said that just after he'd pointed out a house on a dual carriageway that John Lennon from The Beatles had grown up in when he was a little boy.

Wren had stifled the words *I've never had a mate before in my whole life* because it made him feel bad about himself and he didn't want Edgar to think that nobody else liked him.

He looked into the dim light of a lamp in the corner of his room and picked out the picture he had painted on the wall to his left. Captain Cyclone in his full glory, sweeping through a city full of corruption and lies, devastating the homes and offices of the bad guys, crushing them with his power yet at the same time sucking the innocent and good up into the eye of the cyclone that was his body, where they were safe and protected from the storm.

I'll drive you home to Gateacre after I've gone on my message. Is that OK with you, Wren?

It was more than OK. No one apart from Dad ever asked him if things were OK with him. No one apart from Mum before she died asked him if he was OK. No one apart from Mum or Dad or Edgar, that is.

At a set of traffic lights, there was a church across the junction with a poster on the wall that read:

AN HONEST WITNESS DOES NOT DECEIVE BUT A
FALSE WITNESS POURS OUT LIES. PROVERBS 14:5

A good proverb. The sort of thing Captain Cyclone would say at the end of one of his adventures overwhelming murderers and thieves and lowlife scum from the Big City.

He could barely see the wall around his window but he didn't need light to know what was going on behind the veil of darkness because he had painted it himself and knew every square centimetre of the image.

Captain Benjamin Black led thousands of innocent men, women and children back into the ruins of the Big City, with a wren flying over the exodus, and with a simple command coming from the superhero's lips.

Rebuild!

Wren moved into the corner of his room and tilted his lamp so that the light was aimed at the triumphant march back into the redeemed city. He placed the light on his small desk, which he hadn't needed since the day he was kicked out of school for something someone else had done. He opened the desk drawer where he kept his paints and brushes. He selected a broad and a thin brush, a tube of white and a tube of black.

A change was needed to the wall around the window.

Wren took out the step ladder from the side of his pine wardrobe and, setting it up, stepped up from the floor, two, three steps to the top. Brushes in one hand and a tube of paint in the other, he stretched out his arms and moved them in a figure of eight.

This is how Edgar makes me feel, thought Wren. The loneliness that had dogged him for as many years as he could remember was gone.

'My name is Wren. And I can fly!'

26

11.59 pm

Under the dim light of her bedside lamp, Norma Maguire had fallen asleep to the sound of Chopin's Nocturnes whispering from the bedside radio. An empty glass and a bottle of Talisker lay next to each other.

Behind the large black mask that covered her eyes, nose and cheeks, Norma lived through a recurring dream.

In her dream, she walked on a beach, light dancing in the sky above her head and casting every shade of gold on the sand beneath her bare feet. Seagulls called on the wind and circled between the blue sky and the white clouds.

Crosby Beach.

Beneath the transparent white dress that exposed her skin to the light, her feet were elegant, and her legs moved effortlessly.

She turned on the pillow, her face now away from the light.

On the beach, there were rock pools and crabs crawled from the edge of the sea between the pebbles and shells that littered the sand. Dragonflies hovered at her eyeline, flying ahead of her like messengers announcing her arrival to the forces of nature in which she walked; dragonflies, their bodies made iridescent by the sun, the fragile structure of their wings made visible in the morning light.

Somewhere in the house, two clocks ticked out of time with each other, creating a continuous sound that echoed from the high ceilings and the wide walls of the cavernous rooms.

But what was that sound in the sand? What vibration rose from the beach?

Darkness emerged from the sand. A curve of black iron. The shape of a skull. The beginning of a face. The head of a giant man rising from the earth. Throat. Shoulders. Arms. The figure of the man was silent, his face expressionless but his whole being endowed with colossal power.

Another figure and another figure and another and another and another. Rising from the sand, rising from the water, their dark bodies made green by the elements, spaced at different places in relation to the sea and the sand, their silent faces all looking in the same direction, at the horizon and beyond.

She made to run towards the water, towards the nearest Iron Man...

Asleep, Norma made a noise from the depths of her dream, between a cry of despair and a sob of terror.

... but found she was frozen to the sand, now sitting in her wheelchair, as the iron giants of Crosby Beach turned a half circle, some less, some more, but all in her direction. They stared at her in random judgement with sightless eyes, accusing her with dumb mouths.

In the water and on the sand, the Iron Men's arms rose from their ribs and their legs moved as they stepped towards the horizon. With each step, they sank deeper into the water of the Irish Sea.

She watched, dumbstruck and paralysed, as the Iron Men disappeared step by step under the waves for ever while she was rooted in her wheelchair on the sand.

She turned from her side on to her back, felt the tug of consciousness.

Soft, quiet classical music drifted into her head.

Norma sat up slowly, pulled her eye mask down and looked directly into the landing outside her bedroom. There was nothing and no one there.

She looked at the empty pillow next to hers, pictured Fran sleeping lightly, eyes closed, blonde hair spread across the pillowslip. It was a vivid picture, so powerful in her imagination that it was almost real.

Norma reached out but all she touched was the pillowslip and the air above it.

'Goodnight, Fran. Sleep tight.'

A branch from a tree in the garden bent in and tapped on the bedroom window like a caller asking for admission to the house.

'Fran? Can you hear me, Fran? Don't go to him, Fran.' Tears rolled down her face. 'Stay with me. I love you, Fran...'

THE PAST

1979

As she crept down the stairs, moonlight shone through the stained-glass skylight, picking out a path in the darkness for her in amber and red.

With each step, the grandfather clock in the hall hummed and she imagined that in the mechanics inside it there was a real heart, racing at a dozen beats per second like the injured mouse she had found in the garden that morning.

Tiptoeing through the hall in the direction of the kitchen, she felt the vibration of the mouse's heartbeat in her hands, where she had held it for a long, long time.

Other than the hum and tick-tock of the grandfather clock, the house was plunged into the silence of the dead of night.

In the kitchen, she pondered the silence and realised that her baby brother – not a baby now but eighteen months old, though in her heart he would always be her baby brother – was indeed *a very smart cookie*.

A very smart cookie? Her infant teacher Miss Slack's favourite term of praise for children who answered questions correctly, sat up nicely and listened well.

Baby brother had learned a big lesson from his big sister: the total pointlessness of crying.

It was not rewarded with kindness and attention from either mother or father and, very often, provoked the opposite response. Anger.

In her hands she carried a wet nappy. She placed it in the drum of the washing machine, already half full of washing for Mrs Doyle to see to in the morning.

She blew a sigh of relief. No one would notice what she had done for her baby brother just now.

She opened the fridge and was grateful for the outpouring of light from within the chilly box.

She looked up in the general direction of her baby brother's bedroom and recalled the recent memory of her visit to him.

He had stood at the side of his cot, holding on to the wooden rail, his face and head illuminated by a strand of moonlight that shot through a gap in the curtains.

'Hungry?'

He had looked at her in a way that needed no language, not that he had that much anyway. She knew. He was starving.

In the kitchen, she poured milk into his drinking cup and screwed on the lipped top of the vessel.

She found biscuits in a tin and hid them in the pockets of her dressing gown.

When she had been with him five minutes earlier, she had lifted him from his cot and felt that he was suddenly much heavier than his normal weight. His nappy was flooded.

She had laid him on the floor, reminding him with a finger over her own lips and a whispered *hush* of the need for complete silence.

She had unbuckled the safety pins on either side of his nappy, removing the soaked white garment from his body.

In a drawer, she took a clean, dry nappy and wrapped it round his hips and the space between his legs.

Hush now... hussshhhh...

He was lighter when she lifted him from the floor and placed him back inside his cot. His eyes had tracked her as she moved silently across the floor.

'I'll be back,' she whispered to his unflinching gaze. 'I promise you, I'll be back.'

As she reached the top of the stairs with provisions, in a bedroom some doors away her father snored and the sudden sound almost made her scream with fright.

'For fuck's sake...' Her mother's voice sounded in the pit of night.

She hurried along the landing, fearful that her mother might leave the parental bedroom and seek a quieter space to sleep, catching her on the hop, out of bed and stealing food for her baby.

The sheets and blankets rustled in her parents' room and she guessed that her mother had hibernated in their bed, burying her head and ears under the warmth of the materials that comforted them in the cold grip of winter.

She avoided the places on the carpet beneath which the floorboards creaked like demons posted by her mother and father to alert them to the place, time and progress of their children.

His breathing was heavy. Her baby. Her baby brother. Her baby.

The light sharpened as she entered his room, when a night cloud sailed away from the beaming moon.

His hands, his fingers opened and closed, opened and closed, over the wooden frame of his cot. He opened his mouth and the noise of staunched tears made the silence between the walls more dense than it had ever felt to her.

She handed him the cup of milk and watched him drink from the lip as if his life depended on it.

He swayed in the cot and caught on to it with his left hand, stopping himself from falling on to his bottom.

She threw an arm around him and held on to him as tightly as she could, as if the world was... that feeling when she woke up suddenly in the dark... on the verge of collapse.

He stayed on his feet and she let go degree by painful degree.

Whatever was going on, the moon danced in his eyes, and she smiled at him and he smiled back.

His hands, his fingers opened and closed, opened and closed, over the wooden frame of his cot.

She took a biscuit from the pocket of her dressing gown, placed it in his hand and he devoured it before she had time to pick out the next one.

On the landing outside, there was a click. A switch on a wall.

She handed him the next biscuit, thought that she had imagined the noise outside her baby's room.

She heard the creak of the door at her back and saw the deepening band of light fall into her baby's room from the landing outside.

'Well, well, well, what's going on around here?'

DAY TWO

THURSDAY, 2ND DECEMBER 2021

ONEIROPHOBIA

FEAR OF DREAMS

27

3.03 am

Eve Clay sat at the table in her dining room, haunted by a dream that had propelled her from a troubled sleep. The only light in the room came from the screen of her laptop. She muted the sound and watched a clear and gentle tide washing over a gathering of colourful pebbles lodged in clean sand.

Words appeared on the screen.

Pebbles On The Beach.

Her body shivered in the cold of the early hours and the fresh memory of a vivid dream.

She climbed over the metal railings, a precarious barrier between the promenade at Otterspool and the River Mersey below. Tall arc lamps threw light on to the mud and, as she negotiated the concrete steps down to the riverbed, the sky was full of red light and dark contours of menacing clouds.

She opened the fake profile she had posted, masquerading as twenty-something Natasha Jones.

Clay recognised the weight of Thomas' footsteps as he walked down the stairs, and saw that two of the three men she had winked at had winked back at her.

She wrote, Hi, Alan, how yah doing? And then, Hi, Stu, how's it going? as her dream came crashing inside her head.

She walked across the mud towards the dead woman with the sky shifting and the wind howling at her back, her protective suit sticking against her clothes. The waters of the River Mersey disappeared like giant bathwater down a plughole nearby, a vortex in the mud. Clay turned and the line of supporting officers on the promenade weren't there. The light continued pouring above the railings and when she turned to continue her journey to the dead woman, she froze.

'Eve? Are you all right?' asked Thomas from the bottom of the stairs.

'I'm fine. Thank you.'

She heard him moving from the hall in her direction and said, 'In here, the dining room.'

'What are you doing?'

'Do me a favour, Thomas. Keep the light off.'

'Can't sleep?' he asked.

'Bad dreams,' she replied.

The dead woman pulled herself up from the mud, pushing down into the sludge with both hands, her facial skin missing but the muscles on her cheeks twitching into life. With each step Clay took towards her, the woman grew taller and stronger under the shimmering sky.

Thomas pulled a chair up and sat beside her at the table. Clay looked over the laptop and through the French windows at a pair of cat's eyes glinting back at her as it slunk across the top of the wall at the bottom of their garden. She felt the weight and warmth of Thomas' arm as it rested on her shoulder.

'What's this?' he asked, with a smile in his voice.

'What do you think it is?'

'Are you trying to tell me something?'

'Don't worry, it's work-related. The Ghoul...'

'Him?'

'He's pulling his victims from internet dating sites. One in particular. Pebbles On The Beach. We've all set fake profiles, we're all projecting ourselves out there as pretty blondes in our mid twenties. Look.' She pointed at her profile picture. 'This is me. Natasha Jones. Read all about me. Tell me what you think.'

Thomas spent a minute reading through the fiction Eve had projected about herself and said, 'It's nothing like you.'

'Exactly. We pulled the profiles of the victims and noticed similarities.'

'Natasha Jones comes across as a bit of a pushover. When did you last toast a marshmallow on an open fire?'

'I've had a good look across the site,' said Eve. 'In spite of the clichés, the men and women on it seem genuine, solid, dependable types. They come across as worn out by the world. All they want is love and commitment.'

The luxury of her own personal situation hit Clay and she looked closely at her husband in the green light of the screen, saw that he was thinking.

'Go on, ask the question that's on your mind,' said Clay.

'So, when you say you've *all* put up fake profiles, that means everyone?'

'It's a mass phishing trip to get the killer to give himself away.'

'So, what's Karl Stone called?'

'Wendy Bruce.'

'What's Wendy like?'

'Wendy's a cliché-riddled drip, she's blonde and mid twenties and that's exactly the way The Ghoul likes his women.'

The dream played out beneath the surface.

It was in her hands, the thing she had rescued from the mud in which she had been dumped.

'How will you know it's The Ghoul?'

'We're looking at the language he used in his online communication with the Warrington victim, Sandra O'Day. When we pulled up Annie Boyd's online conversations with him, it was a case of comparing and contrasting the two.'

'That's a great idea. But come back to bed soon, Eve. Try and get some sleep.'

She felt Thomas fade away as he left the room and headed back upstairs.

It hung from her hands like a length of slack rubber.

She lifted it above her head and pulled it down over her scalp, face and neck.

The hair was matted with oil and mud and hung from her head like a hex.

Clay stepped closer and, focusing on the woman's face, felt the breath fleeing from her body and her heart pounding against her ribs.

'No…' she whispered to the shadows.

The woman stepped closer and her face was picked out by the lights from the promenade. Clay stared at the woman and saw exactly who she was.

Clay saw herself standing in the mud, stone dead but turning like the living to walk away, barefoot and naked towards the hole in the mud where everything was sucked into the vortex.

She felt her heart beating and the blood rushing through her head.

Clay came out of the Pebbles On The Beach site and looked at her screensaver, Thomas and herself walking in the fallen autumn leaves, at the lakeside in Sefton Park, each holding one of Philip's hands.

Everyone deserves happiness, she thought, *and everyone has the right to seek happiness. Nobody deserves to die because they're lonely.*

28

7.45 am

Neil Wren climbed the stairs with the usual heavy heart for the task ahead. Since he was old enough to go to school, his son had been a nightmare to get out of bed, needing at least ten calls, containing a cocktail of threats and bribes depending upon the mood he was in.

At the top of the stairs, Neil called, 'Wren!' with as much enthusiasm as he could muster. 'Wren! Wren, time to get up, Wren! We've got to go to work, Wren! Please don't make me late, Wren, or the boss will shout at me...'

He knocked on the door and his shoulders sank at the silence behind it.

Neil Wren cursed his sister, Louise, a woman who held sway over Wren, who'd suggested that work experience as an apprentice would be excellent for his one and only son. She had managed to embed the idea into Wren's head that he would meet people and see a different side of life, confiding in him that all the day centre was doing for him was increasing his anxiety levels and making him more autistic.

'Wren, come on, *mate...*'

Neil recalled the time when they'd visited with Wren's Auntie Louise and his son announced that he would like to work with animals, *just like my dad.*

'Wren, I'm coming in!'

His eyes focused on the bed but instead of being a mound under which Wren slept the sleep of the dead, it was made up neatly.

Wren stood in the middle of the room, dressed, smelling of a little too much aftershave and smiling.

'I've brushed my teeth, I've washed myself, I've put clean underwear on, and I'm ready to go to work. Ready when you are, Dad.'

'Well, I never—'

'Surprised, Dad?'

'Very, very surprised. Well done, Wren. Good lad...'

He noticed the smell of fresh paint and his heart rose.

'You're full of surprises, mate.'

Wren eye-pointed to the wall above his head, his Captain Cyclone mural, with new changes to the imagery.

Neil stepped deeper into the room and read the words, '*An honest witness does not deceive but a false witness pours out lies. Proverbs 14:5.* Wow, Wren!'

A dark thought clouded the suddenly bright new horizon.

'You haven't caught religion, have you, Wren? Jesus and the disciples and all that...?' *Shite.* Wren shook his head and flatly said, 'No! Captain Cyclone is my God.'

Wren looked up at the mural and his father looked with him, didn't see the change at first, but when he did see it, he understood immediately the out of character early bird routine.

He had painted over Captain Cyclone's facial features and replaced it with the physiognomy of Edgar McKee.

He double-checked. 'Edgar McKee, right?'

'Right.' Wren smiled in a manner he hadn't smiled since he'd been a small boy before he lost his mother to cancer, and his father felt the welling up of tears.

'You like Edgar?'

'He's my mate. He's cool.'

'Come on, lad. Your lunch box is at the door, the usual, the same as ever, the things you like.'

I will definitely have to buy you a pint or two, Edgar, he thought.

As he walked downstairs, Neil Wren thought about his sister, Louise Fisher, and had to hand it to her. For one thing, she had been bang on the money about work experience. And for another, as Wren had informed her, she was like a second mother to him.

29

9.09 am

Eighteen minutes after a call to the central switchboard from Mrs Alice Hobson, Detective Sergeant Bill Hendricks rang on the doorbell of 235 Allerton Road – one of nine houses from which there had been no reply during the previous day's door to door enquiry – and stepped back next to Detective Sergeant Gina Riley.

Riley turned her back on the house, facing Allerton Manor Golf Course and Allerton Towers and the opening to the public footpath between the two green spaces.

'It looks like Mrs Hobson had a ringside seat.'

'Who is it?' A frail, elderly voice came from behind the front door.

'It's the police,' replied Riley, with as much pleasantness as she could muster on a freezing morning. 'My name's Detective Sergeant Gina Riley and my colleague is Detective Sergeant Bill Hendricks.'

Behind the door, chains rattled as Mrs Hobson loosened them from their catches.

In the narrow space of the partially opened door, a small, bird-like lady in her eighties clutched at the collar of her pink housecoat. On her head was a brown wig. It looked like a cat had curled up and died in its sleep on her skull.

'Trust us, Mrs Hobson,' said Hendricks, working out the angle of the camera pointing down in the direction of the front door and beyond that to Heath Road. 'How did we know to call here other than you called our switchboard and said you had something to tell us?'

'Come in.' She lifted the last chain. 'Brush your feet on the mat and follow me into the front room.'

The walls were white and the front room smelled freshly painted. There was a red leather three-piece suite, with one of the armchairs directly facing a state-of-the-art television set.

Mrs Hobson lifted the net curtain and showed Hendricks and Riley the clear view of the entrance and exit to the public footpath.

'What do you think?' asked Mrs Hobson.

'You have an excellent view of a place we're very interested in,' replied Riley.

'Have a seat.'

Hendricks and Riley sat on the settee, facing Mrs Hobson.

'Were you here all day yesterday?' asked Riley, glancing at the *TV Times* beside the old lady.

'I was.'

'You didn't answer the bell when the constables came knocking door to door.'

'I heard the bell. It rang three times. It was the only call I had yesterday. But I heard on the grapevine the Jehovah's

Witnesses are in the area, so I ignored it and kept on watching telly.'

'Fair enough,' said Hendricks.

'I saw on the Granada Reports round-up after the ten o'clock news that a woman's body had been found on the footpath.'

'Your CCTV, it's working, right?' asked Riley.

'Yes.'

'Have you viewed it, Mrs Hobson?'

'No.'

'What does it cover?'

'It covers the front door.'

'How far does it extend?' asked Riley.

'The top of Heath Road. Do you want to know what I saw just with my eyes?'

'Of course,' said Riley.

'I saw a white van come out of the footpath. It was being driven really slowly. It turned left to get into the lane leading down to Heath Road. And then it took a right down Heath Road in the direction of Mather Avenue. If it didn't stop in Heath Road then it had to turn either right or left on the dual carriageway. What was a white van doing on the public footpath? It's not a road. It's not fit to drive a vehicle down. I tell you...' She looked at Riley and Hendricks in turn. 'I smelled a massive rat.'

'What time did you see the van, Mrs Hobson?' asked Riley.

'Half past three in the afternoon. Just before it started going dark.'

'Did you see who was in the van?'

'No. There wasn't much light. I couldn't see anyone.'

'Licence plate?'

'No. I've told you everything I know.' She reached into the pocket of her housecoat and took out a white envelope. 'This is the CCTV footage. I saved it on to a pen drive. I did an IT For Beginners course at night school.'

Riley stood up and took the envelope from Mrs Hobson.

'Half past three. That's definitely the time you saw the white van?' Hendricks double-checked.

'Definitely the time. BBC 24-hour news was on. I checked the time on the telly,' said Mrs Hobson, pressing her hands down on the arms of her chair to help herself to her feet. 'Would you like to see my IT certificate?'

30

9.33 am

Francesca Christie had the clearest sensation that someone behind her was stripping her naked with his eyes.

She kept her back turned but felt the heat in the office rise and remembered the time when a lipstick went missing from her desk drawer. The only people other than herself who had a key to the drawer were Daniel Ball and Norma Maguire, and that was why she no longer kept personal items in it.

'Francesca?'

At her desk near the window of Maguire Holdings, she heard Daniel Ball's voice coming towards her. She recognised the toadying tone, knew he was about to dump something difficult on her lap as he washed over her with his beady eyes, and she pretended not to hear.

'Fran!'

Caught off guard by his impersonation of Norma Maguire, she looked around and saw that the boss wasn't there to catch Daniel's mockery.

His hands were firmly in his trouser pockets, and his eyes dipped from her face to her breasts and back in the micro-second that she guessed was the fruit of a lifetime's practice.

'Yes, Daniel?'

'You look rather lovely this morning, Francesca.'

As she absorbed the compliment, she recalled the morning of her third day at work in the office and how she'd been filled in and warned at break time. Daniel apparently went to bars in the city centre most nights where he picked up women and sometimes men to take to budget hotels for sex with him. Behind the smart suit, shirt and tie, he was a sex addict. And the conclusion of her colleague's advice had stuck fast. 'Don't be on your own with him.'

'Dean's phoned in sick.'

'Again?'

'I looked in the diary and I see you're free at eleven this morning.'

'Coventry Road?' Francesca anticipated.

'Exactly. The shithole's shithole.'

'With the vendor who doesn't understand that it needs forty grand's worth of work to make it habitable but who won't budge down one bean from the asking price? Postpone the viewing!'

'No. No. Dean's not hacking it. You will. If anyone can build bridges between the vendor and the buyer, it's you.'

Francesca heard the dismal ping of the lift arriving from Norma's office to the ground floor.

'Mama's coming for you, baby.'

'Give me the keys, Daniel. The keys to 431 Coventry Road.'

He placed them on her desk. The lift doors parted. Francesca snatched up the keys and grabbed her wet raincoat from the back of her swivel chair.

'You're rather keen to get out all of a sudden, *Fran*!'

'I need to go and assess the property before I do the viewing. I need to find a way in, a way to convince both parties of a way forward.'

Norma Maguire wheeled herself backwards from the lift into the main area of the office.

'You had three missed calls yesterday, Francesca,' said Daniel, as she stepped towards the front door. 'Three missed calls from Mr Doherty's office. What's going on, Francesca?'

'Nothing's going on. I can't help it if people phone me up. Did you ask for those emails you receive on a daily basis telling you there are dozens of Russian women just dying to meet you?'

Norma turned herself round and smiled into the office, focusing on Francesca and wheeling herself towards her.

'Change the subject, Daniel!'

'Good luck, kid,' he said, walking away.

Francesca half-raised a hand to Norma, threw in a cheery, 'Morning, Norma.'

'In a hurry, Fran?'

'Kind of.'

'Fran?'

Francesca froze, counted to three and smiled at Norma.

'Yes, Norma?'

'A little bird tells me you've been receiving some unwanted attention from a certain someone just down the block.'

Francesca looked around the room for that little bird and saw Daniel disappear into the staff-only kitchen area.

'Just be careful, Fran. The grass may look greener on the other side of the fence but all that glitters, hmm, Fran...'

As Norma spoke, Francesca's eyes were drawn to her mouth, which looked vivid and red.

'What can I do to make you stay? Fran?'

'Leave me... Alone...'

'Pardon?'

'I mean, leave it with me. Your little bird's singing the wrong tune. Listening to gossip? It's not a good idea. Coventry Road. I have to go.'

'Fran?'

'Yes?'

'I'm trying to protect you. Don't take it as anything other than that. I've got your back, Fran. But you know that. Don't you?'

Norma turned herself back in the direction of the lift, the veins in her hands protruding, thick and blue, the muscles around them twitching as she made the manoeuvre.

Francesca headed for the front door with a dozen eyes piercing the nape of her neck and soothed herself with the thought that yesterday James Griffiths had sent her the twenty-four red roses that sat in a vase by her bedside.

31

10.01 am

In the incident room on the top floor of Trinity Road police station, Detective Sergeant Bill Hendricks asked, 'Ready?'

On the screen of Hendricks' laptop was a frozen image of the exit from the footpath between Allerton Manor Golf Course and Allerton Towers on to Allerton Road. The time 3:29:31 pm, the date 01/12/21.

Sitting at his side, Detective Sergeant Gina Riley replied, 'Let's just hope Mrs Hobson's right.'

On screen, the front door of Mrs Hobson's house was covered, and the image extended beyond the corner of the front elevation of the old lady's house and on to the top end of Heath Road.

Hendricks took off the pause and raised his hands to show his colleagues two pairs of crossed fingers.

A blue Orion travelled from the one-way lane leading from Allerton Road into Heath Road.

A fat drop of rain smashed on to the lens of Mrs Hobson's CCTV camera, turning the world it observed into a blur. A gust of wind flattened the moisture. The blurred view of the corner of Heath Road changed in an instant as the slowed-down seconds crawled by.

Hendricks looked at the clock on the screen's corner as it reached 3:30:00 pm and back to the screen, where a piece of discarded newspaper was being bullied by the wind, rolling from Heath Road across Mrs Hobson's path.

'It's coming!' Riley spoke sharply and Hendricks paused. She pointed at the top of the screen. 'It's the front left-hand corner of the van. 3:30:11 pm. Go on, Bill...'

The left-hand side of the white van came into view.

'Look!' said Cole. 'Look in the window on the passenger door.'

Hendricks paused.

'There's someone in the passenger seat,' said Hendricks.

'Keep it rolling, Bill. Let's see what happens as it passes the old lady's house and off into Heath Road.'

The three watched as the van disappeared out of view.

'We've got a partial number plate. That's all we need,' said Cole. 'I'll track its progress using Automatic Number Plate Recognition. If it's turned left or right on to Mather Avenue it'll be easy to follow. Even if it carries on across the junction to the rest of Heath Road, we should be OK. I'll get on to it as soon as we're done here.'

Hendricks rewound the footage back to 3:30:11 pm.

'Let's watch out for the passenger, Bill,' said Riley.

They watched the van come into its fullest view. Hendricks paused.

'This is the best we're going to do for the licence plate.'

'Last three digits,' said Cole, repeating them silently over and over in his head. 'ZDS,' he said out loud.

Slowly, the passenger turned his face towards Mrs Hobson's house, as if his attention was subliminally sucked in by the CCTV camera. In the micro-second before the passenger turned away again, Hendricks paused.

'It's a man,' said Hendricks. 'Fair hair. We need to get this cleaned up by CCTV4U.'

'Are you sure it's a man?' asked Cole, the mantra of three digits echoing inside his head.

'Could be a man, could be a woman,' said Riley. 'But no view of the driver.'

'The thing we now know is whoever's been abducting, killing and skinning women isn't doing this on his own. I'll take this to CCTV4U, get them to drop everything and clean up what we have,' said Hendricks.

Cole walked back towards his desk.

'Thank God for Mrs Hobson. Hopefully, like the last of the little piggies, I'll be able to follow the white van all the way home.'

32

10.14 am

Clay sat next to Poppy Waters and looked at Annie Boyd's two open laptops and two mobile phones.

'The mobile phones are relatively old. As I said when Gina Riley brought the haul in, she must have taken her current mobile out with her when she went on the date. There's nothing on the phones of any note.'

Poppy indicated the older of the laptops, a Lenovo.

'This one's a school laptop. All it contains relates to school work and nothing else.'

'What about this one?' asked Clay.

'This is the one. This is the good news,' said Poppy. 'And this is where we get a lucky break. This laptop is synced to her current iPhone, so anything she'd been doing on her missing iPhone's been mirrored on this. Internet searches, YouTube.'

'What's she been looking up on the internet, Poppy?'

'In the week before she went missing, she's been buying underwear from Victoria's Secret. On YouTube, she's been watching and listening to videos for all manner of love songs.'

Poppy brought up the Pebbles On The Beach website, typed in Annie Boyd's username and password.

'She didn't use the site prolifically. There were two men she entered into a dialogue with.'

'What about the two men she talked to?'

'The language they used is similar. It could be one and the same man. This is the first guy she communicated with. He calls himself Danny Guest.'

Hi Annie, I'd be grateful if you could allow me to have an initial dialogue with you with a view to us getting to know each other a little better. If you don't feel comfortable with this, I can understand absolutely and wish you all the best in finding a man who will one day no doubt, I'm assuming and quite rightly, worship the ground you walk upon. Wishing you all the best, Danny.

Dear Danny, Of course I'm happy to talk to you over the website. Maybe you'd like to tell me a little bit about yourself? On your profile you don't say anything about what you do for a living? What are your interests other than watching football and soul-searching?

Poppy scrolled and scrolled through thousands of words sent back and forth.

'She communicated with him up to four and five times a day and as time passed the messages got longer and more detailed. Then they decided to talk over the phone and that's where the trail went cold.'

'Who was the other man?' asked Clay.

'Richard Ezra. She communicated with him first.'

Dear Richard, I am new to internet dating and am not sure of the way to do this properly. Please let me know what you think of my profile? I am really interested in your profile. Like you I love to drink a glass of wine in front of an open fire. xxxxx Annie

Dear Annie, Like yourself, I am new to internet dating and a little nervous around the whole process. However, I kept coming back to your picture and profile and found myself hoping that we could enter into a dialogue. If you're comfortable with this please reply to me, Annie. If you decide you can't, or don't want to, there will be absolutely no hard feelings. I'm assuming you won't reply to me, so I'd like to take this opportunity to wish you well in your search for Mr Right. I confess, I'm a little jealous of this stranger to me but if he gives you the happiness you deserve, I take my hat off to him.

'It's the same man, same message, same language,' said Clay. 'Have you printed these off for me, Poppy?'

Poppy opened her drawer and pulled out two card files bulging with papers, and handed them to Clay.

'How didn't she see it?' said Poppy. 'I just don't know.'

'Because she didn't want to.' Clay felt dismay for Annie Boyd, for a lack of intuition that went some way towards sealing her sorry fate. 'He's using the same language to filter out clever women, women who aren't that needy. He wants a woman who is so needy that she's suspended her disbelief system. It's the same principle as the Nigerian phishing emails with all their bad writing and spelling howlers. They're aimed at people who think the emails are real, the same people who are stupid enough to hand over money to the scammers. What was the outcome with Danny Boy?'

'It came to the point where Annie was about to speak with him over the phone and – bam! – he completely stopped communicating with her online.

Dear Annie, Something's cropped up. Got to go. Bye, Danny.

'No indicators as to why?' asked Clay.

'None. So, when Danny jumped ship, she started leaning on Richard. *All I want is lasting happiness and to make you happy. If you don't want to have a relationship with me, tell me now and I'll walk away.* These were phrases she bedded into messages to Richard and worded in a dozen different ways nine days into the daily exchange.'

'How did Richard react?'

'It ignited an information storm from his end. *He* didn't want to get hurt again because death had stolen his wife. The last thing he would ever do was hurt another human being because he had been through so much. He had previously claimed he was single. Annie wanted to know why he hadn't told her he was a widower. He didn't want to make emotional capital out of his misfortune. He wasn't playing the sympathy card. She gave him her number and he called her back.'

'We've got his number?' asked Clay.

'Sorry, Eve, no, we haven't. We haven't got an IP address and we haven't got a phone number. She gave him her mobile number. The plan was for him to call her.'

'Did he give any reason why he couldn't leave his number with her?'

'*The gentlemanly thing to do is for me to call you.* Which translated into: It was his suggestion that they speak one to one, it was *his* responsibility as a gentleman to call *her*.'

'The sly bastard. He must've planned well in advance for this day coming. Whose was the parting shot? Him or her?'

'Him. After the practical arrangements, Annie asked him if he minded her asking a question about the death of his wife and his grief.'

'What did she ask, Poppy?'

'Is it possible to die of a broken heart?'

'What was his reply?'

'It is better to have loved and lived and to learn to love again.'

'Screenshot everything Annie had with these two characters and send it to me and everyone else in the investigation. Liaise with Barney Cole. We need to get on to Pebbles On The Beach. We need everything they've got on Danny Guest and Richard Ezra. It's one man playing as a tag team. Danny does the dirty on Annie and Richard comes in on a white charger.'

'No problem, Eve. Do you want me to unlock the rest of Annie's internet history?'

'You've just saved me from issuing an instruction. Thank you, Poppy. I know what I'm looking for now if this man gets in touch with one of us. We'll all know what we're dealing with.'

33

10.33 am

Detective Sergeant Barney Cole looked at the image that the killer had sent to Annie Boyd, the one forwarded to him by Clay.

Mr Handsome.

He pulled up Google Reverse Image Search and clicked on Copy Image URL.

When Google Images filled the screen of his laptop, he clicked on the camera icon.

Richard Ezra. The name the killer hid behind as he lured Annie Boyd to her death.

He clicked Post to URL and Search by Image.

Rain fell down in sheets on the windows that surrounded the incident room in Trinity Road police station, flattening the world outside the building.

Blue letters appeared at the top of the screen.

Best guess for this image: Richard Ezra.

'You're shitting me,' he said to himself.

Underneath this writing a cluster of websites appeared and beneath this dozens of images of physically similar handsome men.

Cole scrolled down slowly through the bank of images until he came to the exact one the killer had sent to his victim. He clicked on the image and visited the website that hosted it.

The picture Cole had run through Google Reverse Image Search had linked up with the Facebook profile picture of a man called Richard Ezra. On the Facebook profile, Richard Ezra was not smiling into a void; he was looking at an incredibly beautiful blonde woman.

Cole skimmed and scanned the home page and saw that Richard Ezra was a partner with Doherty Estates and Properties on Allerton Road, a fifteen-minute ride from Trinity Road police station. There were images of Richard Ezra in a less casual setting, sitting with a group of formally dressed older men. There were pictures of Richard with the same blonde woman who had been edited out of the picture that The Ghoul had so far circulated to his victims.

He recognised the glass front of the office that Richard worked in, situated on the commercial end of Allerton Road, in the cluster of estate agents, legal firms and financial operators.

Cole clicked on the Bio tab and, reading the information, made mental notes.

Richard Ezra wrote about being excited to go on his holidays to Florence, and that was the last post he'd made.

He clicked on the Contacts tab and saw the address and landline telephone number for Doherty Estates and Properties.

He dialled the seven digits and listened to the ringtone. The answer machine kicked in.

'You have reached Doherty…'

At the other end the receiver was snatched up, and Cole got in quickly.

'My name's Detective Sergeant Barney Cole. I'll send you a picture of my warrant card. I'm based at Trinity Road police station a few miles from your office.'

'That won't be necessary.' She was well-spoken and, by the sound of her voice, Cole pictured her as mid twenties and with a cold-fish manner that could have been a front for the workplace or just the way she was. 'How can we help you, Detective Sergeant Cole?'

'I was wondering if I could speak with Mr Richard Ezra?'

She asked, 'Is this a sick joke?'

In moments, the temperature in her icy voice plummeted to arctic depths.

'Absolutely not,' said Cole.

'Excuse me... Mr Doherty?' she called.

He heard her hand smothering the receiver and the phone being passed to the boss.

'If this is a Trojan horse to try and wrong foot us over our client Dale McGee ...'

Dale McGee, thought Cole, *one of the city's most notorious gangsters, currently on remand in Walton Prison.*

'Mr Doherty ...'

'We are a well-established and respectable firm of estate agents.'

But you take the greenbacks from violent criminals, he thought, trying to suppress the grin spreading on his face and leaking into his voice.

'If you want to talk to me or any of our estate agents or administrative staff ...'

He stopped to cough, and Cole wondered if it was his pomposity or self-righteousness that he was choking on.

'Mr Doherty, I need to come and speak to you about Richard Ezra.'

'What's this in relation to?'

'It's a murder enquiry.'

'Then you'd better come in, DS Cole.'

'Richard...?'

'I'm not prepared to discuss Mr Ezra with you on the telephone,' said Mr Doherty through a tightened throat.

Cole wrote down the details of time and place for the appointment. As soon as he'd finished speaking, the estate agent hung up.

Cole dialled Clay's number and was pleased to hear the contrast in tone to Mr Doherty.

'Barney? What's happening?'

'Don't get excited, Eve, but I've got a match for the man in the image the killer sent to Annie Boyd, and an appointment at his place of work, Doherty Estates and Properties. I'd bet three figures it won't be our savage, but it's a way in, a connection.'

'How were they about him?'

'Prickly's not the word. Paranoid isn't quite either but it's closer to the truth.'

'Send me the details and good luck with the appointment. I'll join you in that wager but if this is identity theft, we could be on to something. Barney, I like it. I like this a lot.'

34

10.45 am

Two minutes after connecting with a technical advisor on the Pebbles On The Beach website, Detective Sergeant Bill Hendricks sat back in his seat and sighed from a deep grey inner space.

I understand that you're an IT-based business, he typed into the small box at the bottom of the laptop screen on his desk in the incident room at Trinity Road police station. *And that you do your communication through the internet. But I'd like to cut through this form of us talking, Jayne.*

He pressed send and his message flew across the ether with a breathy note that rose and faded in less than a second.

Ping! His attention was drawn back to his screen by a message sent from Jayne, his contact at Pebbles On The Beach.

How do you want to communicate, DS Hendricks?

I suggest we talk on the phone, Jayne.

How do I know you are who you say you are?

I've sent you a picture of my warrant card through Messenger, confirming that I am who I say I am.

I've seen it. It could be a fake.

Then call Merseyside Constabulary switchboard and ask for my landline number in Trinity Road police station. Call me on that number. You'll hear my voice on my answer machine, my name asking you to leave a message. Surely that's enough, Jayne.

As he gave her the switchboard's number, he completely understood the suspicions of a woman whose working life was spent working on an internet dating site where lies, deceit and misrepresentation largely ruled over truth.

I'm going to talk to my boss. Please hang on.

Hendricks' attention drifted back in time in the direction of the rain-drenched footpath and he pictured Mand-E's scalped and faceless body floating in a muddy pothole.

The phone rang and Jayne came on the line. 'OK, DS Hendricks, we believe you. How can I help you?'

'First up, I need the home addresses for two men who've been using your site.'

'That could be tricky,' said Jayne. 'Data protection...'

'Jayne, this is in connection with a murder enquiry.'

'A murder enquiry?'

An older woman's voice came into the mix and Hendricks realised he was on speakerphone.

'Who is this?' asked Hendricks.

'Emily Jones. I'm the founder and owner of Pebbles On The Beach. I feel like I'm having déjà vu. I've had this conversation with Warrington Police. What's this murder enquiry got to do with me, DS Hendricks?'

'Three women have been murdered. We're almost one hundred per cent certain that the killer connected with them on *your* dating site.'

The silence was long and toxic.

'Is this going to get out into the media?'

'If we're right about the women being selected on your site and we catch the killer, yes, it will. Most certainly, it will come out when it gets to court.'

Across the line, Hendricks felt the weight of Emily Jones' naked disappointment at the impact this information would have on her business.

'I need those addresses, Emily. If the killer carries on and the body count mounts up higher, I'd be very worried if it was my website.'

'What are the names of the men you're interested in, DS Hendricks?'

'Richard Ezra and Danny Guest. We believe they're both from the Liverpool area.'

'OK. I'll provide that information for you. Jayne, speak to Ros. Richard Ezra and Danny Guest. Addresses to begin with, ASAP. Is there anything else I can do to help you, DS Hendricks?'

'The third victim, we're still trying to identify her. I'm going to email Jayne information about her to help you with the search at your end.'

Hendricks looked at the name on the latest victim's left forearm in the photograph on his desk. Mand-E.

'It's possible that her first name is either Mandy, Amanda abbreviated with a y on the end, or Mandie, with an ie ending. She has a tattoo. She spells her name MAND hyphen E, all capitals. If you could look for any woman on your site using this name, I'd be very, very grateful, Emily.'

'My staff and I will do our best. We'll drop everything and concentrate on what you've asked us to do.'

There was a pause as she made her way past a bank of animated voices. The door to her office closed and there was a bleak silence behind her.

'I built this company up from nothing,' she said. 'I've given people work and brought happiness to thousands of lonely hearts. There are plenty of internet dating sites out there. Why mine? Why me?'

'You've been unlucky, Emily. We are looking into other sites as well, to see if the killer's been operating from them.'

He heard the sound of her inhaler and imagined the vice gripping her chest and weighing down on her lungs.

'When this comes out...' She made a noise that was at once loaded with contempt and self-pity. 'Let's just say an expression with the words *rats* and *sinking ship* comes to mind.'

There was a knock on her door.

'Come in. What have you got for me, Jayne?'

'Liverpool-based addresses for Richard Ezra and Danny Guest.'

Hendricks smiled as he picked up his pen.

'Jayne, we're looking for a Liverpool-based woman called Mandy. I'll give you the detail in a minute. What are the men's addresses?'

'Danny Guest's based at 134 Addingham Road. Richard Ezra's at 66 Springwood Avenue.'

Hendricks listened and wrote with thunder rumbling in the distance and the sky above him sagging under the weight of darkening clouds.

'Thank you. Thank you very much.'

35

10.59 am

Detective Constable Clive Winters, a tall, heavily built black man in his forties, watched the second piece of film he'd identified from the high-quality CCTV footage emailed over to him by security from the Echo Arena.

He watched people walking in the general direction of Otterspool Promenade and others walking towards the Museum of Liverpool.

Annie Boyd was a lone pinpoint, identifiable from the smart black coat she wore to impress her blind date and protect herself from the wind blasting off the River Mersey to her left.

'Hello, Annie,' he said to the screen of his laptop as she came closer to the Echo Arena's camera, a black speck turning into a more human form, recognisable from the first piece of footage from the Marina around the corner from the place where she'd parked her silver Renault Megane. She took out her iPhone and Winters guessed she was talking to her friend Cathy Jones, their last conversation as reported to DCI Eve Clay.

You said your goodbye then, thought Winters. *But little did you know it was to be your final one.*

Annie walked further down the concrete promenade, embraced herself tightly against the weather. As she walked towards the Echo Arena's camera, she braved the wind to look up at people overtaking her in the direction of the meeting point at the padlocked railings, no doubt hoping to catch a glimpse of her Prince Charming.

She simply walked under the eye of Echo Arena's camera and out of sight.

Alone.

Winters made a mental note of the time she was last recorded on the first of the Echo Arena's cameras: 7:51 pm for the eight o'clock date, not wanting to turn up late.

He watched the screen as it flipped to the second footage supplied by the Echo Arena, CCTV from the side of the building, starting at 7:48 pm. He fast forwarded it until he reached 7:51 pm.

As the clock changed to 7:52 pm, Annie came under the CCTV camera's watchful eye. It was a sideways shot of her. Winters paused it and counted three other people on screen. A pair of women walking in the direction from which Annie had just come and a man striding ahead of her.

She fought against the wind, which had picked up force, lowering the centre of her gravity as she struggled to get where she was going.

He looked at the CCTV footage from the riverside camera on the wall of the Albert Dock with the final two sequences of Annie.

He looked at the empty space where Annie had just passed through, and felt that he was watching the progress of a ghost.

Winters swapped pen drives, one out, one in, and watched Annie arriving at the railings with the padlocked hearts then standing still, her back to the water, as she waited from 7:53 pm, coat collar turned up, clutching her bag to herself. Time moved on but Annie remained where she was.

7:54 pm, 7:55 pm, 7:56 pm. No one, just Annie.

As 7:56 pm counted up to 7:57 pm, she became animated. She turned her head up and walked away from the railings and back again.

Time collapsed inside Winters' head as he watched her growing colder and more agitated under the overhead street light, illuminating her frustration.

She walked around in a tight circle, stamping her feet and trying to keep warm against the worsening weather.

He looked at the time and saw that it was 8:15 pm.

Winters fast forwarded the footage, watched her perform what looked like absurd little dances as she waited in vain.

At 8:36 pm, he stopped the footage and watched it in real time. She reached inside her bag and took out a handkerchief. Winters zoomed in on her face.

She appeared to be crying and he watched her walk away from the railings and back the way she had come, having been made an utter fool of by a stranger.

Winters paused the footage and called Clay from his landline phone.

'Eve, it looks like Annie Boyd got stood up. He had no intention of meeting her in such a CCTV-rich part of the Albert Dock. She's on her way back to the place where she parked her car.'

'How was she?'

'She looks like she's had seven balls of shit kicked out of her. I'll call you when I've got the bigger picture.'

Winters replaced the receiver and looked at Annie's back, frozen on screen, and imagined how she must have felt after waiting in the cold to be horribly let down.

He turned the footage on and watched Annie walk away into the dark, never to return.

36

11.01 am

The headless carcass of a black and white cow travelled towards Edgar McKee on a moving rail. The cow was suspended by the base of its legs on two metallic clamps.

'Are you ready to have a turn, Wren?'

'Sure, Edgar.'

'OK, so... what's the big word in this process?'

'The big word in the process of skinning the carcass of a cow is *hygiene*.'

'Well done. Great answer. You're a fast learner.'

Edgar drank in the beaming smile on Wren's face.

'Any questions, Wren?'

'Why are they hanging from the rail?'

'It's the most hygienic way of bleeding and stripping the carcass. Bleeding continues until it's a trail and then we can skin it. Why do I use a plastic-handled knife instead of a wooden-handled knife?' asked Edgar.

'More hygienic, Edgar.'

The headless cow swung under the impetus of the vibration that ran through the moving rail. Edgar handed Wren the sticking knife.

'Stick the knife in just above the breastbone at a forty-five-degree angle pointed in the direction of where its neck used to be. Cut.'

Edgar watched Wren's lips move as he performed the action, repeating the information in the silence of his head.

'Am I doing good, Edgar?'

'You're doing just great. Cut away between the hide and carcass and pull the skin away carefully. What must never ever happen, Wren?'

'The outer skin must never touch the carcass because this can cause contamination by the bacteria on the hide, messing up the uncontaminated body of the cow.'

'Cut and pull away, cut and pull away, keep going, fold the outer skin away from the carcass. Leave the left-hand side for a minute and attend to the right. Cut and pull, slow but sure.'

Wren obeyed Edgar, his tongue poking out as he concentrated on the task in hand.

'Carry on, Wren. Anyone says anything to you that you don't like, you tell me. I'm your mate, remember. You and me, best mates.'

Wren continued cutting and peeling away the skin of the cow, centimetres away from his face.

'You are... so... the coolest person I've ever met, Edgar.'

'And you're the coolest person I've ever met, Wren. I swear on Captain Cyclone's super powers, you're my best mate, the best mate I've ever had.'

37
11.00 am

Detective Constable Barney Cole looked at the time on his iPhone and saw that Mr Doherty was making him wait. Ten minutes after the agreed time of their meeting, there was no sign of movement behind the door to the estate agent's office.

Inside the room, voices came closer to the door.

He couldn't hear what was being said, but he recognised the grey pomposity of Mr Doherty and the sweetness of a young woman who was trying very hard to impress.

The door opened and a young woman emerged. She was fit – slim, blonde, matching skirt and jacket – and a face to draw second and third glances on any street.

'Congratulations.' Mr Doherty stepped out of his office and shook her by the hand, seemingly oblivious to Cole's presence. 'I know you're going to be very happy here.'

The handshake went on too long and, as Cole observed it, he took a longer look at the woman's face. Mid to late twenties, there was a sadness in her eyes that spoke of a deep-seated vulnerability.

'Are you happy with the terms and conditions of your employment with me?' said Mr Doherty, lapping up the last drop of gratitude from his new employee.

'I am. Thank you.'

'When do you intend to start working for me?'

'Twelve o'clock today, if that suits you, Mr Doherty.'

'That suits me fine. Excellent. And it's Brian.'

He flirted with her with his eyes, smiled like the sun had come out from behind a leaden cloud. She joined in but her response looked fake to Cole's eyes.

'See you soon, Brian.'

He released her hand and she headed immediately for the top of the stairs.

'Come inside, Detective Constable Cole,' said Mr Doherty, not looking at him as he headed back inside his lair.

Cole closed the door, caught the edge of the young woman's fragrance, recognised it as Chanel No. 5, a perfume his wife liked.

'Sit.' Mr Doherty threw a flick of the wrist at the chair across the desk from where he was now sitting.

Cole placed his hands on the back of the chair, leaned forward and said, 'I have sciatica. It's easier for me to stay standing.'

'Then stay standing. You want to know about Richard Ezra, DC Cole? But before we talk about Richard, there's a question I need to ask.'

'Fire away.'

'Why are Merseyside Constabulary interested in him all of a sudden?'

Cole weighed his words carefully.

'As I said when I phoned you, we're in the early stages of a murder investigation. I can't go into the details but we believe the perpetrator has assumed Mr Ezra's identity in the process of committing his crimes.'

Mr Doherty nodded and his lower lip jutted out.

'In your professional capacity, how long did you know him, Mr Doherty? I gather he no longer works here?'

'No. He was here for six years. He joined the firm in 2014 and was our top agent for five of those years. He became a partner at the end of his first year.'

'A form of golden handcuffs to keep him chained to the firm?'

'Exactly. He was everything you'd want in an employee. Never off sick. Never late. Smashed his sales targets month in, month out. We were perceived as being that good at selling houses quickly that we drew business away from the other agents on Allerton Road.'

'That gives me a clear idea about what he was like as an estate agent. What was he like as a man?'

'He was kind without being soft, and genuinely courteous. People used to take their work and domestic problems to him because he was discreet and offered good advice all round. Most of the girls in the office had a crush on him but he was above all that. He was extremely happily married to Sarah. They were culture vultures, always visiting art galleries, watching world cinema, reading quality literature and going to Europe to soak up the art and culture of the past. Until it all went horribly wrong for them.'

'Have you got a picture of Richard?'

Mr Doherty opened the top drawer of his desk and, reaching inside, took out a framed photograph, which he offered to Cole. He took the picture from his hands and turned it over.

In between Mr Doherty and the beautiful blonde he'd seen on Google Images was a slim, handsome man with jet-black collar-length hair and sky-blue eyes, who smiled into the camera as he clutched a cut-glass statuette.

'That's when he won North West Estate Agent of the year, back in 2017. That's me, obviously. The woman next to him was his wife, Sarah.'

'Was?'

'They were in Florence. They'd spent the day visiting art galleries. It had been particularly hot. It was in the evening. They were in a pizzeria near The Fountain of Neptune. They'd just ordered when Sarah went to the ladies. Five, ten minutes went by. Richard thought she'd been taken ill. He asked a waitress to go into the ladies to see if Sarah was OK. The waitress went in. The screaming brought the restaurant down into a terrible silence. Richard ran into the ladies and Sarah was lying in an expanding pool of blood. There were over thirty stab wounds to her body. There was an open window. The killer escaped the same way that he got into the building. There were no witnesses.'

'Was the killer mentally ill?'

'I assume so but I don't know. Nobody knows why he or she did what they did. The Florentine police didn't get near anyone. The killer was never caught.'

Cole gazed into Mr Doherty's eyes, saw a welling of emotion.

'Can I get a colour copy of this picture, Mr Doherty?'

Mr Doherty held his hand out and, taking the picture from Cole, stood and walked to the photocopier in the corner of the room. His shoulders sagged as he copied the picture and it occurred to Cole that these memories were deeply personal and painful to him.

Mr Doherty walked back to the desk, with the same picture in each hand and an expression in his eyes like he was locked in a time bubble.

He sat down, slid the colour copy across the desk to Cole and placed the framed picture back inside the cold darkness of his drawer.

'What happened to Richard Ezra?'

'When he came back to England it took just under twelve months for him to completely fall to pieces. It started when Sarah's body was repatriated. He refused to accept that the body in the coffin was hers. He insisted the Florentine authorities had planted another body and it was all part of a conspiracy to protect the killer. I was there when the coffin was opened and he could see it was Sarah. I saw something in his eyes, a wildness that made me sick to the core because I knew in that moment he was doomed.

'He never returned to work and wound up in a haze of pills and alcohol. We offered to help him, we tried to intervene; many, many people did but he retreated into himself, stopped answering the phone and the door.

'I believe he killed himself.'

'Can you tell me a little more, Mr Doherty?' asked Cole.

'His car was last caught on CCTV on Jericho Lane leading down to Otterspool Promenade. The car was discovered on a parking bay overlooking the prom. I believe he threw himself into the water and drowned. His body was never recovered. It wasn't just one life that got taken that day in Florence. It was two lives. It just took Richard longer to go, during which time...'

Mr Doherty looked sick to his core.

'What happened to Richard Ezra during that year?'

'He completely changed. Grief, alcohol and drugs. When he disappeared, I went to his house with the police looking for a suicide note. We found his laptop but no note.'

'What did you find on his laptop, Mr Doherty?'

'He'd taken to downloading pornography in the last twelve months of his life. Violent pornography from the dark web. Rape. Torture. Horrific abuse.'

'Who were the victims?'

'Women.' The wind pushed a volley of rain into the window behind Mr Doherty's head. 'He used the internet to find prostitutes. He was a good man who completely collapsed.'

'Have there been sightings of Richard Ezra?'

Mr Doherty nodded. 'But I don't believe in any of them. I think he had a moment of clarity. He saw what he'd become, remembered the man he'd been and decided to end it all. That's what I like to think happened.'

The initial antagonism Cole had felt towards the estate agent completely evaporated.

Mr Doherty stood up and, turning his back on Cole, looked out of the window as rain raked the glass.

'Is there anything else you'd like to ask me, DC Cole?'

'Yes, Mr Doherty, there is. You said that you were there when Sarah's coffin lid was lifted.'

He nodded at the pouring rain.

'In my view, that was well above and beyond the call of duty for an employer.'

Mr Doherty turned and Cole placed his contact card on his desk.

'You asked me about professional capacity. First and foremost, I wasn't just his employer. I was his friend and mentor. I don't have many friends but Richard was one of them.'

'I've left my details there, Mr Doherty. Do you still have his work laptop, work telephone?'

'He took them away with him when he first came back to the UK. At first he made a show of attempting to work from home. He didn't, of course. After he disappeared and his house was cleared, there was no trace of them. Just his personal laptop, riddled with filth.'

'Did he have an address book in work?'

'Yes... yes, we still have that somewhere in the office. Everyone who works here keeps a paper copy of their contacts in case of technology failure.'

'That's a good idea. If you find Richard Ezra's professional address book, can you call me and I'll collect it. Or if you think of anything else you haven't mentioned to me now, call me.'

When Cole got to the door, Mr Doherty said, 'What do you want his address book for?'

'The name of the person using Richard as a shield could well be in that address book.'

'I'll instruct the office junior to find that book and deliver it to you. How dare they pour dirt on Richard's memory?'

'That's right, Mr Doherty. How dare they?'

38

11.25 am

As Detective Chief Inspector Eve Clay turned left on to Woolton Road on her way to Springwood Avenue, she realised what the stretch of road she was heading for was like in reality.

This is a piss take of the highest order, she thought as she headed to the lights at the junction with Springwood Avenue, all hope fading away as she turned on to South Liverpool's expansive Death Row.

A phone call from Hendricks had already confirmed that Danny Guest's given address – 134 Addingham Road – was a fake, with the numbers on the doors of the terraced houses ending in the high seventies.

Clay was acutely aware of the caravan of vehicles behind her, the rapidly scrambled marked and unmarked police cars in a procession of fools.

She glanced over her shoulder at Stone following behind her and shook her head. He responded with a thumbs down. Behind the railings to her left, she passed the solitary Pub in the Park, then slowed as she came to the only house on the road.

'But you're not 66,' she said, listening to the sour note in her own voice.

She slowed down even further as she caught up with a procession of funeral cars and resisted the temptation to overtake.

Clay watched the hearse at the head of the queue turning left into Springwood Crematorium and saw the white flowers against the coffin bearing the word MUMMY.

The notion of her own funeral went through her like a cold wind. She imagined Thomas and Philip sitting in the car immediately behind the hearse as it inched up the path to the crematorium.

She pulled over near the entrance to the crematorium and, as she got out of her car, watched the five cars behind her slow down and stop. The officers emerged from their vehicles in puzzled silence.

'Sorry, everyone,' called Clay. 'This is a bum steer. Karl,' she addressed Stone. 'Come with me. Thank you to the rest of you for supporting. Go back to Trinity Road and resume other duties.'

Clay followed the course of the hearses up the path towards Rose Chapel, her knuckles white as she grasped the steering wheel, and turned on to the small car park overlooked by the glass-fronted crematorium.

'God help them!' said Clay, as two girls, one aged eight years, her sister two years younger, and a man in his early thirties emerged from the lead car. The girls sobbed hysterically and their father stooped to gather both of them into a single embrace at the front of Rose Chapel. He kissed them in turn and whispered words of comfort from the depths of his own private hell.

Six undertakers shouldered the children's mother's coffin, the floral MUMMY desolate in the back of the empty hearse as Clay watched the mourners follow the dead mother into the chapel, and felt the weight of her own mortality like an iron anvil on her heart.

The music of Gerry and the Pacemakers filtered into the daylight.

With each breath, Clay felt time collapsing around her and it made the enclosed space of her car shrink, forced her to open the door and get out as the last of the mourners crept into the chapel.

Clay spotted a gardener pushing a wheelbarrow and walking in her direction. Locking her car, she caught the man's eye and held up her warrant card. She looked over his shoulder and behind him the sheer breadth and width of the cemetery stood out like an infernal riddle.

The gardener squinted as he placed a pair of reading glasses on his nose.

'How can I help you?' he asked.

'Sixty-six? Does that mean anything to you?'

'The cemetery's divided into plots. The plots are numbered. One of the plots has the number sixty-six.'

'Can you take me to it?'

He left the wheelbarrow and its load of perished flowers where he stood.

'Follow me...'

Clay gathered her coat at the collar and she and Stone walked after the gardener into the mean wind and the dying strains of *You'll Never Walk Alone*.

39
11.30 am

Norma Maguire's brain was alive with dark instinct.

Fran wasn't answering her landline phone in the office downstairs or her mobile. Three times her landline voicemail kicked in and three times Norma listened with growing impatience to her employee's voice grinding in the fact that she just wasn't there.

Hi, Francesca Christie speaking. I'm currently unavailable. Leave a message after the tone or try again later.

She dialled Daniel Ball, the office manager, the man who knew everything about everybody.

'Norma?'

'Where's Fran? She's not answering her office phone and as far as I'm aware she isn't out at a viewing.'

'I don't know where she is, Norma.' The neutrality in his voice incensed her.

'You're the office manager, for God's sake. If you don't know where my people are, who the hell does?'

'Please don't shout at me, Norma. What do you want me to do? Follow people down the street?'

'Have you seen her today?'

'Yes, she left the office at twenty to ten. Norma, you were there. You saw me with her when you came downstairs just after half nine.'

The noise of voices in the office behind Daniel died down and she imagined them all listening in, all knowing what was going on while she was in the dark.

'Oh!' said Daniel, with a note of levity. 'Speak of the Devil. Francesca just came into the office.'

'Send her up to me. Now.'

The familiar tap on the door – the way only Fran's fingers could connect with glass – didn't happen and, instead, for the first time, she walked into Norma's office without warning.

Norma pretended to be studying a set of papers on her desk and feigned surprise when she looked up and made eye contact with her employee.

'I didn't hear you coming in, Fran...'

Francesca Christie looked around the room, as if looking for some other person.

'Fran?' Francesca touched herself under the throat. 'Who's Fran?'

Norma felt a worm turning in between the hemispheres of her brain.

'What's wrong, Francesca?'

'I won't be coming back to work for you.'

'You have a contract with me. One month's notice.'

'I'm not coming back to work for you. Contract or no contract.'

'You've been head-hunted then. Haven't I been good to you?' Norma felt hurt translate itself into a blade that cut into all her vital organs in the same moment. 'What's the problem? Is it me?' asked Norma.

'I don't feel comfortable around you.' Francesca's gentle voice stiffened into something much harder, more abrasive.

'What do you mean?' Norma heard herself match it.

'The way you look across the office at me.'

'You're imagining it.'

'It's not just me who's noticed. It's the talk of the office. The anonymous Valentine's Card that arrived at my house. Not a word on it. Block print letters on the envelope but do you know what, Norma? I could smell your perfume on it. Literally. Chanel Coco. There were creases on the card where you'd dripped it on to…'

'Francesca, stop right there! I did no such thing. It was a prank, a prank by one of your colleagues.'

'Why is it, Norma, every time you take us out to eat, you sit at the top of the table and I sit at your side? Why is it when a table is booked, you call the restaurant and give them place settings and those name cards are set out on the table? Why is it your hand or foot always touches me under the table?'

'I'm crippled and have no sensation at all from the waist down.'

'Every picture taken of every night out, your left arm's around my shoulder and your fingers are hovering over the top of my breasts.' She pointed at a framed picture on the wall. 'Look, if you think I'm imagining it. Look, if you don't believe me!'

'I didn't know you had this in you, Francesca. There are codes of conduct for estate agents. We have rules. You cannot break your contract.'

'That's exactly what I am doing.'

'I'm going to take this further, you'll see.'

'Go ahead. I've been talking to a barrister about you and your harassment. If I take you to tribunal, you'll get roasted alive.'

'Roasted alive? Will I now? Well, if I was you I wouldn't rely on any support from your so-called friends downstairs. They wouldn't dare go against me. I'm their bread and butter. You're just somebody who used to work here. But on that note, on that very sorry note, just who are you going to work for?'

'Mr Doherty.'

The first stirrings of a storm brewed inside Norma and the new-found hurt shifted into rage.

'Then I'll take both of you to the cleaners.'

'Leave him out of it. He didn't approach me. I approached him. And I can prove it.'

Norma pictured Brian Doherty, pompous and bulbous-lipped, and imagined Francesca Christie fawning over him and working hard to win his affection and admiration.

'Get out! Get out of my office now. Collect together any last pieces of personal tat that you have downstairs and get off the premises.'

'I don't keep personal belongings in that drawer. Someone started going into it and taking my personal items. Who could that be?'

Francesca Christie stopped at the door.

'You want to watch your blood pressure, Norma.' She turned and looked at her former boss. 'Your face has gone purple and your eyes look like they're about to explode out of your head. You'll have to excuse me. I have to go to work.'

40
11.40 am

Clay stood in a maze of hundreds of graves next to the head gardener, who had taken her to what looked like the middle of a stone-studded nowhere.

She turned a full circle and asked, 'Where does the plot begin and end?'

'The grave you're standing next to is the bottom right-hand corner of the grid, Springwood 66. Three graves in front of you from there is the top right-hand corner. Three to the left is the bottom left-hand corner. Four rows of four. A square of sixteen in all, DCI Clay. 66 Springwood Crematorium.'

Clay counted the sixteen headstones set out in a square and asked, 'Is there anything significant about this plot?'

'No. They were all born, they all lived, they all died. No poets or martyrs that I'm aware of. If you're looking for their company, try plot 157.' He laughed, wheezed like an old accordion and smelled of tobacco and earth.

'Mind if I get some pictures?'

'I'm sure none of the residents will object.' Walking away, he pulled the collar of his coat together. 'Death's a demanding mistress. I'm a busy man. If you have any questions, you can contact me through the office.'

'Karl?' Clay looked at Stone. 'Get pictures of each grave in plot 66, please.'

He walked to the bottom left-hand corner of the plot and asked, 'You want me to check them out with the crematorium office?'

'Please.'

Clay walked forward, read the headstone of a very old man who had died decades earlier and who had probably not been spared a second thought after his death. She paused at the grave ahead of it and saw three tired red silk flowers in an urn and noted that the person had died before she was born.

As Stone took multiple shots of each headstone, Clay walked to the white marble angel, the standout headstone on the plot. The angel's head was inclined to the left, her eyes downcast on the grave beneath her feet.

Clay read the headstone.

CATRIONA WEST
WIFE AND MOTHER
STOLEN IN AN INSTANT
1940–2001

Behind a glass oval in the marble was a picture of a mature and attractive woman, a moment snatched in time. *Remember me this way.*

'Karl. Lots of shots of this one, please.'

Stolen in an instant? The words lit fuses in Clay's head. *Sudden death? An accident? Suicide? Murder?*

'I'm interested in all of them, but Catriona West's getting right under my skin,' said Clay.

Her iPhone buzzed with an incoming call and Clay felt the temperature take a sudden dip, with the wind whistling from the wide spaces at her back and the black clouds above her spitting out the first notes of what promised to be a heavy downpour.

In the silent acres of the dead, Stone stood beside her, taking pictures of Catriona West's headstone. Clay focused on the picture of Catriona's face, felt her scalp crawl and her face flush, her mind's eye filling with her first impression of Annie Boyd's scalped and faceless body. A form of paralysis possessed Clay.

Answer the phone, she urged herself. *Answer the phone.*

She dug deep, shook off the invisible shackles that weighed her down and prepared to connect the incoming call.

41

11.55 am

Detective Sergeant Bill Hendricks waited with growing impatience for Clay to pick up as he called her from the landline phone on his desk in Trinity Road police station. He counted the ringtones in his head and, in the final moment before the answer machine kicked in, she connected the call.

'Bill, how are things?'

She sounded extremely cold, with the wind sobbing behind her, and Hendricks was grateful for the warmth of the incident room.

'Pebbles On The Beach have got back to us on the victim on the footpath linking Menlove Avenue and Allerton Road. Mand-E turns out to be Amanda Winton.'

'Are we sure it's her?' asked Clay.

'There are three Amandas in Liverpool who go on their dating site and only one spells her name or refers to herself as MAND-E. I double-checked.'

'Where does she live?'

'Flat 3, 189 Princes Road, Liverpool 8.'

'Karl, come on...'

Hendricks heard the sound of two sets of feet moving at speed through gravel.

'The landlord?' asked Clay.

'I'm still trying to track him down.'

'Then get on to the duty magistrate, Bill. We need a warrant to get into her flat and search it. I'm going there directly.'

'I'll ask the duty magistrate to send the warrant to your phone.'

'Tell Gina Riley to meet us there.'

'Anything else?'

'Go through the National Police Computer. See if there's anything on Amanda Winton. When you've checked out Amanda... It may be something, it may well be nothing, but have a look for anything on a Catriona West.'

'Jesus, have we got another victim?'

'She was born in 1940 and she died suddenly in 2001. Wife and mother. That puts her outside the prey profile for what's going on in 2021. She wasn't single. She wasn't blonde. Karl Stone's going to circulate a photograph of her when she was middle-aged.'

'Who is she, Eve?'

'She could be a complete waste of time. She resides in Plot 66, Springwood Crematorium. We need backup. 189 Princes Road.'

Hendricks heard music piped from a loudspeaker. *Unforgettable* by Nat King Cole. And beneath the music, children crying hysterically, a combination of sounds that went straight through him.

A car door opened and closed, killed the dreadful sorrow. Hendricks heard Clay turn the ignition on in her car.

'I'll get on to Gina and the duty magistrate right now.'

42

11.59 am

Francesca Christie walked over the threshold of Doherty Estates and Properties with a sharp mixture of nervous tension and profound relief. It felt like the air in the office was clean and easy to breathe.

'You made it with a minute to spare, Francesca.'

Sally Manson, a tall middle-aged woman with long black hair, walked towards her, arm outstretched, hand extended and smiling. As Francesca shook hands with her, she felt the ever-present vice of oppression that Norma Maguire could tighten with a glance, unlock around her skull. She looked around the office, saw that they were the only people in the space.

'Hello, Sally,' said Francesca.

'Office manager and head girl. Pleased to be at your assistance. Step this way, Francesca.'

Francesca followed Sally to a desk. 'This is your desk. It's a rather small goldfish bowl, the world of estate agents in this neck of the woods. Everyone knows everyone. Do you like to keep busy?'

'I like to keep really busy.'

'Well, we can certainly offer you that option. Look at us now. Up the wall. And just wait until new year: January, the busiest month in the year for divorce lawyers and estate agents.'

Francesca felt the steel clamp that was permanently locked between her shoulder blades in Maguire Holdings vanish. She laughed, felt the glow of the dawn of a brand-new era in her life. New job? Certainly. New man? How she hoped it would work out with James.

'I've got your mobile number, Francesca. Brian gave it to me.' The smile in her eyes dipped. 'How did Norma take the news you were leaving?'

Francesca half-shrugged. 'She was angry. She made all kinds of noises about what would happen to me because I'd walked early from my contract. But I couldn't care less. I'm just so happy to be here. Away from the oppression.'

'Yup!' said Sally. 'We have heard. Anyway. New chapter and all that. Brian's delighted you're on board, we all are. He's wanted you to join our team for ages, and we're a tight-knit bunch. You're going to fit in just fine.'

'Thank you so much, Sally.'

'One thing. It is Francesca, isn't it?' Sally checked. 'Not Franny or...?'

Francesca laughed.

'You can call me Francesca. You can call me Franny if you like. But please, please, never ever Fran...'

'I've got you, Francesca.'

43

12.20 pm

Detective Chief Inspector Eve Clay and Detective Sergeant Gina Riley followed Mr McGann, Amanda Winton's ground floor neighbour, up the staircase to the third floor of a large Victorian terraced building on Princes Road. He stopped on the first landing, out of breath, clinging to the banister, his stained white vest and boxer shorts clinging to his flabby bulk.

'Murdered?' he wheezed.

'Yes,' said Clay. 'How come you've got the key to her front door?'

'The landlord pays me as caretaker, so I have the keys in case of an eventuality...'

'I see you're struggling. How about you hand the keys to me?' Clay held her hand out.

'Won't argue with you...'

'Go downstairs, gather your thoughts on what you know about Amanda Winton.'

Clay and Riley hurried up the remaining two sets of stairs, past the competing sounds of daytime TV and robotic dance music leaking from the separate flats. At the plain door of Amanda Winton's top floor flat, as Clay slid the skeleton key into the lock she imagined how Pandora felt when she unlocked the forbidden box.

She turned the key and pushed the door open at the top right-hand corner with her index finger.

A narrow corridor led into the heart of the attic flat, with rooms on one side of the passageway.

'Nothing in the bathroom.' Riley checked to the left.

'Nor the kitchen,' confirmed Clay, inspecting the room ahead of it.

Clay stopped at the closed door of the main living space. On the door was a collage of pictures of the same woman, a slim blonde in her mid twenties; there was no sign of anyone else in the collage, just her.

'They're all selfies,' said Clay, making a mental note of the smiles and the pouts that Amanda should have grown out of when she was in her late teens.

Carefully, she pushed the door with the merest touch and it swung back with a pronounced creak from the hinges. Clay reached around the wall and turned on the light.

A huge bunch of red roses sat in a vase next to Amanda's double bed.

'I wonder who sent them?' said Clay.

Clay stepped into the cold attic room but felt something colder run down her spine, something alive, inhuman and wet.

She took a mental picture of the room, the modern ornaments, the colourful throws and Laura Ashley cushions, a single woman's attempt to imprint a feminine, homely touch on a drab space.

Clay walked to the table at the centre of the room and looked at Amanda's laptop, next to the photograph that The Ghoul had sent to Annie Boyd in his incarnation as Richard Ezra, gazing lovingly into the space where his wife had stood with him in reality.

She turned the picture over and quietly read the writing. *Dear Mand-E, with love Thomas.* Clay showed it to Riley. 'Same picture, different pseudonym.'

Outside the building, Clay heard the arrival of cars, the slamming of doors and sirens coming closer in the distance. She glanced at Riley, saw that she was taking a video portrait of the scene on her iPhone, systematically covering each piece of the cramped living space.

Clay took out her iPhone and called DS Terry Mason on speed dial.

'Terry, what are you up to?'

'Where do you need me to be?'

'189 Princes Road, top floor flat.'

'I'm on my way, Eve.'

Clay unplugged Amanda Winton's laptop from a socket in the wall.

'Gina, hotfoot Amanda's laptop down to Poppy Waters.'

Riley walked away quickly, dropping the laptop into an evidence bag.

On the bedside closet, make-up compacts, lipsticks and bottles of fragrances stood to attention around a circular mirror.

At the bottom of the stairs, Clay took in Mr McGann.

'Mr McGann, what do you know about Amanda Winton?'

'Nothing. She was the only tenant in the building who went out to work. I tried to talk to her a couple of times but she brushed me off.'

'When was the last time you saw her?' asked Clay.

'She went out about seven o'clock one night. She was all dolled up. I watched her from my front room window. It was like she was walking on air.'

Clay wondered if Amanda Winton had looked back over her shoulder as she left her flat, whether she'd had any primal inkling of the danger she was walking into.

She recalled the size and the colour of the roses by Amanda's bedside, the fraudulent picture of her handsome suitor next to her laptop.

No, Clay concluded. *If she had experienced any dark warnings, she must have drowned them out with hope.*

Amanda Winton didn't walk towards her date with death. She skipped there.

44
1.30 pm

Detective Constable Barney Cole sat at his desk with a map of South Liverpool spread out in from of him.

On the map were asterisks where the Automatic Number Plate Recognition cameras had picked up the white van on its journey away from Allerton Road in the direction of the River Mersey.

Detective Chief Inspector Eve Clay sipped her coffee, noticed how the asterisks had the appearance of a constellation of dark stars, and said, 'Talk me through it, Barney.'

'From the CCTV at the old lady's house on the corner of Allerton Road and Heath Road, we had the last three digits of the licence plate of the white van, ZDS. It's a Ford Transit Custom 2.2 TDCi panel van. So far so good. ZDS. Those digits were enough for the ANPR cameras to pick up as the van headed away from the scene of the body drop-off on the footpath between the golf course and the public park, Allerton Towers. The full registration is OD53 ZDS. Guess what, Eve?'

'You phoned the DVLA and it's a genuine plate.'

'It's registered to an eighty-six-year-old lady called Dolores Green.'

'Does she live in Liverpool?'

'She lives in Trinity Gardens in Brixton, South London.' Cole took out his iPhone. 'A couple of WPCs from the Met have been round to see her, to reassure her.' He showed Clay a photograph of a chocolate box granny.

'He's copied her plate then, or had it copied for him.'

'Spot on. However, The Ghoul's left a trail in its wake.'

She looked at Cole's asterisks and the way they led to a rectangular box in the Grassendale district, butting on to the River Mersey.

'From the footpath, they went to Gateacre. There are five readings. There are seven readings of the van heading from Gateacre to Grassendale. The van gets picked up on Aigburth

Road, by the Cricket Club, then again further down Aigburth Road by St Austin's Church. Then it goes off the radar. Last reading, 4:13 pm, Wednesday, 1st December.'

'What's this with the box, Barney?'

'The four corners of the box are where the ANPR cameras are located. The van was picked up by the ANPR near the corner of St Mary's Road and Grassendale Road. There were no readings from the ANPRs situated on the three other corners of the grid. I checked the CCTV cameras fanning out away from the river towards Garston. No show for white van OD53 ZDS. It's a strong probability that the van disappeared in that geographic box.'

Clay looked at the grid of roads leading down to the promenade. Grassendale Park.

'It adds up, Barney. Annie Boyd's body showed up five minutes away from this grid of roads.' She pictured the houses in her head; tall, detached, set back from the quiet roads with their well-established gardens and air of overarching affluence.

Clay looked closely at the roads leading away from the grid. She pointed at Beechwood Road.

'It could have made it out of the grid through that road, got itself away through Aigburth Road.'

'It's entirely possible, Eve, and I'm waiting for CCTV footage to come in so I can check that possibility.'

The grid seemed to rise from the map, the roads drifting into Clay's head where she made a mental journey past tree-lined pavements and the houses beyond them.

She imagined Annie Boyd and Amanda Winton imprisoned somewhere in a house that most people could only aspire to live in and asked, 'Are you positive that the van didn't slip the net?'

'I've checked and checked and checked the ANPR cameras outside the grid. Nothing.'

'I'm going to draft in some help for you, Barney. We're going to have to blitz the ANPR cameras leading away from the rectangle, and double-check your conclusions.'

Clay looked at the grid and the streets leading away from it.

'Bear in mind, there are ways out of the grid other than Beechwood Road.'

She looked at the winding side streets leading to the maze of semi-detached roads on the blind side of Aigburth Road and, wondering how knowledgeable The Ghoul was of the surveillance cameras in the neighbourhood, concluded that he knew them like the knuckles of each of his fists.

'I'm going to say it for you, Eve, because your scepticism's going to make you sound mean-minded. The journey from the body drop-off at old Allerton Road to Gateacre and the van's disappearance into the rectangular grid that I've identified could be twenty-four-carat bullshit, a ruse on The Ghoul's part to waste our time.'

'No. I wasn't going to say that. I wasn't even thinking that. This is sharp deductive work, Barney. Double-check again the surveillance cameras leading out from the grid you've drawn. Look for all white vans heading away from the grid. Let's bomb-proof your theory.'

45

1.35 pm

The Ghoul was growing hungrier by the hour for female company.

Three women had winked on Pebbles On The Beach in the space of one hour. The Ghoul settled back to check their profiles, to find a suitable woman to share the space next door.

Hungry. Hungry. Hungry. For love. The hunger for more sharpened with each passing minute. One or two women were somehow too many but The Ghoul knew a million bitches would never be enough.

Checking the profile of the first woman, who'd winked forty-seven minutes ago, it was obvious at a glance that she was no good. A red-headed cow in her thirties. Wrong-coloured hair and old as the fucking ocean.

The second woman was no better. Forty-plus with the face of a goat, even on a profile picture that was meant to flatter her.

'Let it be number three.'

Number three.

'Fuck you, bitch!'

A black woman in her forties.

The urge to throw the laptop against the wall was reined in by a simple thought. No laptop. No woman.

Walking to the cell door and turning the lock, The Ghoul opened it and looked inside at the empty mattresses.

Lying down where Annie Boyd had been, caressing the chains that had bound her, something tender broke inside The Ghoul, marbling the mounting hunger, the void within.

Gripping the chain tightly, The Ghoul felt the swell of loneliness, and it wasn't good.

Next time, tonight.

No more loneliness.

There would always be someone in the cell.

As one went, another would arrive.

The Ghoul dropped the chain and headed back next door, the light from the laptop glowing in the red light from the bare bulb in the ceiling above.

On the laptop, another woman had just winked on Pebbles On The Beach.

Blonde. Pretty. Mid twenties. Sally Haydn.

The Ghoul winked back at her.

'Look at me… Look at me… Lurammeeeee…'

46

5.30 pm

With the door closed for business and alone on the pavement outside the office of Doherty Estates and Properties, Sally said, 'I've got a duty of care towards you, Francesca. If someone upsets you, colleague, vendor or buyer, you tell me. I'll do what I can to help you. Have a great evening.'

'Yes, you too. Thank you.'

Francesca walked towards the pelican crossing and, as she pressed the WAIT button, she had a strange feeling that she was being watched. She looked around and there were people there but no one was looking at her.

When the green man came up, she crossed Allerton Road quickly, with the wind whipping at her ankles and the dust of the day playing havoc at her feet.

In the pocket of her coat, her iPhone rang out and, as she reached the other side of the road, she connected.

'Francesca?'

'James…' Her good mood became instantly better.

'Can you talk?'

'Of course.'

'Look, I know this is short notice, Francesca, but I was wondering if we could meet tonight?'

She counted to three, to stop herself appearing over-eager, and said, 'Yes, we could meet tonight. Where?'

'The railings with the padlocked hearts near the Albert Dock. Do you know it?'

She knew it well. Her own name and that of her ex, Patrick, were written on one of the padlocks, a detail known only to her and as many people as he had chosen to brag to about breaking her heart.

'Yes, I know it, James.'

'Shall we say eight o'clock, Francesca.'

'That should be fine.'

'Pick any restaurant you'd like to go to and don't be a cheap date. I've got plenty to celebrate at the moment, plenty. Winning the case yesterday. Seeing you tonight.'

Crossing Church Road, Francesca was again possessed by the unsettling feeling that she was being watched or followed.

'Are you there, Francesca?'

'Yes…'

'You went very quiet.'

'Just crossing a busy road, on my way home.'

'Well, I guess I better leave you to it.'

'Thank you, James. For asking me out.'

'Thank you for agreeing. Eight o'clock. The padlocked railings.'

As he disconnected the call, Francesca looked back at a bus stop full of school children and elderly men and women in the glare of a fish and chip shop's bright light.

Bath. Hair. Make-up. Nails. Black cocktail dress. Heels.

She planned it out in her head as she turned left to the car park outside ASDA.

I'll tell my mother, she thought, *that I'm going to Bryony's. I'll slip out of the house, so that she doesn't see me dressed for a date. It'll just be a thousand and one questions...* She glanced at her watch as she sat in her car... *and I don't have the time.*

From the driver's seat, she called Bryony.

'Hi, Francesca. How are things?'

'Fine, thanks. I need a small favour. A white lie. I'm going on a date tonight and I don't want my mother to know. You know how nosy she can be.'

'What time are you coming round to mine?' laughed Bryony.

'Eight-ish.'

'I've got a bottle of Prosecco in the fridge. Where did you meet him, Francesca?'

47

6.00 pm

The Ghoul sat on the bed on which Annie Boyd had spent her final hours chained to the wall and recalled the sound of her crying and begging for mercy, a sound better than music, a longed-for song that needed to be heard again and again.

Laptop open and signed into Pebbles On The Beach, The Ghoul saw that another woman had winked at the fictional man called Geoff Campbell, its latest online incarnation.

Opening the first online profile, The Ghoul didn't read what she'd written about herself because she was a brunette and looked like she was pushing forty, even though the number 28 jumped from the screen.

An incoming message arrived. Sally Haydn.

Hi Geoff. I'm a single woman looking to meet a caring guy. I love it when I'm being pleased but I love to please you back in return. Perhaps we could talk really soon. xoxo Sally Pretty please lol.

She was desperate and in a hurry and, between the lines, she made suggestive promises that spoke of her need to be rescued from the loneliness.

The Ghoul looked closely at Sally's profile picture and wondered if the rouge glow of the basement had turned 20:20 vision into deceptive goggles.

The Ghoul wondered if Annie Boyd and Sally Haydn were in some way biologically related and shared the same lowest common denominator. LCD. Lonely. Cunt. Doormat.

The Ghoul skimmed and scanned Sally Haydn's profile and translated the words into the bones of reality.

Lonely. Looking for love. Eager to meet. Eager to please.

Willing to have sex. Doormat. Pushover. Easy to manipulate. Exploited in the past. Exploitable in the future. Unintelligent. Unimaginative.

On every level, she came over as the perfect woman.

On closer inspection, the likeness between Annie Boyd and Sally Haydn was astonishing, and demanded an immediate response.

Hi Sally, Thank you so much for getting in touch. I'm glad you've opened up this initial dialogue. Reading between the lines, I guess you'd like for us to get to know each other a little better. Say, talk on the phone, maybe. If I'm reading too much into this please forgive me and I wish you all the luck in

the world in finding a man who will quite rightly worship the
ground you walk upon. I take my hat off to him. xoxo Geoff
Send.

Fresh meat was on its way.

And there was a never-ending supply of it.

48
6.08 pm

When Clay entered the incident room at Trinity Road police
station, there was an air of industry in the space, and many
of the faces sitting around and close to Cole were unfamiliar
to her.

She looked at the door, waiting for Poppy Waters to arrive,
and, sitting at her desk, she opened her laptop and winked
back at four men who had winked at her over Pebbles On
The Beach.

Clay took a paper transcript of the online exchanges
between Annie Boyd and Richard Ezra from her drawer and
spread them out on the desk.

'Thank you so much, everyone. Great work. Couldn't have
got here so quickly without you,' said Cole, standing and
stretching his limbs.

Clay raised her arm to attract Cole's attention as Hendricks
and Riley emerged from the group. Cole walked in her
direction with a smile on his face and a map in his hand.

'What have we got, Barney?' asked Clay.

He placed the map down on her desk and she looked at the
black rectangle with North Road and Grassendale Road on
the left, and Salisbury Road on the right.

'I've double-checked. We've got the main road, St Mary's Road, forming the top of the rectangle and Grassendale Promenade on the bottom. We've got fourteen roads inside the grid.'

'There's absolutely no way out, no way of getting out of the grid without getting caught on CCTV or ANPR at some point nearby?' asked Clay, staring long and hard into the mouth of the gift horse.

'We can check the roads west of North Road and Grassendale Road but the CCTV on Beechwood Road hasn't thrown anything up, and east of Salisbury Road, there are no roads to travel down.'

Hendricks gave two printed sheets to Clay, a CCTV image of the white van and a generic picture of a vehicle of the same make and approximate age.

She looked at the pictures of the van and the small area outlined on the map.

'Bill, ring round the duty superintendents. We need every available body for the Grassendale Park door to door. Gina, oversee the operation. Everyone reports back directly to you.'

'Anything comes up, Eve, I'll be right on to you.'

'We need every garage open,' said Clay, turning to Cole. 'Barney, get on to the duty magistrate. We need an emergency search warrant, pronto. And pull up all the men who live in the grid from the electoral roll. Check them against the National Police Computer, please, and let's see what comes crawling from the woodwork.'

She looked at the map, the network of roads inside the rectangular grid.

'I hope you're right, Barney.'

'So do I. All that time and effort. I'm going to look like dick of the year if I'm wrong.'

49
7.01 pm

Doors away from the junction of North Road and West Road, Hendricks pressed a musical bell for the fourth time and, stepping back from the ramp that rested on the steps in front of the double-fronted house, looked at the garage at the side.

The mid-Victorian house and the late-twentieth-century garage were unlikely neighbours. The 1970s' metal-doored garage was wedged between the side wall of the house and the wall that fenced in the grounds. The security light above the garage went out and he waved his arms above his head to turn it back on.

On the other side of the door, there was no sound of anyone approaching but, behind a stained-glass oval, the light went on in the hall.

'Who is it?' A woman's voice came through the front door.

'Police. It's nothing to worry about,' said Hendricks, hoping he was wrong.

The search had started at the north end of the grid and the hastily assembled team of constables and community officers was working systematically down to the river.

Hendricks looked down and saw a woman peeping through the gap at waist height. He saw her right foot resting on the metal plate of her wheelchair.

He held his warrant card at a level where she could read it. Her face was partially hidden behind the door and his first impression was that she was extremely shy.

'I need to look in your garage, Mrs...?'

'Ms Norma Maguire. What are you looking for, DS Hendricks?'

'A white Ford Transit van.'

'I don't have a white van.'

'Fair enough, but I need to look in your garage.'

She pulled an expensive-looking bag from the handle of her wheelchair and on to her lap, and unfastened the chain.

'Excuse me,' said Norma Maguire, opening the front door and wheeling herself down the ramp and ahead of Hendricks without looking at him. She took out her car key and pressed the fob. Without making any noise, the garage door rose up.

She wheeled herself under the rising door and turned the light on in the garage, revealing a red Vauxhall Combo and a folded-down wheelchair propped against the interior wall.

Hendricks weighed up the interior of the garage. The back wall was solid brick and there was no way of driving a vehicle to the rear of the property.

The garage was a dead end.

'No white van, just my red Vauxhall Combo WAV.'

'WAV, Miss Maguire?'

'Wheelchair Accessible Vehicle. I need it to get to work and back. So, what's the big deal with the white van?' asked Ms Maguire.

Hendricks moved to look at Ms Maguire directly. She shifted her wheelchair a little to the right and looked away from Hendricks.

'Are you all right, Ms Maguire?'

'I'm extremely shy and I'm not used to having people call to the house. If you could give me my personal space, I'd be grateful.'

'I apologise for making you feel awkward. It certainly wasn't my intention, Ms Maguire.'

There was something desolate in the air and Hendricks wondered if it was Ms Maguire or the large garage that radiated negativity.

'Just as a matter of interest, do you own the house?' asked Hendricks.

'What kind of a question's that?'

'You might be a tenant. Your landlord might have a white van. I may need to talk to your landlord.'

'I've lived here all my life. I own the house outright.'

'Do you live alone?'

'Yes. The house is customised for my needs. I know what you're thinking, DS Hendricks. That's an awfully big house for one woman.'

'It's none of my business. I was wondering if there was anyone else in the house because I've got questions to ask.'

'Fire away.'

'Have you seen a white van driving past your house, or on any of the streets around here?'

'I've seen several white vans. People in the houses around here have workmen call to repair and decorate.'

Hendricks showed her the CCTV picture of the white van.

'Have you seen this one?'

'No. All the white vans round here have their owner's name, trade and contact details advertising their services. There are no such distinguishing marks on the van you're showing me. Can I close my garage up now, please?'

'Sure. Thank you for your help, Ms Maguire.'

As she reversed herself out of the garage, Hendricks got the clearest sight of Norma Maguire's face and her eyes were bloodshot and cloudy.

Hendricks walked down the path and felt sorry for her because it looked like she'd been crying for hours.

50

7.05 pm

Alone in the incident room, Clay looked closely at the first messages that Annie Boyd had sent to Richard Ezra, and the initial exchanges between Amanda Winton and Thomas Saddler.

Richard Ezra wrote: *Hi, Annie. Thank you for winking at me. I love your profile.*

Annie had replied: *Hello, Richard. Great to hear from you. I love your profile too. You come over as a really fun guy.*

Clay skipped over the short, initial exchanges, the polite yet probing messages, and came to Richard Ezra's first substantial volley of words. She held the page under her desk light and read out loud, *Hi Annie I'd be most grateful if we could have an initial dialogue with a view to getting to know each other better. Hopefully, you'll be comfortable with...*

She took the transcript supplied by Warrington, the exchange between Sandra O'Day and a man claiming to be Michael Towers, and picked out his first major line of attack.

Clay skimmed and scanned Ezra's and Towers' words, eyes flicking left and right, staying right and back to left, and read, 'Ezra, *initial dialogue*; Towers, *initial dialogue*. Ezra, *getting to know each other a little better*; Towers, *getting to know each other a little better*. Both of them, *if you don't feel comfortable with this... wishing you all the best in finding a man... worship the ground you walk on...*'

Clay looked up as Poppy Waters entered the incident room.

'I've got the full transcripts from Amanda Winton's communication with Thomas Saddler. Like the others, Eve, the trail goes somewhat cold after he gets her mobile phone number and tells her he's going to ring her.'

'Let me guess. Michael Towers, just like Richard Ezra and Thomas Saddler after him, didn't want to get hurt again because his wife had died. He didn't tell her he was a childless widower because he didn't want to make emotional capital out of his tragic misfortune. Did Amanda ask him if it was possible to die of a broken heart?'

'No, he volunteered the information willingly.'

'If this wasn't so vile, there'd be a funny side to it. If he was just a guy playing fast and loose on the internet – I mean, think of it, Poppy. He comes over as a nice young widower wearing his heart on his sleeve. He could have wiped up. It could've been pussy galore for him.'

'Under the name Thomas Saddler, did he say anything different, anything that stood out?' asked Poppy.

'No. Same guy. Different alias,' said Clay.

'Same old language?'

'Same old shit,' concluded Clay.

51

8.45 pm

As she made her way from the Albert Dock and past the Marina, heading for her car, Francesca Christie felt completely stupid.

Stupid cow, standing in the wind and the rain, waiting for a man who would never show up. Ha ha ha... Even the waves of the river seemed to laugh at her.

Half an hour earlier, she'd called him but he was unable to take her call. Phone off. Try again later.

She felt the rising storm of tears as humiliation sank its teeth into her heart, and wondered what was so terribly wrong with her that the world, in the form of a solitary man, could treat her so very badly.

Hand in hand, a couple laughed as they walked past her, their happiness and closeness drilling a nail into her head that sank down and spiked her heart.

Hi, Francesca! Bryony's voice. *How did the big date go?*

He was OK, I guess. He asked me out on a second date. I'll make excuses, let him down gently.

As she manufactured the lie, she took a left turn towards the place where she'd parked her black Vauxhall Corsa. She walked towards her car, opening the doors with her fob.

A vile thought assaulted her, triggering a string of humiliating possibilities.

What if he's got a Facebook page? What if he's done it for a bet? What if he posts my picture? What if he tells the whole wide world what a fool I've been?

She could see the pitying looks of her new colleagues in the office of Doherty Properties and Estates, hear the silence that greeted her in a thousand dismal places.

Francesca opened the driver's door of her car and made a decision.

No more internet dating, ever. Loneliness, though brutal, was better than humiliation. First job, as she stepped over the doorway of home, take down her profile from Pebbles On The Beach. The bitter end.

'Excuse me!' The voice was insistent but polite, mechanical and androgynous.

She turned, felt like she'd been hit in the face by a brick. Her legs gave way and the thing behind her held her up, turned her round and bundled her into the driver's seat, closing the door after her as the back door opened.

Lights went on and off in her head as she placed the key in the ignition, tried to get the car started, but it was too late.

The back door of her car slammed shut.

'I am The Ghoul.'

Sitting right behind her, oozing into the pores at the back of her neck, she felt breath, hot and insistent.

'Get the car started, Francesca.' She turned the key in the ignition.

In the rear-view mirror, two points of light danced immediately behind her, a pair of eyes lurking in the dark.

She shuddered and her stomach turned when a large hand landed on her right shoulder and there was a sharpness against her throat, a lethal edge of a sharpened blade.

'Hello, Francesca. Can you hear me?'

She nodded, felt the roll of the edge of the blade pressing left to right and back again.

'This is what you're going to do. If you don't do as you're told, you will die.'

She heard words and found herself driving down a straight stretch of road that ran parallel to the Mersey, Riverside Drive, and knew she was following instructions.

As she came up to the Britannia pub, a marked police car came in her direction, heading towards the city centre, and as quickly as wild hope blossomed inside her, so did The Ghoul's mounting rage, translated into harsh language spat into her neck as the blade came away from her throat.

'Don't even look sideways, don't even think about trying to attract their attention. Look at me! Look at me! Lurrraaammmeeee...'

Eternity passed in a handful of seconds.

She pulled up at the roundabout at the bottom of Jericho Lane and watched a car turn off, heading in the direction of Aigburth.

'Wait!'

She watched the car travel further and further up Jericho Lane, its rear lights turning into illuminated pinpricks before dissolving into the dark.

'Go!'

Francesca took a long in-breath through her nose, tasted blood in her mouth and on her lips as she turned on to Jericho Lane and caught the edge of The Ghoul's natural body odour.

'When I tell you, when we get near the top of the road, you turn right and stop your car near the gateway into Otterspool Park.'

She turned into the darkness at the gateway.

'Turn your engine off. Get out of the car. Walk.'

The point of the knife was in her back; she could feel its jagged tooth through her clothes and a ripple of electricity ran down her spine. Francesca made out the shape of another vehicle in the shadows at the gateway and, fifteen metres away on Aigburth Road, she heard streams of traffic heading in two directions.

The parked car. She was marched round the back, her eyes almost blind with tears. The boot was thrown up.

'Get in. Shut the fuck up with the tears.'

She wiped her eyes and watched as The Ghoul opened a vial of liquid and noticed there was no smell as it was handed to her.

'Drink it! All of it!'

A fist formed high above her head.

She swallowed the tasteless liquid and curled into the foetal position.

'And, so, off she floats to nowhere.'

The Ghoul slammed the boot down and condemned her to the darkness.

Francesca heard the engine come to life, felt the motion of a moving vehicle, and had the urge to shut her eyes as the ropes that tied her to consciousness unknotted quickly. Within moments, she was no longer locked in the boot of a car.

She was gone.

52

9.59 pm

Norma Maguire sat at the wheel of her Vauxhall Combo WAV, driving down Regent Road on to Crosby Road South, her head full of Francesca Christie.

She imagined her sitting in her bedroom communicating on her laptop with some creep or other, passing sick-making lovey-dovey notes and blithely turning her back on the real love that she had to offer.

Norma opened her window and heard the sound of the Irish Sea as it lapped against the sands of Crosby Beach.

She marvelled at the sudden and brutal manner in which Fran announced her departure.

'If you can't beat them, join them, Fran,' she whispered into the darkness.

She remembered the small but significant band of ungrateful defectors. They walked through her mind like restless ghosts, the expression on their faces as they told her they were leaving seared on to her brain.

One, two, three, four and five and now a sixth. Fran.

She pictured the two front bedroom windows of Fran's house and imagined a light going on and Fran appearing, not looking out but closing both curtains, on the many nights she'd sat outside on Druid's Cross Road, watching, watching.

What are you smiling for, Fran?

Norma revisited the same fantasy that played out in her head when she sat outside Fran's house in every kind of weather. She pictured her sitting on the bed and taking her top off, the sound of bathwater running a few doors away. Fran slipping out of her skirt, both thumbs hooking on to the sides of her thong, standing and stepping out of her clothes on the carpet. Smiling in the mirror as she unclasped her bra, her rosebud nipples puckering on a cold winter's night.

Tears rolled down Norma's face and she felt the weight of them pressing down on her bad skin and ugly, ugly face, the depth of the hurt Fran had caused her kicking in with full force, as the cruel music of her self-defeating fantasy cackled in her ears.

'Why did you do it, Fran?'

Norma heard brokenness in her voice where only moments earlier she had listened to the deep defiance and anger that burned inside her. The hurt Fran caused was deeper and harsher than all the others who had betrayed her put together.

'If you only knew how much I totally love you, Fran. But you don't. You're a good person really, the best, but you're young and you've been totally foolish.'

Norma fell silent and remembered the nights she'd watched the front door of Fran's house opening and Fran's mother putting out an empty milk bottle, and the fear of being caught, wondering what would happen if her mother just marched over the road and confronted her, called for the police and sparked a scandal in which Norma would be cast as both central villain and laughing stock.

Time dissolved.

She was no longer driving. Instead, she stared ahead at the dark sands of Crosby Beach where Iron Men gazed at the water of the Irish Sea, but all was blurred by the haze of tears and the throbbing inside her head.

'I love you, Fran. But you're a bitch.'

She turned the key in the ignition.

'How could you?'

Her tyres screeched as she performed a three-point turn and headed back towards Liverpool.

'How could you?' she screamed at the windscreen, her fists pounding the steering wheel.

THE PAST

1980

It was the same routine every lunchtime during the holidays and the days she wasn't well enough to escape the house and go to school.

When the front doorbell rang, she was to stay in her bedroom and was told to remain there until a large chunk of time passed, the front door closed and the visitor hurried away at a speed between striding and sprinting through the gravel at the front of the house.

She stood at her bedroom window, tall enough now to see the whole of the grounds before the front door.

He walked through the open gateway – they all did – and she wondered why none of her mother's visitors could drive or own a car or park it where her father's Bentley went when he was home.

As the visitor approached the front door, she looked closely at him. Like she did with all her mother's visitors. And like all of them, this newest caller was totally unlike her father.

She recalled watching her father that morning as he walked from the house to his fancy car. Wearing a grey suit with a white shirt and a purple tie, he was only slightly taller than he was wide. Unlike the man approaching the house, who was dressed in jeans and trainers and a brown leather coat that kissed his ankles as it flapped in the breeze at his feet.

Tall and thin and much, much, much, much younger than her mother, he looked like an actor or an artist or one of those other men her mother constantly argued about with her father.

He looked left and right, and then left and right again as if he was playing an extremely dangerous game of hide and seek. In his hand was a thin book.

The man looked like... what were the words her father gave to men such as this on the street and the television set? Yes, yes. He looked like *an arty-farty piece of shit.*

She couldn't see it but the front door was opened – by her mother, it must have been, she was the only one in the house apart from her and her baby brother, who was in his room at the back of the house – and the man was sucked into the belly of the house by an in-breath of her mother's making.

'What's this?' her mother giggled in the hall below.

'My new book of poetry. *And, so, off she floats to nowhere.* It is for you.'

Their voices dipped and their words became incomprehensible as they came up the stairs at speed.

Just as they'd zoned out, they faded back in.

She spoke. 'Do you not like what you see?' It was her sad voice.

'But you're the most beautiful woman I've met in my life,' said the young poet.

'Is that all?' she asked, the dent in her pride evident in the injury in her voice.

'Helen of Troy. Yes, this is who I see when I look at you.'

In the pause that followed, she sensed in the poet the same struggle she had for ideas when her mother asked her questions about the way she looked.

'You're divine. You could be Venus.'

'Could be?'

'Are! Are...'

She worked out that Mother and her visitor had arrived at the top of the stairs because the words stopped and there was a silence punctuated by a sucking noise, and sighing. The kissing game. They all liked to play it.

The ball of sickness in her stomach tightened and swelled.

What was it? she asked herself. *What was it with these men, man after man after man visiting her mother?*

She heard her mother's bedroom door close and, behind it, the swish of curtains closing.

Her head hurt. The pain swelled. And it rocketed through her nervous system to the parts of her brain where compulsion ruled.

For the first time in her dark life, without making a decision, she found herself opening her bedroom door.

Walking down the corridor towards her mother's bedroom, she saw with dread that her baby brother's bedroom door was open. She looked inside but he was not in his bed. His absence went through her like horrid fire and she felt like her brain was frying in the dreadful heat.

Where are you?

Panic invaded her.

Where are you, baby brother?

Please be anywhere, her voice echoed in her head. *But please don't be in there, behind that closed door of hers. Please.*

She crept towards her mother's bedroom door, drawn by mounting terror for the little one.

Behind the door, she heard the poet's voice.

'Er, what's this?' he asked.

'Ignore it,' replied her mother. 'If you don't like it, get out now!'

There was a silence.

'Don't you want me?'

'I'm staying,' he replied.

She got on to her knees and looked through the keyhole, saw flashes of the poet and her mother as they took their clothes off, lunging at each other as they did so, fumbling with their hands and kissing with their mouths.

'Tell me again,' said her mother. 'Tell me what you said on the telephone. How beautiful am I?'

'You're beyond beautiful.'

'Do you think any man could resist me?'

'No man could resist you.'

He sucked at her breast like a baby should.

Where are you, my brother?

She could see her mother's lower legs and feet, lying down on the bed, and then the man's legs and feet, his toes to her ankles.

A noise came from the space around the bottom of the bed, a sniffling that was drowned out as Mother and her visitor started making noises like animals fighting to the death.

'What can you see when you look into my eyes?' asked her mother.

His legs were moving up and down, his toes clamped on to the mattress.

'I can see the ocean, clear blue water sparkling in early morning light.'

'What do you see when you look at my face. Look at me. Open your eyes and look at me!'

'I can see the most beautiful sunset.'

'What about my body?'

'Your breasts like... like those of a... a teenage goddess. You've got the figure of an angel and legs like Venus de Milo.'

'That's right, that's exactly what I'm like.'

She opened the door a fraction and gained a wider view of what was going on.

The man was bouncing up and down on her mother, whose legs were wrapped around his backside, a tight knot to seal him to her.

'I'm the best you've ever had, right?' said her mother.

'I'll never get better. You're the best, you're the best, you're the best!'

She opened the door some more and saw that her mother was looking into the huge mirror on the wall to the right of the bed. Her eyes were locked into her reflection as if they were glued to the image on the glass that entranced her.

'I am gorgeous, I am beautiful, I am...'

It was as if their bodies seized up in the same pattern of moments. They cried out together as if they were both utterly lost and completely in pain.

She opened the door wider and saw that her baby brother was at the bottom of the bed, standing and watching in the silence that constantly defined him. In his mouth was a dummy and he watched his mother and her visitor without any emotion, and she guessed he'd seen and heard everything, more, much more than she had seen.

The man rolled off her mother and lay on his back beside her.

Her mother stared at her face in the mirror, her long blonde hair fanning out across the pillow.

'And, so,' said her mother to her own reflection. 'Off she floats to nowhere.'

He reached out towards her breasts but she threw his hand away.

'Get out!' It was the voice her mother used when she was boiling with rage, usually during and after the shouting matches she had with her father.

Her brother fell to his hands and knees and crawled around the corner of the bed towards the door. She urged him forward with both hands and her mouth, which opened and closed, opened and closed as she urged...

Come on, come on, come on, and away...

'And take your juvenile poetry shit with you.'

'What did I do wrong?' asked the young poet, the rising of unshed tears in his question.

Silence, the kind that bit down hard into the deepest place where sorrow reigned with a rod of jagged ice.

She reached out and swooped up her baby brother.

'What did you do wrong?'

Her mother sounded like she was going to explode.

She ran down the landing with him in her arms, urging him *hush, hush, hush...*

'Ask yourself a different question.'

She ran to her room, clutched him to herself as if their lives depended on it.

'What did *you* do *right*, arsehole?'

DAY THREE

FRIDAY, 3RD DECEMBER 2021

MONOPHOBIA

FEAR OF BEING ALONE

53

0.05 am

Francesca Christie's mother pulled back the curtains in her living room and looked out on to the street, her anxiety peaking as she tried her daughter's mobile for the twelfth time since eleven o'clock, to hear the same frustrating automated message.

Sorry, the person you're calling is currently unavailable. Try again later.

'We have an agreement, set in stone. You said you'd be back by eleven, half past at the latest...' Margaret Christie talked to the framed picture of her daughter on the wall. 'Why have you turned your phone off? Whenever you go out or I go out, we keep the phone on at all times in case of an emergency or a problem. This just *isn't* you.'

With a balloon of sickness inflating in her stomach, she marched into the hall and took the address book from the drawer beneath the landline phone.

She flicked to the B page and looked for Bryony's phone number but it wasn't there. She remembered the book was ordered alphabetically according to surname but, in that moment, she couldn't remember Bryony's family name even though she'd known Francesca's best friend since she was eleven years of age.

Going to the front door, she opened it and walked quickly on to the pavement, looked down the road and hoped she'd see Francesca's car turning the corner and heading home. There was no sign of any traffic.

Marsh! Through the blinding fog of panic, it came to her. Bryony Marsh...

Closing the front door after herself and turning to the M page of the address book, she dialled her number. The phone rang out and she imagined the alarm in the house at a phone call coming in after midnight.

'Come on. Pick up! Pick up!'

'Hello!'

'Bryony, it's me, Margaret, Francesca's mum.'

'Hi...'

'She's been with you this evening?'

'Er, yeah, yeah...'

'Is she there with you now?'

'No, she left.'

'When?'

'An hour ago.'

'She's not home.'

'Isn't she?'

Another voice drifted into play, and she recognised Bryony's mother's voice joining the tense exchange.

'What's going on, Bryony?'

'It's – it's Margaret... I'll deal with it, OK?'

'Put me on speakerphone please, Bryony. Hello, Cheryl, can you hear me?'

'What's up? Why are you calling this late at night?'

'I'm sorry but Francesca's been at yours this evening and isn't home yet.'

Silence.

'Hello, Bryony, Cheryl, are you still there?'

'I'm sorry,' said Bryony's mother. 'There's been some sort of confusion here. Clearly. Francesca hasn't been here this evening. She hasn't been here for at least a fortnight.'

'Then I'm afraid Bryony's been lying to me.'

'What?' Bryony's mother sounded like she'd been stung by a wasp.

'OK, OK, OK,' said Bryony. 'She asked me to cover for her. I'm sorry for lying to you, but Francesca asked me to. She's gone out on a date. I'm not sure if it's someone from the internet but she's been doing online dating sites. She said it was a blind date... shit! Oh my God...'

There was an ugly silence before Margaret asked, 'Bryony, what do you know about the man Francesca's been out with?'

'Nothing. She wanted to keep quiet about the date. She asked me to cover her tracks. I'm sorry.'

Francesca's mother replaced the receiver as the balloon within her swelled by the moment and threatened to swamp her vital organs.

She picked up her car keys and hurried from the house.

54

0.10 am

Savage pain woke her up; a deep throbbing pressure down in the stem of her brain. She felt something cold, metallic and heavy on her stomach and she knew that she was naked. She opened her eyes and found she was in a bare room doused in flickering red light.

Red. Black. Red. Black.

Everything flashed through her head in a heartbeat, and she was filled with horror at what she could remember and terrorised by what may have been when she was unconscious.

She reached a hand towards the space between her legs but was held back by the chain that bound her.

Francesca shuffled up the bed a little, took a series of deep breaths and analysed her entire body. There was no pain or sensation in her vagina or anus. She touched herself to double-check but there was no sign of invasion.

She closed her eyes and took a series of deep breaths, retraced the steps of a living nightmare, felt the point of a blade against her throat, a weapon that wasn't there in the cell but the sharpness felt like it had left an indelible stamp on her skin.

'Owwww!' She mouthed the cry, not wanting to attract attention to herself, and recalling the force and speed of the first blow that had overwhelmed her as she tried to get into her car.

She thought she'd driven in silence but her useless words came back to her.

'Let me go. Please. Let me just pull up by the pavement. You can have my car. You can have my bag and purse. I won't tell the police, I promise. I won't tell anyone.'

As she drove past the empty industrial units of Sefton Street to her left and the crowded bars overlooking the river to her right, she had willed someone to rescue her from her new-found hell. No one did.

Francesca looked into the rear-view mirror, saw the glinting of The Ghoul's eyes, sensed the joyous smile as they danced in the dark and drank in her desperation.

The police car. Jericho Lane. Alone and powerless with The Ghoul.

There was the absolute darkness of the boot of The Ghoul's car, the tasteless drug that knocked her out and after that, nothing.

'Jesus, where am I?' she whispered, the flickering red light above her head invading her eyes and disorientating her ragged senses.

A dot of light appeared in the darkness within her, a dot of light that grew a little bigger with each breath she took. And she knew as it expanded that it was recent memory, before she was plunged into the nightmare of the moment she was living in.

She closed her eyes and saw a window that was familiar to her and a patchy, fractured view on to Allerton Road with the sound of a police helicopter overhead, flying in her direction. There was a desk. The door to the office closed for privacy. She was nervous in Norma Maguire's office, she was always nervous around Norma.

She sat opposite Norma, who handed her a card file. She opened it and saw a record of her excursions on to Pebbles On The Beach. She closed the cover.

Words were exchanged and Norma was acting mysteriously. She wheeled herself around so that she could look out of the window.

'I'm careful,' she had said to Norma.

Words poured from Norma's mouth.

'I suppose the woman whose body was washed up in Warrington in the summer would have said she was careful too... you look puzzled. You didn't hear about it?'

'No.'

'He scalped her and took the skin from her face. According to the police, she met him on an internet dating site.'

The helicopter blades chopped the air, a stolen car screamed in a trail of chaos.

'I heard a report on Radio Merseyside this morning on my way in to work. There's another body been found closer to home. Otterspool Promenade.'

She opened her eyes, heard footsteps above her head and two voices, arguing, their words indistinct, their mutual tone furious.

Somewhere else in the building above, a televison was playing.

The full weight of Norma Maguire's warning hit her.

She touched her face and hair.

A scream built up inside Francesca Christie. She pressed her face into the stinking, wet mattress and screamed until all she had left in her was the air she needed to breathe.

55

0.21 am

Clay picked her car keys from her bag and, with heavy legs, headed for the door of the incident room, hoping that within the next hour she would be showered and asleep at her husband's side.

She reached the door and the landline phone on her desk rang out.

Clay stopped. *Should I? Or shouldn't I?* The temptation to ignore the ringing phone was immense but its insistence was enough to drag her back to her desk.

She picked up the receiver.

'Eve, I'm so glad that I've caught you.' It was Sergeant Harris, the custody sergeant. 'I've got a woman in reception, she's asking for you. She knows you're the SIO on the Otterspool Promenade case.' He raised his voice to normal volume. 'Mrs Christie wants to report her daughter as missing.'

'Has she been on an internet date?'

'Yes, she has.'

'Take her to Interview Suite 1, I'll be down immediately.'

Minutes later, in Interview Suite 1, Clay took two chairs from behind the desk and placed them facing each other.

'Sit down, please, Mrs Christie.'

The woman opposite Clay looked like all the blood had been drained from her veins.

'Tell me what's been going on?' said Clay.

'As I understand it, my daughter, Francesca, went out tonight on a date with a man she met on the internet, a man she's never met before in real life. I didn't know that she was visiting internet dating sites, and she lied to me about where she was going. She told me she was visiting her best friend. I learned from Bryony that Francesca had actually gone on a date. That's about all I know. Her phone's been turned off. She never turns her phone off. She's got work in the morning. She never gets in later than eleven when she's got work the next day.'

'Where does Francesca work, Mrs Christie?'

'Maguire Holdings on Allerton Road.'

Mrs Christie's eyes were red and her face was a knot of intense anxiety.

'Do you have a picture of her, Mrs Christie?' Clay leaned in a little closer as Mrs Christie opened her shoulder bag and took out her iPhone. 'The most recent one if possible, please.'

Mrs Christie swiped through the images on her phone. 'This is the most recent one.'

Clay looked at the picture of Francesca Christie – blonde, slim, attractive, mid twenties – and shuddered inside.

'Send all the pictures you have of her to me, Mrs Christie.' Clay handed her a contact card. 'Do you have her address book?'

'It's the family address book.' Mrs Christie handed it to Clay.

'She may have gone visiting someone on the way home.'

'She wouldn't just do that. It's out of character.'

'In my experience, Mrs Christie, most people do things that are out of character at some or several points in their lives. We have to go through a process of elimination here. Does she have a laptop?' Mrs Christie nodded. 'We need to look at it.'

'I thought you might ask.' She produced a laptop from the bag.

'The pictures, please, Mrs Christie.'

As Mrs Christie sent the pictures of Francesca to Clay's phone, she said, 'You're taking this very seriously, DCI Clay.'

'We take all missing persons cases seriously.'

'I don't believe you. I'm sorry, but I don't. You're thinking what I'm thinking. Francesca's in serious trouble.'

'Mrs Christie, I don't know where Francesca is at the moment but these are very dangerous times for young women in this part of the country. My aim is to find Francesca and not jump to alarming conclusions. Have you left all your contact details with Sergeant Harris on the desk?'

'Yes.'

'What was Francesca wearing?'

'I don't know. She called goodbye from the front door as she was leaving the house. I was in the kitchen.'

'What car does she drive?'

'A black Vauxhall Corsa.'

'Licence plate?'

'It's a personalised plate. FC 1.'

'We'll be in touch with you as soon as we know anything, Mrs Christie. Is there anything else you'd like to add?'

'Francesca lost her father a year ago, and her so-called boyfriend jilted her weeks after the funeral. It broke her into pieces. Her confidence plummeted. She doesn't normally lie to me. But she's a very proud person. She lied to me about these wretched dating sites because she was embarrassed to have to stoop that low. She's a good daughter. She's a good human being.'

'I believe you, Mrs Christie.'

Clay read the anguish on the woman's face and positioned herself directly in her place.

'If Francesca shows up, call me immediately, I don't care what the hour is,' said Clay.

They left Interview Suite 1 in silence and Clay escorted Mrs Christie to the door leading out of Trinity Road police station.

Clay felt the burden of Mrs Christie's anxiety and knew that Francesca's mother shared the same instinctive and certain knowledge.

Francesca had been abducted.

When she had gone, Clay walked quickly to the desk and showed Sergeant Harris a picture of Francesca Christie on her iPhone.

'Missing. Internet date. Probably Pebbles On The Beach.'

'Shit,' said Sergeant Harris.

'Ring round everyone on the team, please,' said Clay. 'Ring switchboard and put out an instruction to all officers out there on duty. We're looking for a black Vauxhall Corsa. Licence plate, FC 1. I'll be in the incident room. They're to meet me there as soon as possible.'

56

0.28 am

Francesca Christie heard the sound of a hatch opening in the ceiling of the cell in which she was imprisoned. Instinctively, she sat up on the bed, covering her breasts with both arms and folding her legs at the knees.

The Ghoul.

Feet came down the stairs, one hand holding the rail, the other carrying a canvas bag; she watched a body materialise, arms and body clothed in black, face concealed by a black balaclava with a head light that acted as a blinding screen.

The Ghoul stood at the bottom of the stairs, she guessed, looking directly at her.

'And, so, off she floats to nowhere.'

The Ghoul's voice was mechanical, robotic, and she tried to remember what had been said to her and the way the words had been spoken when she'd been taken at knifepoint, but her memory felt like it was swathed in twisting clouds.

Francesca looked away, memorised the first words spoken to her since she'd awoken in captivity. She clenched her body and paid attention to the metal table between herself and the empty cot on the other side of the cell.

'I'm thirsty,' she said.

The Ghoul walked to the metal table and placed the canvas bag on its surface.

Polite, be polite, don't say a word that is offensive. The words rose up from deep inside her. *Show that you are listening.*

'What do you mean: And, so, off she floats to nowhere?' she asked.

The bag was unzipped and out of it came a hypodermic needle and a scalpel. The noise of the scalpel against the table told her that it was made of metal.

Francesca counted in silence. *One, two, three, four.* Out came four scalpels of different sizes.

The head light shone directly in her face.

She felt the contents of her stomach lurch, held on to her breath as if it were her last one and battled down the urge to throw up, to give away another victory to The Ghoul.

'Do you like my mask, Francesca?'

She nodded.

'I can't hear you?'

'I like your mask.'

She could hear the dryness in her throat, the rasp of her tongue against the parched walls of her mouth. Above her head, in the building, she heard a kettle whistle and voices talking, but knew that they were coming from a radio because as soon as they stopped, a Radio City jingle played, normality on the edge of the abyss.

I'm still in Liverpool then, she thought, *or the area just outside the city.*

'Sit up and sit perfectly still, Francesca...' The Ghoul came closer.

She sat up and rested her chained hands at the top of her legs. A right-hand index finger appeared in front of her face.

Francesca shut her eyes tightly and pictured herself at the bottom of the wooden ladder running up the steps...

She felt the weight of an index finger at the middle of her chin.

...and into the kitchen, which she'd never seen before, but she looked all around in a moment...

The finger was light as it travelled left along her jawline to the base of her ear and, once there, just under her hairline.

...and saw the back door, and a drawer near a huge sink. She hurried to the door, turned the handle this way and that but it was locked...

It travelled smoothly under her hairline to the middle of her neck, where it stopped and rose from her puckered skin.

She ran to the kitchen drawer, opened it and took out a kitchen knife...

Another finger continued towards her right ear and down towards the centre of her chin, where the journey across the flesh of her face had begun.

The Ghoul roared from the hatch, rising into the kitchen and flying at her at full speed. Lifting a fist to punch her in the face, it stepped forward, didn't see the knife coming as she plunged it into that miserable heart...

She felt her cheeks being squeezed between a thumb and index finger.

'Look at me!' She opened her eyes but everything was a blur. 'You've got good skin. You've got nice hair. You're pretty. You're just what I need.'

The head light was turned off. Its face came towards her. She felt the musty wool of a black balaclava rubbing against her cheek, saw the darkness behind the eye holes, held her breath as The Ghoul pulled back and stood up from the bed.

Francesca watched its distorted form as it walked away, to the table, to the stairs, and she felt a weight land next to her on the bed.

It disappeared through the entrance, closed the cover and was gone.

Francesca fumbled across the mattress and felt the pliable plastic of a water bottle. She trapped it between her knees and with the hand that could reach, she unscrewed the cap.

Wait! She heard her own voice, warning. She raised it to her nose and could smell nothing. She dipped a finger in it and licked the tasteless fluid. Water? It seemed to be exactly the same as the fluid in the small vial that had knocked her out.

She dipped her tongue into the neck of the bottle, coated as much of it as she could with such a small amount.

Dip. Repeat. Wait.

Through the ceiling above her head, she heard voices.

She listened as hard as she had ever listened to anything in her life and made out one word.

Francesca… Francesca… Francesca…

Silence.

57

0.49 am

Clay stood in front of Hendricks, Riley, Cole, Stone and Winters in the incident room, each of them holding a printout of Francesca Christie's photo, as Poppy Waters sat at Clay's desk unlocking the missing woman's laptop.

'Has anyone had any luck online? Anyone turned up on your profile pages who sounds like The Ghoul?' asked Clay.

They were silent and collective disappointment marbled the air.

'Me neither,' said Clay.

'Maybe he's getting a little spooked,' said Hendricks. 'Maybe after his prolific activity, he knows he's left a trail behind him...'

'You could have a point, Bill.'

'What's the plan?' asked Stone.

'I've ordered in CCTV footage from in and around the Albert Dock. All the CCTV footage from the different venues feeds into a central monitoring centre operated by the Dock's 24-Hour Security Services. It's on its way over now. I'm banking on him being a creature of habit and I've asked for footage leading down the front towards the padlocked railings from seven-thirty pm onwards. If he told Annie Boyd and Amanda Winton to be there for eight pm, I reckon he'll have given the same instruction to Francesca Christie. So far so good from his point of view. It's working. Why make changes to a winning game plan?'

'I've made my way into it,' said Poppy Waters. 'I'm on to Francesca's desktop.'

'How are you going to get on to her Pebbles On The Beach profile? asked Clay.

'In the first instance, I'll try using the letters Francesca Christie to crack her username. Did you know there's a top twenty of most commonly used passwords in the English-speaking world? Guess what comes up at number five. iloveyou, all lowercase. Tens of thousands of people use it.'

'What about when the rest of the world wakes up in the morning?' asked Riley. 'What then, Eve?'

'Francesca worked at Maguire Holdings on the commercial end of Allerton Road. I'm going to show up there tomorrow before the doors open, talk to the people who worked with her, ask if she'd told anyone about her communication with this man, or if she'd let anyone in on any information about her date last night. Karl.' She looked to Stone. 'I'd like you to come with me, act as a second pair of eyes.'

Clay turned to Riley and said, 'Gina, in the morning I'd like you to chase up CCTV4U, see how they're getting on with cleaning up the footage of the white van heading away down Heath Road from the Amanda Winton body drop-off. See if we've got a clearer shot of the man in the passenger seat.'

Poppy Waters stood up, stepped back from Francesca Christie's laptop and looked down at the screen as if it had just dished out an insult to her.

'I'm not having much luck with this method,' said Poppy. 'And I don't want to get locked out by the system.'

'What are you going to do?' asked Clay.

Poppy turned the screen so everyone could see the brightly coloured pebbles sitting on golden sand and being washed over by clear water. The irony of the purity of the image hit Clay hard.

'I'm going to hack her computer. I'll use Metasploit, it's powerful, a product of Rapid 7. I'll use it with WEB UI. I'll run an individual exploit on her Pebbles On The Beach account. If that fails, I'll try a basic penetration test. It should work. If she's like millions of other people on the internet, her security system's going to be completely inadequate.'

'Will it take you long?' asked Clay.

'No,' replied Poppy, sitting down and fixing her attention on the screen. Her fingers danced over the keyboard. 'Won't be long before you know who she's been talking to and what's been said. Same old, same old, bet you?'

58

4.00 am

'Eve?'

Clay looked across the incident room at the sound of Poppy Waters' voice. She caught Stone's eye, and knew that something important had come up on Francesca Christie's laptop.

As Clay walked over to them, Poppy said, 'The Ghoul's been masquerading as James Griffiths. That's the fake identity he's been hiding behind in hunting down Francesca Christie.'

Clay sat next to Poppy Waters and looked at the online endgame between Francesca Christie and The Ghoul.

'I've taken it back to the point where James Griffiths' other self, Thomas Saddler, who's been as lovely as can be to Francesca, suddenly goes off the planet, leaving James with a completely free hand.'

Clay skimmed and scanned James Griffiths' sugar-coated poison and quoted, 'You deserve a man who worships the ground you walk on and how jealous I would be of that stranger even though I take my hat off to him.'

She recognised the way he teased Francesca out and how her desperation mounted with each passing message and her need not to be hurt rocketed.

'It's like...' Clay touched the screen where the word *hurt* sat like an open wound itself in Francesca's message. 'It ignites the word hurt in his reply and sparks off the whole yarn about the dead wife and how he claimed he was single because he didn't want to make emotional capital from his bereavement. Which is when he offered to phone her because that was the gentlemanly thing to do.'

'Oh, well,' said Stone. 'It got results for him. Do you know what I'm reading into this? Like all good con men, when he's typing this bullshit he believes it in his heart of hearts. When he's spoken with them on the phone, he's believed every single word he's said, and it's made him super plausible to the lonely and vulnerable women he's targeted. But once he's got them where he wants them, lined up for a date, the switch flicks inside him and he turns from Rudolph Valentino into The Ghoul.'

Clay looked back at the dead end on screen.

Francesca Christie's mobile number: 07700 937374.

'Sent with love and kisses, 07700 937374, Francesca's eleven-digit pin code to a date with death with The Ghoul. Where this strand of evidence ends, the words we can't know are spoken over mobile phones.'

Clay picked up Francesca Christie's laptop and handed it back to Poppy.

'Go and have a look around her documents, emails, Facebook, Poppy. See if you can find anything that can lead us to this James Griffiths. Work through the other laptop and phone we took from Francesca's bedroom. Thank you. You've confirmed through the pattern you've uncovered that she's been abducted.'

Clay worked it out. Just over seven hours had passed since Francesca was last seen on CCTV at the waterfront. In five days, her mutilated body would show up after a four- to five-day window in which she'd be a captive, ending with her being murdered.

'Eve, do you want me to go and visit Francesca's mother, let her know what we know?' asked Stone.

'I'd be grateful if you could do that, Karl. Call Samantha Green from family liaison and make the visit together.'

59
4.08 am

The Ghoul was ready.

It typed in one of its usernames and its matching password to access Pebbles On The Beach, the only hunting ground it needed, the one that had yielded success upon success.

Sandra.

Annie. Amanda.

Francesca.

She would need company, a mistake The Ghoul had made in his naive opening excursion.

It was one thing to keep a single woman imprisoned and terrified to the portals of hysteria and madness, but that was half the story, half the potential of the pleasure to be had balanced against the risks undertaken.

Two could comfort each other, but that was fleeting.

Two could feed from each other's weaknesses, stoke up each other's fault lines and raise the temperature of terror as The Ghoul prepared their separate endgames.

Sally Haydn? Annie Boyd's lookalike and soundalike...

The Ghoul typed: *Dear Sally, I am new to internet dating and am a little nervous around the whole process. However, I kept coming back to your profile picture and felt compelled to enter into a dialogue with you. Perhaps you could get in touch with me, maybe give me your mobile number and I could call you?*

The Ghoul wrote words, more words, words that seemed to flow through the tips of those meaty fingers as they typed, fingers that would have an altogether different function at the endgame.

The Ghoul signed off the message – *Fond regards* – and remembered the name of the latest incarnation for this particular hunt. Geoff.

The Ghoul sent the message to Sally Haydn and smiled.

Next door, the sound of Francesca Christie crying seeped through the adjoining wall.

The Ghoul walked to the wall and picked out the place where her noise was loudest.

It stuck out a tongue and licked the bricks.

The Ghoul pressed its lips to the roughness of the brick, drank in the moisture of pain and terror.

'It won't be long now!'

60

4.35 am

The lights were on in the front room of Francesca Christie's house when Detective Sergeant Karl Stone arrived at the gate.

Sergeant Samantha Green, family liaison officer, was already there, waiting.

'Has her body been discovered?' she asked.

'No,' replied Stone. 'We're updating Mrs Christie on what we know. Preparing her for the worst.'

He walked up the path and heard the rattle of a milk float travelling away down Hornby Lane, and for a moment, as he pressed the bell, he wanted to swap places with the milkman.

'Who is it?' A voice travelled to the front door.

'Police, Detective Sergeant Karl Stone, and Sergeant Samantha Green, family liaison.'

The door was opened by a woman who looked like she'd been ravaged with anxiety and sorrow.

'Margaret Christie?' asked Stone.

'Yes. Have you found her?'

'No, I'm sorry.'

'Bring them in.' Another woman's voice came from deeper inside the house.

In Margaret Christie's living room, Stone sat next to Sergeant Green and made eye contact with Francesca's mother and aunt.

'What's happening?' asked Francesca's mother.

'We've looked at Francesca's online communications with a man posing as James Griffiths and the language he used when talking to Francesca was almost identical to the words used with other women who went missing.'

The two sisters looked at each other, and dread clashed with terror.

'We've seen footage of Francesca at the Albert Dock. It looks like he didn't show up at the allotted place and time. He's done this before. Francesca went off the CCTV radar at around twenty-five to nine...'

'Oh God, no...' Margaret Christie fell forward suddenly, forehead and face on her knees as if she'd been suddenly and completely snapped near the base of her spine. Her sister caressed her back and whispered, 'It's not over yet. We still have hope.'

'Based on previous cases, Francesca's got some time on her side,' said Stone.

'How long?' asked Francesca's aunt as her mother sobbed a fresh wave of unbridled tears.

'Days. We're pretty certain we've located a geographic area in South Liverpool where we think Francesca is being held captive. We're working round the clock to locate her. We have

CCTV footage of a man we're keen to question. His image is going to be extensively circulated in the media.'

'There's more than one of them?'

'Yes, we believe there's more than one.'

The horror in Francesca's aunt's face reached breaking point.

'I have to say there was no sign whatsoever,' said Sergeant Green, 'of any sexual violation with the previous victims.'

Mrs Christie uncurled slowly.

'As soon as we learn anything new, we'll be in touch with you immediately. We are doing our best, I promise you,' said Stone. 'Samantha will stay with you, and if you want to get a message to us or you remember anything that may help, tell Samantha and she'll pass it on to us.'

Stone walked to the front door with a monumental silence at his back.

Leaving the house, he heard the oncoming rattle of the milk float and a cat yowling in the dark as he headed towards Druid's Cross Road.

His iPhone buzzed with an incoming message.

CLAY

Francesca Christie's black Vauxhall Corsa has been discovered near the gates to Otterspool Park, just off Aigburth Road. It's in our garage at the Speke Industrial Estate.

He walked back up the path, wondering what words he was going to use to deliver the latest grim news.

An owl sang in the sky as night slowly uncoiled to dawn.

In the imminent grip of violent death, the rhythm and music of life rolled on.

61

6.01 am

Her brain and body wanted nothing more than to shut down and fall into a deep sleep, but this was one compulsion that Clay knew she had to ignore.

She looked at the cup from which she'd consumed several strong coffees and wondered if she was only imagining Gina Riley walking towards her across the incident room from the corner of her eye.

Clay turned to look closely and saw that Riley was lost between deep agitation and raw excitement, carrying her open laptop towards her. She remained deadpan but guessed what Riley was going to say next.

'I think we've got a hit from The Ghoul,' said Riley.

'Are you sure?' asked Clay.

Riley looked like she was in need of a forty-eight-hour lie-in and Clay questioned the wedge in her own brain that was too keen to believe her friend and colleague was right.

'On the profile I posted as Sally Haydn.'

Riley placed her laptop in front of Clay.

'He's had Francesca Christie for nine to ten hours,' said Clay, clawing back information from his most previous pattern. 'He had Annie Boyd and Amanda Winton together in a five-day window, Annie first in, Amanda next day. He must have loved every minute of it and now he's looking for company for Francesca.'

Clay read the opening sentences in response to Riley's coy bait.

Hi Sally, Thank you so much for getting in touch. I'm glad you've opened up this initial dialogue. Reading between the lines, I guess you'd like for us to get to know each other a little better. Say, talk on the phone, maybe. If I'm reading too much into this please forgive me and I wish you all the luck in the world in finding a man who will quite rightly worship the ground you walk upon. I take my hat off to him. xoxo Geoff

She looked over the rest of the message, the same condensed contents of messages to Annie Boyd, Amanda Winton and Francesca Christie, and said, 'You're right, Gina. It's The Ghoul. I see he's signed himself off as Geoff Campbell this time. He's on the minutes. He doesn't usually ask for a mobile number at this stage. Have you written back to him yet?'

'No, not yet.'

'Write back, something like, *Hi, Geoff, you're right lol there's no time like the present.* We'll work off my phone. I'm going to need it down the line. Be affectionate but equally desperate with it.'

Clay handed Riley her iPhone and she typed at speed with the thumbs of both hands.

'Give him a specific time to call you. Tell him you can't wait to talk to him. Let's make it hours, not days. We'll book an interview suite with a strictly do not disturb sign on the door.'

Riley looked up from the iPhone.

'What time, Eve?'

'Half past ten this morning. It's bordering on indecent haste but we haven't got time on our side. Stay put right here. Between now and half past ten don't get drawn into anything other than the phone call to him. I don't care if World War III breaks out, that's the only thing you have to do. Go over your Sally Haydn profile and learn it word for word. Rehearse your phone call with Bill Hendricks.'

'Half past ten. It's good,' said Riley. 'It makes me look super needy. *Can't even wait for the evening to talk to you, Geoff.*'

'Keep sending him messages, butter him up. See what language he comes out with, so we can rule out all possibilities of this being a linguistic fluke.'

There was silence as both Clay and Riley reread his message, a silence broken by the sound of a domestic running a vacuum cleaner outside in the corridor as Hendricks entered the incident room.

'Bill, over here.'

Clay made a multitude of connections in her head.

'Bill and Gina, I want you to book a block of time in a quiet place. You both know everything we have about how The Ghoul presents to women he's entrapping. Go over and over it because there's a grey area. We don't know how he performs on the phone. Based on what we know from his writing, it's a fairly safe bet to say it'll be more of the same. Practise that phone call.'

'I'll be Beauty,' said Riley.

'And I'll be The Ghoul,' replied Hendricks.

'What is it, Bill?' asked Clay. 'You've got that *shit's about to hit the fan* look on your face.'

'That's because it is, Eve. Big time. Gina gets on the phone to him, he offers to take her on a date, who's actually going to go on that date with death?'

'You think I haven't thought about that, Bill?'

'I'm sure you have, Eve, but I'd like to know what is your thinking on it?'

Without hesitation, Clay said, 'I'm going on the date. We'll organise a covert but extensive firearms presence and flood the area with plain-clothes officers.'

Hendricks and Riley looked at each other and the following silence was dense and filled with an intense prickly heat.

'Well, say something?' said Clay.

'Have you told Thomas yet?' asked Hendricks.

'I've been in much worse danger, Bill, you know that. If The Ghoul tells me through Gina to meet him at the padlocked railings, there'll be more coppers floating round the Albert Dock than at Goodison Park or Anfield on match day. I'll be perfectly safe.'

'Are you sure, Eve?' The anxiety on Riley's face was raw and came from deep within.

'I'm sure. What option do we have? This is a golden opportunity to catch him. If the past is anything to go on, Francesca Christie's got four and a half days before she shows up in a ditch or a river with no face and scalp. It's our primary duty to protect the public. We can't leave her to that bastard's tender loving care.'

'You don't fit the physical profile, Eve,' said Hendricks.

'That was tactfully stated,' said Clay. 'Even if it was a little cack-handed.'

'I'm sorry, Eve. I'm looking at safer alternatives, strategies...'

'There are none. OK, I'm a long way past twenty-five and I'm a brunette. I'll dye my hair blonde and make myself up like Francesca Christie on her profile picture. If he gets close enough to see my face, then he's going to shit himself hard and fast because I'll be carrying a fully loaded Glock and I will use it if he gives the game away and tries to attack me.'

She looked at them in turn, read their minds. 'I'm not sending in some ambitious twenty-five-year-old WPC. There is an element of risk. This is my plan, this is my responsibility. This is down to me and no one else.'

Clay took out her iPhone and scrolled through her contacts. 'Who are you on to, Eve?'

'I'm calling the duty superintendents from all the stations on Merseyside in the first instance. We can't sit around on this one. We need to square it all up with senior management, and get this one out of the nest and flying.'

'You mean business then, Eve?' asked Riley.

Clay remembered her first impression of Annie Boyd on the mudflats on the River Mersey, and the subsequent visit to her parents.

She remembered the despair on their faces and imagined the lifelong road of devastation that lay ahead of them.

'Yeah, I really mean business,' said Clay. 'Bring it on!'

62

8.45 am

Detective Chief Inspector Eve Clay got out of her car when she observed a painfully thin man in his forties opening up the front door of Maguire Holdings.

A little further ahead, on Allerton Road, Detective Sergeant Karl Stone got out of his car and headed towards the estate agency.

Clay noticed a disabled parking bay directly outside the estate agency as she showed the man with the keys her warrant card.

He introduced himself. 'Daniel Ball. Office manager.' He looked at Stone, who also showed him his warrant card. 'Please, come in.'

Daniel Ball turned on the lights and closed the door after himself. He indicated empty seats behind unmanned desks but Clay said, 'It's OK, thank you, Mr Ball.'

'What – what's this about?'

The complete attention he'd been giving to Clay and Stone faltered and he looked directly out of the window, where a red Vauxhall Combo arrived in the disabled parking space.

'This the boss?' asked Clay.

'Yes. What's this about?'

'Francesca Christie works here, right?'

Daniel Ball looked like he'd just had a ball of wet dung thrown in his face. 'Until yesterday lunchtime she did.'

He looked out of the window again, where a middle-aged woman was opening the car door.

'That suddenly?' asked Clay. 'Lunchtime? Not even until the end of the day?'

'Yes,' said the office manager. 'That suddenly. Shocking.'

'What's your boss' name?' asked Clay.

'Norma Maguire.'

'Was there an argument?' Stone chipped in.

'Not exactly. More of a unilateral bombshell from Francesca.'

'I spoke to Francesca's mother last night,' said Clay.

Outside, the door of the red Vauxhall Combo closed with a slam and the car beeped as Norma Maguire locked the vehicle. As she wheeled herself from the road to the shallow ramp leading on to the pavement, Clay sensed a mounting agitation in Daniel Ball's eyes.

'Norma's not happy about Francesca walking out. If you have questions to ask Norma on that matter, *please* tread carefully.'

Norma Maguire stopped on the pavement and looked into the front office with a dead-eyed stare.

'She was very fond of Francesca. She was like the daughter Norma never had. But when it came down to the end, Francesca dropped Norma like she was a diseased dog.'

Norma wheeled herself towards the front door.

'Why are you looking for Francesca?' he asked.

'We're not sure yet,' replied Clay. 'Are you OK, Mr Ball?'

'How do you mean?' he replied.

'You seem a little stressed.'

The office manager opened the door for his boss.

'I see we have visitors. This early?' asked Norma Maguire.

Clay showed her warrant card to her. 'Can we go to your office, Ms Maguire?'

'With respect, why are you here on my business premises?'

'It's about Francesca Christie,' said Clay.

'I need to stay down here and talk to your staff,' said Stone. 'Once the staff are over the front door, I need to keep it closed to customers for as long as it takes to find answers to my questions.'

'If you're going to talk to my staff,' said Norma. 'I'd like to be here also, at least for a few minutes to try and support them. We're not used to having the police around here.'

'By all means reassure your employees about us being here,' said Clay, walking towards Norma Maguire. 'But please don't keep me waiting too long. Where's your office?'

'Upstairs.'

'I'll meet you up there shortly,' said Clay, heading out of the office and towards the stairs.

63

8.59 am

Alone in Norma Maguire's office, Clay was drawn to a wall of framed photographs of the happy teams who had worked at the estate agency down the years. On her iPhone, she took three pictures of each portrait, the last one with Francesca Christie sitting at her boss' right-hand side in the office downstairs.

There was something about the group portraits that made Clay feel as if a large bird had landed on her head and was steadying itself on the curve of her skull by digging its talons into her scalp.

What is it? she asked herself. *Who is it?* She skimmed the smiling faces of the most recent portrait, saw Francesca Christie on the seated front row, her shoulder connecting with Norma Maguire's, and felt bitterly sorry for her.

Clay stood at Norma Maguire's desk and went through the pictures she had taken, noting the change in fashions and hairstyles as time passed and that, over the years, staff turnover was negligible.

She emailed the images to Cole with a message.

Barney – print off the best picture of each group and stick it on the noticeboard with the other images. Sandra O'Day. Annie Boyd. Amanda Winton. The real Richard Ezra. Springwood Cemetery Plot 66, etc. Cheers, Eve.

She heard the lift arriving and, moments later, Norma Maguire wheeled herself into the office.

'Please sit down, DCI Clay,' said Norma Maguire, wheeling herself behind her desk.

Clay smiled at Norma Maguire and, in the cold grip of the overhead fluorescent light, noticed just how much make-up the estate agent was wearing. In a glance, Clay saw that the beige foundation that covered the surface of her face looked three layers thick; her eye shadow looked like it had been smeared across her eyelids with a pair of thumbs. The only part of her make-up that was well-applied was her lipstick but, in her view, it was redder than it should have been for a Friday in the office. She was clearly a woman who felt under-dressed without a heavy slap of war paint on her face.

The landline rang on Norma Maguire's desk. She looked at Clay and said, 'Excuse me.'

'Excused.'

Clay looked around the room and her eyes were drawn to the back of a framed photograph on the desk. She glanced back at the wall lined with group portraits and concluded that every last man and woman was smiling a little too enthusiastically.

Norma placed the receiver down and faced Clay directly.

'Is Francesca in trouble?'

'Possibly.'

'In what way?' asked Norma Maguire.

'Are you happy for me to call you Norma?'

'Yes, of course.'

'I understand that Francesca left your employment yesterday, Norma?'

'It came as a huge and unpleasant shock. I thought we had a good relationship. I was obviously mistaken. She presented as a pleasant young woman but she was also our out and out best salesperson by a country mile. It's been a double blow.'

'Why did she leave Maguire Holdings?'

Norma shrugged her shoulders and looked utterly puzzled. 'I don't know. When she resigned, she was in no mood for a meaningful dialogue. It was completely out of the blue.'

'Do you know if or where she went to?'

'Doherty Estates and Properties. Just down that way on Allerton Road. Can I ask you again, DCI Clay. Why are we talking about Francesca Christie?'

'She went on a date last night and she hasn't shown up.'

'I tried to warn her!'

'How do you mean, Norma?'

'The last significant conversation we had before the one in which she told me she was leaving.'

Norma Maguire opened a drawer in her desk and placed a card file in front of Clay. She noticed how Norma's eyes were troubled, dithering as she processed a string of unpleasant ideas.

She took a deep breath and explained, 'Francesca had technical problems with the laptop I gave her for work. I sent it away to be repaired and, when it came back, the technician flagged up to me that Francesca had been using her work laptop to conduct discussions with men on an internet dating site.'

'Which dating site?' asked Clay.

Norma thought about it. 'Pebbles On The Beach.'

'What's in the file, Norma?'

'Have a look. The names of the men she's been talking to on the internet. Dates and times on which she accessed the dating site and transcripts of her conversations with men. One or two in particular.'

Norma looked over her shoulder and turned her wheelchair round. 'I took her to this window. Follow me, DCI Clay.'

Clay stepped beside Norma Maguire and looked out at the junction of Allerton Road and Penny Lane.

'I tried to show her how men she may meet online weren't like men she could meet face to face. I used the example of the street outside. I tried to tell her that she couldn't possibly read the important signs of first impression in cyberspace, and how much information was lost from real-life encounters. I warned her, there were so many predators out there and that internet dating just wasn't a safe game.'

Clay weighed it all up and said, 'Norma, I understand that you caught her using your equipment to visit internet dating sites. But can you see how that conversation might have been viewed by some as a little inappropriate, with you being her employer and Francesca being your employee?'

Without hesitation, she shook her head.

'I thought of her as a surrogate daughter, that's how I perceived our relationship. *There's no fool like an old fool* as the saying goes.'

Clay observed Norma as she looked out of the window, her eyes becoming moist and her shoulders sagging. 'Silly, silly girl. The whole thing makes me feel embarrassed. But that's not the main issue now. There might be something in the file on my desk that will help you find Francesca. I don't know the details of what's in there. I just took the technician's word for it and skimmed the information.'

Clay looked across Norma Maguire's desk and stifled herself from showing any sign of surprise when she saw the picture in the frame that faced the estate agent all day long.

'She's incredibly beautiful,' said Clay.

'Francesca Christie?'

Norma turned around from the window and Clay stayed right where she was, looking at the framed picture on the desk.

'No,' said Clay. She pointed at the picture. 'Who is she?'

'She's my mother.' Norma picked up the framed black and white photograph.

'She's dressed differently,' said Clay, observing the white pleated gown that exposed her elegant shoulders, visible because her hair was tied up in intricate curls.

'She was an actress. This one was taken when she was playing Jocasta in Sophocles' *Oedipus Rex* at the Everyman Theatre in the late 1960s. It was a publicity photo. She didn't go out in the street dressed like that, for heaven's sake. No, she was a smart, fashion-conscious woman, a woman of her times.'

'What was her name, Norma?' Clay smiled. 'I kind of recognise her.'

'Cecily Levin.' She pointed at neat cursive writing at the bottom of the picture. 'That's her autograph.'

'Did she work mainly in theatre?'

'She did a lot of TV and some films.' Norma placed the framed photograph back in its place on the desk.

Clay placed her contact card down in front of Norma.

'Is there anything else you have to add about Francesca Christie?'

'No. I hope she comes back safe and sound, and this missing business has all been a horrible mistake.'

'I need to take the file containing Francesca's internet activity away with me, Norma, and her work laptop and any other devices she may have used that you issued her with.'

'Yes, of course. See Daniel Ball. He'll sort you out. Good luck, DCI Clay.'

'Call me if you think of anything you haven't told me so far, Norma.'

64
9.25 am

In Interview Suite 2, Detective Sergeant Bill Hendricks faced Detective Sergeant Gina Riley across the table. Between them were the transcripts of online conversations between Sandra O'Day and Michael Towers, Annie Boyd and Richard Ezra, Amanda Winton and Thomas Saddler, and Francesca Christie and James Griffiths; sweet nothings to and from The Ghoul.

Riley looked at the clock on the wall and observed, 'An hour and five minutes until he's supposed to put in his call. Do you think he'll follow through?'

'He's the one in a hurry. He's got Francesca Christie. He wants Sally Haydn in captivity with her.'

'Never mind the *ifs, buts* or *maybes*. We'll find out for sure at half past ten. Focus on this. Let's go again,' said Hendricks. 'Keep those two d words spinning at the front of your mind. Diffident and desperate.'

His face filled with a cheesy grin and he winked across the table. Riley laughed, but said, 'This is serious, Bill.'

Hendricks fixed his face and said, 'Hi, Sally, thank you so much for letting me call you.'

'No problem, Geoff. Thank you for suggesting we talk rather than use the dating site. You get a much clearer idea of who a person is and what they're like from direct conversation.' Silence. 'You're quiet?'

'I'm just a little nervous around the whole internet dating scene. I'm brand new to it, you see.'

'Well, I'm a little nervous too.'

'Don't be nervous, Sally. I kept coming back to your profile over and over again and found myself hoping that we could enter into a real dialogue. I'm so glad we have.'

'Me too, Geoff.'

'Your picture on the website?'

'It's not a very good one.'

'You're mistaken. You look great.'

'You're teasing me?'

'I am what I said I am in my profile. I'm a stand-up guy. I don't tell lies and I don't say things I don't mean. Look, I'm going to put my cards on the table. I don't know if I am the right man for you. Or even if you're the right woman for me. There's only one way to find out. We need to meet up. Sooner rather than later, Sally, because I don't want some other man to snatch you out of my hands.'

'I'm not communicating with any other man. I picked you because of the things you said in your profile. I know we haven't met but I feel like I know you already. I feel like you could be the perfect man for me.'

'Then if you're comfortable to do so, please meet up with me, Sally. Tonight. At eight o'clock.'

'That would be great. Where, Geoff?' Riley looked across the table at Hendricks. 'What's up, Bill?'

'You micro-paused before accepting. Soon as he asks you out, bang, accept immediately. Otherwise, very good. Back to Sally and Geoff. Sally, do you know where the padlocked railings are by the Albert Dock?'

'That's soooo romantic.'

'We'll meet there. Is that OK?'

'Brilliant.'

'If I could just say, Sally, if it doesn't work out between us, I sincerely hope and wish you well in your search for Mr

Right. I confess, if that happens, I'm a little bit jealous of this stranger but if he gives you the happiness you deserve, if he worships the ground you walk on, I take my hat off to him.'

Hendricks leaned forward.

'Eight o'clock. The padlocked railings.'

'I'm so excited to meet you, Geoff. Bye for now.'

'OK, Gina. I'd put money on it that he's going to go down that route or a very similar road when you speak on the phone. Diffident and desperate to The Ghoul. Right between his eyes.'

65

9.26 am

Around the corner and out of sight of Maguire Holdings, Clay sat at the driver's wheel of her car with Stone at her side.

'How did you get on with the troops, Karl?'

'They seemed over-cautious when I asked them about Francesca Christie. Nobody knows anything at all about Francesca going on dating websites or going on a date…'

'That's interesting. Francesca got pulled for using her office laptop to go on the sites. Daniel Ball, he was in the dark too?'

'No. He took me to one side when I was on my way out and told me that Norma wanted to keep the information about Francesca going on the dating sites between themselves. She especially didn't want anyone to know that Francesca had been using Maguire Holdings IT equipment during office hours to look for men.'

'Any reason Norma wanted it like that?' asked Clay.

'She was trying to protect Francesca, spare her from any embarrassment. Even after yesterday when she walked without notice, breaking the terms of her contract with Norma and basically treating her boss like shit. She didn't want Francesca exposed as an internet dater. I feel sorry for the woman.'

As she spoke, Clay reconsidered the information and wondered, *but just why did you leave so suddenly, Francesca?*

'Anything else, Karl?' asked Clay.

'Yes. I asked Daniel Ball for a list of names, employees of Maguire Holdings present and past. We need to know exactly who's on Francesca's radar.'

Stone looked out into the rain.

'Spit it out, Karl,' said Clay.

'When I asked, he was guarded. I threw in a spoiler. Francesca resigned. Anybody else resigned from Maguire Holdings? He said he'd look into his records and let us know.'

'What about the girls and boys on the office floor? What did they know about Francesca?'

'Nothing. She was popular, hard-working, kept herself to herself socially after work finished. Except for the staff nights out when Norma used to take them to a restaurant and pay the bill for them all.'

'Was this a regular occurrence?'

'Monthly. She's a bit of a task mistress but she's a popular boss. I asked Daniel Ball how long he'd worked at Maguire Holdings. Twenty-two years. So what he doesn't know isn't worth a penny. But he had nothing more to add than the people who'd been there for a much shorter time.'

He sat up, covered his mouth with his hand to conceal a lengthy yawn.

'Ever heard of Cecily Levin, Karl?'

The picture on Norma's desk danced in Clay's mind.

'No. That name means nothing to me, Eve.'

Clay found the picture from Norma Maguire's desk on Google Images and showed it to Stone.

'The face rings a bell though.'

'I thought as much, Karl. You love your retro TV and movies.'

'Who is she?'

'Norma Maguire's mother. She was an actress, 1960s and 70s, theatre, TV and film. I'll ask Barney Cole to go on a fishing expedition on the internet.'

'I know her face but I don't know where from.' Stone looked closely at the screen of Clay's iPhone. 'A twentieth-century actress?' he asked himself out loud. 'How is she of interest to us, Eve?'

Clay half-shrugged. 'The way I see it, Norma Maguire's a little strange around Francesca Christie. This picture of her mother's making me itch. I just want that itch scratched and then let's move on.'

As she watched Stone's eyes processing information, the silence between them became deeper.

She pricked the silence with a pair of words. 'Cecily Levin?'

'Feels like I might have had a dim and distant crush on her when I was a kid. Mind you, which actress didn't I have a crush on?'

He laughed out loud at the memory of his adolescent self and Clay waited for him to turn and look at her in the silence.

'Karl, you're the only person who hasn't told me not to go on a date with The Ghoul. Do you have anything to say on the matter or do I just take your deafening silence at face value?'

'I've been in an incredibly dangerous situation with you, Eve. When we were tracking down Adam Miller in the bell tower of the Anglican cathedral. Remember?'

'God, yes.'

'When I was knocked unconscious and you covered my back. I could have ended up as a box of ashes on the shelf in my ma's front room but I didn't. I've got every confidence in you. And this time, it's my chance to cover your back if anything does go wrong. We need to catch this fucker before he does any damage to Francesca Christie, and you're the woman to lead from the front. End of. My silence was a vote of confidence. I'll be on the waterfront with you, and I'll be carrying a loaded gun. Get the bastard but, know this, you're not on your own.'

Clay looked at the time on her dashboard, felt the stirrings of emotion and humility and snapped herself out of it.

'Nine-thirty, time's marching on. I need to get back to Trinity Road. Gina's got a phone call coming and I need to sit in on it.'

66
9.30 am

Wren paced in his father's cupboard-sized office, three steps to the window, three steps to the door, wishing he could summon up that final flake of rage and transform himself into Captain Cyclone.

'Where are you? Where are you? Where are you?'

He stopped at the window, watched as a lorry backed in to the arrivals depot, heard the lowing of a truckload of cattle as the doomed cows edged closer to the clamps, saws and knives that awaited them, wondering no doubt, he thought, where their fields had gone to and why the barn that had housed them in the dark country night since they were calves had suddenly disappeared.

'Where are you? Moo, moo, moo!'

The door opened and Wren froze as his father squeezed into the cramped space.

'Where is he?' nagged Wren.

'Calm down, Wren. Deep breathing, remember.'

Wren made a show of breathing deeply but it did nothing to calm the red-hot ball in his stomach and the jagged spike of ice that pierced his heart.

His father threw the only chair in the room in front of Wren and ordered, 'Sit down!'

'Where is he? Where's Edgar?'

'Sit down!'

Wren sat down, drew the hands that knew how to make mischief under his thighs and fixed his entire attention on a dark spot on the opposite wall, where a tiny patch of old paint had long since flaked away from the plaster.

His father stooped to get into his eyeline.

'Edgar's not coming in today, Wren. That's why he's not here. He's got diarrhoea and vomiting. He couldn't possibly come in to work in that condition. Think of the hygiene implications.'

'Oh, noooooo...'

The rumble of machinery on the floor below the administration offices moaned through the tiny room.

'When's he coming back?' asked Wren.

'When his condition gets right. When he no longer has diarrhoea and vomiting, he has to stay away from work for at least another two whole days, otherwise he'd be a health and safety hazard. Do you understand me?'

Wren absorbed the information, felt the heat and ice of anxiety collide into a ball of sorrow.

'He's going to be away for ages, isn't he, Dad?'

'Days, days…'

'Then I want to go home.'

'I think that's wise, Wren. Later. I can't just drop everything now and take you home. I have to reorganise the skinning platform around Edgar's absence. It'll most likely be during my lunch break.'

'I don't like change.'

'I know you don't, son.'

'Can I go and see him?'

'He's not well. He needs to recover in peace and quiet.'

'Peace and quiet! Peace and quiet! How do you *know* he's sick?'

'He made a telephone call in to the main office. We *know* he's sick. He's not a malingerer.'

Wren jumped up, flailed his arms.

'Take me home. This place is nowhere without Edgar.'

'Later. I'll take you home as soon as I can. But until then you'll have to wait here in my office. Not everyone in the abattoir is as nice as Edgar McKee. You understand?'

'I understand, Dad. I'll be a good boy.'

'And, Wren. One last thing. Thank you for holding it a little bit together and not having a complete meltdown out there in front of my men.'

'No, Dad. Nobody heard me screaming. They were wearing ear defenders and the machinery was working well.'

67

9.45 am

Cole recalled asking Clay, *why?* and her answer, *maybe it's just the stuff that killed the cat.* Normally open and as available as it was humanly possible to be, Clay had issued a statement to him by email. Planning was going ahead for the liaison with the perpetrator, and was awaiting a rubber stamp from the chief constable and his team. Armed officers were on call and, like every other police officer in the operation, they were all undercover. She was off limits for the whole of Friday morning but more about that would be revealed before the day was done.

Cole sent an image of Cecily Levin in classical Greek mode to the printer.

He pulled up Clay's email address and summoned up his thoughts about the actress, who he'd read about on her Wikipedia page and some retro fan sites. He wondered if Eve had roped him in to give her a mental pressure drop.

Dear Eve,

Cecily Levin was a London-born actress whose career was at its peak throughout the 1960s and early 1970s. She toured extensively as a repertory actress performing in plays by numerous playwrights including Oscar Wilde, Noel Coward and William Shakespeare, to name but three. She joined the company of the Liverpool Everyman Theatre in the early 1970s alongside actors such as Jonathan Pryce and Julie Walters and lay down her roots here. She started breaking into TV with increasingly bigger roles in *Z Cars, Coronation Street, Till Death Us Do Part, Dixon of Dock Green* and the BBC's *Play For Today* series. With TV exposure came parts in British films, mainly for Hammer, where she had solid parts in *Twins of Evil, The Vampire Lovers, Lust For A Vampire* and *Dracula AD 1972.*

She gave up her acting career when she married Terry Maguire, a local business mogul whose wealth came from building, tarmac, palettes, a fleet of taxis and several nightclubs across the north-west of England.

When she stopped acting she went completely off the radar and was effectively never heard of again.

You can see her acting on YouTube. All the Hammer Films are on there and some of the TV shows she was in.

Best wishes and take care,

Barney.

He picked up the image of Cecily Levin from the printer and pinned it on the board near the image of Richard Ezra gazing lovingly into the space where his wife, Sarah, had been airbrushed out of existence, the picture The Ghoul had sent to Annie Boyd and other women.

Cole walked down the noticeboard, looked at the images of Sandra O'Day, Annie Boyd and Amanda Winton dead in the watery places from which their bodies were recovered. He compared their images in death to their online profile photographs and was saddened enough to want to turn his back on the women.

But he didn't do that. Instead, Cole looked at the images as a whole and, in the part of his brain where the dots formed that needed joining, he felt the pressure of their emerging existence.

The door of the incident room opened and his chain of thought was interrupted. A young constable who he'd never seen before entered and approached him, carrying an A4 envelope.

'Detective Constable Cole?'

'Yes. And you are?'

The constable handed the envelope to Cole. 'Michael Bennett. Sergeant Harris asked me to come and give this to you. It was handed in at reception, just now.'

'Thanks, Michael.'

Cole sat back and slid the contents from the envelope, a stylish black leather book. He turned it over and saw the words Address Book embossed in gold. The word Fiorenze was pressed into the leather. He opened the book and a piece of Doherty Estates and Properties headed notepaper fell on to his desk.

DS Cole,

Please find enclosed Richard Ezra's address book. I would be grateful for its safe return when you have finished using it in your investigation.

Yours sincerely

Brian Doherty

Cole opened Richard Ezra's address book at the A page.

68

10.29 am

Outside Interview Suite 2, Clay heard Sergeant Harris, standing guard on the door.

'It's a no-go area for the foreseeable. If there's anyone else who didn't get the message, tell them fucking straight and direct them back to me if they've got a problem with the concept.'

The stern outburst broke the tense and lengthening silence between herself, Hendricks and Riley.

'Gina, don't pick up the phone when it first rings out. Count it in, three or four rings.'

Clay looked at Hendricks' laptop screen, saw the map of Garston where his mobile was located in Trinity Road on Geolocator, and the box inviting him to type in the mobile number that he wanted to locate.

She looked at the clock on the wall, at her iPhone in Riley's hand, and made eye contact with Hendricks.

'As soon as we get a location for his phone on Geolocator, I'll message Cole and get him to send in the troops. It's all set up to roll on red alert.'

The minute hand touched the curve of the six's body and slowly leaked further into the digit, the hum of clockwork in the stillness and quiet of the room. Clay's index finger hovered over the record button on the audio box on the table.

The display panel of Clay's iPhone lit up and within a heartbeat the ringtone of an old-fashioned landline rang through the air. She pressed speakerphone and Clay pressed record.

'He's calling from a mobile,' said Riley. '07700 913133.'

The second ring.

Hendricks typed the digits into Geolocator.

On the third ring, Riley connected.

'Hello?' said Riley. 'Is that you, Geoff?'

'It is.' He sounded happy and light-hearted to the point of oblivion. 'And that is you, isn't it, Sally?'

There was a rumble of traffic in the background and it sounded like the call was being made from a street.

A map of Grassendale Park came up on Hendricks' laptop screen, a small icon, a phone close to the junction of Aigburth Road and Grassendale Road.

Clay sent a message to Cole.

Call switchboard to make a general red alert. All officers to flood Aigburth area near Grassendale Park. Focus on Aigburth Road and Grassendale Road. The Ghoul is outdoors and on the street. Full speed. No sirens. Trace this number. 07700 913133.

'Yes, it's me,' said Riley. 'I was worried you wouldn't call, Geoff.'

'Don't be worried. Of course I was going to call you. You have a lovely voice by the way, Sally, lyrical, lilting. Are you a singer by any chance?'

'I'm not a singer, Geoff. I could never stand up on a stage and sing in front of people.' Clay smiled at the display of diffidence. 'You're not from Liverpool, are you, Geoff?'

'I am from Liverpool.'

'You have an accent.'

'Oh yes, I know what you mean,' he laughed. 'I spent a lot of time growing up in North Wales. Some of that accent rubbed off on me, I guess.'

'Whereabouts in North Wales?'

'Flintshire.'

'That's a nice part of the world, Geoff. I've been there. I'd love to go again.'

'Maybe we could go together? I could show you all the beauty spots. You did say in your profile that you liked long romantic walks in the countryside.'

In the background, they heard a bus speeding past him.

'Did you know, Geoff, if you look across the river near where I live on a clear day, you can see the outline of Moel Fammau?'

'Where do you live?'

'Off Riverside Drive, just by Otterspool Promenade. Do you know it?'

'I haven't been there for a long time, but yes, I know the prom.'

'Where do you live, Geoff?'

'Gateacre. I've got a cottage.'

'A cottage? Sounds cosy.'

'It's lovely. You mentioned in your profile you love real coal fires.'

'I love roaring log fires. Drinking wine and making pictures in the glowing coals.'

'Maybe when we've been walking in the countryside we could come home and light the fire, settle in front of it with a nice bottle of red wine.'

'You've got a real coal fire, Geoff?'

'Yes, I have. Just no one to share it with.'

'Well, maybe that's all about to change,' said Riley, her face set and her eyes burrowing into the phone on the table. 'Geoff, I know your profile by heart but I was wondering...'

'Yes?'

'... if you could tell me something about yourself that isn't in your profile?'

'Oohhh, well…' He fell into a silence that was difficult to read. 'I kind of get the feeling you want me to make a confession of some sort.'

'No, I just want to know more about you. I feel like I know you so well already, but I'm really keen to get to know you just that little bit better again.'

'I do have a confession of sorts to make.' His tone shifted down a gear.

'Go on?' Riley pushed.

'On my profile I said I was single. It seemed like the simplest way to convey my situation. I'm new to internet dating and a little nervous around the whole process. Maybe I should have given this thing between us a little more time before diving in at the deep end. I mean, we only connected yesterday.'

'What are you telling me, Geoff? Are you trying to tell me you have a girlfriend? I mean, I really don't want to get hurt…'

'The last thing I'd do is hurt another human being because I've been through so much. I don't want to get hurt again. The truth is I am and I'm not single. My wife died at the end of last year. I've been on my own since then. But I'm terribly, terribly lonely. I know I can trust you to tell you that.'

'Thank you for trusting me with that. Thank you for telling me that you're a widower. I'm so sorry to hear that.'

'Please don't think I'm trying to make emotional capital out of my misfortune.'

'I don't think that. I think you're being upfront and honest about what's happened to you. It takes guts to be honest, and I respect you for that.'

'You do?' He appeared to sound surprised. Clay couldn't decide if it was part of the act or if it was the sound of advancing cars speeding at seventy to eighty miles per hour down Aigburth Road towards him from either direction.

'Do you have children, Geoff?'

'No. We nearly did. Lucy was six months pregnant when she died.'

There was a pause that turned into a silence that Riley span out to give the officers descending on Grassendale the advantage of time.

'Are you still there, Sally?'

'I'm so... so... sorry. It sounds busy where you are. Where are you?'

'I'm on Lister Drive near Old Swan. The traffic is busy. Listen, Sally, are you busy tonight?'

'No.'

'I know we hardly know each other but...'

'But?'

'Does this sound crazy? I feel like we've made a connection already, a real connection. From your profile and the messages we've exchanged. I – I've just got this gut feeling, especially now I've heard your voice. I mean, we've talked on and off all night over the internet and it's like you've already lifted a weight from me. I think we should meet up soon, get talking to each other face to face.'

'Yes! I'm ready. I just hope I don't disappoint you, Geoff.'

'You won't. And I hope I don't disappoint you. Do you like the Albert Dock, Sally?'

'It's my favourite part of the city to go out in.'

'Me too.' He laughed and Riley joined in with a pair of stones for eyes.

As the laughter faded, Riley said, 'Geoff? Can I ask you a question?'

'You can ask me anything, Sally.'

'Then if you don't mind me asking, just how did Lucy die?'

'How about I tell you when I see you, when we can see and hear each other directly?'

Behind him, Clay heard the sound of speeding cars slowing down and his footsteps picking up speed as he walked away from the main road. It sounded like he was disappearing around the corner and away from the dual carriageway.

'Sally, something's just cropped up. How about we say, eight o'clock tonight at the padlocked railings. You know it?'

'I know it. It sounds perfect, Geoff.'

'It's all on me, Sally. You can pick anywhere that you like to eat. No expense spared.'

More cars approached, splitting off from the main road and down the streets leading off from it.

'You're worth it. You deserve kindness. You deserve a man in your life who'll worship the ground you walk on and celebrate the air that you breathe. See you at eight, Sally. Oh, one last thing. Are you driving there?'

'Yes.'

'Where are you parking?'

Riley looked at Clay. *In the place where there'll be six hidden marksmen.*

'Usually when I go to the Albert Dock, I leave my car in the Marina's car park and walk along the promenade.'

'That's a good place to park. But a friend of mine turned up one minute after his pay and display ran out, and they clamped him and hit him with a hefty fine. I don't want us to be watching the clock when we should be watching each other. What do you think, Sally?'

'I'd better not leave it in the Marina's car park.'

'You could always park it round the corner near the apartments. It'd be pretty safe there.'

'Thanks for that tip, Geoff. I'll do that.'

'Don't want a great night out being ruined by a car park fiasco. I'll see you at eight, Sally.'

Before Riley could reply, the dead tone filled the interview suite.

'Do you believe him?' asked Hendricks as Clay pressed stop.

'He lied about his location,' said Clay. 'I think he's putting the accent on. Why would he tell us anything about the truth of his background? Why would he tell the truth about anything? All we are in his mind is meat to be preyed on.'

69

10.43 am

The Ghoul walked slowly down Dugdale Close, away from Aigburth Road and on to Montfort Drive.

Why? Why all these police cars here, so suddenly? The mind danced as it leaped over itself at what it saw and heard.

At the end of Montfort Drive, as it ran into Grassendale Road, a marked police car cruised past and out of sight. It provoked a feeling of overwhelming paranoia that made the simple act of breathing like hard labour.

The policeman in the driver's seat looked straight ahead; relief came in floods like sudden rushes of blood from the heart.

The recent memory of Sally's voice came as a consolation. She sounded as thick as she was insipid, a lifelong loser who thought she had something to offer in life when all she really had to offer was her corpse.

Planning out the night ahead was the best way to cut through the stress that constantly chewed at the gut and pressed down on the skull like an invisible clamp.

Watch Sally from a distance, savour her mounting agitation as she realised she was being stood up by Geoff, and follow her sagging shoulders to the place where she had parked.

As she arrived at her car, perform a quick but thorough three hundred and sixty degree check to make sure there was no one and nothing around to witness the first words hitting the back of her neck. 'Excuse me!'

Dread mounted as another car came closer on Grassendale Road.

The car slid past. It wasn't a marked police car. But that didn't stop it being an unmarked vehicle. It carried on. *Was it from the neighbourhood? Could've been; no way of knowing for sure.*

As soon as possible, Sally would receive a picture of Richard Ezra to her iPhone that would surely get her hopes up so high that when she fell she would land with a mighty crash.

Carry her down the wooden steps like a bag of potatoes but enjoying the warmth and vulnerability of her body against the power of The Ghoul.

Picturing the look on Francesca Christie's face when she saw she had a roommate, stress gave way to joy, joy gave way to ecstasy.

'Look what I've got, Francesca. Look at me, Francesca. Look at me with the look of love, love, love. Lurrraaammeeeeee!'

70

10.55 am

'Eve, I was just about to call you,' said DC Cole as she entered the incident room. 'How did the call to Geoff go?'

'He's a slimeball who knows how to press all the right buttons. He's also a slimeball who doesn't know it yet but he's bitten off far more than he can ever chew.'

Cole held up a black leather book.

'What's this, Barney?'

'Richard Ezra's address book, as supplied by Brian Doherty, his last employer before he died.'

Clay sat next to Cole.

'Anything?'

'It's mainly business contacts, contractors, solicitors, surveyors, advertising agencies, printers, other estate agents and the like. How did your meeting with Norma Maguire go just now?'

'Norma Maguire?' Switches tripped in Clay's brain. 'She's of interest to me because she employed Francesca Christie. And on the day Francesca Christie suddenly walks out of her employment, she goes missing. Norma tried to play the mother hen over Francesca's internet dating, and had her fingers in her employee's online activity on Pebbles On The Beach. She may come up with something that we can use. Let's put it this way, I'll be in touch with Norma very soon, no doubt whatsoever.'

'OK,' said Cole, turning the pages of Richard Ezra's address book to the M page and handing it to Clay. 'Richard listed the business address of Maguire Holdings but he also listed Norma Maguire's private residence at 73 West Road.'

'Is that the only double listing relating to one individual?' asked Clay.

'No. If you go to the D page you'll find Brian Doherty's business address on the commercial end of Allerton Road, a couple of blocks away from Maguire Holdings, and his home address in The Serpentine. It wasn't unusual for Richard to have double takes of business and private contacts. But I'm flagging up Maguire and Doherty because on the day Francesca Christie went missing, she walked out on Maguire and went in to work for Doherty. Could be something, could be nothing.'

'Keep that plate spinning, Barney. What's wrong?'

Clay saw an undertone of sorrow play out on Cole's face.

'I saw her yesterday morning, Eve. Francesca Christie.'

'Yeah?'

'When I went to talk to Brian Doherty. She was in his office while I waited outside. He'd just given her the job. She looked like she'd just had a massive burden lifted from her. She was like really grateful to him. I didn't know who she was at the time or where she worked but she couldn't have been more thankful to him. I can only conclude one thing. She must have been as miserable as sin working at Maguire Holdings.'

Clay looked at Norma Maguire's home address, at Richard Ezra's elegant handwriting, and felt the sadness of his presumed suicide and his wife's violent death.

'Up close and personal, Francesca Christie's a really lovely-looking young woman. I could tell she was a really decent sort,' said Cole. 'I'd go as far as to say, she's gorgeous. I don't know why on earth she needed to use internet dating sites.'

'Barney, the way we see ourselves isn't always the way others view us. Sometimes, some people love themselves for no good reason. Sometimes, some people undervalue who and what they are. I bet when we sift through all this, we'll find Francesca was in the latter category. She must've had her own good reasons for internet dating.'

Clay handed Richard Ezra's address book back to Cole.

'I've photocopied it. I'll get the book back to Brian Doherty. He comes over like a pompous shit but he's really hurting over Richard Ezra. Guess what, Eve?'

'What?'

He held up the address book and pointed to Norma Maguire's home address.

'She lives in the Grassendale Park grid.'

71

11.05 am

Francesca Christie's mother hurried towards the front door, the ringing of the doorbell drawing her to it like a siren song.

'Francesca! Is that you, Francesca?'

She reached the front door but there was no reply from behind it.

When she opened the door, her first impression was that there was no one there. She looked down and saw Norma Maguire looking up at her from her wheelchair. On her lap was a large bunch of roses.

'Can I come in, please?' asked Norma.

Margaret Christie opened the door wider.

'If you could just help me over the step, please.'

When Norma wheeled herself inside the house, Margaret slammed the door shut out of sheer disappointment.

'Follow me. We'll go into the kitchen at the back, Norma.'

Norma wheeled herself after Francesca's mother. From the top of the stairs, her sister called, 'Who is it?'

'Norma Maguire, Francesca's boss.'

In the kitchen, Norma handed the roses to Francesca's mother and said, 'It's just to let you know that I'm thinking of you at this extremely difficult time. I know there's not much I can do but if you think of anything, please don't hesitate to ask.'

Francesca's mother stood leaning back against the sink where she'd placed the roses.

'Thank you for the flowers.'

'Has there been any news?'

'Her car was found near Aigburth Vale. The police are certain she's been taken by the men who've been picking off women from internet dating sites.'

'Men?'

'It's not a lone individual, Norma. She was last seen around half-eight last night on CCTV and the police called at just after half-four this morning. In between times, they unlocked her laptop and have drawn certain undeniable conclusions.'

Francesca's aunt walked into the kitchen, holding a rag doll.

'You found Kizzy,' said Francesca's mother, the ghost of a smile floating beneath the gridlock of terror and anxiety on her face.

'In the drawer under Francesca's bed,' she replied, handing the doll to her sister.

Margaret lifted the doll's skirt to reveal a frayed manufacturer's label. 'Look!' she said, showing Francesca's childlike handwriting on the label. 'She wrote her name so that if Kizzy was lost, whoever found her would know who to send her back to.'

Francesca's mother looked at Norma. 'It was Francesca's favourite doll all through her childhood. She wouldn't go to sleep without her.' She clutched the doll to herself tightly. 'Was there anything going on in work that you noticed, Norma? Anything odd?'

'I found out she was going on internet dating sites. I kept this information strictly between me and my office manager, but I did speak with Francesca on the quiet and warned her of the dangers of...'

'Why didn't you inform me?'

'She's a grown woman. I couldn't pick up the phone and tell you. There are data protection issues here. But what I did do was say exactly what you would have said, Margaret. The police came to see me this morning just before the office opened for business. I told them everything I know.'

'Is there anything else, Norma? Anything about Francesca?'

'Francesca has been my best performing agent, month in and month out, since she's been with me. She's good at her job and I thought she was happy in her work. But she decided to leave me rather suddenly, to go and work at Doherty Properties and Estates. I've no idea why she left...'

'When did this happen?' Francesca's mother sounded mystified.

'Yesterday, at around lunchtime.'

The sisters looked at each other.

'She didn't say anything to you?' Norma looked directly at Francesca's mother, who paced in the confined space of the kitchen and placed the rag doll down on the table.

'No.'

'Do you have any idea why she left my firm?'

'I have no idea. She didn't say a word to me,' said Francesca's mother to her sister as she stuck the plug in the sink, filled it with water, and placed the roses in it. 'Secrets on secrets on secrets. I just don't get it. Francesca, what were you thinking of?'

A brand-new wave of anguish and agony swept over Francesca's mother.

She said, 'Excuse me.' And she walked quickly out of the room, fresh tears flooding her face.

'You'll have to let yourself out, Norma,' said Francesca's aunt, following her sister.

'I'm so, so sorry,' said Norma. 'Truly I am.'

She looked at Kizzy as the women ran up the stairs.

'Don't worry about me,' said Norma, quietly. 'I can manage the step going down.'

72

11.59 am

Eve Clay closed the door of Thomas' surgery and he stood up to pass her a chair.

'This is a surprise,' said Thomas. The smile on his face faded. 'Are you OK, Eve?'

'Thomas.' She sat facing him, held out her hands and folded them tightly around his.

'What are you going to tell me, Eve?'

'Hear me out. Please...'

'Fire away.'

'The Ghoul has bitten on the bait we threw out over the internet dating site Pebbles On The Beach. He actually responded directly to Gina Riley, and has had a direct phone conversation with her this morning.'

She paused to frame the words she had come to say directly to him.

'It's definitely him?' asked Thomas, darkness forming in his eyes.

'Most definitely. He's arranged to meet Gina Riley at eight o'clock tonight around the Albert Dock. She's posing as Sally, a twenty-something lonely heart.'

'Gina's not going though, is she?'

She felt him pulling his hands away and tightened her grip on them.

'Please, Thomas. I'm the SIO on this case. I've decided to go in her place.'

'Oh, for fuck's sake, Eve...'

'Please, Thomas.'

She saw mounting panic in his face, felt the pain that her unwelcome news was causing him, and black guilt overwhelmed her.

'Listen, Thomas, listen to me.'

'Let go of my hands.'

She loosened her grip and watched as he folded his arms across his chest, the tell-tale body language she'd come to read in every major argument down the years.

'Go on, Eve, I'm listening.'

'There was no other way to tell you other than straight. But here's the thing. This is a massive sting involving over fifty plain-clothes officers, most of them armed. I'll be carrying a Glock handgun and I'm not frightened to use it. There's no evidence so far to suggest that he uses firearms. And even if he does, he's heavily outgunned. If he turns up there's no way out for him.'

Thomas was unusually still and quiet, as if he was digging down deep inside himself.

'Please say something, Thomas.'

'Why you, Eve?'

'Because the whole thing was my idea. I couldn't put this plan on the table and allow someone else to go in for the fight.'

The tension and anger she saw in him dissolved and gave way to something fragile and afraid.

'You told me and Philip you wouldn't take any unnecessary risks. This strikes me as being just that. A massive unnecessary risk.'

'It's a risk, certainly. I won't lie.'

Thomas stood up and walked to the window and looked out. She watched his back, saw the slowly forming stoop of his shoulders, the thin strands of grey that seeped into the darkness of his hair.

'We've got a victim in captivity, Francesca Christie. If she's lucky she's got days to live. We've manufactured a chance to save her. Tonight is probably the only chance we'll get to catch him and rescue her.'

He turned from the window and she recognised the look on his face. He was furious but trying to mask it by staring blankly into space.

'How have you organised the sting, Eve?'

'I'm meeting him at the padlocked railing at the Albert Dock at eight o'clock. Chances are, he'll stand me up and off I'll wander back to my car further on past the Coburg Marina. I'm sure this is where he's hit his victims in the past, away from the public and CCTV cameras. We're going to have six concealed marksmen in and around the place where I'm going to park my car.

'When I'm not in that place, I've got a constant string of plain-clothes officers around me. As long as I'm out I'm never going to be more than three metres away from an armed colleague. I'm going wired for sound and wearing a discreet body cam.'

She saw his thoughts playing out across his face and said nothing.

'You told me last night that you know the grid of streets where he's operating from. Why not make a series of raids?'

'Barney Cole's Grassendale Park grid was a great piece of deduction but it's flawed. There are ways in and out that mean the place we're looking for mightn't be in that rectangle. It's not a foregone conclusion that Barney's got it one hundred per cent right. Your idea's a valid one but it's a risk we can't afford to take. Say The Ghoul is operating inside the grid – if he gets we're closing in on him, he'll panic and run away and we'll lose him. The other option is he stays put and tries to balls it out; either way, if we make a mistake, we'll be bringing Francesca Christie out in a body bag.'

'I see.'

But quite the opposite seemed true to her.

'Thomas?'

There was a knock on the door.

'Go away, I'm busy.' Thomas spoke with a note in his voice that the world wouldn't recognise but that she knew clearly, and it spoke of the depth of his anxiety and fear. The guilt inside her intensified.

'Thomas, please, come and sit with me.'

He was still for what felt like a long time but he moved towards her, slowly, and sat down.

'You're killing me, Eve.'

'I didn't come here expecting you to dance for joy. It's not ideal, I grant you that. But I did come here hoping to level with you and give you something to hang on to. When I went down in the Williamson Tunnels with three psychotic members of the Red Cloud, that was infinitely more dangerous than tonight's exercise. When I was in the Bell Tower of the Anglican, Karl Stone nearly lost his life. Think about it, Thomas. I could list you example after example of me taking unnecessary risks in the past. I've got great cover and backup tonight. The dress rehearsal is getting organised right now.'

Thomas looked at her and she saw him reliving their time together in a passage of seconds, the faltering but joy-inspired early days through the cementation of years – acceptance, compromise, parenthood – to the place they'd arrived at in the present, a realistic and hard-won happiness.

'I knew what I was getting into when we first got together. You made it clear to me about the risks you had to take and the reality of people you hunt down for a living. I accepted it then. But I'm conflicted. There was just the two of us. We've got a son now. There are no guarantees in life. You cannot guarantee that tonight you'll be safe.'

'This isn't a competition between you and me, Thomas.' She looked at the door to his surgery. 'But do you know what's coming next through that door?'

'You don't have to remind me, Eve. The paranoid schizophrenic who stopped taking his medication and walked in here carrying a knife and wondering why his GP was Satan.'

She held his hands, shivered inside at the memory of the attempted attack on her husband in the space where they were sitting.

'None of us know the moment when the hammer's going to fall,' said Eve.

'So this could be the last time we speak face to face?'

'It won't be.'

'I see you've made your mind up, Eve.'

'It was made up for me. By the situation. By the brutality at work here. By the fact that the only person I can totally trust in this is me.'

He looked at her intently and his gaze penetrated deep inside her.

'I've loved you since the moment we met and I always will love you, Eve. Take that one away with you and I hope it helps you get through this. But I'm telling you now, it's very, very hard at times being married to you. You're not the only police officer who could have done this. But I agree with you. You're the best choice for the job, even if you say so yourself.'

'I appreciate your understanding. I'm grateful for your patience and I don't take your support for granted.'

'You don't need a scowling husband, especially not at a time like this. I'll tell Philip you're busy and you'll see him in the morning.'

They stood up and he wrapped his arms around her.

'I know I've upset you, Thomas, and I'm really sorry. I love you, and I love Philip.' She took comfort in his embrace. 'Say something, Thomas.'

'You're carrying a Glock?'

'Yes.'

'Don't hesitate to blow his brains out if you have to.'

'Don't you worry, Thomas. If it's me or him, I won't hesitate for one second to do just that.'

73
12.25 pm

Detective Sergeant Barney Cole looked at two lists, one long and one much shorter, that related directly to his Grassendale Park grid.

The long list supplied by the librarian, Margie Rivers, had yielded five names with historic criminal convictions from the National Police Computer from the two hundred and five males listed on the city's electoral register.

There were two convictions for petty fraud, one for drink driving, one for drunk and disorderly and a fifth for shoplifting. All convictions were over twenty years old and all the petty criminals had pleaded guilty to the charges against them.

Cole sent a round robin email to Clay and the team outlining the disappointing trawl from the Grassendale Park grid with a note.

Hardly the CV of The Ghoul.

As he sent the email, Cole felt a sudden heavy weight on his head and shoulders and an even heavier burden inside himself.

What if? he asked himself in the cold light of a rain-sodden day. *What if my ego and inbuilt need to look smarter than smart has led me to concoct the Grassendale Park grid? What if I've allowed myself to wander up a flawed geographical dead end, and taken others with me?*

Cole stared into space and felt sick at the prospect of the point in time when he would have to hold up his hands and deliver a damning self-verdict: Twenty-four-carat idiot.

He looked at the shorter list of names from the city's electoral office, twelve males in the Grassendale Park area who had opted to leave their names unpublished on the publicly available register of voters. There wasn't a criminal blemish against any of the dozen men and Cole's already dark mood deteriorated further.

'Have you looked at the names of the women on the registers?' he whispered to himself. 'What's the point?' he replied silently, but he started with Grassendale Road and drew his right index finger down the list, hoping to catch a glimmer of light from the females on the list.

'Barney, how's it going?' asked Stone at his back.

'Badly. There's not a single sign of anyone with the potential to become The Ghoul.'

'If it's any consolation, look at what I've pulled from the CCTV footage of people driving out of Grassendale Park on to Aigburth Road.'

Stone placed a small pack of printed-off images from the CCTV trawl in front of Cole and he flicked through it.

An old man driving with an old woman at his side in a VW Passat. An old woman driving on her own in a Ford Orion. A woman in her thirties with a baby strapped in on the back seat of her Peugeot 108. A man and a woman with two teenage children in the back of their grey Range Rover. A middle-aged woman alone in her red Vauxhall Combo.

'It's just more and more of the same.'

Cole placed the rest of the unviewed images down on the desk.

'There aren't any hits for two men or one man on his own making a getaway from Grassendale Park,' said Stone. 'The men who did show up on camera are either with elderly people, kids or their wives or girlfriends. I couldn't see anyone who looks like they have the opportunity or desire to keep young women hostage and then strangle and skin them. I'll put them on the noticeboard and see if anyone has any different ideas to mine.'

Cole looked at his map of Grassendale Park and pointed to a turning off Grassendale Road, the way out of the grid. 'Shit idea or what?'

'I think you've got a strong idea, Barney. It's a relatively small area but there are a lot of houses in there, and a lot of places to hide.'

Stone stood next to Cole, watching the images of the people in vehicles leaving Grassendale Park mount up as he pinned them on the noticeboard. As he put up the picture of the single woman in the red Vauxhall Combo WAV, Stone asked, 'Do you know this woman at all, Barney?'

'No. Who is she?'

'Her name's Norma Maguire.' Stone pointed to the portraits of the staff from Maguire Holdings. 'Did you put those pictures up?'

'Eve sent them to me, told me to cherry-pick the best and get them on the board.'

'Norma Maguire's staff, past and present.'

Stone went back to looking at the group portraits of Norma Maguire's employees, focused on Francesca Christie and said, 'Little did she know the truth around the corner when that picture was taken.'

He looked at the previous picture to the left. There was no sign of Francesca Christie. *Before your time*, thought Stone. He looked at the next picture down the chronological line and examined each face, lingering on each employee and wondering, *who are you?*

He looked at the centre of the display board and took down one picture in particular, which he carried back to the third group portrait.

'Have you noticed the way Norma Maguire conceals her face on the Maguire Holdings group portraits?' asked Stone. 'Tinted glasses, scarves that are knotted so high they obscure the bottom half of her face. Bill Hendricks met her on the door to door of the Grassendale Park grid. He said she's super shy. Did you know she's in a wheelchair?'

Cole looked at Stone and said, 'Yes, I've heard that.'

Stone looked at the photograph in his hand and at the third group portrait, picking out a man standing next to Norma Maguire and smiling broadly into the eye of the camera.

'Are you all right, Karl?'

'Come here, Barney. Double-check this for me, please.'

Stone showed the photograph he had taken down from the board and pointed at the man in the third group portrait.

'Oh, God, yes, yes it is. Hair's shorter in the group portrait, but the smile's undeniably his.'

Stone dialled Clay on speed dial.

'Karl, what's happening?' asked Clay.

'Look at your photo gallery on your iPhone, Eve. The group portrait, Maguire Holdings, two back from the latest featuring Francesca Christie. Look at the man standing next to Norma Maguire. He's not in the next two portraits after that one. Richard Ezra, the real one, the one the killer's claiming is him. Ezra worked for Norma Maguire before he worked at Doherty Estates and Properties. Just like Francesca Christie.'

'Get your coat on,' said Clay. 'Get yourself over to Maguire Holdings and grab the office manager, Daniel Ball. Richard

Ezra leaves and his identity gets stolen by The Ghoul. Francesca Christie leaves and she gets abducted by the bastard. We need a list of names of former employees. I'm going to Doherty Estates and Properties. I need to speak to Mr Doherty.'

74

12.30 am

As Neil Wren drove past Broadgreen Hospital and over the flyover on Queens Drive, his son wound the window down in the passenger door.

'Wind the window up, Wren, or the rain'll soak you to the skin!'

Wren wound the window up and asked, 'When's Edgar coming back to the abattoir?'

'I've told you before. I've told you dozens of times. When his symptoms have cleared up, he's got to wait for at least forty-eight hours before he can come back to work.'

'Well, when will his symptoms clear up?'

'I... don't... know...'

'It's Friday, half past twelve. If his symptoms have cleared up now...'

'There's no point in speculating, Wren.'

'Saturday lunchtime, Sunday lunchtime, he could be back in on Monday morning. Yay! Dad, Dad, Dad. Why don't you give him a ring and ask him if his symptoms have cleared up?'

'I've explained to you over and over, I'm Edgar's line manager. As his line manager, I'm not allowed to contact him because he's off sick. If I contacted him, it would be rightly read as harassment. So, no, Wren, and please don't ask again. I am not going to phone Edgar, end of.'

'How long's he worked at the abattoir?'

'Years and years. He was there before me.'

'Did he ever meet Mum?'

'No.'

'Did you ever talk to him about Mum?'

'After she died. Yes, when everyone else in work was pretending that nothing had happened half an hour after I got back there. He's a very good listener. He gave me some great advice. Can we stop talking about Edgar now!'

'What great advice did Edgar give you, Dad?'

'Cling on to your memories of your wife tightly, but cling on to your son with all your heart and soul.'

Keeping perfect time with the windscreen wipers, Wren said, 'Whoosh, whoosh, whoosh, whoosh.'

'Listen, Wren! OK, now I've got to go back to work, which means I'm going to have to trust you on your own in the house. What are your plans for this afternoon?'

'TV, PlayStation, drawing.'

'Don't go out on your own. The weather's stinking, stay home, stay safe, stay dry. Promise me you'll stay at home.'

'I promise you I'll stay at home.'

Neil pulled up at the lights and looked at the unique artwork on his son's Captain Cyclone lunch box and felt the same sucker punch each and every time. Such a talent, such a child, such a shame.

'You promised me once in the past, and you went out. I'm going to come home early today and I'm afraid, if you're not at home, as you've just promised me, then you'll have to stop working at the abattoir and go back to the day centre. It's as simple and as harsh as that, Wren. There'll be no more Edgar, ever. Ever... ever!'

'Oh no, I don't want to go back to the day centre. I want to work in the abattoir with Edgar McKee, my mate. Has Edgar ever had diarrhoea before?'

'No.'

Neil Wren pulled up at a red light at the Childwall Fiveways.

'I'm not answering any more questions about Edgar. Is that clear?'

'OK.'

'Think on, Wren. I've spoken to your Auntie Louise and she's going to pop in to see you at some point. Understand?'

'I understand.'

Neil Wren followed the traffic past the green light.

'Edgar? Does he have other mates or does he only have one mate? Me.'

75

1.15 pm

Detective Chief Inspector Eve Clay faced Brian Doherty across his desk and noticed that he looked like he was in physical pain.

'Are you all right, Mr Doherty?'

'In all the years I've been here, I haven't had any dealings with the police, and then two back-to-back visits all of a sudden.'

Clay focused him on an imperative that wasn't Brian Doherty centred.

'Your newest employee, Francesca Christie, she's still missing, by the way.'

'Is that what you've come to tell me?'

'No.'

'Then how can I help you, DCI Clay?'

Clay noticed the way the framed family portrait on his desk was angled so that anyone facing him could see him with his wife and two teenage daughters.

'I've come here to have a highly confidential talk with you, Mr Doherty, and I need a reassurance you won't divulge the content of our conversation with anyone.' She pointed at the picture on the desk. 'Even your family. And especially not your employees.'

'I don't see how I can help you, DCI Clay. Francesca Christie only worked here for half a day before she went missing.'

'You enticed her away from Norma Maguire, right?'

'Wrong. Francesca approached me. I got my fingers singed last time I head-hunted from Maguire Holdings.'

'Richard Ezra?'

'Yes.'

'We sussed it out,' Clay explained. 'He worked for Maguire Holdings before he came to work for you. Tell me the story. What happened?'

'I approached Richard directly behind Norma Maguire's back. He was the top agent at Maguire Holdings. I needed him on board here. At the time we were in a slump, to say the very least. I offered him a deal he couldn't refuse. If he helped us to drive up our sales and lettings to the place they'd once been in and he could captain that sustained performance for twelve months, I'd make him a profit-sharing partner in the firm. He bit my hand off.'

'How did Norma Maguire take this?'

'She went ballistic. She sent me legal hate mail when Richard started with me. What she wasn't going to do to me wasn't worth mentioning. She was going to close me down and sue me in the highest court in the land if she had to.'

'Did Richard know about this?'

'Yes. I showed him the letters, played back the toxic messages she left on my answer machine. On the last occasion I played him her poison he quietly asked to be excused and left the room. When he came back he told me he'd called Norma on her personal mobile and had a private conversation with her. Norma immediately stopped banging the war drums. I never heard from her again.'

'Did he tell you much about Norma?'

'Is she in trouble?' A light glinted in his eyes; it was the glimmer of hope.

'Please answer the question, Mr Doherty.'

'He didn't tell me that much about her, just that she was consistently over-familiar with him. There was nothing overtly sexual about it but he felt uncomfortable around her.'

A clear pattern emerged in Clay's head.

'Did Francesca Christie say anything about Norma Maguire to you?'

'That she wasn't going to work her notice, and that she'd personally take the fallout from that decision. Richard Ezra was a little less hasty. He worked his month's notice and spun a yarn to Norma that he was going travelling for a year. I told Francesca to wait but any time I mentioned Norma it was like someone had stepped on her grave.'

'How do you mean, Mr Doherty?'

'She shuddered at the mention of her name. Norma Maguire was a touchy subject.'

'Is there anything you'd like to add?'

'Will I be receiving another visit from you or your colleagues, DCI Clay?'

'It's more than likely. Thank you for your time and discretion. Let's hope your silence on my visit to you helps us to bring Francesca Christie back safe and sound.'

When Clay stepped on to Allerton Road outside Doherty Estates and Properties, her iPhone rang out. She looked down the busy street in the direction of Maguire Holdings, connected the call and asked, 'Karl, how did you get on?'

'Daniel Ball's gone home, thrown in a sickie, and he's not answering his landline home phone or his mobile number.'

Clay's suspicions escalated.

'Where does he live?'

'721 Loreburn Road, over the road from Mosspits School.'

'You can make it there in five minutes, Karl. I need that list of names of people who've walked out on Norma Maguire. Was she there?'

'No, she was out at a meeting. No one knew the answer to my question. At least that's what they all claimed.'

As Clay walked towards her car, the pattern in her head became clearer.

Richard Ezra – Maguire Holdings to Doherty Estates and Properties; his wife ends up murdered and a year later, so the story goes, he threw himself into the Mersey.

Francesca Christie – Maguire Holdings to Doherty Estates and Properties; she is kidnapped and goes missing, and is almost certainly in the hands of The Ghoul.

Clay fired up the ignition and drove away on autopilot as the line between bizarre coincidence and grim pattern blurred from static black and white into a moving cloud of grey.

76
1.55 pm

Clay sat at her desk in the incident room and drank a mouthful of cold coffee to wash down a painkiller. She didn't hear the door open but was drawn by Poppy Waters' voice.

'Eve?'

'Poppy…'

She walked towards Clay with Francesca Christie's open laptop in her hands, and sat next to her.

'You've found something, Poppy?' she asked, trying hard not to become instantly intoxicated with hope.

'Yes. I think I know why she left her job so suddenly.'

'Go on?' Clay sat up, shook off her fatigue and gave her attention to Poppy.

'She kept a diary of things that went on at work in Maguire Holdings. She didn't like her boss, Norma Maguire.'

Clay pictured the woman in a wheelchair to whom she'd spoken hours earlier.

'Norma harassed Francesca. She's listed dates and times when Norma said or did things to her.'

'Are we looking at sexual harassment here?'

'Yes and no. Norma was clever, so she did things like touch Francesca but never in an overtly sexual way. But what she did, for example, was touch Francesca's elbow and slide her hand down to her wrist. Take that on its own and its pretty much nothing, but that sort of thing happened over and over. *Fran*, as Norma very annoyingly insisted on calling Francesca, was forever being called into Norma's office for motherly one-to-one chats about things that had absolutely nothing to do with the business of selling houses. As time went on, the gaps between these cosy chats grew shorter and shorter. Then there were the monthly meals out, a reward for the whole staff for good performance on the surface but Francesca didn't see it that way. Francesca always had to sit next to Norma. It was a running joke in the office. Everyone went out on Norma and Francesca's date nights.'

'How many of these incidents did Francesca log, roughly?'

'Specifically, three hundred and seventy-three over eighteen months.'

'Ouch! Norma Maguire told me she had no idea why Francesca left.'

'Well, there's your answer.'

'Send the log to me but, also, give me a specific example of Norma's unwanted attentions. The most vivid one you can think of, Poppy?'

An incoming message pinged on Clay's iPhone.

'Well, if it was me I can tell you now. The one that would make me come out in goose bumps was the office Christmas party last year. They had it in the Dovedale Towers. Francesca was understandably down because her father had died suddenly prior to Christmas and her boyfriend decided to dump her soon after that. Norma had consumed a few too many whiskies. She lured Francesca into the disabled toilet and closed the door. She laid it on with a trowel about how lonely she was. It was high octane emotional blackmail. She wanted Fran to come to Crosby Beach with her on New Year's Day, to go for an afternoon out and have food somewhere. Francesca got out of it by playing the bereavement card. New Year's Day was her dad's birthday and she couldn't leave her mum on her own.'

'I need to have another word with Norma Maguire.'

She opened the message from Stone.

Eve - No one home at Daniel Ball's house. I knocked a few times. According to the neighbour, Daniel would be in work. His wife, Lydia, goes to town most days. Sorry, no sign of.

77

2.03 pm

When the landline telephone on Detective Sergeant Gina Riley's desk rang out, the only person in the incident room was Detective Constable Barney Cole.

Cole moved three desks down and picked up.

'This is DC Cole on DS Riley's telephone.'

'Oliver Brown, CCTV4U. She called us to hurry up on the footage you sent us.' He sounded like a busy man who was just about at the end of his tether. 'I was ringing to inform her that I've emailed the cleaned-up footage to her.'

'I haven't got access to Gina Riley's laptop. Can you do me a favour, Oliver? Can you email the footage to my laptop and I can distribute the images to DCI Clay and the rest of the team.'

He told Oliver his email address.

'No problem.'

'And thank you for doing such a swift job.'

'We'd have had it to you sooner but the quality wouldn't have been as good as it is now. I'll resend it to you right now.'

Before Cole could reply, Oliver hung up.

As he returned to his desk, he called Clay and, when she connected, he heard immediately that she was in her car.

'Eve, we've got the cleaned-up CCTV footage of the white van leaving the Amanda Winton body drop-off.'

'What's it like, Barney?'

'I don't know yet, I'm opening my emails now. OK.' He counted to five as he cued up the footage. 'I'm watching. Oh, that's great. Where it was overcast and grainy, the footage is much brighter and clearer. The white van's coming away from the footpath and turning left to make it into Heath Road. It's coming closer to the old lady's house, it's about to draw level with her CCTV camera. Jeez, I'm pausing it on the image of the passenger.'

'What's he like?'

'It's a male. Eighteen or nineteen years of age. Blond hair. White. Thin face with a prominent nose and forehead. I'm looking directly at him because, as the van pulled level with the CCTV, bingo, right on cue, he looks left directly at the camera. He's not your run of the mill teenager. He looks like there's something not quite right about him.'

'That's one way of putting it, Barney. Anything on the driver?'

'We couldn't see him at all, remember? He's like a bulky silhouette now. He's a big man. I can see his hands on the wheel. I can see his forearms, they're knotted with muscle, and there's some sort of tattoo just above his left wrist. I'm guessing he's quite mature, but that's a guess, Eve.'

'Anything of his face?' asked Clay, crossing the fingers of her mind.

'No, the hands and the forearms, yes, but the rest of him is in shadow. I'm taking it off pause. And watching the van disappear down Heath Road.'

'I'm pulling over, Barney. Can you send it to me now, please?'

Cole heard the screech of her brakes, clicked on forward and sent the footage to Clay's iPhone.

'Got it, Barney.' She fell silent and after several moments said, 'That's great. The kid should be dead easy to identify.

Circulate this CCTV footage to the team and give it to our PR people. I want this image of the lad on local news at teatime, Granada and the BBC. I want it repeated after ten o'clock and throughout tomorrow's local news daytime bulletins. We'll issue it with your landline number.'

'Leave it with me. I think we're going to have him in custody before the day's done.'

At the other end of the line, he sensed Clay turning very quiet.

'He doesn't look like he's capable,' said Clay.

Cole heard the spark of her ignition and her shift into first gear.

'Where are you off to, Eve?'

'Norma Maguire and then home for an hour, to get ready for tonight.'

'Good luck with that, Eve. I'll hold the fort here and relay anything that comes in to you.'

Cole watched the footage through again and when the young man came fully into view, he was forced to agree with Clay.

He looked like a child trapped in the body of a young adult.

Cole didn't know who he was or where he came from but he was sure of one thing.

The passenger was going to lead them to The Ghoul.

78

2.35 pm

Detective Chief Inspector Eve Clay stood alone at the window in Norma Maguire's office and processed recent events.

She had arrived at the estate agency ten minutes earlier and found that Norma was still out of the office. She had told Carolyn Wilkes, the most senior of the estate agents, that she'd wait in Norma's office for the boss to return and had given her an instruction to call Norma and ask her to return as quickly as she could.

Now, from the window, she saw Norma parking in the disabled bay in front of Maguire Holdings. She watched Norma get out of the car and into her wheelchair, a manoeuvre she performed with dexterity and speed.

Clay waited, heard Norma's imminent arrival in advance with the ping from the lift.

The door to the office opened and Clay stayed still and where she was.

'DCI Clay? What's the matter?'

Norma wheeled herself to her place at the desk.

'Thank you for coming back so quickly, Norma.'

'Can I help you?'

'I was just wondering about Francesca Christie?'

'Have you got news for me about Francesca?'

Clay heard a note of concern.

'Sadly, no. She's still missing. Do you think her leaving could be linked to you speaking to her about her activities on the internet dating site?'

Norma frowned.

'No. You've asked me that before.'

'Double-checking, now. She didn't give any reason why she was leaving?'

'She must have been offered a lot of money. Or been given a lot of unlikely promises. That's all I can think.'

'It's just while I was waiting for you, I looked at the pictures on the wall of your staff. It's a pretty stable history.'

Norma smiled but as soon as it surfaced it sank down beneath the grim cast of her face.

'I pay good bonuses and I'm understanding if people need to stay off when their children are sick. People tend to leave when they retire. The turnover of my staff is the envy of all the estate agents on Allerton Road.'

'Has anyone else ever left Maguire Holdings to go and work for another estate agent?'

'Francesca isn't the first. There've been others down the years. It happens.'

'Like who?'

'I've been here for nearly thirty years, DCI Clay. Do you remember the names of everyone you worked with, decades ago?'

'Your office manager, he was here this morning. He's gone home sick.'

'No. I don't know where you got that piece of misinformation from but he's taking some long overdue paid holidays. He came in this morning to give me a brief rundown on where and what everyone was up to. Daniel's like a lot of men. He puts a brave face on it, DCI Clay, but he suffers from stress and anxiety. I insisted, take time off.'

The image of Francesca Christie smiling as if her life depended on it, sitting side by side with Norma Maguire, rolled around inside Clay's head.

'You didn't notice anything odd about Francesca in the days leading up to her resignation?'

'I thought everything was perfectly fine. Clearly, it wasn't.'

Clay stood up.

'Thank you very much for your time, Norma. I hope the holiday makes Daniel feel a lot better.' Clay stopped at the door of the office and asked, 'As a matter of interest, where have you just been to, Norma?'

'I've just been to see Francesca's mother to show some support, and to let her know I was thinking about her under these horrible circumstances.'

'How is Mrs Christie?'

'Distraught, as you can imagine. Will you keep me posted on any developments?'

'One thing, Norma. Who was Richard Ezra to you?'

'A star that burned out before its time.'

'Francesca Christie followed in his footsteps, didn't she?'

'How do you mean?'

'Stellar sales person who left you to go and work for Brian Doherty. Richard Ezra. What a sad story that was. I'll be in touch with you again shortly, Norma. Make yourself available at all times for the foreseeable future.'

79

4.05 pm

Eve Clay sat at the dressing table in her bedroom and, staring into the mirror, wondered if she was gazing at herself or some other woman, a flirty blonde who had suddenly taken over her body. She studied the picture of Francesca Christie propped up against the mirror and carried on straightening her hair in the same style as the missing woman.

She looked through a range of shades of foundation and chose porcelain over ivory, the one most suited to Francesca

Christie's pale skin tone. Looking straight into the mirror, she carefully applied the base to her skin with a brush.

As she did so, she listened to the silence in the house and wished that Thomas and Philip were there to fill the empty space it triggered inside her.

Thomas was at the surgery and Philip was at a friend's house for a birthday tea.

Clay spread the foundation evenly across her forehead, softening care-worn wrinkles that she usually didn't have time to notice. She looked at the left-hand parting in her long blonde hair and the way the hair hung behind her ears.

There were four lipsticks in the dressing table drawer. Clay took them out and opened them to compare them to the shade on Francesca's lips. She picked the palest red, almost bordering on a pink, and drew the flattened point over her top lip.

Wondering if Francesca Christie was still alive, Clay tried to give herself some grey reassurance and did the maths, based on The Ghoul's past patterns. She drew mascara through her eyelashes as she concluded that if things stayed as they were, Francesca Christie's body would show up on Monday, after she'd been killed and scalped on Sunday.

She checked the application of lipstick in the mirror and noted how it altered the dynamic of her mouth.

Standing in front of the full-length mirror on the wall, Clay saw that the coat of make-up had taken years off her and, though she could never pass for a woman in her mid twenties, she looked considerably younger than her usual forty plus years.

Clay opened her wardrobe and asked herself, *what would I wear if I was going on a first date?* She took out a black cocktail dress, a black coat and a pair of black flats. Opening the drawer of the wardrobe, she took out a pair of black tights and underwear, and placed the clothes in her overnight bag.

At her dressing table, she put the make-up bag in her handbag and assessed the space it took up. She was satisfied that there was more than enough room for a Glock handgun.

There was the sound of a key turning in the front door lock. She looked out of the window and saw Thomas' car parked outside the house.

The front door opened. 'Hello!' he called. 'I can smell hair.' He walked up the stairs. 'Have you been using those straighteners I bought you for Christmas?'

She smiled as his voice came closer and kept silent to build up the dramatic impact of her physical transformation.

'I phoned Barney Cole and he told me you were home. I thought I'd give you...' Thomas stopped in the doorway and stared at Eve. '...a surprise. Quite the other way round, then? Wow, look at you...'

'What do you think?'

'Your make-up's really...' He walked to her and kissed her on the lips. 'That felt a little bit like I was cheating on you.' Looking into her eyes, Thomas smiled.

'You have my full permission to cheat on me with the blonde who showed up in our bedroom. Well, what do you think, lover boy?'

'It's you, but it's not you. You look kind of different and you look kind of the same, which is just great. God, my head's spinning.'

She took him by the hand and sat next to him on the end of the bed. She watched his attention drift to the dressing table and he asked, 'Who's the girl in the picture?'

'Francesca Christie.'

He placed an arm around her shoulders and looked back and forth between her and the picture of Francesca.

'When you look at that woman and think of what happened to the others, it makes me realise your operation's totally necessary. It's an excellent idea, in fact. But I can't stop asking myself, *why you*? You don't have to answer, Eve. We both know the answer to that.'

She rested her head on his shoulder.

'Thank you,' she said.

'What for?' he asked.

'This lovely surprise, you turning up from nowhere, filling the emptiness I felt when I was alone in the house just now. Thank you.'

She placed her hand just above his right knee, a part of his body where she knew he loved being touched.

'Thank you for not trying to pressurise me over decisions I make in work. Thank you for allowing me to do my job the best I can. Thank you for putting up with my absences. Thank you for being the best dad in the world. And thank you for waiting for me.'

She looked up at his face and pressed her mouth against his lips.

'Did you like that, Thomas?'

'I loved it.'

'Would you like some more?'

He kicked off his shoes and unbuckled his belt.

'I'll take that as a yes.'

Eve stood up, walked to the window and closed the curtains.

She turned. 'And this is what you get for being a really, really good boy.'

On the dressing table, her iPhone rang out.

'Leave it,' said Thomas. He pulled her down on top of himself and planted a kiss on her mouth. The ringtone stopped and her answer machine kicked in.

'This is Eve Clay. Leave your name, number and message and I'll get back to you.'

'Hi, Eve, Karl Stone. Everyone and everything is in place at the Albert Dock. We need you down here to run through the dress rehearsal. The armoury sergeant's got your Glock. Wants you to sign for it and a few rounds. Oh, and white van boy's getting his picture shown on the local Granada and BBC news.'

Thomas put his hands on her shoulders.

'I'm sorry, Thomas, really I am...'

'You've got to go, Eve.'

'I do love you, Thomas. You do know that, don't you?'

'Yes. And I love you. I must do.' He smiled at her. 'Or I must be barking mad. Maybe a bit of both.'

'I'm sorry for leaving you high and dry. We'll pick it up where we left off the next time I'm home. You're on the biggest promise I've ever made you.'

She cupped her hand over his ear and whispered.

Thomas was silent for a moment and then he laughed.

'That much?' he asked.

'And there's a whole lot more where that's coming from!'

80
5.15 pm

Wren looked out of his bedroom window at the falling rain and the yellow street lights as they spluttered into life. He felt like he'd been locked up in the house for five years, rather than the not yet five hours he'd actually been there.

Downstairs, the landline telephone rang out and, without thinking, he followed the sound.

Halfway down the stairs, the ringing stopped but started up again immediately.

'Hurry, hurry, Wren…'

In the front room, he snatched up the receiver and said, 'Yes?'

'Wren, how are you?'

'Oh my God, Edgar, it's you. It's really you. How are you?'

'Not very good, to be honest.'

'You don't sound sick.'

'It's a tummy bug.'

'Will you be back in work on Monday?'

'I'm pretty certain I will be, Wren. OK, now listen. I want you to remind me of what we said about the message we went on the day you started in the abattoir.'

'What message? We didn't go on any message.'

'Because?'

'It was a top-secret mission taken out on behalf of Captain Cyclone. If details of it became known, it could endanger Captain Cyclone's life and the lives of his agents in the field.'

'Wren, you have remembered everything, word perfectly. I will inform Captain Cyclone in my next secret briefing with him. He will be proud of you and pleased with your loyalty and dedication to duty. You should be made into a lieutenant in Captain Cyclone's elite unit of men of honour. I salute you,

Wren. Await your commission to officer status in Captain Cyclone's super elite band of warriors fighting the forces of evil in a planet of grime.'

As Wren saluted, he heard the door of his father's car slam shut.

'Dad's outside, Edgar.'

'Hang up and make no mention of this top-secret telephone call.'

Wren hung up and sat in the armchair, listening to his father opening the front door.

'Wren? Wren?'

'Here, Dad…'

His father appeared in the doorway.

'Why haven't you put some lights on? You're sitting in the dark.'

His father put on the light in the hallway and in the front room.

'Anything happening?'

'No,' replied Wren.

'Any callers?'

'No. Your big sister didn't show.'

'What have you been doing?'

'Nothing. I didn't notice.'

'You didn't notice what?'

'That it had all gone so very dark.'

81

6.38 pm

Detective Chief Inspector Eve Clay looked at herself closely in the mirror of the female toilet adjacent to the incident room in Trinity Road police station and, dimming the light, saw herself as the image she had constructed of Francesca Christie.

Blonde. Pale skin. Pinky-red lipstick, black eyelashes. A cosmetic version of a different woman.

She turned her back on the mirror and faced the closed cubicle doors.

Hi, I'm Sally Haydn. I'm a woman with a lot to offer the right kind of man who I can make precious memories with and who wants to make dreams come true...

The words of Riley's fake profile ran through her head like firestorms.

'Jesus...'

She turned back to the mirror and said, 'I love nothing more than sitting in front of a roaring log fire with a glass of wine and some romantic music. I like long walks in the countryside, picnics and winter strolls on empty beaches.'

Clay heard The Ghoul's voice on its call to Riley and it made her skin feel wet.

On my profile I said I was single. It seemed like... new to internet dating...

The Ghoul's words span around her head.

The truth is... wife died... on my own... terribly, terribly lonely...

She turned up the dimmer switch and looked beneath the coating of make-up, stared into her own eyes, picked out who she really was, the last thing The Ghoul wanted.

Clay opened her bag, took out the Glock handgun she had signed for and double-checked it was fully loaded.

On the corridor outside the ladies' toilet, footsteps approached and she slipped the gun back inside her bag.

'Eve?' Riley's voice drifted through the wooden door.

'Come in, Gina. I'm kind of decent. I guess.'

Riley opened the door and, stepping inside, looked at Clay with a mixture of amazement and amusement.

'You really suit being a blonde,' said Riley.

'No, I don't. Being blonde in this neck of the woods gets your face torn off and your head scalped. I can't wait to go back to brunette.'

Riley looked Clay up and down.

'Well, how do I look?' asked Clay.

'You look the part.'

Heavy rain fell on the building.

'How are you feeling, Eve?'

'Up for it. How are things here? I've been in my own little bubble for hours.'

'Things here have been strange.'

'Have we heard from Daniel Ball, Maguire Holdings?'

'No. We need to stick his head into a mangle ASAP.'

'Anything else?' asked Clay.

'Barney Cole's on one,' Riley smiled.

'How so, Gina?'

'The image system on the board in the incident room. He's pulling his hair out.'

'Good. Barney Cole's agitated spells usually bring results.'

A pipe rattled deep in the building and the wind wrapped itself around the walls and windows like a requiem hymn defying the night.

'Great night for a first date,' said Riley. 'Everyone's ready and in place. I'll be two or three cars behind you as you drive down to the waterfront. You're not on your own here. But we have to go right now.'

Clay felt the weight of her bag, the solidity of the handgun against the make-up.

'Then let's go right now,' said Clay. 'Let's get this sorted.'

82
7.10 pm

Neil Wren stared straight ahead, tried to drown out his son's voice, the verbal battering ram banging incessantly against his skull and his ears.

'Dad, Dad, Dad, talk to me, Dad. This is the fifth time we've driven under the Garston bridge, fucking Garston Bridge...'

'Wren, cut the language, now!'

'You're going round in a circle, Garston Village, the high street, under the bridge, turn left and carry on and slow down at the police station, and on, and on, and on...'

Wren fell silent, then made a clucking noise with his tongue against the roof of his mouth.

'You're acting weird, Dad. What's wrong with you?'

'I'm trying to think. Shut up and let me get my thoughts in order.'

The moment when Neil Wren saw his son on television, caught on CCTV in the passenger seat of Edgar's white van, hit him again at full force.

The police want to talk to this man in relation to the discovery of a woman's body in the Allerton district of Liverpool.

As the newsreader's words went through him, he wondered if he was imagining that it was Wren or if he was mistaking another man's white van for Edgar's, but he knew at his core there was no mistake.

'What happened when Edgar took you home early on your first day in the abattoir?'

'Nothing.'

'He told me he was going to take you home but that he was going to go on a message on the way there. Where did he go to on that message?'

'Nowhere.'

'Answer the question. And don't lie!'

Where words had cascaded, they now came in drips.

Neil Wren pulled up at a red light and took out his iPhone. He scrolled through the gallery of pictures until he came to a photo he had taken of Wren's bedroom wall. He showed the image to his son and said, 'Read it to me. Read what you wrote on your wall in the name of Captain Cyclone.'

Wren turned his face away, looked into the darkness outside the window.

'I'll read it to you then. *An honest witness does not deceive but a false witness pours out lies. Proverbs 14.5.*'

Behind them, a pair of car horns sounded. Neil Wren looked up and saw that the lights had turned green. He pulled away.

'Captain Cyclone doesn't like liars. In fact, Captain Cyclone hates liars and can't stand lies. Where did you go with Edgar when you left the abattoir with him?'

'Nowhere.'

'You're not going to tell me, are you?'

With the front entrance of Trinity Road police station metres away, Neil Wren slowed down and stopped.

'Why have you stopped by the police station?'

Neil turned the engine off, took the key from the ignition and unfastened his safety belt.

'Why, Dad? Why have you stopped here?'

'Edgar's not the only one who can go on a message. I'm going on a message. I'm going on a message into the police station and you're coming with me, Wren!'

'But only police officers and dirty low-life scumbags go into police stations. I am neither of those things, so why? Why should I go into a police station?'

A constable stepped on to the pavement from the police station and looked up and down the street.

'Get out of the car!' Neil Wren opened the driver's door and got out of the car.

'You're acting weird, Dad. I don't like this game.'

Neil slammed his door shut and walked around the front of the car to the passenger door.

Wren lifted his feet from the floor, folded his arms tightly around himself and made himself into a human ball on the passenger seat.

'But I haven't done anything wrong, Dad...'

'Then you've got nothing to worry about, have you, son? Get out of the car and come with me.'

Neil opened the passenger door and, raising his arm, called, 'Excuse me, officer!'

The constable walked directly to the car.

'Take me home, Dad.'

'You either get out of the car on your own, which makes it look like you've got nothing to hide, or the policeman will make you get out and that way you don't look so good.'

Wren unfolded his arms, shut his eyes tightly and stuck his index fingers in his ears.

'Is something wrong?' asked the constable.

Neil pointed in the direction of his son and there was a silence that seemed to stretch all the way to the sky and right back down again.

'His name's Robin Wren. He's my son, and he's on the autistic spectrum.'

Wren opened his eyes and saw the constable standing right in front of him in the place where his dad had been, looking like he'd just won the lottery.

'What on earth is all this about?' asked Wren.

'Out of the car, Robin,' said the constable.

Wren undid his safety belt and, getting out of the car, walked to the pavement.

'You're coming with me, Robin,' said the constable.

'I am?'

Wren burst into a sprint but, moments later, found himself face down on the pavement, rugby-tackled from behind. Pain flooded through his senses from his forehead where he'd landed on the ground. His hands were behind his back and the metal cuffs placed on his wrists pinched his flesh.

'Ow! Owwwwww, you're hurting me.'

Somehow or other, Wren found himself back on his feet, the constable holding his right arm.

'Don't even think about trying to run away from me, Robin,' said the constable.

As he marched towards the front door of the police station, Wren looked over at his father and wondered why he was crying.

Wren spoke to his father and he replied, 'I didn't catch that, son. What did you say?'

His father's footsteps followed him into the police station.

'I want my mum, I want my mum, I want my mum.'

83

7.25 pm

In her mind, Detective Chief Inspector Eve Clay processed a string of macabre thoughts.

I am like Annie Boyd, and Amanda Winton, and Francesca Christie. I have come to meet a man I have never met before in my life. Through Riley, he told me his name is Geoff Campbell. This is a lie in a network of untruths that he has been peddling. If he succeeds in abducting me, if the operation goes horribly wrong, the next time I'm seen by another human being I will be dead, scalped, my face missing.

The twisted bottom line hit her with colossal force.

Clay looked at her watch as she walked along the shoulder of the River Mersey in the direction of the Albert Dock and the padlocked railings.

Hendricks walked towards her but looked directly ahead and she recognised another officer, whose name she didn't know, lighting a cigarette as she leaned against the railings and laughed as the officer beside her cracked a joke.

A group of half-drunk young people dressed in Santa hats and costumes blocked her path as they headed for the Albert Dock, singing along with the Christmas music that blasted out from a loudspeaker inside a nearby pub.

As she came closer to the padlocked railings, Clay watched the coloured lights linking the lamp posts, swaying in the wind.

In her bag, her iPhone rang out. She found herself a pocket of space away from other people, opened her bag and took out the iPhone sitting next to the loaded Glock handgun.

Connecting, she identified herself with, 'Sally speaking.'

'Hi, Sally. It's Barney. Do you have time to speak briefly?'

'I'm early. I've got time.'

'The TV appeal worked a treat. I don't want to distract you, but we've got the kid in the white van in custody. His name's Robin Wren and his father walked him in here. We've had a lot of calls identifying him as Robin Wren.'

'Is he talking?'

'No, but his father is. The kid's denying it's him in the van. If that's the truth, he must have a doppelganger.'

'Has the father any idea who the driver was?'

'His name's Edgar McKee. They work together in the Stanley Abattoir on East Prescot Road in Old Swan.'

'Have we got a home address for McKee?'

'Flat 6, 199 Moscow Drive. Winters is on his way over there right now with a search warrant and a couple of shooters for backup.'

'What's the kid like?'

'He's as bright as a button but he's extremely autistic. His father says that when he gets something locked in his head, he's almost impossible to break.'

'Where is Wren junior at the moment?'

'He's in the cells.'

'Keep me posted up until eight but after that communicate any developments to Bill Hendricks.'

Clay walked on along the back of the Echo Arena and watched people pouring in to see an American stadium rock band.

She took in the city skyline, the two cathedrals illuminated by powerful uplighters, the Albert Dock close to her left and mirrored in the surface of the water at its base.

She recalled the footage of Annie Boyd walking away from the padlocked railings, her head down, and imagined what must have been running through her mind.

I've been stood up by a man I've never met before because I am worthless and unattractive, and nothing can change that.

Behind her, Clay heard footsteps and sensed the presence of someone following her. She stopped and let the stranger past, a bald man in his thirties who said, 'Excuse me.'

'I'm sorry? I didn't catch that,' she checked.

He looked back over his shoulder and said, 'I said, *excuse me.*'

He didn't sound anything like the man who called himself Geoff Campbell.

She looked towards the padlocked railings and saw that there was a group of older men and women there but no police officers, an observation that unsettled her for a moment. The group was approached by Riley and Clay's unease was dissipated.

She checked the time – 7.31.

Clay called her husband on her iPhone and, three rings in, she heard his voice.

'Eve? Where are you?'

'I'm at the Albert Dock. It's freezing.'

'What's it like?'

'Heaving with work Christmas dos, and crawling with armed coppers. As we speak, Gina Riley's four metres away from me. No one's looking at me, no one can hear me. I'm blending in perfectly.'

'How are you feeling, Eve?'

'A little nervous. I'd have to be a fool not to be. But I'm surrounded by bodies. Nothing can harm me here. You? Are you OK?'

'No.' His voice dipped in volume. 'It's like I've got pins sticking into the soles of my feet.'

'I'm really sorry, Thomas. How's Philip?'

Her hair blew up at the sides of her face and, for a moment, she didn't recognise it as her own hair, felt in that one disconcerting moment that she was residing in another woman's body.

'He's fine. He's in his bedroom writing a wish list for Christmas. He asked me to send you his love if you called. He wanted to call you but I said we couldn't. You were in a very important meeting. He accepted it.'

She noticed a black firearms unit van parked up and saw there was no one in the cab, just like there would be no one in the back. Covert rifles were already in place from the Albert Dock to Mariner's Wharf, to the Coburg Marina Club and beyond.

'What are you going to do tonight?'

'There's a Championship League game on TV. It starts at eight. I've promised Philip he can stay up and watch it.'

She imagined herself on the sofa in their front room, herself on one side of Philip and Thomas on the other side of their son, watching second tier footballers slogging it out against each other in the wind and the rain.

Another missed evening with her husband and son twisted the conflicted knife in her core. She heard the sound of a whistle carried on the wind and imagined picking up her sleepy son as the match ended, carrying him upstairs and laying him down to sleep in his bed. The soft blue light from the bedside lamp picked out his features as he drifted into sleep. She brushed his hair to one side and whispered in his ear, 'Sweet dreams, sweetheart...'

'Eve, are you still there?'

'I am. God, I wish I was at home with you.'

'So do we, we wish it very, very much. But I understand. There's a monster out there. It's got to stop, love.'

In the background she heard Philip shout, 'Dad!'

'I love you both.'

'And we love you back just as much. Call me as soon as you can, Eve.'

'Dad, how do you spell reindeer? Is it with an a or an e?'

'Of course I will.'

She disconnected the call and, placing her iPhone back in her bag, checked again that she had a loaded gun at her disposal.

As Gina Riley walked away from the padlocked railings, Clay walked towards them.

'We've got the kid in Trinity Road and we've got a name for The Ghoul. Edgar McKee.'

Riley nodded and carried on as if she'd heard nothing.

Clay stood with her back turned to the padlocked railings. The people walked away, as if they'd been magically alerted to leave on cue with her arrival.

On the promenade to her right, the wind pushed something metal against a street light, an irregular clanging of metals like a defective bell summoning mourners to a funeral by the river.

Clay stopped and waited as the cold wind bit down on her and pinched her face, just as it had done to Annie Boyd, Amanda Winton and Francesca Christie.

84
7.31 pm

In 199 Moscow Drive, there were six flats spread out over three floors. Winters stepped over the threshold with five armed officers at his back, past the man who had opened the front door of the tall building.

He showed the man his warrant card and said, 'You're to stay in your flat. Keep the door closed and don't come out until we've left.'

Winters turned to his colleagues. 'I'll have one man on each floor to keep the neighbours indoors. One, two, come with me.'

On the landing of the top floor, he pressed in the timed light and identified the door of Flat 6. With one hand he knocked on the door three times, each time a little louder, and in the other hand felt the weight of the ram.

'Open up, Mr McKee. It's the police. I've going to give you a count of five. If you haven't opened the door on five, we'll ram your door.'

On five, Winters opened the door with one swift blow.

The flat was in complete darkness. Instinct told him that it was empty. There was a concoction of competing odours, musk and sweat at the heart of it, thinly masked by body sprays that did nothing to eradicate the ingrained stench.

Winters stepped inside and turned the light on in the narrow hall. After the armed officers had checked the rooms either side of the corridor, Winters knew that his instinct had been right. McKee wasn't home.

He turned on all the lights in the bedroom, bathroom, kitchen and living room and took in how clean and tidy it all was, despite the stale smells.

Stepping into McKee's bedroom, he saw that the sheet was folded over at the top of the single bed. *Fastidious bachelor*, thought Winters, opening the wardrobe where shirts, jackets and trousers were lined up in neat rows, the hooks of the hangers all pointing in the same direction.

There was a wooden box at the bottom of the bed. Winters lifted the lid and saw heavy dumbbells of different sizes, imagined what it would be like to get into a fight with a fastidious bodybuilder.

He stepped across the corridor to the kitchen and saw a picture of a cow, labelled to identify each cut of meat on its body. Winters was drawn to the drawers of a sparklingly clean but old-fashioned unit. He opened the drawers at once and saw cutlery lined up in neat sections in one of them and, in the other, a range of professional carving knives that went from an extremely small blade through a rising range of lethal sharps and ending with a plastic-handled cleaver.

Winters pictured the images he'd seen of Annie Boyd and Amanda Winton, post-mortem, their faces and heads flayed, and he shivered at the gleaming metal in the drawer, wondering if these sharp objects had been used to skin them.

A voice came from the living room. 'DC Winters, can you come in here, please?'

The armed officer stood in front of a tall bookshelf full of DVDs. Winters read the titles on the spines, took one from the shelf and looked at the writhing bodies on the cover. He turned it over to read the blurb and slipped it back on the shelf.

Apart from the bookcase, the room was dominated by three objects. A widescreen television that looked like it had cost at least four figures, a DVD player and a solitary armchair facing it.

Winters let out a heavy sigh and looked up and down the shelves at the titles of the DVDs in Edgar McKee's living room.

'He's got quite a collection of hard-core pornography here,' said Winters, feeling the urge to run the hand that had touched the DVD under boiling hot water.

He looked around the bare walls.

'He's got a state-of-the-art Technogym running machine in the bathroom,' said the second officer. 'What do you want us to do, DS Winters?'

'Ask the guys on the floors beneath us to find out all they can about McKee from the neighbours. Then wait here for Scientific Support to arrive. They'll pull this place apart.'

85
8.38 pm

Walking back to her car, Detective Chief Inspector Eve Clay took out her iPhone and called Stone.

'Eve, I can see you heading back to your car. He didn't show!'

'Are you surprised?'

'No.'

'This is a quick one. I want to keep my line clear. I need everyone on their toes. They're looking out for me but they're also looking for any lone males in the vicinity. I want those lone males followed and confronted.'

She disconnected the call and remembered the automated message she'd listened to when she called Geoff Campbell's mobile phone and his answer machine kicked in.

Clay glanced over her shoulder at Detective Constable Emma Simpson from Admiral Street police station, who had been assigned to follow her back to her vehicle. Simpson's presence did nothing to stop the tightening in her stomach as she came closer to her car.

As she walked in the footsteps of the dead and abducted, she smiled bleakly at the irony of John and Yoko's *Happy*

Xmas War Is Over carried on the bitter wind from the Marina Clubhouse.

She caught sight of Detective Sergeant Gina Riley approaching her on the edge of her vision but turned her head so that she didn't make direct eye contact with her.

There was an incoming message to her iPhone.

Geoff

She opened the message.

Dear Sally I am so very sorry to have let you down. I am also extremely sorry to have to tell you the reason why I couldn't make our date tonight. My mother died suddenly at 6.30 in the evening. She was crossing a road near where she lives and was hit by a drunk driver and was pronounced dead on the spot by medics. I am currently in the family room of the mortuary at the Royal Liverpool Hospital. I apologise profusely for not turning up for our date and hope you will understand my sad predicament. Love Geoff xxx ps I will make it up to you if you are good enough to give me a second chance. pps I know I should have called you direct but I am unable to speak due to the depths of my grief and I just keep on breaking down.

She stopped at the back of her car and forwarded The Ghoul's message to everyone on the team.

At the driver's door of her car, she looked around, turned a whole circle, but the only person she could see was Simpson with one hand on the gun in her coat pocket and the other holding her mobile phone to the side of her face.

Despite the absence of immediate danger, as Clay opened the car door she expected to be attacked from nowhere. Nothing happened.

She turned on the overhead light inside her car and checked the back seat, wondering if Annie, Amanda or Francesca had experienced any sense of imminent danger as they slumped away in defeat at being stood up.

Clay closed the door as she sat behind the wheel and felt her heart pumping, adrenaline flowing through her, and a mixture of emotions; relief that she was physically unharmed and profound disappointment because she didn't get the chance to face him down and stick him in custody.

Her car rocked in the wind as she clicked to reply.

Oh my God Geoff what can I say? I am so sorry to hear of the tragic news of your mother's sudden and awful death. If there is anything at all I can do to help you in this dark hour please do not hesitate to let me know immediately and I will be there for you. I am currently still on the waterfront. That is not so far from the mortuary where you are behind the Royal Hospital. I can come and see you within the next fifteen minutes if you think that would be of any help to you.

Clay looked in her wing mirror, saw Riley get into her car, five metres behind hers, and her cocktail of relief and disappointment escalated.

'If you'd showed up, you bastard, we'd have had you in custody right now in this very moment,' she said, speaking her thoughts out loud, comforting herself with the sound of her own voice.

Clay recognised a marksman she didn't know by name, emerging from the darkness and heading towards her car as she returned to composing her message.

If you don't want me to come to the mortuary, please say so. Otherwise when and only when you are ready please contact

me and we can arrange to meet. Love and condolences Sally
xxx ps can you pls let me know your mother's name so that I
can mention her directly as I pray very long and hard for both
you and her. pps do you have family and friends around you
who you can lean on for support?

Clay pressed send as the marksman walked by the passenger
door, giving a single reassuring tap to the roof of her car. She
guessed at his meaning.

You're safe...

And her deepest instinct responded, *but don't bank on it.*

Clay called Stone on her iPhone.

'Karl, call off the red alert.'

'Are you sure, Eve?'

'Certain. Tell the arms sergeant I'll give him the Glock back
in the morning.'

'Any reason?'

'The general red alert's off. Mine's still on. Pass on a
message for me. Thank everyone involved in the operation
and tell them to go back to their stations.'

She opened Messenger and typed:

Thomas, I'm in my car and safe. He didn't show. Talk later.
Ly xxx

Clay drove in the direction of Sefton Street and watched
Riley's car overtaking her, headlights dazzling as she drove
away at speed, putting more distance between them with
each passing second.

Clay shifted gears in her head and prepared her next
moves – a visit to Moscow Drive and then to return to Trinity
Road to question Robin Wren.

As Clay passed the Coburg pub, another message came on to her iPhone. She pulled up to the pavement and opened it.

Dearest Sally your kind words have come as a great comfort to me. Thank you for offering to come to the mortuary to help me but I really don't want you to see me in the state I'm in. I am quite alone in this world with no family and the friends I do have are scattered far and wide in Australia, Canada and Hong Kong. Thank you for praying for me and my mother. I will be in touch with you as soon as I am able but for now have to go as I am about to formally identify my mother's body in the viewing suite. I have dreaded this moment of my mother's death for years but never imagined that she would be stolen in an instant.

Clay felt as if something toxic had penetrated her scalp and was eroding the surface of her skull. Stolen in an instant?

God bless you Sally. Love to you, Geoff xxxxx ps For the sake of your prayers my mother's name is Catriona West.

Clay skipped back in time to the day before and she found herself standing in the rain in Springwood Cemetery, Plot 66. She recalled looking at the finest headstone in the group of sixteen graves and the words carved into the marble.

CATRIONA WEST
WIFE AND MOTHER
STOLEN IN AN INSTANT
1940–2001

She called Riley on her iPhone.

'Gina, track down anything you can about Catriona West on the NPC and HOLMES. Where's Robin Wren?'

'He's in the interview suite with Barney Cole.'

'If he's being awkward and refusing to co-operate, he needs to know what McKee's been up to. If he's not talking now, he will do when I get back to Trinity Road. I'll show him pictures of McKee's handiwork on his victims.'

As she closed down the call, a message came on to her iPhone.

My dearest Sally, I have now identified my mother's body. I was wrong. I need your support desperately. Can we meet ASAP?

She typed back.

Of course. Where?

She waited, staring ahead into the darkness.

Clay watched unmarked police cars heading away from the Albert Dock and it sparked a feeling of isolation combined with personal power deep at the root of who she was.

She heard the next incoming message ping.

Sally my love, I'm on the fourth floor of the multi-storey car park at the back of the Royal, overlooking the mortuary.

Jesus, she thought, tactical nightmare. *Like trying to storm a castle on top of a mountain.*

Geoff. I'll be there in ten minutes. xxxxx

Clay worked it out as she turned her car around and headed back in the direction of the mortuary. From the fourth floor of the multi-storey car park, he had a powerful overview of any approaching vehicles.

Pictures flooded her mind. Women, dead, skinned and scalped.

For a moment, she wanted to stop, to turn back.

The tactics deployed at the Albert Dock hadn't worked and her deepest hunch was that he had been there and had been spooked by something he'd seen but was still on the hunt.

Sandra. Annie. Amanda.

The Ghoul knew it was a sting.

If I call in help, the words passed through her mind, *he'll see us coming for miles, flooding into the area around the mortuary and multi-storey car park. The best shot of catching him would be blown.*

She pulled up at a red light, took the Glock from her bag and placed it in her coat pocket.

The red light seemed frozen in time.

A message came in.

No pressure Sally but my mood is swinging. Please be there ASAP. Please.

She messaged back.

Please wait for me, Geoff. You need me. I need you.

The red light turned green and she switched to contacts on her phone.

She called Riley but her line was busy.

Clay called Stone and she guessed he was on to Riley.

A message came in.

How far away are you, Sally my love.

She looked out of the window, saw the illuminated tower of the Anglican cathedral. She pulled up to the pavement.

Geoff, I'm three minutes away. Stay.

She called Hendricks and felt another incoming message.

Sally, I feel like throwing myself off the fourth floor.

'Eve, what's up?' asked Hendricks.

She drove down Hope Street towards the Metropolitan Cathedral.

'Eve, are you there?'

Her thoughts raced and clashed. Alone, she had control. If the truth came out, she lost control of decision-making, and risked losing The Ghoul.

'I'm checking out a lead at the mortuary. Making sure that the shit about his mother dying in an RTA was a total lie. That's where I'll be if anyone needs me. There or thereabouts.'

Her pulse quickened and her mouth turned stone dry.

'Francesca. Are you still alive?' she asked herself.

I am your best and only hope, thought Clay.

She headed towards the multi-storey car park.

Clay could smell and taste blood, realised she had bitten her lower lip.

The Ghoul was waiting.

86

8.40 pm

Sitting between his father and the duty solicitor, Mr Robson, Robin Wren was less than a metre away from Detective Sergeant Barney Cole but looked as if he may as well have been on Mars.

'Robin?' Cole tried.

'He really can't stand his first name,' explained his father. 'He likes to be addressed as Wren.'

In Interview Suite 1, Wren looked at the space above Cole's head and chewed the heel of his hand. Wren's father settled a hand on his son's shoulder and Cole observed that the tender, well-intentioned gesture drove the young man deeper into himself.

'Wren, just tell the truth, son...'

'Do you know what, Wren,' said Cole, leaning forward to get into his eyeline. 'I told my boss, DCI Clay, about our first chat and how you weren't answering my questions. So, this is the second time of trying to sort out this horrible mess and I'll tell you what I told you first time round. I don't think for one minute that you're involved in any wrongdoing. When you were at the desk with Sergeant Harris and he was explaining why you were here and what had been going on, I thought maybe you were involved in disposing of a body. But I just don't buy it. The end.' Cole sat down. 'Look at me and let's sort this whole thing out for good.'

Slowly, Wren lowered his gaze.

'Thank you,' said Cole. 'Thank you for looking at me. Stay with me. OK?'

'K.'

'Wren, when was the first time you ever met Edgar?'

'Wednesday just gone. First day of December. On my first day in the abattoir.'

'So until two days ago, you'd never met, seen or spoken to Edgar?'

'Correct.'

'Wren, did you tell Edgar about Captain Cyclone on the first day you met him?'

Wren made a noise deep inside his throat, a sound that was impossible to interpret.

'Was that a *yes* or a *no* or an *I don't know*, Wren?'

Cole looked at Wren's father and back at Wren, and pictured himself in the same position with one of his sons. Sorrow sliced through him and then pure relief at the normality he had taken for granted for years on end.

'That was a yes,' said Wren.

Light appeared on the darkest horizon.

'Your dad told me quite a bit about Captain Cyclone. You made him up, right?'

'Right.'

'He showed me pictures you painted on your bedroom wall. You're quite an artist. I'm impressed. Dad even sent the pictures to me. He's as proud of you as would I be if you were my son.'

Cole turned his laptop round on the desk so that Wren could see the image of Captain Cyclone on his bedroom wall.

'So, Captain Cyclone's face changed on the day you met Edgar. Now Captain Cyclone looks like Edgar, right?'

Wren nodded as if his brain was made of concrete. 'Yeah.'

'Thank you for telling me the truth, Wren. I think the greatest thing I learned from your dad when he told me about Captain Cyclone is the importance of telling the truth and being a good witness. You created Captain Cyclone out of your own brain and your own imagination. I believe that Captain Cyclone's core values are your core values. I read what you wrote on your bedroom wall and I need you to step up to that. I want you to be a good witness, not a bad witness. You got me, Wren?'

Wren nodded and, as Cole picked up his chair and sat to the young man's side, he noticed how he looked years younger and much more vulnerable than he had appeared at the desk as Sergeant Harris booked him in.

'I'm going to show you some CCTV footage. I'll stop it at various points and ask you some questions. I'll talk you through the footage as you watch it so that you're absolutely clear about what's going on. Are you OK with that?'

'K.'

'Keep your eyes on the screen the whole time, Wren.'

Cole pressed play.

'The white van you can see coming from the footpath between Allerton Manor Golf Course and Allerton Towers belongs to Edgar.' Cole paused the footage. 'Do you recognise the van?'

'Yes.'

'Do you accept that it belongs to Edgar?'

Wren shrugged. 'Don't know.'

'Let's put that another way. Could it possibly belong to Edgar?'

'It could do. It could belong to you. How many white vans are there in existence?'

Cole pressed play.

'The driver of the white van's turning his vehicle left to get into the lane of Heath Road leading away from the golf course and in the direction of Mather Avenue. It's coming up to a house on the corner of that road. It's now directly aligned with…' He paused. '…that house. This is what the CCTV camera picked up. Don't look away, Wren.'

Mr Robson touched Wren's sleeve and said, 'Listen to DC Cole. Look, Wren!'

Wren's eyes shifted like dead weights back to the screen of Cole's laptop.

'Who's that?' Cole pointed at the screen. 'Who's that sitting on the passenger seat?'

Wren stared intensely at the screen, as if he was trying to wipe it clean by the power of his mind.

'That's you, Wren, isn't it?' Cole prompted. 'Remember what we said about being a good witness?'

The only sound in the room was the hum of the clock on the wall.

'If Captain Cyclone was sitting in the room in your place, what would he say?' asked Cole.

'He'd say it was me,' replied Wren.

'What do you say, Wren?'

'I'd say it was me.'

'That's a great answer, Wren.' Cole touched the screen. 'See my finger. Whose hands are those, just above my finger? Whose hands are on the steering wheel?'

'I don't know.'

'They're Edgar's hands, aren't they?'

'I don't know.'

'You've just driven away from the public footpath between the golf course and the park. That's nowhere near your house in Gateacre, or the abattoir in Old Swan. Why did Edgar drive you to the footpath?'

'I don't know.'

'Did you ask him why he'd driven you there?'

'I don't know.'

'How far up the footpath did you travel?'

'I don't know.'

'What did you see?'

'Nothing.'

'What did you hear?'

'Silence. Birdsong. The rain.'

Cole watched Wren shrinking inside himself, the front of his mind closing down. He threw him a line.

'What are you thinking, Wren?'

'I don't know.'

Wren closed his eyes, stuck his thumbs in his ears and double-sealed his lips with his index fingers.

'I'm sorry, Wren, but Edgar McKee is not your friend.' Cole looked at Wren's dad and Mr Robson. 'I don't think there's much more that I can do to help Wren at this point. I'm closing this interview. I'm sorry, Wren. You're going to have to go back to your cell.'

87

8.53 pm

As Clay drove up the ramp and onto the fourth floor of the multi-storey car park, she turned her headlights off and parked at a space overlooking the Royal.

She waited.

Clay looked into the shadows to her left but couldn't make out anything other than darkness.

She turned on her reverse lights and looked over her shoulder where the red glow oozed into the gloom.

Clay gripped the Glock in her hand as she stepped out of the car, moving sideways and at a defensive angle towards the wall near the front of her car.

Below, at the edge of her vision, traffic flowed in either direction at the ground level of the multi-storey car park.

She turned to face the darkness and sensed that hers was the only car on the fourth floor.

'Geoff? Are you there, Geoff?'

Silence.

Does this sound crazy? Words from the telephone conversation he'd had with Riley echoed from her memory and breathed through the cold spaces of the car park. *I feel like we've made a connection already. A real connection.*

Silence.

She took the first step into the shadows, heard her footstep echo from the low concrete ceiling.

Listening hard, Clay heard breathing, tried to locate its source and realised it was her own.

'Geoff?'

This time a little louder as the gun in her hand became coated with a film of sweat from her palm.

She took three or four cautious steps closer to the red light that leaked from the back of her car.

Beyond the doors leading up to the level, footsteps rose up the concrete staircase.

Taking the Glock from her coat pocket, she moved at speed to the doorway leading onto the fourth level concealing herself at the side of the entrance.

The footsteps came closer and closer and arrived at the fourth floor.

They stopped and she pointed the gun at the doors.

The footsteps carried on towards the fifth level.

'Geoff? I've come to support you. If you don't reply to me, I'll have to get back into my car and drive away. Please, Geoff, talk to me. I want to help you.'

I've got this gut feeling... the memory of his words to Riley crawled from the darkness... *especially now I've heard your voice...*

Light from the concrete staircase filtered onto the level through the glass panels in the double doors.

She peered into the darkness ahead of her and tried, 'Geoff? Please, Geoff, if you can't speak and God knows I understand having just lost your lovely mother, please make a noise to let me know you haven't thrown yourself over the side of the car park.'

Her voice and slowly advancing footsteps were now flattened as she imagined the space closing down on itself, condensing into a cube of crushed concrete, metal and flesh.

She looked to the left and saw sodium streetlight pouring past a concrete column supporting the weight of the floor above her head.

'Geoff?' A plea from the heart of a forlorn tease.

She turned again at the descending footsteps beyond the doors leading from the level. The footfall was followed by a bizarre and eerie whistling that sounded like it was pouring though a broken and tattered heart hung up to dry.

Clay looked through the glass in the doors and saw a blonde woman pass by the fourth floor. The blonde carried on and, although her hair looked vibrant and natural, she had the freakish air of an individual who had undergone too much poorly delivered plastic surgery.

And as quickly as she'd come into sight, she was out of sight.

This is my danger. This is my decision. This is my responsibility, she told herself as she walked deeper into the darkness. I opted to be the bait. And then I opted to go it alone.

Below, an ambulance screeched towards the front of the Royal and she either heard or imagined she heard something go click behind her.

She turned. Nothing.

'Hello?'

I think we should meet up soon, get talking together face to face...

Just a memory.

'Geoff?' Nothing other than shadows as she made her way backwards towards the doors.

She turned, made out a broad band of switches and pressed them down, one after the other up to the eight.

Overhead in the ceiling in the ceiling, lights flickered and burst into life, drowning the shadows in blue illumination and swallowing the darkness whole.

She looked around at the space and saw that she was completely alone.

Clay put the Glock back inside her coat pocket and felt the deepest disappointment as she made her way back to her car, the only vehicle she could see on the fourth floor.

I won't tell anybody, she replied to a voice inside herself. *I won't tell anyone on the team about what I did. I won't tell Thomas about the risk I took. No one needs to know.*

She pressed the car key to open her car and, hearing the action of the car locking, realised she hadn't locked it. Clay pressed again, opened the car door and sat behind the wheel. Closing the door over, she heard herself let out a long sigh.

Clay looked down and leaned forward to turn the key in the ignition.

'Excuse me?'

A voice behind her.

She reached into her coat for the gun.

The first blow to her skull was heavy but deflected by the head rest. She saw stars and random patterns of light.

She squeezed the Glock from her pocket and looked into the rear-view mirror as the second blow came down towards her. Clay dipped but the heavy instrument clipped her head and sent her sense of gravity spinning upwards in a wild spiral.

Clay saw. Clay forced her eyes wide as the tug of unconsciousness turned into a restraint that couldn't be denied.

Clay looked.

A thick head of blond hair, freakish, and something sad and wild glinting across the surface of a pair of dark eyes.

She raised the gun and the effect was immediate.

The back window was smashed. The door opened.

The gun fell from her hands and, in those last moments of wakefulness, she felt the Glock skitter under her seat.

She slumped forward, felt the goodnight kiss of the steering wheel as her forehead made contact with its curve.

As darkness took over, the last of Clay's senses told her that there were ambulances and traffic out there and someone had been there who smelt of something expensive.

Her senses dulled and, within a moment, Clay was buried alive in darkness.

88

9.30 pm

Detective Sergeant Karl Stone stood in the space beneath the floorboards in Edgar McKee's living room and looked around at the bagged-up contents of his flat. DVDs, CDs and magazines were in three separate sacks. Each item of clothing from his wardrobe was in a bag of its own, waiting to be ferried back to Trinity Road for forensic inspection.

Detective Sergeant Terry Mason walked to the door of the living room with an air of intense disappointment and two bags containing a bottom bed sheet and a plain duvet cover.

'Anything on the sheets?' asked Stone, glancing at the mammoth collection of pornography on DVD.

'The bed sheet and the duvet cover look like they're freshly clean on. To the naked eye, there are no traces of semen or saliva. McKee had a dirty mind but his living space is squeaky clean. There's no way he could've held a cat captive here, let alone a couple of women. Anything from the neighbours, Karl?'

'Clive Winters has spoken with all of them. Nothing to report. McKee keeps himself to himself. They're all singing the same song. He'll say *good morning* or *good afternoon* as he passes you on the stairs, but that's the end of it. He goes out to work in the morning, returns early evening. No one knew his name or what he does for a living.'

'Anything about his white transit van?' asked Winters.

DS Mason's assistant, Sergeant Paul Price, appeared behind him in the doorway.

'None of them have ever seen him in or around a white van. He walks out of the house, he walks back into the house. No white van,' said Mason.

'What have you got, Pricey?'

'A passport. An address book. A diary.' Price showed the bagged haul to Mason. 'From a drawer in his bedroom. He travels to Thailand most years by the stamps on his passport. The diary's just a functional one, times and dates of appointments, nothing about the inner workings of his mind. He visits three different prostitutes on a regular basis. He's heavily oversexed but so far there's nothing to connect him with abduction, murder or mutilation. Not from here anyway.' Price looked directly at Mason. 'Shall we start loading the van, Terry?'

'Let's make a start.'

Stone made his way out of the living room and into the spartan bedroom. The floorboards were propped up against the wall near the bed and mattress, which were covered in bubble wrap. The wardrobe was open and empty, and next to this was a bench press, a barbell and a collection of heavy free-standing weights. He made a series of snapshots of Edgar McKee's life and felt a wave of depression.

In the cramped kitchen, he opened the freezer door and saw a huge range of expensive cuts of meat in the top drawer. In the second drawer down, there were plastic boxes containing what looked like frozen soup, each box labelled by days of the week.

Detective Constable Clive Winters walked past the kitchen doorway with a sack of pornographic DVDs in one hand and magazines in the other.

'Clive?' He stopped. 'Ask Pricey for the contact details of his three lady friends. We'll have to talk to them about Edgar McKee. I'll leave that one with you. OK?'

'I'll do it as soon as I've offloaded this filth on to the van.'

As Stone headed for the narrow hallway and the door leading out, his iPhone buzzed in his hand.

'Karl, where are you?'

It was Sergeant Harris.

'Edgar McKee's flat. What's up?'

'Do you know where Eve is?'

'No, I haven't seen her since she was down at the Albert Dock.'

'No one knows where she is and she's not answering her iPhone. She told Bill Hendricks she was going to the mortuary but when we spoke to the duty mortician, he hadn't seen or heard from her at all. We're tracking the progress of her car on CCTV. She did an about turn on Sefton Street and headed towards the city centre.'

'Where's she at?' asked Stone, a ball of anxiety forming inside him.

'At the moment, as far as we know, in the direction of the Anglican cathedral. Look, there's something pretty major turned up here.'

There were voices in the background, animated and loud, but Stone couldn't make out what was being said.

'What's going on?' he asked.

'Edgar McKee's going on. He's just walked in off the street and presented himself to me.'

'Keep him there, Sarge. And I want a running commentary on the progress of Eve's car on CCTV. Guide me into her path.'

Stone hurried down the stairs towards his car and worked out the quickest route to the Anglican cathedral.

As he got into his car, Clay's words echoed inside his head. *The general red alert's off. Mine's still on.*

89

9.44 pm

Detective Sergeant Karl Stone led a stream of police cars heading up London Road and crossing the junction on to Prescot Street in the direction of the mortuary where Clay's car had last been seen on CCTV entering the multi-storey car park.

As he drove into the car park, he opened his window and smelled the heaviness of petrol.

He recalled the instruction he had issued to all cars following him.

When you get inside the car park, wind your windows down.

On the first floor, he surveyed the handful of cars but Clay's wasn't one of them.

He looked over his shoulder and called, 'First two of you, block off this floor!'

There weren't many cars on the second floor, and no sign of Clay's vehicle.

As two cars peeled off to secure the second floor, Stone saw Hendricks directly behind him.

'Call the officers behind you to seal off floor three. I want you to come with me, Bill.'

'What do you think happened?' asked Hendricks.

'Gina Riley told me The Ghoul communicated to Eve that he was in the mortuary attending to his dead mother and identifying her body. She reckons The Ghoul's been hanging around in this neck of the woods at some point this evening.'

Driving up the ramp on to the fourth floor, Stone could hear the blood pumping in his ears and felt his pulse quicken as he turned on to the level.

'It's her car! It's her!' he called back to Hendricks.

Stone turned his headlights on fully on to Clay's car and felt sickened to his core when there was no sign of anyone sitting in the vehicle.

On the concrete ground at the back of Clay's car, fragments of broken glass were scattered.

He pulled up, heard Hendricks slam his door shut. Stone joined him and they hurried towards Clay's car.

'Why did you come here on your own, Eve? For fuck's sake...'

No reply.

Stone arrived at the back of the car, saw the ceiling light flickering inside, but no one and nothing on the back seat.

With mounting dread, he looked at the empty space behind the wheel and made out blood spray on the windows.

He opened the driver's door and saw Clay slumped forward, the back of her head matted with blood.

Gently, he lifted her head from the lower half of the steering wheel and said, 'Eve?'

He lowered her back on to the seat and checked. Her airways were unblocked. She was breathing, and with his index and middle finger he made out a pulse.

'Eve?'

Stone lifted her from the driver's seat and lay her on the ground at the side of the car, placing her in the recovery position.

As he did so, her eyelids fluttered and she winced.

In the background, Stone heard Hendricks calling for an ambulance.

'Eve, it's me, Karl Stone. Bill Hendricks is here. You've been attacked but you've survived and medical help is on its way. Can you hear me?'

She gave the slightest nod of the head and spoke a word that Stone couldn't make out.

'Don't strain yourself, Eve, just stay still and listen to my voice.'

In the background, there was an approaching siren.

'That's the paramedics. Listen, we followed you on CCTV. You turned around on Sefton Street and headed directly to the multi-storey car park. That's how we found you. Try and get your thoughts straight. Why did you come here, alone? What happened when you arrived here?'

Little by little, her eyes opened and her voice became clearer, but the meaning was still lost to Stone.

The paramedics' car turned on to the fourth floor, its siren dying.

She whispered.

'Closer ...'

Stone placed his lips as close to her ear as possible.

Clay straightened up.

'Slow down, Eve,' said Stone.

'Slow down?' She turned, looked at him and blinked herself into consciousness.

'I saw it! I saw. The Ghoul. Its eyes.'

90

10.05 pm

As Detective Sergeant Gina Riley walked into Interview Suite 1, Edgar McKee looked directly at her, his legs outstretched under the table and feet poking out on the other side. He smiled at her, appeared happy and relaxed, and when she sat opposite to him, he extended his hand.

'Keep your legs in, Mr McKee.'

He withdrew his legs and his hand.

She weighed him up with a penetrating glance and looked to Cole at her side.

Close-cropped ginger-grey hair with the stiffness of velcro hooks, a glimmer of youth still lurking beneath his smiling face, he looked like he had been born in a gym and bottle-fed with whey protein from his very first day.

'Who are you?'

'My name's DS Riley and the man to my left is DC Cole.'

He looked at Cole. 'Are you in charge here?'

'DS Riley's in charge. You'll need a solicitor, Mr McKee.'

McKee returned his steady gaze to Riley and she wondered if he was imagining what she would look like without any clothes on.

'I won't be needing a solicitor.'

'You most certainly will,' replied Riley. 'Why have you handed yourself in?'

McKee laughed and shook his head slowly.

'I haven't handed myself in. Handing myself in explicitly suggests I've committed a crime. I haven't committed a crime. I've walked in here of my own accord to this police station because I figured you'd have a young man called Robin Wren in custody. I saw his picture on television, caught on CCTV in my van. Just like me, he hasn't done anything wrong. His father phoned me, told me what I'd already worked out. I came in here to make it clear. Wren and me have done nothing wrong.'

'Were you driving the vehicle in which he was a passenger?'

'I most certainly was. It's my van. I'm the driver. He was the passenger.'

'Mr McKee,' said Cole. 'I'm going to reiterate the message DS Riley gave to you just now. You are going to need a solicitor. You're looking at some incredibly serious charges here.'

'Such as?' His smile broadened as he sat back in the chair and swept Riley up and down with his eyes. She gridlocked him with her whole being, kept him pinned down on the other side of the table, and waited until the sharp edges of his smile faded and he blinked beneath her unyielding gaze.

'Such as murder,' said Riley.

'Murder?' McKee grinned. 'The only person getting killed around here is me.'

Cole pushed a piece of paper across the table towards him.

'Here's a list of duty solicitors. Choose one.'

McKee looked at the space between their heads and randomly jabbed his finger on the paper in front of him. He looked down, lifted his finger and read, 'Monica Davis. She can keep me company while you run yourselves around in ever-decreasing circles.'

He stood up to his full height and his physical presence was imposing. As he stretched his limbs, the sleeves of his anorak rode up and the bottom end of a black and white tattoo became visible on his left wrist. He sat down heavily.

'You clearly don't want to interview me without legal representation. Fine. I'll go and sit in the cells until Monica Davis gets here. But I'd be grateful if you could release Robin Wren from custody right now. He's a highly intelligent and sensitive young man on the autistic spectrum and this experience will be causing him unprecedented levels of stress.'

'Who is he to you?' asked Cole.

'He's my apprentice in the abattoir. He's a vulnerable young man and he really shouldn't be subjected to any of this.'

Cole stood up. 'I'll go and call Monica Davis,' he said as he walked to the door.

'Ask Sergeant Harris to come here and take Mr McKee to the cells,' said Riley.

The door closed and, alone in the room with him, Riley leaned forward.

'Do you understand what Robin's here for, the crime in which he's implicated?'

'The abduction, murder and mutilation of young women. It's all over the media. Got it, DS Riley. As if I'd walk into a police station on behalf of another human being with that sword hanging over my head.'

The concrete certainty that Riley had entertained as she walked into the interview suite deserted her and was replaced by an uncomfortable and rapidly growing vacuum.

'I've given all my details to Sergeant Harris so you can run background checks on me. I'm afraid you're going to be sorely disappointed.' He looked like he'd just had a great idea out of nowhere. 'A woman went missing last night, DS Riley? I was with a prostitute last night. Marlene Black. From the Dream Girls agency. Have a look in my address book.'

He smiled at Riley. *Fuck you!*

'Where's your van?'

'In a lock-up on Derby Lane, a few streets away from where I live.' He dropped a set of keys and a fob in front of Clay. 'It's number seven. It has a blue door.'

A DATE WITH DEATH

'Your licence plate?'

'What of it?'

'It's not legitimate. It's a clone of another legitimate licence plate.'

'I bought the van three weeks ago for cash, through an ad in the *Liverpool Echo*. I haven't registered my details as the new owner with the DVLA because I simply didn't get round to it. I'm not on top of my game when it comes to paperwork. That doesn't make me a murderer, Riley.'

'Have you got the previous owner's contact details?'

'I've got a mobile number on my iPhone for someone called Dave.'

He placed his mobile phone in front of Riley.

There was a knock at the door and Sergeant Harris came into the room.

'Sergeant Harris will take you to the front desk to book you in. Then your twenty-four hours in our custody begins.'

On the way out, Riley closed the door as Sergeant Harris escorted Edgar McKee in the direction of the cells.

'Mr McKee? What job is it you do exactly in the abattoir?'

He looked over his shoulder and smiled.

'I'll tell you when Monica Davis gets here.'

91

10.23 pm

In the reception area of A&E in the Royal Hospital, Karl Stone waited and marvelled at the sights that greeted him.

A woman in her forties in Winnie-the-Pooh pyjamas, suede boots and with rollers in her hair limped past a homeless man stretched out and asleep two rows down. A man dressed as Elf, worse for wear, clutched a blood-stained towel to his head.

He looked at the clock and saw that Clay was well into her treatment for the three punches that she'd received on the back of her head and the wound on her forehead.

Stone walked to the doors leading into the treatment area, opened them and took in the bustle between the curtained-off bays.

A young nurse walked towards him and he showed her his warrant card.

'How is DCI Clay?'

'Ask her yourself in a minute.'

Halfway down the room, Clay emerged from behind a pair of curtains.

Her head was bandaged and, as she walked towards Stone, she looked as if she was fighting a huge internal battle.

'She's all yours,' said the nurse, walking past him into the reception area.

'Eve, what's happening?'

She didn't reply.

'Aren't you staying in for observation?'

'No, Karl. The CAT scan's clear and I'm discharging myself.'

'Are you sure?'

He looked into her eyes and tried to read absence but all he could see was grim determination.

'I'm sure. As you drive me back to Trinity Road, fill me in on anything I've missed.'

92

10.43 pm

'I've sifted through some depressing crap in my time but Edgar McKee's worldly goods are out there in a league of their own.'

Detective Sergeant Terry Mason eyed the contents of Edgar McKee's living room, separated into sections on the long central table that dominated the room he shared with his assistant, Sergeant Paul Price.

On the floor, starting at Price's feet and rising to the level of the tabletop, was a tower of evidence bags. He picked up the top bag and carefully took out a blue denim jacket. He placed the jacket down on a clear plastic sheet on the table and unpeeled a sheet from a lint roller.

'Have you noticed the way the smell from his flat has carried over into our room?' said Price, pressing the sticky sheet on the fabric of the collar.

There was a knock at the door.

'Enter the cesspit,' said Mason.

Poppy Waters, civilian IT expert, entered the room and the normally ever-present smile on her face dissolved instantly as she saw the vast collection of pornographic DVDs on the table.

'Oh, wow,' she said. 'The joy of things to come.' She looked away and a deep blush climbed across her cheekbones.

Mason pointed at two evidence bags at the centre of the table.

'We pulled the laptop from McKee's flat. Sergeant Harris took his iPhone from him before Riley took him into the interview suite.'

'Is he in the cells now?'

'Yeah. We're going to have to motor on this one. What's your brief from Eve?'

'Find anything at all on his devices that link him to the dead women and the missing, abducted woman, Francesca Christie.'

'Then we're singing from the same hymn sheet, which is good.'

Poppy picked up the two evidence bags.

'We worked super-fast,' said Price, 'once we had the laptop and the phone. They're both sticky because we used sellotape to pull any fingerprints, palm prints and fabric fibres.'

'I'll be wearing a double layer of latex gloves,' she said, reaching the door.

'If you come up with anything, Poppy, as soon as you've spoken to Eve, let us know. It could influence the complexion of our search.'

As she closed the door after herself, Mason took in a slow in-breath, his nose wrinkling.

'Raw meat, sweat disguised by too much cheap body spray. McKee's obviously neat and tidy but some smells you just can't wash away or mask. He must have worked out a lot in his flat.'

Price looked at the sheet of lint roller in his hand and showed the tiny blue fibres lifted from Edgar McKee's jacket to Mason.

'OK, Paul, just keep going. All we need is one stroke of luck and that'll leave him needing a million.'

Mason took the next evidence bag from the pile, removed a blue check brushed cotton shirt and laid it down on the table.

He checked the clock on the wall. Since Edgar McKee had been booked in to custody, the passage of time in his head seemed to have accelerated to double fast. The clock told a similar story.

'I wonder how Winters is getting on with Marlene Black?'

'Who?' Price seemed miles away, engrossed in the task at hand as he opened the front of the jacket and pressed the sticky sheet of lint roller on the inside of the garment.

'The working girl who McKee claimed was entertaining him on the night Francesca Christie went missing.'

'Yeah, yeah. Marlene Black. I heard he wasn't a bit embarrassed when he told Riley about it. I'd feel like somehow my whole life was a failure if I had to pay a woman to have sex with me.'

Mason indicated the DVDs. 'It was clearly a way of life for him. Goes into the newsagents for a paper, then pops into the nearest knocking shop for a shag. Equally weighted financial exchanges.'

'I wonder if he was ever married? My tenner says he was,' said Price.

'My tenner says he was never married. He doesn't like women. That's what his DVD collection's telling me. We'll sort through it after we've been through his clothes.'

'Do you think Marlene Black's going to be a reliable witness?'

Mason carried on lifting fibres from Edgar McKee's brushed cotton shirt and thought about the consequences for her if she wasn't.

'She'll be in a whole lot of shit if she doesn't tell the truth. She'd be looking at jail time. Perverting the course of justice.'

As Mason worked on Edgar McKee's shirt, he offered up a prayer of thanks to the god of forensics. The thought of directly touching anything that had come into contact with Edgar McKee's skin made him want to puke.

Outside, the wind rumbled and rain lashed down.

'OK with you if I open a window, Paul?'

'I was about to ask you the same question.'

The central heating in the room was drawing the sour smells from Edgar McKee's possessions.

As he opened the window, Mason said, 'I tell you who I feel sorry for. Poppy Waters. I can only guess at the shit on his laptop and iPhone.'

93
11.05 pm

The naked arrogance that had defined Edgar McKee during his first visit to Interview Suite 1 was replaced by a calm neutrality that Clay guessed had been prompted and strongly advised by his solicitor, Monica Davis.

McKee stared at the digital clock on the audio recorder to his left as Clay formally opened the interview; he appeared to neither listen nor care.

Monica Davis chipped in, 'Before you start questioning Mr McKee, he's asked me to read a statement on his behalf. He wants it to be formally reiterated and recorded that he walked into Trinity Road police station with the express purpose of supporting Robin Wren, who should not be here under any circumstances whatsoever. Edgar McKee and Robin Wren are innocent of any criminal charges relating to the abduction, murder and mutilation of young women in the north-west of England, namely Warrington and Liverpool.'

Clay eyeballed McKee. 'I hear you.' She looked at his fists bunched on the table in front of her and they were massive. 'Let's start with your van, Edgar, your Ford Transit van. Problem number one.'

'For?'

'You. Just before I came downstairs to interview you, I received a phone call from Detective Sergeant Stone, the officer I assigned to go to your lock-up. The van wasn't there. The lock-up was completely empty.'

Clay took out her iPhone and pulled up the roll of images Stone had sent to her. She showed the screen to Edgar McKee, who frowned.

'Is that the door of your lock-up?' asked Clay, pointing to a dark door with a number 7 painted crudely in thick strokes of white paint.

'Yes.'

She scrolled. 'Is this the interior of your lock-up?'

'It looks like.'

'There was nothing there, Edgar. Certainly no white van. Nothing. What do you say to that?'

'Was there any sign of tampering to the lock or damage to the door?' asked Edgar McKee.

'No.'

'Where's the van, Edgar?' Hendricks waded in.

'I really don't know.' He looked thoughtful as his fists tightened on the table. 'I can only assume two things here. One. Someone's managed to open the lock-up and steal the van. Two. Your colleagues have removed the van in an attempt to stitch me up.'

'Do you really believe that we're living in the year 1973, Edgar?' Hendricks sounded in a place between disbelief and amusement. 'We've got a lot of people out there looking for your van. Why don't you cut yourself some slack and tell us where it is?'

'If I knew where it was I'd tell you, because of the complete lack of forensic evidence linking me to these murders.'

'The way it looks at the moment, Edgar, you're concealing a massive piece of evidence linking you to multiple murders. What were you doing on the footpath between Allerton Towers and Allerton Manor Golf Course late in the afternoon on Wednesday 1st December?'

'I was taking Wren home. He was going on about a fictional superhero of his own making. It was pouring down with rain. The traffic was a nightmare. I saw three near crashes. I told him to be quiet so I could concentrate on driving, but that I'd take him some place where I'd park up and he'd tell me about Captain Cyclone. The lad's father is my line manager in the abattoir and had just thrust his son under my wing. I wanted to get the relationship off to a good start but I couldn't drive safely and listen to him waffling on.'

McKee looked sideways at his solicitor, who kept her head down and made notes in a spiral-bound book.

'That's not how Wren's telling it,' said Clay.

'How's he telling it?'

'Wren's version of events has you taking him there from the abattoir.'

'The thing I don't get is this,' said Hendricks. 'You work in Old Swan. Wren lives in Gateacre. Wouldn't the most obvious route from the Swan to Gateacre be to go down Queens Drive and get into Gateacre through the Childwall district? The footpath in Allerton is nowhere near there, not even for a *diversion* as you call it. Especially on a day when you said you'd seen three near crashes.'

'I just took him there because it was quiet and he told me he was enjoying the ride.'

'You like watching films, don't you, Edgar?' asked Clay. 'We're going to show you a sequence of CCTV films that have been edited together of your journey from Old Swan to Allerton and then back to Gateacre. Before you watch it, I'm going to give you a potted account of that journey. You drove from the abattoir to Queens Drive. You proceeded to the footpath via Allerton Road. You drove to Heath Road and Mather Avenue after you'd stopped at the footpath. You made your way up to Menlove Avenue. Up to Woolton Park and down to Gateacre.'

Clay turned her laptop round, pressed play and drilled her eyes into Edgar McKee's face as he watched the CCTV footage of his van travelling around South Liverpool. He was deadpan but Clay noticed a sound under the table. A slow, heavy rhythm of a foot tapping against the floor of the interview suite.

'You recognise your van? The journey you went on with Robin Wren?'

'Yes.'

'You can say "no comment" at any point in the interview. I did advise you to do so,' said his solicitor.

'Only guilty people say "no comment". I've got nothing to hide...'

Seeing that he was giving nothing away in his face or eyes, Clay noticed his hands, the thickness of his fingers, the bulging veins and the network of faded freckles beneath the forest of stunted ginger hairs.

'All done?' Clay turned her laptop round. 'Anything to say, Edgar?'

'Yes. So what?'

His solicitor ripped a piece of paper from her pad and slid it along the table to him. He read it.

'Yes,' said Edgar. 'It puts me at the place where a body was dumped. But how many vehicles go past the top of the footpath at the Menlove Avenue end and the Allerton Road end at the bottom? Get real, all of you. I was one of thousands.' He pointed at Clay with a look of pure moral outrage, jabbed his index finger at her and said, 'You're clutching at straws and you know it.'

'No, I'm not clutching at straws, Edgar. I've got *you* down to the last *full stop*. Put your finger down, it makes you look petulant.'

'Go no comment, Mr McKee. Really.' McKee looked at his solicitor. 'You've gone above and beyond being co-operative in this situation and it's not doing you any favours. You've made a salient point about the volume of traffic in and around the Allerton footpath. These two officers are gunning for you. Trust me. I've seen it many times in this police station.'

'Bent coppers. No comment it is then.'

'Thank you for that, Ms Davis. It's advice for sure, but it's bad advice,' said Clay. 'Edgar…'

'It's Mr McKee to you, Clay.'

'Mr McKee, I'm not going to ask you any more questions because I don't want to hear you saying no comment over and over like a parrot. I'm going to tell you what's been going on.

'Wednesday 1st December was Wren's first day at the abattoir, that was the first time you met him. You knew in advance that your line manager's autistic son was coming to be apprenticed to you. You drove to work that day with the scalped and faceless corpse of Amanda Winton in the back of your white van. When you dumped her, you took Robin Wren along for the ride because no one would ever believe that a murderer disposing of a body would take along a young man with learning difficulties. You'd started grooming him and you cynically used him as a smokescreen. On TV, you saw Robin Wren on CCTV in your van at the scene of a body drop-off. You came here because you had nowhere else to go.

'Later, you saw us crawling over the building you live in. You turned up protesting Robin Wren's innocence, to further distance yourself from your crime. *Mr* McKee, you're a misogynist, a murderer with the brain of a high stakes gambler.

'In the abattoir, your job is to skin the corpses of cattle. According to Robin Wren's dad, you're the fastest skinner of corpses and the most talented skinner of corpses that he's come across in over twenty years. You applied these skills post-mortem to Sandra O'Day, Annie Boyd and Amanda Winton.'

Silence.

'Question. Where is Francesca Christie?'

Edgar McKee shook his head and, sitting back in his seat, looked across the table at Clay with his former show of arrogance.

'See what I mean, Mr McKee. Me. You. Down to the last full stop.'

94

11.14 pm

In Edgar McKee's address book there was a contact card for Dream Girls and Marlene Black's name was written on the back of it. All major credit cards accepted.

As Winters pulled his car into Armitage Gardens, three sides of a square of semi-detached houses built around a large central green, he went over the process by which he had tracked down Marlene Black.

A call through to Dream Girls had been met with suspicion by a woman who sounded like she had been a heavy smoker from the age of six. When he offered to send his warrant card through to the agency's email address, the woman he'd spoken to on the phone had wanted to know why the Merseyside Constabulary were interested in Marlene Black.

The words *murder enquiry* altered everything in the stop-start conversation.

At his desk in the incident room at Trinity Road police station, he'd hung up and waited. Within two minutes, his landline rang out. Marlene.

Winters got out of his car and looked for 97 Armitage Gardens, the address Marlene had given him when she called him.

93. 95. 97 Armitage Gardens.

Winters tapped the double-glazed front door as Marlene had politely asked him to. The hall light came on instantly and a woman's form hurried to the door.

'Is that the police? DC Winters?'

'Yes.'

The front door opened without hesitation.

Her face was clean, without any trace of lipstick, and her black hair was snatched back in a bunch.

Winters showed Marlene his warrant card.

'Come in,' she said, in a voice made up of multiple whispers.

She closed the front door and said, 'Follow me.'

Barefoot, she was dressed in a red check shirt with grey jeans, and she looked nothing like she'd sounded on the phone. As he passed the closed door of the front room, Winters heard a movie playing on the television set, and it sounded like a romantic comedy.

As Winters sat at her kitchen table and she closed the door, he noticed a baby monitor plugged into the wall. She sat down and faced him, anxiety pouring from her.

'What's the matter?'

Listening to the quietness in her voice, he wondered how many other people were in the house and why she'd invited him to her home as opposed to meeting him in a neutral space, an option he'd given her up front.

'Who's in the house apart from you?'

'My two small children and my mother.'

'This is a sensitive matter. Where are they?'

'My mother's in the front room watching TV and my children are in bed. Can you please tell me why you're here?'

'It's in relation to your work as an escort, Marlene. We have a man in custody at the moment in relation to a very serious offence...'

'My mother has no idea of what I do,' she interrupted. 'She thinks I work in a pub in town.'

'Marlene, I'm not here to upset your apple cart. I just need to know if you could confirm or deny his alibi.'

'There's probably going to be a huge problem here. I'd say most of my male clients are married, and so are many of my female clients. They don't give me their real names. I certainly don't give them mine. I'm not Marlene Black. My real name's Susan Hurst. Who do you have in custody?'

'Edgar McKee.'

'Edgar? Edgar McKee? Are you serious?'

'Yes, I'm serious, Susan.'

'What on earth's he done?'

'You sound surprised.'

'Edgar's a regular. He's kinky but he's gentle. And he told me from the word go that he wasn't going to hide anything from me. When he told me his name, he showed me his driving licence. I didn't tell him my real name. This was his choice. That was mine. I've spent time with him this week.'

'When?'

'Last night. Thursday, 2nd December. The Travelodge.'

'What time?'

'Eight o'clock until ten at night.'

Shit, thought Winters, the CCTV footage of Francesca Christie walking away from the Albert Dock just after half past eight replaying in his mind, the last time she was seen.

'Are you absolutely certain about this, Susan?'

'It was last night, for heaven's sake. Of course I'm certain.'

'What room did you use?'

'The room we always use if it's available. Room 1002.'

'Whereabouts in the building?'

'Top floor. Do you know what?'

She walked to the freezer in the corner of the kitchen, opened the door and pulled out a frozen leg of lamb.

'Whenever I service him, he always brings me a gift from the abattoir where he works. Last night it was this leg of lamb. The time before that...' She thought about it as she placed the leg of lamb back in the freezer and shut the door. 'It was a load of top-end T-bone steaks. He doesn't have to do that. Hardly any of them do express gratitude or give me gifts. With most of them it's like, *I've paid for it now so suck my dick or kiss my snatch and act like you're grateful.* Not Edgar. He's a gentleman. What's he up for?'

'Murder.'

'Oh, fuck right off, pardon my French. Some of the punters are rough. He's not one of them.'

She fell silent, listened hard to a noise in the house that Winters couldn't make out.

'OK, change the subject. I never quite know what she hears or understands.'

The kitchen door opened and an elderly woman peered in as if looking through a dense fog. Winters worked out she was well advanced in her dementia.

'Who? Who is this, Susan?'

'It's Clive, the manager of the Philharmonic pub. We're having a business meeting.'

'Don't be silly. It's your dad, Susan.'

'I'm not your husband, sorry, Mrs Hurst,' said Winters.

'Mum, go and watch the ending of *Silver Linings Playbook*. I'll come and join you soon.' Susan's mother nodded even though she looked a thousand miles from certain. 'Go on, Mum. See you soon.'

She stood up, gave her mother a gentle push on the shoulder and closed the door. From the baby monitor came the sound of a young child smacking its lips as it turned over in its sleep. It sounded exactly like Winters' son when he was two years old, and an unfathomable sadness filled his being.

'Mind if I take a picture of you, Susan?'

'OK, but why?'

'To show Edgar McKee we aren't bluffing when we say we went to see you. He's questioning just about everything.'

Susan sat back down and Winters took a picture of her on his iPhone.

'My mother's got Alzheimer's. I don't know how much longer I can keep her at home. I don't want to put her into care but the periods of clarity are diminishing and the confused times are getting longer and more severe.'

'Just as a matter of interest,' said Winters. 'Why are we having this conversation here?'

'I couldn't work tonight because my regular babysitter...' She rolled her eyes. 'And *mother* sitter couldn't make it. Like I was going to meet you somewhere else and leave my mother in charge of Charlie and David.'

'I did wonder.'

Her face lit up as if she'd had a moment of pure inspiration. Susan walked to the pad of shopping lists on the wall unit next to the oven, tore off the top sheet and removed the pen that was held next to the paper by a magnet. She placed the paper on top of the nearest unit and, briefly, wrote down a few words.

Walking towards Winters, she folded the paper into four.

'Ask the person interviewing him to ask him what he got up to in the Travelodge with Marlene Black. The answer's on this piece of paper.'

As Susan handed Winters the folded paper, through the baby monitor there were the opening notes of a very young child waking up in the night.

'I have baby monitors in every downstairs room in the house. You never quite know where you're going to be when they need you most.'

She opened the kitchen door and headed to the stairs.

'Can you see yourself out, Clive. I'm not being rude.' The sound of one of her sons crying floated down the stairs as she hurried up them. 'I'm sorry, but you've completely got the wrong man.'

95

11. 15 pm

Francesca Christie blinked.

It seemed to take a whole minute for her eyelids to open and reconnect.

She blinked again, felt the weight of her eyelids like a pair of wall-mounted tapestries.

She counted slowly as she blinked again. Four seconds, not sixty.

Francesca heard her own breath and listened for other clues in the building beyond the impenetrable darkness around her, but all that came back was silence.

Pulling at the chains that bound her, there was no slack and no sign of weakness where the first metal link was buried in the wall.

I cannot move. I cannot escape...

Her flow of thought was interrupted by a sound from the next room.

It was an in-breath, followed by a sigh of the deepest satisfaction.

Someone, something, was moving behind the adjoining wall and door.

A key turned in the lock and her heart overflowed with dread.

The door opened and the hinge creaked like a pair of deaf people attempting song.

Red light poured in through the open doorway and she tried not to think what was coming next.

A human form appeared in the red glow, stepping into her cell as if on tiptoes.

There was a click and she was astonished as a wall-mounted light flooded the space with steady and continuous white light.

She blinked and blinked until the blinding light settled and the walls around her came into focus. She heard footsteps coming towards her and wished with all that she had left that they'd go away.

The sound of a tuneless melody came towards her and she shut her eyes, wondering if she'd tripped over the edge of sanity and was on a rapidly shifting downward spiral.

'Open your eyes, look at me!'

She opened her eyes, made out a dark human form that could have been carved from stone.

'Listen to this, Francesca!'

She heard the recorded sound of a door opening and a woman's voice announcing, 'The Judge wants to see you in his chambers.' Her voice became softer, quieter. 'I think you're going to be pleased.'

'Thank you, Rhonda.'

She heard the sound of a door closing and recalled the telephone conversation she'd had with a man she had thought was a barrister called James Griffiths.

'Want to hear it again, Francesca?'

'No.'

'Fooled you. Look at me…'

She blinked and the figure standing over her came more into focus. Making out the head, she noticed that it had long hair that hung over its shoulders. The face between the hair was pink but she couldn't make out the features.

'Look at me.'

'I am looking at you but I can't see you properly because I've been plagued with all kinds of broken light and pitch darkness and now this blinding white light.'

Francesca felt as if her soul was rising from her body, lifting through each pore of her skin and floating to the ceiling above her head, forming a cloud in the shape of her being.

She felt a hand against her face, the fingers flowing over her cheek. The smell triggered a sharpening of her senses and she was able to make out a vividly painted mouth and two dark circles either side of the nose.

The person sitting on the mattress next to her was lit from behind and Francesca could make out that the hair was blonde.

'Help me!' said Francesca, battling to get a much better impression of the thing before her.

Moment by moment, breath by breath, the facial features became clearer to see, and it was her first impression that the person beside her was young and pretty.

Another smell hit her, expensive and applied subtly.

Under the fragrance came the edge of another smell, a sour chemical aroma that drifted from the face and the hair of the person sitting on the bed.

Francesca looked into its eyes and, as they came alive, there was something very wrong about them and the way they sat within the skin around them.

'Look at me...'

Francesca looked at the nose, saw that the skin beneath the nostrils rose and fell slightly with each breath.

'Look at me...'

The skin around the mouth continued to move in the silence that followed the husky, whispered instruction.

Francesca closed her eyes, wanted the person on the mattress to disappear into thin air.

'Look at me...'

Francesca opened her eyes and drew in a breath to stop herself from crying out at the shock of the close proximity of the face to hers.

She looked down at the line of the chin. There appeared to be a scar running along the jawline. The hair hung down on to Francesca's face.

The eyes were close enough now for the eyelashes to brush against hers.

The eyes glinted and Francesca had a flashback to the eyes in the rear-view mirror of her car as she drove away from the Albert Dock with a blade at her throat and a maniac at her back.

She felt its lips pressing against hers and a tongue sinking into her mouth, lapping against her taste buds.

Francesca found a piece of herself on the ceiling and looked down at the scene below.

She was being passionately kissed by a young blonde woman who sounded like an animal.

Francesca sank down into her body and pressed a hand into its hair.

Chemicals flooded her nose and throat as it snatched her hand away and sat up.

The thing before her was wearing a mask. The mask shifted. It was made of skin and hair.

Everything became crystal clear.

The thing stood up.

'Look at me!'

It was wearing the scalp and face of a dead woman.

Francesca held her breath.

'Look at me...'

It turned and walked towards the door, turned off the light and disappeared into the room next door.

The eyes beneath the skin seared her mind.

In pitch darkness, Francesca Christie screamed as the thing next door wept with joy.

96
11.18 pm

'I just called you on the off chance you'd be free,' said Thomas.

Clay looked around the incident room, saw that Gina Riley was busy skipping between two laptops.

'It's lovely to hear from you, Thomas.'

'I wanted to hear your voice before I go to bed.' She could hear the relief in his voice.

She made an involuntary noise, a sigh that could have passed for a solitary laugh. 'I so wish I was going there with you, love. How's Philip?'

'He's fine. He didn't quite make it to the end of the second half of the match. I had to carry him to bed.'

The tender image softened the sharp edges of the day's disappointments, frustrations and fears.

'How's it going there?'

'Not so well.' She dropped the volume of her voice. 'The evidence so far says our prime suspect's the wrong man. Don't quote me on that just yet. Every part of me says I should believe what I've just said is true, but at the same time every part of me says *no, I don't believe that.*'

'You've been here before. Trust your instinct. Go with your hunch. Is he a vile fucker?'

'To quote Shakespeare, yes.'

Across the room, Riley looked in Clay's direction and held up her right thumb.

'Thomas, I'm so sorry to cut this short. Something's just come up.'

'No worries.'

'Go into Philip's room. Kiss him for me. Tell him I love him, even if he is asleep. And I love you.'

'I love you back.'

'Goodnight, love.'

Standing, she replaced the receiver and walked over to Riley.

Clay looked at the two screens on Riley's desk. On one screen was the Home Office computer system, information sharing for all constabularies across the UK, HOLMES. On the other was the National Police Computer.

'Catriona West, 1940–2001,' said Riley. 'There's not much. The bulk of what we have is from our investigation on Merseyside. She had no criminal convictions and the only references we have to her on both systems relate to her death in 2001. She was the victim of a hit and run, she died on Mather Avenue before the ambulance got there.'

'Did we pull the driver?'

Riley shook her head.

'If it'd happened now, we'd have easily pulled the driver with the amount of CCTV out there. She died in the June of 2001. It was only after terrorists flew aeroplanes into the Twin Towers in New York in the September of that year that the West went ape shit about security. Hence, the dawn of the golden age of CCTV.'

'Is that it?'

'That's it. I've trawled through the systems for hours looking for some other crumbs. Let's put it this way. It wasn't an in-depth investigation because there were no witnesses and no evidence and no realistic chance of catching the driver.'

'Thank you for trying. Hit and run. *Stolen in an instant.*'

Clay pulled up the image on her iPhone of Catriona West, taken from her grave.

'At least we know what happened to you now, Catriona.'

But what's your link to The Ghoul? Clay asked herself.

97

11.30 pm

Five minutes after Clay outlined her plan to Sergeant Harris, the custody sergeant opened the door of Robin Wren's cell and Clay found the young man sitting on the bench staring ahead of himself, with a grey blanket over his head and shoulders.

Clay stepped inside the cell and said, 'Wren, take off your blanket and step this way with me, please.' He didn't move. She took the kindness out of her voice and replaced it with iron. 'Now!'

He stood up immediately and the blanket slipped from his head and shoulders on to the floor.

'I want to go home right now.'

'We're working very hard to make that happen for you, Wren,' said Clay. 'But you've got to play your part too if you want to make it happen. Come with me.'

'Where are we going?' he asked, as he followed Clay out of the cell and into the corridor.

Clay allowed him to position himself behind Sergeant Harris and ahead of herself. She placed a hand gently between his shoulder blades and spoke softly. 'Keep going, Wren. You're doing just great.'

They turned a corner and passed through automatic sliding doors.

'Are you going to interview me again, DCI Clay?'

'Not just yet.'

'Then where are you taking me?'

'For a walk. OK, we can stop right here.'

Wren read out loud the metal plate on the door. 'Interview Suite 1. I don't like this room, take me away from it.'

Clay's iPhone rang out in her bag. She took it out and saw WINTERS on the display.

'Sergeant Harris, can you go on that message for me. Please go back to the cells and return as quickly as possible.'

Clay connected the call.

'What's going on?' asked Wren.

'Wait a minute, Wren,' said Clay. 'Clive, how did you get on?'

She walked away from Wren's hearing.

'Badly. She was with him last night during the time window in which Francesca Christie was snatched. They were in the Travelodge on the edge of Liverpool One. She genuinely seems to like him. Like he was her star trick. She told me to check the CCTV in the hotel. That would back up the alibi she was providing for him.'

'Anything else?'

'She's written down what they did together during that time. If you ask him about that and his version of events tallies up with hers, that'll confirm that they were together.'

'Where are you?' asked Clay. 'Hey, turn around, Wren, or else!'

'Or else what?' He turned his back on Clay. 'What have I done wrong now?'

'I'm on the edge of Garston Village, a minute away from Trinity Road.'

'Put your foot down, get here as quickly as you can. Come directly to Interview Suite 1 with that piece of paper.'

She closed the call down.

'Can you hear that, Wren?'

'What?'

The corridor was completely quiet.

'Listen...'

Around the corner came the hiss of a pair of automatic doors opening and a voice talking softly to someone else.

'What's going on?' asked Wren.

'The man you just heard was Sergeant Harris.'

His voice came closer.

'Is he talking to himself?'

'No.'

A female voice blended into the mixture of muffled sound.

'Then who is he talking to?'

Clay turned her iPhone on to video, went to stand behind Wren and pointed it at the back of his head and the corridor in front of him.

McKee turned the corner, in between his solicitor, Ms Davis, and Sergeant Harris. Wren's hands flew to his mouth and Edgar stopped dead in his tracks.

'Wren, I worked out you'd be here. I came to rescue you, to show the police that it was all a dreadful mistake you being in here. I'm so sorry you're here,' said McKee. 'I blame myself but I am trying to save you and I will save you one way or another.'

Wren seemed to grow over ten centimetres as he stood to attention and dropped his hands to his sides. With his right hand he gave McKee the stiffest, most formal of military salutes.

'Wren, put your hand down,' said McKee.

Wren didn't move, kept his hand frozen in mid-air.

Clay walked in front of Wren, filmed the look of righteous solemnity on his face as he walked towards Edgar McKee.

'Hand down, Wren. That's a good lad.'

Wren held an index finger to his lips and made a soft shushing sound.

'Captain Cyclone and agents in the field are safe, Edgar. Thanks to you and me.'

'Captain Cyclone isn't real, Wren. I really don't know what you mean. There are no agents in the field.'

'Pardon?' asked Wren.

'It's a game we play.'

'It was all in my head. You made it come to life. And now you're saying it's not real? Is that what you're saying, Colonel Edgar McKee?'

The light in Wren's eyes faded and was quickly replaced by darkness and hurt.

'It's all right, Wren. We can work all this out,' said Clay. 'Separate the fact from the fiction.'

She turned her iPhone on Edgar McKee, saw him tailspin into sudden confusion.

'This is all really highly irregular,' said Ms Davis with a moral outrage that simply didn't ring true.

The door leading into the corridor of interview suites opened behind Clay, and the coldness of the night outside came in with the caller.

'Ms Davis, it's not as irregular as young women being murdered, scalped and having their faces ripped off post-mortem,' said Clay. 'We're going to talk Captain Cyclone to you, Wren, after we've talked Captain Cyclone to Edgar, here.'

'She's tricking you, Wren,' said McKee. 'You've done nothing wrong, neither have I. But she wants to make you feel like you've done something wrong. That's her role in this world. Say something, Wren. Let me know that we're still mates.'

'We're still mates.' Wren looked as if he was about to break down into floods of tears and was digging down to his deepest grit to hold himself together. 'Are you feeling better, Edgar?'

'I'm right as rain, mate.'

'Have you stopped going to the toilet?'

McKee looked at his solicitor and at Clay.

'Are you going to interview me or what?'

'That's what I brought you down here for. Sergeant Harris, please escort Mr McKee into the interview suite and then take Wren back down to the cells.'

McKee walked past Clay as he followed Sergeant Harris into the interview suite, looked at her, the rising darkness inside him forming in his eyes. 'You're clutching at straws. You're pathetic.'

'Take a seat in the interview suite, Mr McKee. Detective Sergeant Hendricks is waiting for you. And calm yourself down.'

Winters handed Clay a piece of paper.

'It's what he got up to last night with Marlene Black, aka Susan Hurst.'

Clay unfolded the paper, noticed the neatness of the writing and the filth within it.

'Charmed, I'm sure. Clive, go check out the CCTV at the Travelodge.'

98
11.51 pm

Clay took her place next to Hendricks across the table from Edgar McKee and his solicitor, and didn't take her eyes away from his reptilian gaze.

'I've got some good news for you, Mr McKee. For now, at least.'

'You saw it with your own eyes, Clay, and heard it with your own ears just out there. Anything Robin Wren may or may not have said to you counts for shit. He's intelligent, yes. But he's disabled and lives in a world of his own. What do you say to that?' asked McKee.

'I'd say that it's my place to ask questions and yours to answer them.'

Clay looked at the words on the page in her hand, felt the sharpness of the irony of the pastel flowers that adorned its borders.

'What were you doing, Mr McKee, between eight and ten o'clock last night?'

He smiled as he gazed back at Clay.

'I told you the first time we met. I was in the Travelodge by Liverpool One with a prostitute.'

'Her name?'

'Marlene Black.'

'Is that her real name?'

'Don't know.'

'How long were you with her?'

'I booked her for two hours.'

'Are you a regular client of hers?'

'Pretty much.'

'What did you do together?' asked Clay.

'Sex. What do you think we'd do? Play Monopoly?'

'Specifically, what kind of sex did you have?'

Edgar McKee looked at his solicitor, the smile on his face now gone.

'I don't see where this is going, DCI Clay,' said Ms Davis.

'We've been to see her. She wrote down on this piece of paper what kind of sex Mr McKee had with her. She suggested to DC Winter that if I asked Mr McKee what kind of sexual activity had passed between them, that it would make the alibi she was giving him more concrete. I'm giving Mr McKee a break.'

'Answer the question, Mr McKee,' instructed Ms Davis.

'Oral sex and anal sex,' said Edgar McKee, in a flat voice that sounded like it could have been ordering fish and chips.

Clay slid the paper across the table to Edgar McKee and said, 'Bullseye. Well done. She speaks very highly of you, according to DC Winters.'

'I don't know anything about her. I don't even know her real name. But I give her a lot of work because she's good at her job, end of.'

'There's no personal relationship between the two of you?' asked Hendricks.

'Get real. It's money for sex and sex for money. That's what I call an honest relationship. I've got an alibi. I didn't fucking kidnap anyone. I was with a pro. Can I go home now?'

'No, certainly not,' said Clay. 'Your twenty-four hours isn't up yet. And besides, your flat's being treated as a crime scene. If you do get out from here, you're going to have to find somewhere else to stay until we're ready.'

Ms Davis turned to McKee, held her hand up to cover her mouth and whispered in his ear.

'Do you want to bring it up?' he asked.

'DCI Clay,' said Ms Davis. 'The murders and abductions in Liverpool are linked to a murder in Warrington last August. Correct?'

'It's the same killer,' confirmed Clay.

'My client, Mr McKee, wasn't in the country during that time. I've contacted easyJet and they're going to send confirmation that he flew to Amsterdam on July 30th 2021 and returned to Liverpool John Lennon Airport on August 18th.'

'We'll do the same,' said Clay. 'Had Mr McKee mentioned this to us, that would have been the very first thing we'd have done.'

'I didn't mention it, Clay, because I wasn't even aware that some poor woman in Warrington had been abducted and murdered last August,' said McKee.

'It was a massive news story,' said Hendricks.

'Not in Amsterdam it wasn't.'

'The story rolled on into the autumn, the investigation by the Warrington police. You had no idea?'

'I don't follow the fucking news, for God's sake, it's depressing shit.'

'When did you first become aware of the murder of Sandra O'Day?' asked Hendricks.

Edgar McKee looked again at his solicitor with a puzzled expression and a shortening fuse.

'That's the name of the Warrington victim,' said Clay.

'When Ms Davis told me, about half an hour ago, when we had a meeting. Are you seriously still going to keep me in custody?'

'We can approach the Dutch police for assistance. Is there anyone in Amsterdam who could confirm you were there in the suggested time window?' asked Hendricks.

'Funnily enough, I didn't swap contact details with any of the prostitutes I visited on my summer holiday. And guess what? I didn't get any selfies with them either. Also, also... it was, like, four fucking months ago. They get through dozens of men a day. Do you think they're going to remember me? I don't think so, because I wouldn't remember them, if I tripped over them on the street.'

'How are you feeling, Mr McKee?' asked Clay.

'How do you mean?'

'Coming back to more recent times. As in yesterday. Wren just asked you how you were.'

Edgar McKee shrugged. 'He's autistic. He's random.'

'No, he wasn't being random. I've spoken to his father, Neil. You phoned in sick to the abattoir with diarrhoea and vomiting. How can you have a two-hour sexual marathon with a woman if you've got gastroenteritis?'

'I phoned in sick because I wanted a breather from Wren. How would you feel if he was on your neck every minute of your working day? The lad was driving me nuts, and I'd only been with him for a couple of days. When I woke up on Friday, I just couldn't face it.'

'Well, as the saying goes, Mr McKee...' Clay looked up at the CCTV camera filming the interview. 'Every cloud has a silver lining. If you are found to have done nothing wrong, maybe this could be the lever you can use with the management in the abattoir to get Wren off your neck.'

McKee stood up and folded his arms across his chest.

'Try to help someone. End up in a cell. You're damn right I'm not having any more to do with him. Wren? That's a fucking joke name. He's more of a fucking albatross. What are you smiling at, Hendricks?' asked McKee.

'That was quite a witty play on words. Wren, neck, albatross. I am allowed to smile, Mr McKee.' Hendricks looked at Clay. 'We done for now?'

'Just for now.' She took out her iPhone and called the front desk. 'Sergeant Harris, can you come and collect Mr McKee and take him back to his cell. And can you ask Detective Constable Cole to download some CCTV footage from the interview suite on to my laptop.'

She looked at Edgar McKee, read the twists and turns inside his head.

'Something wrong, Mr McKee?'

THE PAST

1982

From her bedroom window, she could see her little brother standing perfectly still on the snow-dusted gravel in front of the house, in between the front door, the evil wind that pressed down on the earth and the black taxi that throbbed near the wide-open gateway.

Dressed in a grey coat and woollen hat, with socks that stretched up to below his knees, his lower thighs were exposed to the fierce cold.

She could feel the cold that pinched at his skin.

'Aren't you at least going to say goodbye to him?'

Her mother's voice rose from the downstairs hallway.

'No!'

Her father sounded like he had no feelings, as if he was colder than the weather outside, like there was nothing solid beneath the shape of his skin.

'Please?'

'I'm going to count to three...'

She filled in the silence that followed this phrase of her father's, the threats, the curses, the darkness, the promised agonies that were housed in his language each time he mouthed it.

Her mother spoke but her voice was like babble, the meaning of the words lost in the bricks and mortar between downstairs and her bedroom.

She looked down at her little brother, standing at an angle to her as he looked at the taxi and the black fumes that poured from the exhaust pipe.

He coughed and shivered but remained like a statue in the place on which he stood.

She tapped on the glass, softly so as not to alert her father to the fact that she was disobeying him during her little brother's final days at home.

You're not to look at him! You're not to talk to him! You're not to say goodbye to him!

Her bedroom door creaked open and she froze, dreading what was coming into the space where she slept, the space where she escaped.

'It's only me...'

She felt the vice around her head unlock. It was Mrs Doyle stepping closer to her. Not *him*. Not *her*. Not *them*.

'Where's he going, Mrs Doyle?'

Silence.

'Away.'

'Away where?'

'Away somewhere. I don't know the details.'

'Is he coming back?'

'I don't know.'

'Will I ever see him again?'

'I don't know.'

She looked out of the window and applied all her concentration to the image of her little brother as the snow started a fresh falling. Still he didn't move, didn't shift his head to watch what was drifting from the sky that pressed down on his little head.

I want to remember, I want to remember you, I want to remember what you looked like the last time I saw you.

Her parents' voices tangled in the space beneath her.

The same tangled sound that had drawn her down the stairs and made her listen to the exchange between her parents.

She recalled the snatches of speech that had made it out of the living room.

'Mrs Doyle?'

'Yes, love?'

'Out of the city.'

'Out of the city?'

Mrs Doyle sounded confused.

'He's being sent away from Liverpool? Right?'

'I don't know.'

'That's miles and miles away. On his own. He's so little.'

Below, her parents' voices faded into a worrying silence.

'I don't know,' said Mrs Doyle. 'I've come to tell you. I'm also leaving today.'

She felt the pain inside her swell but said nothing, knew she'd have done the same thing if she had the chance.

She recognised the sound of her father's footsteps clumping up the stairs.

'You'd better go, Mrs Doyle.'

'Just for now, I'm going nowhere, little girl.'

She felt the warmth of Mrs Doyle's body at her back. The old lady's hands settled on her shoulders, a gentle weight that assisted gravity and kept her feet firmly planted on the floor.

The front door of the house closed and her mother stepped out, carrying two small suitcases. Her long blonde hair floated behind her as the wind bit down.

Her little brother turned to his mother and she said, 'Get into the taxi.'

The door of her bedroom opened and her father said, 'What's this?'

'This, sir, is what will happen if you take another step into this young lady's room. This, sir, is the police. This, sir, is scandal. This, sir, is the end of you in this city. This, sir, is the sum of the terrible things that I know. This, sir, is you versus me.'

Her mother shepherded her little brother towards the taxi.

'You wouldn't dare!'

'I keep a diary, sir. I would dare. Would you?'

He slammed the door and she felt the lack of his presence in the room.

Her little brother stopped at the open back door of the taxi and looked up at her window, looked at her directly in the eyes. He waved his hand and mouthed, 'Goodbye, big sister.'

She waved back.

'Goodbye, little brother.'

Her mother followed him into the back of the taxi and the driver headed the black cab towards the gate.

She knew in her heart that she would never see him again.

The taxi disappeared from view.

'And, so,' she said. 'Off he floats to nowhere.'

DAY FOUR

SATURDAY, 4TH DECEMBER 2021

THANATOPHOBIA

FEAR OF DEATH

Winters looked at the printout of the reservation that Edgar McKee had made at the Travelodge on Thursday, 2nd December and felt a weight forming in his heart. During the time window of his reservation, McKee had booked in at 7.31 pm and booked out at 10.13 pm, according to the information provided to him at the reception desk.

Tommy Hart, head of the hotel's security unit, cued up the CCTV footage from the previous day and asked, 'Which room? Which floor?'

'Room 1002, top floor, please.'

'I can put the footage on fast forward and slow it down any time someone appears on screen, otherwise we're going to be spending a lot of time looking at an empty corridor. We've got CCTV on each stretch of corridor on every floor. Give me a minute and I'll tee up the section where Room 1002 happens on the top floor.'

'Take your time, Tommy. Whenever you're ready...'

Winters pulled up the picture he had taken of Susan Hurst on his iPhone and showed it to Tommy.

'Her working name's Marlene Black. I took this picture of her in her kitchen a few hours ago. She most probably looks entirely different when she's working, make-up, clothing and hair, but this is the woman we're looking for on CCTV.'

Tommy broke off from what he was doing and looked at the picture.

'OK. I know her. By sight. I've seen her round and about in the hotel. I knew what she was up to but she's a discreet operator. Most of the working girls are. We don't like our hotel being used as a knocking shop and we certainly don't encourage it, but what happens behind the closed door of a hotel room is private to the people in it. Unless someone's behaving in a screamingly obvious way, what can we do? Challenge a guest who'll come back with, *how dare you refer to my husband or wife as a hooker?* There's nothing we can say.'

'It's a tightrope you're walking on.'

Winters pulled up Edgar McKee's mugshot, looking directly into the eye of the camera.

'This one was taken tonight when he was booked in at Trinity Road. Do you recognise him?'

'I've seen a lot of him. Edgar McKee. Didn't know his name but it's on last night's reservation. Most of the guys up to his tricks come in using pseudonyms and pay with cash. At least he's not hiding behind a false ID. We'll go from 7.29 pm and take it from there.'

Five minutes passed on fast forward and there was no one on the top floor where Room 1002 was situated. As 7.34 pm rolled into 7.35 pm, someone stepped out of a lift. Tommy Hart paused and slowed down the footage. It was a man talking on an iPhone and walking towards the camera but it wasn't Edgar McKee.

Fast forwarded from 7.35 pm to 7.40 pm.

Edgar McKee seemed to step out of the wall on to the corridor.

'He's actually used the stairs rather than the lift,' said Tommy. 'That's a lot of flights of stairs to climb.'

In slow motion, Edgar McKee walked towards the camera. He stopped at the door of a room.

'Can you pause it for me, Tommy?'

'No problem.'

'And can you print that image off for me, please.'

Tommy sent the frozen on-screen image to a printer in the corner of the room which instantly came to life and spat out the picture of Edgar McKee.

'This is going to go down so badly at Trinity Road. We really thought we had our man. OK, can we roll, please?'

As Winters watched Edgar McKee disappear into the hotel room, he noticed that he was carrying a bag and remembered the leg of lamb he'd brought along to keep sweet the woman he knew as Marlene Black.

'We'll fast forward again,' said Tommy.

At 7.55 pm, a woman stepped out of the lift where the first man had previously emerged. Tommy paused it on a clear frontal shot of the woman walking directly to the room where Edgar McKee was waiting. It was Susan Hurst.

She was dressed in a smart black winter coat with boots that came up to the hemline below the knee and her hair hung down from a black hat. On her shoulder there was an expensive handbag and her hands were encased in black leather gloves.

'You've got to hand it to her,' said Tommy.

'She doesn't look like a sex worker. I see how difficult it must be for you, Tommy.'

'I guess we're not going to be that interested in anything until quarter to ten.'

'For now. I'd like to see what happens from a quarter to ten, but if you could send us the whole footage from beginning to end, we can check if they stayed in the room the whole time.'

At 9.45 pm, the corridor was full of a group of people that didn't include either Edgar McKee or Susan Hurst.

Ten minutes later, the door of Room 1002 opened and Susan Hurst emerged, carrying the bag that Edgar McKee had taken into the room. She swung her handbag squarely on to her shoulder and spoke into the room.

Edgar McKee came out of the room.

'He's not our guy,' said Winters, thinking aloud.

Edgar McKee walked side by side with Susan Hurst and Winters noticed how relaxed their body language was around each other; they could have been a regular happy couple.

As they made their way towards the lift, Winters saw that Edgar McKee appeared to be struggling, his confident swagger from hours earlier completely gone.

Why are you limping, Edgar? Winters asked silently.

'He looks like he's worn himself out,' said Tommy. 'I mean, half an hour to an hour's pretty standard, but two hours?'

'From what we've found so far, he's a sex addict. Can you do me a favour, Tommy? Can you pull together the footage of the two of them arriving at the room and the two of them leaving and put it on a pen drive for me so I can show my colleagues.'

'No problem.'

When the lift arrived at 10.03 pm, there was a discussion between Edgar McKee and Susan Hurst. With a hand gesture, he indicated for Susan to get into the lift first. She shook her head and mirrored his action.

With some reluctance, Edgar McKee got into the lift and Susan Hurst stayed where she was and he was gone.

'It's quite usual. They're being discreet. They weren't seen arriving together, they won't be seen leaving together.'

Susan Hurst stepped back from the lift and placed the bag Edgar McKee had given her on the floor. She swung her bag round and, opening it, took out her purse. Pressing for the lift to return to the top floor, she opened her purse and took out a wad of banknotes.

With a quick and careful glance both ways, she flicked through the money before putting it back in her purse.

'She had a good few hundred there. Does he have some super high-paid job?' asked Tommy.

'No, he doesn't. Maybe he spends all his money on paying for sex and lives on thin air.'

Edgar McKee? wondered Winters. *The more we learn about you, the less you add up.*

100

0.39 am

Clay watched Wren as he walked into Interview Suite 1, flanked by his father and the duty solicitor, Mr Robson. He made a moment's eye contact with Clay and looked as scared as he was confused.

'Where's Mr Cole?' he asked, frozen on the spot when he looked at Hendricks.

'He has other things to do, Wren. My name's DCI Clay. I'm going to ask you some questions. Would you please sit down and listen very carefully to the things I'm going to say to you.'

'Then, who's that?' asked Wren, sitting down and pointing across the table.

'My name's Detective Sergeant Hendricks and I'll also be asking you questions.'

Clay stared across the table at Wren as Hendricks formally opened the interview and she felt a collision of emotions as she glanced down at the frozen image of Edgar McKee on her laptop in front of her.

'Wren,' said Clay, burying any empathy she felt for him in those moments by recalling the condition of Amanda Winton's body in a flooded pothole on the bleak footpath between a park and a golf course.

'I'm tired, I want to go to bed,' said Wren.

'You stay up until all hours most nights,' said his father sharply. 'That's why you're such a nightmare to get out of bed most mornings. You're getting this sorted here and now.'

'I don't think you were telling the truth to DC Cole when he interviewed you. You denied knowledge of anything happening when you were on the footpath with Edgar McKee on Wednesday. You kept saying, *I don't know, I don't know* to most questions. Did Edgar tell you to say, *I don't know?*'

'No. I told myself.'

Clay leaned back and said, 'Look at me, Wren. I think you're building up a wall around yourself so that you don't have to tell the truth. I think you're doing that because you want to be a good mate to Edgar McKee. Is he your *mate?*'

'He's my mate, I'm his mate. He told me you'd try to twist things.'

'I'm not trying to twist anything. I'm trying to work out what really happened and weed out what hasn't happened.'

Clay turned the laptop around in front of Wren.

'So, Edgar's your mate?' asked Hendricks. Wren stared at the screen and said nothing. 'Because he's your mate you're not telling us what happened when he parked up on the footpath.'

Clay watched Wren closely.

'I'm going to tell you what I think happened when you were on the footpath,' said Hendricks. 'I think Edgar got out of the van.'

Clay watched Wren look away and his hand rise to his face briefly.

'I think he told you to stay in the van and went away for some time. I think he told you to keep looking ahead, to guard the van and not to get out.'

Wren's eyes dithered and Clay watched the mounting discomfort in the young man's face.

'I think when Edgar got back to the van, he was out of breath and sweating even though it was a particularly cold afternoon.'

'What do you say, Wren? Is DS Hendricks coming close to the truth?' asked Clay.

'I don't know.'

'At some point, Wren, you're going to have to tell the truth,' said his father. 'Do it now, rather than later.'

Wren looked at Mr Robson. 'Your father's right. Listen to him.'

'As a matter of interest, would he ever say bad things about you, your mate, Edgar McKee?' asked Clay.

'Of course he wouldn't say anything bad about me. He came here to rescue me. That's why he's in the cells. It's my fault he's in this pickle.'

'It's not your fault, Wren. You're quite certain he wouldn't say anything bad about you?' Clay held his gaze.

'I'm certain he wouldn't.'

'I'd like you to watch and listen carefully to a short sequence of film. It's Edgar McKee being interviewed in the same room you're sitting in now.' She pointed out the CCTV camera aimed at him. 'Do you want to see and hear? Then look at the screen of my laptop.'

Clay leaned over and pressed play.

'*How are you feeling, Mr McKee?*' Her own voice sounded ghostly as it drifted from the laptop.

'How do you mean?'

'*Coming back to more recent times. As in yesterday. Wren asked you how you were?*'

'*He's autistic. He's random.*'

'Turn it off,' said Wren.

His father grabbed his hand and said, 'Watch and listen!'

On the laptop, Clay challenged Edgar McKee about his absence from work and the improbability of him engaging in a two-hour sexual marathon while suffering from gastroenteritis.

'Listen to what he said about you, Wren.'

'*I phoned in sick,*' said Edgar McKee, '*because I wanted a breather from Wren. How would you feel if he was on your neck every minute of your working day?*

'*The lad was driving me nuts, and I'd only been with him for a couple of days. When I woke up on Friday, I just couldn't face seeing him, spending time with him.*'

As she listened to herself explaining to Edgar McKee that his current situation could be the lever that could cut him loose from Wren, she looked at the young man and saw he was on a fast-mounting arc of rage.

'*Try to help someone,*' said Edgar McKee, his bitterness growing with each word. '*End up in a cell. Wren? That's a fucking joke name. He's more of a fucking albatross...*'

Clay paused the footage.

'Do you know what an albatross is, Wren?' asked Hendricks.

'No.'

'It's a large sea bird. A sailor in an old poem, *The Rime of the Ancient Mariner*, killed an albatross and had to wear the dead bird around his neck. An albatross is a curse. In referring to you as an albatross, Edgar McKee is basically saying he sees you as a curse, and he wants rid of that curse. He's not your mate. He's lying. He's using you. He's using you to make his story sound plausible. I'm sorry. You need to know the truth. Ignorance isn't bliss, it's just ignorance. Ugly deceitful ignorance.'

'Here's the plan, Wren,' said Clay. 'We're going to close the interview now. There's a lot for you to process here. I suggest you have a heart to heart with your dad and Mr Robson. After that, Sergeant Harris will take you back to your cell where you can think things through. I'd like you to stick this at the centre of your thoughts. Ask yourself, am I prepared to lie and get into a heap of trouble for a man who thinks of me, in his own words, as *a fucking albatross*, a curse?'

'I want to go home.'

'As soon as you tell us the truth, you'll be free to go home.'

Clay looked at the clock on the wall. The time had come to execute the next piece of her strategy. She formally closed the interview and said, 'Let's go, Wren.'

Clay opened the door and Edgar McKee stood against the wall facing it, in between Sergeant Harris and PC Tom Morgan, two men whose combined weight in muscle and bone was over thirty-five stone.

Wren stepped out of the interview suite and became very still. He stared at Edgar McKee.

'What's up, mate?' asked Edgar McKee.

Wren made a noise in his throat like a wild dog on the verge of frenzy. He lurched at Edgar McKee but was held back by Harris and Morgan.

'You little bastard, McKee!' Wren spat in Edgar McKee's face.

'What have you said to him, Clay?' demanded Edgar McKee. 'What have you said to turn him against me?'

'I didn't say a word to turn him against you. You said all the words that were needed to turn him against you.'

'Start walking back to your cell, McKee,' said Sergeant Harris, restraining Wren on the floor.

Clay held up the key to his cell door. 'You heard Sergeant Harris. I'll make sure you get locked up.'

'You're the fucking albatross, McKee!' screamed Wren at Edgar McKee's departing back. 'Not me. You. You're a fucking enemy agent.'

101

1.15 am

Clay hung on to the sides of a mug of coffee as if it was a life raft as she watched the unfolding edited highlights of Edgar McKee's visit to the Travelodge for his sexual encounter with Susan Hurst. At the point when he followed her out of the hotel room, she asked Winters, 'Have you watched the unedited CCTV footage? From the time he first arrived until they both left?'

'I rolled it forward at double speed,' said Winters. 'He wasn't physically capable of snatching Francesca Christie. He was getting his nasties off on Susan Hurst behind the door of Room 1002. That door didn't open during the time they were both behind it. No one went into the room. No one came out.'

She considered the news Gina Riley had given her half an hour earlier, when she'd shown her the supporting evidence from easyJet, confirming Edgar McKee's story that he'd flown out to Amsterdam in late July and had returned to England after the middle of August. Sandra O'Day had gone missing on August 1st and her body was discovered on August 11th.

Clay walked to the window and stared out through the rain-streaked glass at the lights on the Mersey Estuary.

Turning to Winters, she said, 'I don't care what information comes in to corroborate his alibis, I'm holding Edgar McKee in custody until the very last second of the twenty-four hours we can keep him. He might have been in the wrong place at the wrong time when he was with Wren on the footpath, but where's his van now? That's enough for me. He's part of a tag team and he's up to his neck in it.'

The landline phone on her desk rang out. Despite the fact that good news never came over the phone at that small hour of the night, she wished for it as she picked up the receiver and said, 'DCI Clay.'

'Eve, it's me.' Detective Sergeant Terry Mason sounded down. The good news she'd hoped for just wasn't going to happen.

'Hit me with it, Terry.'

'We've been through every stitch of Edgar McKee's clothing. We've been through the drum of his washing machine and the dust filter from his tumble drier and there's isn't a single stray blonde hair that could match Annie Boyd. There's nothing for us to test.'

'What about the U-bend from his sink and the out pipe from his washing machine?'

'We've been through everything. His armchair, his furniture, his bed, his bedding, his carpets, his laminate flooring. I'm sorry. There's nothing doing. We just didn't find anything.'

'Anything from the garage on Francesca Christie's car?'

'Nothing yet. Sorry.'

Clay's mind went into top gear as the bad news had the reverse effect of what it should have done: it galvanised her.

'Have you been to the abattoir where he works, Terry?'

'No.'

'Leave it with me. When I've alerted the abattoir's twenty-four-seven security team that they're going to have to open up, that's going to be your next port of call. Given the nature of the work he does, there's going to have to be some changing facility. He's probably got an individual locker with his personal belongings and spare clothes. I'll ring you when I've sorted it out. Stay on stand-by and thank you for trying so hard. If anyone's going to find the forensic evidence that's going to nail the bastard, it's you and Pricey.'

As soon as she put the receiver down, her phone rang out again and, within half a second, she raised it to her ear.

'Eve?'

'Sergeant Harris? What's up?' She dismissed the pale hope of a turnaround confession from the holding cells.

'I've got two women in reception. They're demanding to see you immediately.'

'About?'

'They wouldn't say. But they're insistent on speaking to you personally. It's a matter of life and death. Neither of them are pissed or high. My gut believes them.'

'Did they give you their names?'

'Lydia Ball and Janine Ball.'

Ball? thought Clay, processing dozens of names that had cropped up in the space of the past three days.

'I'll come down straight away. Ask one of them what her husband's name is?'

Harris asked the question and a fractured voice came through the receiver.

'Daniel Ball.'

'I got that, Sarge,' said Clay, seeing a speck of light on the dark horizon.

As she headed for the door, Winters asked, 'Want me to square things with the abattoir people for Mason and Pricey?'

'You're a star, Clive. ASAP please.'

102

1.21 am

'Are you OK if I record our conversation?' asked Clay.

'I have no problem with that, DCI Clay,' replied Lydia Ball.

Lydia looked at Janine who said, 'That's fine.'

Clay pressed record.

'So, Lydia, Daniel Ball is your husband and, Janine, you're his sister.'

The women nodded.

'I'll start with you, Lydia. Tell me what's been going on with your husband Daniel. Take your time. Don't be afraid of silence if you need time to think.'

'Daniel left for work as usual yesterday morning. He seemed perfectly all right, up-beat even, talking about what we were going to have from the Chinese takeaway because it was Friday night and he had the Saturday off. The last thing he said to me was *I'll see you at six. Have a great day.*

'Six o'clock came and went and he didn't arrive home. If he's running late he always calls and tells me.'

Lydia Ball took a tissue from the box on the table and dabbed the corners of her eyes. Her first minutes in Interview Suite 1 had been spent sobbing and, although she felt very sorry for the woman opposite her, Clay's impatient streak had been tweaked.

'I called him on his mobile but it was turned off. I got in touch with Janine because I thought maybe, maybe he might have gone round to his big sister's.'

'He wasn't with me,' said Janine. 'I called him on his mobile but it was turned off. It just wasn't like him. He never turns his phone off.'

'I called our girls but they hadn't heard from their dad,' said Lydia. 'I started to get really worried so I called Norma Maguire on her home number. I asked her if everything was OK with Daniel.'

'What did Norma say?'

'She was quiet, didn't say a word for a few moments. But then she said, *Daniel wasn't in work today.*'

'Norma Maguire said, *Daniel wasn't in work today?*' Clay double-checked, as the vivid memory of him opening the office for her with a set of keys played out in her recent memory.

'Yes, she did. Is there something wrong with that?'

'No, no, I'm just checking, Lydia. Go on.'

'She told me he'd booked leave and Daniel had said to her we were going away for a break. I couldn't believe my ears. I asked if she was sure he'd said that. She told me she was one hundred per cent positive. I asked her was anything wrong? Had he been having problems in the office? I was crying at this point and she tried to reassure me that everything was fine, everything was normal, no problems other than the niggling little things that happen all the time. There was nothing going on in his working life that could make him want to behave strangely and disappear.'

Lydia took a sip of water and Clay made a pointed mental note. Norma Maguire had not only misled Lydia Ball about Daniel's presence in the office during the previous day, she'd failed to mention the fact that the police had descended on Maguire Holdings, and had made informational demands on her husband.

You're a liar, Norma, thought Clay.

'What was her tone like with you, Lydia?'

'She sounded worried for Daniel and sorry for me.'

Clay noticed the red veins in Lydia's eyes and the sourness of her breath.

'I phoned him every ten minutes but his phone was off. It was the same for the girls.'

'And me,' said Janine.

'I phoned round all the people in our address book but no one had seen or heard from him.'

'Before you last saw Daniel, did he ever say anything about former employees of Maguire Holdings?'

'How do you mean?'

'Did he ever talk about people who'd quit Maguire Holdings?'

She frowned and thought about it. 'Richard Ezra was the biggest fish who jumped from the pond. There were others, I'm sure, but I couldn't tell you who they were. Daniel worked there for a long time.'

'Could you do me a huge favour, Lydia. Could you dig down deeper into your memory for the names of anyone who quit working at Maguire Holdings?'

'It'll take my mind off things, I guess. I'll try.'

Lydia Ball rubbed her eyes hard with her fingertips and Janine wrapped an arm around her sister-in-law's shoulder.

'It'll be OK, Lydia.'

'Did you do anything else to try and find him?' asked Clay.

'We drove to his favourite place, hoping to find him, but he wasn't there.'

'What was that place, Lydia, Janine?'

'Otterspool Promenade. Every so often, he used to drive down there at night. He loved the sound of the river.'

Clay focused on Janine, who looked as if a deeply buried family secret had just been leaked on the internet.

'And it was well-lit, the prom... I told myself to start gearing up for the worst possible news. Maybe he had taken himself down to the prom and thrown himself into the river.'

'Was he or has he ever been on prescription medication for his mental health?'

'He's never had a problem with his nerves as such.'

'Has he ever gone missing before?'

The women looked at each other.

'Yes,' said Janine.

'No, he wasn't really missing,' defended Lydia. 'It was a blip, a bit of a mid-life crisis. He kept in touch when he went to find himself, didn't he, Janine?'

'When did this happen?' asked Clay.

'Last August,' replied Lydia.

'What happened after you couldn't find him on Otterspool Promenade?'

'We just had to sit it out, fear the worst and hope for the best,' said Lydia. 'Then round about half-eleven, the phone rings and it's Daniel.'

Lydia started crying and, Clay guessed, they were tears of jagged relief.

'And how was Daniel?' asked Clay, focusing Lydia, dragging her back on track.

'He sounded terrible, like he'd been drinking heavily and didn't quite know the time of day.'

'Tell me, as accurately as you can, what was said, Lydia. The detail you offer could make a massive difference.'

'He said, *I love you and I'm sorry for what I've done but I don't know what else to do.* I asked him if he was in trouble and he told me he didn't know. I asked him for more detail but he said he couldn't. And then he mentioned your name. Detective Chief Inspector Eve Clay. He said he wanted to get in touch with you. He mentioned your name over and over, as if it was stuck in his head like a scratched record. One moment he wanted to talk to you, the next he didn't know if he could do it. It was like he was talking in riddles. I tried to calm him down by asking him simple questions. *Where are you? Are you with anyone? Have you had anything to eat? Have you got somewhere to stay?* But all he came back with was how conflicted he felt.

'I asked if he had your number. He told me he did have it. I asked him why he had your number? He told me the police had been into the office over Francesca Christie's disappearance. I thought maybe that's the thing that's pushed him over the edge. Francesca. He said he was going to hang up. I told him, you must get in touch with DCI Clay. *You haven't done anything wrong. She'll help you if she can.* I insisted. I made the point over and over. Then he hung up and I haven't heard from him since.'

Clay refilled the glass from the water jug and Lydia downed it in one.

'So, he *had* been in the office despite what Norma said,' concluded Lydia. And she didn't even mention the police calling in. What's she playing at?'

'I'm not sure. Thank you so much for coming in and telling me. I know how difficult this must have been for you.'

She placed the glass down on the table, held on to the edges with a claw-like grip.

'Is he in trouble with you, DCI Clay?'

'No, not as far as I'm aware.' Clay drank in the woman's profound unhappiness as they engaged over the short expanse of a wooden table. 'I want you to do something for me, Lydia. If Daniel does get back in touch with you, I want you to keep hammering home the message that he must call me directly. Reassure him that you've spoken to me and that he's not in trouble. Tell him I very much want to help him. But he must make that call.'

Lydia nodded and Clay read unspoken words in the heaviness of her eyes and the lines on her face.

'If I turn the audio recorder off, Lydia, anything you say to me can be treated in confidence as long as it doesn't relate to a criminal offence.'

Clay pressed pause, keeping her left index finger ready to take off the pause depending on what came next out of Lydia's mouth.

'Is having a mid-life crisis a criminal offence?'

Clay tried not to smile too broadly at the question, the absurdity cocooning tragedy.

'In itself, not at all. If the crisis involves criminal offences, then yes it does.'

'I'm pretty sure...' Lydia looked down at the desk.

'At the moment, Lydia, the machine's not recording. I sense you have a personal problem of an extremely sensitive nature.'

She looked up. 'Yes! Yes...'

'Woman to woman,' said Clay. 'I'm listening.'

'Francesca Christie. I think my husband is in love with her. It was just the way he was when he spoke about her. I could tell. There. I've said it.'

'What do you think, Janine?' asked Clay.

'I don't know,' she replied, with an expression on her face that told Clay she would have much more to say under different circumstances.

'Maybe, Lydia,' said Clay, 'the mid-life crisis isn't the sole domain of men. Women have problems when they hit middle age. Looks fade, figures fill out, regrets for what could have been mount up as possibilities for what could be diminish. You met Francesca?'

'Yes.'

'What was your view of her?'

'Young, pretty, an absolute sweetheart of a woman in her prime.'

'You in your twenties, then?'

'I guess so.'

'Just because Daniel fell in love with you all those years ago doesn't mean he's going to fall in love with a version of your view of how you used to be. I think you've been tormenting yourself over phantoms. Mistrust your doubts. Your husband loves you. If he didn't, he wouldn't have called you tonight.'

Lydia was quiet for a long time.

'I think you're one of the kindest people I've ever met, DCI Clay.'

'If there's anything I can do to help, let me know, Lydia.'

A smile appeared on Lydia's face like a pale moon forming in the sky on a clear winter evening.

'I'm glad it's you he wants help from.'

***

In reception, as Clay watched Lydia and Janine Ball walk through the main doors, she called, 'Janine, have you got a minute?'

'Back in a tick, Lydia.'

Janine walked back inside Trinity Road police station and Clay asked, 'What's going on?'

She looked around and, Clay guessed, was checking to make sure no one could overhear.

'Daniel's got a problem. His sexuality's all over the place. It kills me to tell you this but I'm telling you because if he's in trouble, you need to know the truth. I've known him since he was a baby and we're close. He's been massively oversexed since he hit puberty. He's been playing around behind Lydia's back since the day they met. He confesses to me. Yes, he goes with women. Yes, he goes with men. Yes, he goes with prostitutes. And, yes, he had a massive, massive thing about Francesca Christie. He didn't have to tell me that last thing. Whenever she came up in conversation, I could see it in him. I'm his big sister. I know more about him than his wife does. I love him. I love her. I'm in the middle of an ongoing nightmare. He refuses to seek it out but he needs help, DCI Clay.'

'Thank you for being so candid with me, Janine. I appreciate how hard this must've been for you.'

'He needs a lot of help. Something's got to give with Daniel.'

103
3.05 am

The silence inside the abattoir amplified the erratic beat of the rain as it crashed on the roof of the building. In the ceiling, fluorescent lights blinked into life as the site manager, Christopher Paisley, guided Detective Sergeant Terry Mason and Sergeant Paul Price towards the changing rooms.

'The boss sends his apologies for the no-show. He's delegated it down to me. He's been at a Masonic dinner and he's had a few too many sherries to drive over here.'

The huge bunch of keys jangled in his hands as he walked ahead of Mason and Price.

'Edgar McKee?' Christopher sounded puzzled. 'It's definitely his locker you want to look into, right?'

'That's right,' said Price.

'We've got some right scallywags working here. He's not one of them. He's one of them pillar of the community types. Ask anyone who works here. What's he in trouble about?'

'I can't tell you,' said Mason. 'Sensitive investigation, early stages.'

Christopher turned his head and tapped the side of his nose. 'Gotcha.'

Without looking, the site manager selected a single key from the crowded forest on the ring and stuck it into the lock of a plain white door. When he opened it, the smell of bleach and stale sweat was undeniable. He turned on the light to reveal a row of wooden benches down the centre of the space and metal lockers lining the walls on both sides.

'I'll open his locker with the master key.'

Christopher walked the line of grey metal doors, each labelled with the name of the person assigned to it.

'As we speak, is he in police custody?' asked the site manager.

'Yes, but that's as much as I'm going to tell you,' said Mason.

Christopher stopped at a drab door, turned the master key and the door creaked as it opened into another corner of Edgar McKee's world.

'Christopher.' The site manager turned and Mason showed him a search warrant on his iPhone. 'The duty magistrate issued this an hour ago. Is this the only locker Edgar McKee has?'

'Yes. Staff are only allowed one.'

'Is there anywhere else on the site where he could keep other possessions?'

'No, absolutely not. Health and safety's God Almighty in this place. Has to be. The only personal possessions are stored in the lockers in the changing rooms.'

Mason looked at the row of shower cubicles at the far end of the changing rooms, the adjoining toilets, and the wisdom of the abattoir written on a laminated poster on the wall.

A CLEAN WORKER IS A SAFE WORKER

'I'll sit on the bench here as you go through his stuff.'

'No. Can you please wait outside the door? Sergeant Price and myself may have to exchange sensitive information during the course of our search.'

The site manager got up reluctantly and walked towards the door with profound disappointment stamped in his slumped shoulders.

'Christopher. The warrant allows us to seize his property and take it away for forensic investigation. You understand? Please close the door as you leave the room.'

Price opened a large black holdall containing a stack of evidence bags as Mason snapped on a pair of latex gloves.

They looked into the locker at the small haul of Edgar McKee's clothing.

Price opened a pair of large evidence bags and Mason knelt at the foot of the locker. He picked up a pair of worn and scuffed white wellingtons, the letter E painted crudely on the left boot and M on the right.

'Light them up, Pricey,' said Mason.

Price shone torchlight inside the left boot and said, 'It's riddled with all kinds of matter.'

'Wait until we get deeper into the boot, from the end of the heel to the tips of the toes.'

Price repeated the illumination in the right boot and said, 'Same.'

'What was the first thing I said to you, Pricey, day one when you joined me?'

'There's so much evidence that can be picked up from the head and the feet.'

'Let's bag them, one boot in each bag. Thank you.'

Price placed the evidence bags on the wooden bench and shone light on the empty floor of Edgar McKee's locker.

'I'll lint the whole interior when we've emptied it,' said Price.

Mason stood up and from a hook on the right-hand side of the locker lifted a white leather apron with a brown fibre lining. Price opened a large evidence bag and the apron was secured inside and placed alongside the bagged boots.

There were three shelves. Mason took a small stack of plain white T-shirts from one shelf, a few pairs of white boxer shorts from the middle shelf and from the bottom shelf a thin blue nylon jacket and a bundle of white hairnets.

'What do you think?' asked Price as they bagged the clothing. 'Do you think we're going to get anything from this?'

'If we do it'll be the boots or the hairnets that come up trumps.'

Price explored the empty surfaces with his torch.

'This place gives me the creeps. I bet it's full of bustle and noise during the day but now it feels like a haunted house,' said Price.

'Don't overthink it, mate. We've been in better places, we've been in worse. I'll hold the torch. You lint the interior.'

Price tore a strip of four sheets from the lint roller and placed them on the ceiling of the locker. He ripped them off and Mason shone light on the sticky surface, where there was nothing other than particles of rust.

It took three minutes and the best part of a roll to print the inside of the locker.

'We'll do the outside of the door even though it's going to be heavily contaminated by McKee's workmates,' said Mason.

Outside, the rain slackened but the wind picked up and wrapped itself around the almost deserted abattoir like a celestial fist.

'Done?' asked Mason. 'Let's get out of this place.'

104

3.44 am

Clay looked through the observation slot in the door of Edgar McKee's cell and stared into the darkness. She made out his form, lying under a blanket on the bench, and he was completely still, apparently asleep.

'Eve.' She turned her attention to the whispering of her name and saw Poppy Waters standing nearby. 'Sergeant Harris said you'd be here.' She carried an evidence bag in each hand, one small, the other medium-sized.

Clay closed the observation slot with dismay. In her experience of watching what happened in the closed eye of night, the guilty paced while the innocent slept. She walked towards Poppy and together they walked away to the automatic doors leading to the staircase.

'What have you found on Edgar McKee's computer?'

'It's riddled with the most horrendous filth. I haven't seen it all. I'd be watching until Christmas and beyond to check it all out. I didn't find anything that showed a preference to overt violence towards women. There was a lot of rough sex but it cut both ways, men dominating women, women dominating men.'

'How about his phone?'

'The same.'

Their voices and footsteps mingled and echoed against the glass walls that housed the staircase as they ascended to the incident room.

'Here's the big one, Poppy. Has he been on any internet dating sites?'

'No. I've been through his history on both devices stretching back to last June, including the evidence he's deleted from the surface of his hard drive. On the evidence I've seen, he's never been on an internet dating site.'

'How sure are you?'

'One hundred per cent.'

'Chat rooms?'

'Doesn't do them.'

'Emails?'

'No communication with any of the victims on email or Messenger. I simply didn't find anything to link him to Sandra O'Day, Annie Boyd, Amanda Winton or Francesca Christie.'

'Have you looked into his adventures on the dark web or the deep web?'

'That's my next job. God knows what I'm going to find there porn-wise.'

'No sign of anything to do with Richard Ezra in his photo galleries?'

'No. He's taken some pretty rancid selfies.'

'Naked selfies?'

'He's in love with his own body.'

Clay considered Poppy's words.

'Is he masturbating in the selfies?' asked Clay.

'No. Strangely enough.'

'What's your verdict on Edgar McKee?'

'Depressing loner, sex maniac but not involved in the crimes you're now investigating.'

They walked towards the top floor and through the sliding doors of the incident room. The room was lit by a quartet of lights dotted around the desks. Clay walked through the dark spaces towards her desk. She pulled up a second chair and indicated for Poppy to sit down in the glow of her desk light.

'Show me the devices please, Poppy.'

Poppy took a pair of latex gloves from her coat pocket and slipped them on. She placed Edgar McKee's iPhone on Clay's desk and his laptop next to it.

'Are his selfies on the phone?' asked Clay.

'Yes.'

'Any pictures of himself on the laptop?'

'No.'

'Are they littered around the photo gallery?'

'He's a neat and tidy narcissist.'

'Show me.'

'They're all in one camera roll and he's the only person starring in it.' As Poppy spoke, she picked up the iPhone and pulled up the gallery.

'Do you want a coffee, Eve?' Poppy handed the iPhone to Clay.
'Thank you, Poppy.'

One hundred and ninety-six pictures and all of himself, thought Clay, sensing a chink somewhere in his gruff armour. She put on a pair of latex gloves from her desk drawer.

She tapped on the first image and saw a rear view of Edgar McKee naked in front of a mirror, head tilted to look up at his iPhone, his powerful shoulders and muscular arms the product of years of working out.

She swiped the screen and saw a head and shoulders shot of Edgar McKee on his bench, the silver of a weights bar above his head.

Clay swiped and swiped and saw that the content and theme of the pictures was repetitive: the wonder of me.

'Poppy, are there any selfies that stand out from the others?'

'Yes,' she called back from the kitchen area. 'Go into the middle section. There's two standout shots.'

Clay pictured Edgar McKee's sleeping form in the cell on the ground floor as she made her way into the central block of images. She slowed down and said, 'Yeah, I see what you mean.'

She looked at a picture of Edgar McKee lying on a bed, knees bent and legs wide apart, with a large, open jar of Vaseline at his right hip. In his right hand he held a wooden rolling pin, which he had inserted into his anus.

The next shot was a close-up of his hand moving the rolling pin deeper inside himself.

'Have you found the anal shots, Eve?'

'Yes.' Clay moved back to the close-up of his hand. 'I hope he doesn't roll out pastry with it afterwards. God!' she said, as she touched the screen and honed in on the tattoo on his wrist.

Mum

1940–2001

Poppy walked back with two mugs of coffee.

'Can you send this close-up to my phone, please, along with a selection of other pictures and definitely the two butt snaps.'

She dialled the front desk.

'PC Watson, how can I help you?'

'A message for Sergeant Harris, please. I want Edgar McKee in the interview suite first thing. Book him in for 8:30 am. Message his solicitor and tell her to be there sharp. Unless anything major happens in the meantime, I'll see him then.'

Sipping her coffee, Clay pictured his face as he penetrated himself, the tattoo on his wrist and his muscles taut and tense. She heard a thump at the window and saw a seagull on the window ledge illuminated by the bright uplighters on the ground.

'This isn't natural,' said Clay, to the beady black eye staring at her. 'This isn't natural at all.'

105

4.08 am

The walls of Mason and Price's room were lined with Edgar McKee's clothes all in evidence bags, ready to be picked up for deeper investigation by Galton Solutions, the independent forensic laboratory.

Price surveyed the smaller haul from Edgar McKee's locker in the abattoir. He took his camera and took pictures of the hairnets, the white wellingtons, the T-shirts, the underpants, the white leather apron, all separated out on the table.

'Are you ready to start working through these?' asked Price.

'Yeah.'

At the other end of the table, Mason surveyed Edgar McKee's library of pornographic DVDs and laughed.

'What's amusing you, Tez?'

'They're ordered alphabetically. How OCD is that? Starts with *Aching For Anal* and ends on *You Wanna Fuck Me Right Now* 2.' Walking down the table to the clothes, Mason said, 'What I don't get is that he doesn't have a copy of *You Wanna Fuck Me Right Now*, as in the first in the brief series?'

'Maybe it's like *The Godfather*,' said Price. 'A lot of people prefer *The Godfather II*, to the exclusion of *The Godfather*. Anything else about the DVDs?'

'I haven't had a chance to look properly. We'll start with his head and feet, the rubber boots and the hairnets.'

'Sounds like a plan.'

'Pass me a scalpel, Pricey. Let's get the soles separated from the boots.'

106

6.01 am

The landline phone on Clay's desk rang out, bringing her out of a shallow slumber. As she awoke, the ringing sounded distant and hollow but with each tone it became swollen and more demanding. She lifted the receiver, shaking off the shackles of sleep, and said, 'DCI Clay.'

There was complete silence at the other end.

'Who is this?'

She tried to identify background noise but there was none and she wondered if the caller was in some kind of vacuum.

Stone walked towards her across the incident room and Clay hit speakerphone.

'I'm going to count to five and then I'm going to hang up.'

Stone sat on the edge of Clay's desk, pressed record on his iPhone and extended it towards Clay's landline.

'DCI Clay?'

'Yes?'

Silence.

'You know who I am,' said Clay. 'Who are you?'

'I've got something to tell you.'

'Go on? What do you have to tell me?' she pressed.

'You asked me for a list of names…'

'Daniel, take your time.'

She picked up a pen and poised it over a notepad on her desk, heard the breathing of a man on the verge of tears.

'You've got nothing to be afraid of, Daniel. Just give me the names of people who walked out of Maguire Holdings. I don't have to tell Norma anything. If you're worried about your job, and she asks me where I got the names, I'll tell her I spoke to other estate agents and pieced the information together.'

She sensed that he was about to hang up.

'I've spoken to Lydia. She's worried to death about you. So are the girls. Go home, Daniel. Whatever's wrong can be worked out.'

His breathing became more ragged.

'What made you run away? Why are you so unhappy?'

'She knew.'

'Norma? What did she know?'

'Yes, Norma. About my affair with him. She blamed the affair for him leaving, therefore she blamed me. She threatened to tell Lydia and the girls. She held it over my head for years, like a fucking sword. If I ever left, she'd tell everyone.'

Clay looked at Stone and then at the noticeboard, at the pictures of Norma and her employees down the years, and saw through the falseness of the smiles on their faces, the enforced projection of a great big happy working family.

'Does she have any material proof of this affair?'

'No.'

'Are you on good terms with your ex?'

'Yes.'

'Is he likely to blow the whistle on your relationship?'

'Absolutely not. He's got as much to lose as me.'

'Well, I've learned something about Norma Maguire, Daniel, since I spoke to Lydia. She's an out and out liar. If she makes allegations about you to anyone, I'll be the first one to climb on the roof and shout out about her lies. She's got no credibility and if she tries to denounce you, she's got me to contend with. I'm going to put it to you directly, Daniel. You didn't have an affair with anyone, did you?'

'Sorry?'

'Say it. *I didn't have an affair with anyone.*'

'I – I didn't have an affair with anyone.'

'Norma Maguire is a sad, lonely woman who makes malicious allegations.'

'Norma Maguire...' Clay heard key notes of conviction creeping into his voice. '...is a sad, lonely woman who makes malicious allegations.'

'She can't beat both of us, Daniel, and she can't prove anything at all against you. All you need to do is stick to your story. *Nothing happened between me and any man.*'

Clay looked at the clock on the wall, saw the seconds ticking away, chipping into Edgar McKee's time in custody.

'Norma Maguire has lied through her teeth to your wife already,' encouraged Clay. 'Lydia came to that conclusion herself and I can back that up one hundred per cent.'

Daniel Ball spoke two words and the skin on Clay's spine puckered as her whole body turned cold. She wondered if fatigue was making her hear things.

'Repeat that name, please.'

'Michael Towers. He left for another firm. We were close, Michael and me.'

'Go on.'

'Richard Ezra. Thomas Saddler. James Griffiths. Geoff Campbell. Francesca Christie. That's it.'

'Repeat those names for me, slowly.'

As he spoke, Clay had the sense that a massive corner was being turned.

'Thank you. Daniel, where are you?'

He hung up immediately.

Clay spoke to Stone. 'Round up the troops. I want you to come with me to West Road in the Grassendale Park grid, to Norma Maguire's house. We're going to pull her in. Every person who's walked out on her with the exception of Francesca Christie became a pseudonym for The Ghoul's alter egos, hunting down lonely hearts. She's on my shit list.'

107

6.23 am

Waking up from a sleep full of lost dreams, Norma Maguire heard the iPhone at her bedside ring out.

She pulled the eye mask from her face and looked at the ringing telephone, knowing that whoever was calling at that hour wasn't going to hang up until she replied.

Norma saw the name DCI CLAY on display, connected the call and turned on speakerphone.

'DCI Clay?'

'I'm sorry to wake you so early, Norma.'

The words hung in the air like circling vultures.

Norma Maguire listened hard, heard that Clay was in a moving vehicle.

'Has there been some news on Francesca Christie?' asked Norma.

'We're still looking for her, Norma.'

'Excuse me, I'm still here, I'm just unfolding my wheelchair.'

She pulled the arms apart and tasted last night's Talisker at the back of her tongue.

'Is everything all right, DCI Clay?'

'No.'

'Why are you calling me?' She checked her alarm clock. 'At just after twenty past six?'

'I'm on my way to see you, Norma. You need to be up and dressed within the next few minutes.'

'Why?'

'Have a look outside your window, Norma.'

She made her way into her chair and wheeled herself to the bay window overlooking West Road. Pulling back a curtain, Norma saw a vehicle blocking her drive.

'Why is there a police car outside my house?'

'That was exactly the same question I was about to ask you,' said Clay.

'You're talking in riddles, DCI Clay. Where are you going with this?'

'At the moment, I'm going left off Aigburth Road on to Grassendale Road in the direction of your house.'

'Why?'

'Stay on the line, Norma. Do you hear me?'

'Yes.'

Norma watched two constables get out of the car and walk towards her front door.

'I don't feel well. What's that? In his hand?'

'It's a ram, Norma, to knock your front door open.'

'I don't feel well. I'm having a dizzy turn.'

'We'll let the duty medic give you the once-over in Trinity Road.'

Norma saw Clay, iPhone in her hand, getting out of her parked car. Clay pointed at her.

'Get dressed. Get down the stairs and get outside as fast as you can!'

'What's that noise?'

'Your front door's just been rammed. We haven't got time on our side.'

108

6.27 am

Clay stood in Norma Maguire's hall, watching her as she descended on the stair lift, the top half of her face concealed by a large pair of sunglasses. Norma Maguire opened the wheelchair at the bottom of the stairs as Stone entered the house, follow by uniformed officers. He showed Clay his iPhone.

'The search warrant from the duty magistrate.'

Riley followed Hendricks into the hall.

Norma looked at Hendricks. 'You! Tell them you looked in my garage for a white van and you found absolutely nothing.'

Stone showed Norma the search warrant.

'What on earth's going on here?' As she transferred herself from the stair lift into her wheelchair, Norma sobbed, 'What are you looking for?'

'Do you have a loft, Norma?' asked Clay.

'Yes.'

'How do we access your loft?'

'There's a metal arm by the entrance hatch. The hatch is near the bathroom.'

Winters came into the hall and Clay pointed up.

'The loft please, DC Winters.'

'Got it, DCI Clay.'

'Do you have a basement?'

'Yes.'

'How do we access the basement?'

'Through the kitchen. The hatch is beneath the mat by the back door.'

'Give me your car keys, house keys, mobile phone.'

Norma opened her bag and handed Clay her keys and phone.

'You can open the garage door with the fob on the car key ring,' said Norma.

'Take your glasses off. It's not a bit sunny.' Norma didn't move. 'Take them off and look me in the eyes,' insisted Clay.

Norma lifted the glasses from her face and looked at Clay. 'I don't know what you're up to but you're making a huge mistake.'

Cole walked into the hall.

'This is Detective Constable Cole. He's going to take you to Trinity Road police station. Before you go, would you like to tell me where Francesca Christie is?'

'What are you talking about?' Norma Maguire looked at Clay as if she was completely insane. 'I'm not saying another word until I have a solicitor with me.'

'Now that is sensible, Norma. Take her away, DC Cole.'

He positioned himself behind Norma's wheelchair.

'Take your hands off my chair. I'll push myself, thank you very much.'

'I'll see you soon, Norma. Interview Suite 1's been booked for you in Trinity Road police station. Hurry up, Norma. From now on, every second counts.'

109

6.33 am

In Norma Maguire's kitchen, Clay lifted up the plain mat at the back door and flicked on a torch. She raised the hatch, the entrance to the basement.

'Hello,' she shouted. 'Police.'

The silence that came back filled Clay with horror.

She shone torchlight down the wooden stairs leading into the basement.

Clay identified a switch on the wall near the top of the stairs. As she descended, she flicked on the light, watched irregular red light flickering, interspersed with crackling darkness. She turned the faulty fluorescent light off and used the torch to guide herself down the steps as she combed the space with light.

'Hello!' she called again, even though there was no one in the basement, just a smell of damp and earth, and something vaguely chemical. Beneath the blanket aroma there was a stench of what could have been human waste or just a dead animal decomposing in the soil around the walls of the basement.

On the wall near the stairs was a long rectangular chunk of exposed brick that looked like it had been hacked out. A mound of plaster dust and chippings lay on the ground and particles of dust danced in Clay's torchlight.

There was a door in the wall to her left.

'Hello,' she tried again. 'Police.'

In the lock, there was a key. She turned it, built herself up for whatever was behind the door.

She pushed the door and a blast of stale sweat hit her in the face, but a quick inspection showed that the only thing in the room was a large mirror on the wall. She walked around the walls, sensed a vibration in the air that chimed in her marrow.

The sweat in the air was fresh.

'Someone's been here. Recently. Not long ago.' She spoke to the glare from her torch on the surface of the mirror.

She walked back to the wooden steps and weak light from Norma Maguire's kitchen filtered into the basement.

Clay called Mason on her iPhone and asked, 'How are you getting on, Terry?'

'We're working on McKee's boots from the abattoir.'

'Anything?' she asked, hoping against hope.

'We've got one long hair from inside his right boot, but it's impossible to give it a colour. It's like it's been there since Noah was a baby. We're about to start looking at his hairnets. What are you up to?'

'Searching Norma Maguire's house.'

'Whoa! Norma Maguire? Why?'

'You'll find out soon enough.'

Mason disconnected and Clay listened to the sound of the search above her head. She stooped to the pile of plaster and lit it up.

She found a chunk covered in black paint, the form of the letter s. She rooted through the plaster debris, found a letter n and an f, and concluded there had been writing on the wall that been hastily destroyed.

Walking up the wooden stairs to the kitchen, she called Hendricks on her iPhone.

'Bill, ask around. Is there anyone on the search good at jigsaw puzzles?'

110

7.00 am

'Wren,' said Detective Constable Barney Cole. 'We've given you a lot of time to process the information you were given in your last interview with DCI Clay. You spoke with your dad and Mr Robson?'

'Yes.'

'And you're ready?'

'Yes.'

'You heard what Edgar McKee said about you?'

'Yes.'

Wren looked through Cole and it was impossible to tell what was going on in his mind.

'What do you think of Edgar McKee?'

'Edgar McKee is a very bad man who has lied to me by saying he was my mate but was calling me a curse behind my back. And coming here to say he was rescuing me. Lies! All lies!'

Cole could tell that Wren's dad's words and the advice given by Mr Robson had sunk in as Wren spent the night stewing in his cell.

'Tell me what actually happened on Wednesday afternoon when Edgar McKee drove you home from the abattoir. Don't leave anything out,' said Cole.

Wren nodded.

'We know you were in Edgar's white van and that he drove to the footpath. What we don't know is what happened when you were on the footpath. Did you ask him why he'd driven you there?'

'*Ours is not to reason why. Ours is but to do or die.* That's what he said. He said those were Captain Cyclone's words.'

'What else did he say?'

'*Clear the city of low-life scum.* He said we could be endangering the lives of Captain Cyclone's agents in the field if we talked. But I no longer accept the words of a liar.'

'I see what you're saying, Wren,' said Cole. 'But I don't get the reference to endangering the lives of Captain Cyclone's agents in the field?'

'That's exactly what the lying McKee said to me when he got out of the van. *Stay right where you are, Wren, and watch out for enemy agents. If you get out of the van you could be endangering the lives of Captain Cyclone's agents in the field. These are not my orders, these are the orders of Captain Cyclone himself.*'

'Do you know how far up the footpath you parked?'

'How do you mean?'

'Did you see anything out of the window while you were waiting?'

'In the wing mirror, I saw a green sign with white writing and there were white words – Bridle Path – and a white picture of a rider on a horse.'

'That's interesting,' said Cole, working out the proximity of the place where McKee had parked to the flooded sinkhole in which Amanda Winton's body had been discovered.

'When Edgar McKee got out of the van, what did you hear?'

'I heard Edgar opening the back of the van. I heard Edgar slamming the back doors of the van. I heard his feet squelching in the mud as he walked away. I heard a yappy dog coming closer. I saw a speck of light in the van's wing mirror. I thought I heard someone screaming. I heard Edgar's heavy breathing as he got in the van. In the driver's seat. *Let's get you home now, Wren.*'

'How did Edgar appear when he got back into the van?'

'He was shaking. He was in a hurry to get away.'

'He told us that you explained to him about Captain Cyclone as you were parked there?'

'No, I said nothing about Captain Cyclone. We weren't there long.'

Under the desk, Cole crossed his fingers and made a mental journey from the bridle path to the drop-off site of Amanda Winton's body.

'How long was Edgar McKee out of the van?'

In his mind, Cole walked there with the weight of a woman's corpse in his arms and ran back to the van empty-handed.

'Four minutes and nine seconds,' said Wren, with supreme confidence.

'That precise?' asked Cole blandly, in spite of the flame that the answer ignited inside his head.

'I counted time in my head when he was gone. It was four minutes and nine seconds exactly. I have a clock.' He touched his forehead. 'Inside my head.'

Cole looked at Wren's father, who smiled.

'We don't need to have a clock of any description in our house. Do we, son?'

'No. I am it. DC Cole, can I ask you a question, please?'

'Fire away.'

'What on earth was Edgar McKee doing on the footpath? And why did he take me there with him?'

'Because McKee thinks he's a genius who's better and more clever than everyone around him, when he's an altogether different thing in reality,' explained Cole. 'He thinks other people are really stupid and that no one can get the better of him.'

'What is he?' asked Wren.

'An idiot. He took you there thinking you'd back up everything that he said, to cover his tracks. He underestimated you, Wren, and that insult to your intelligence is just about to come back and chew his lying arse.'

The tension in Wren's body slackened.

'Is there anything else you'd like to add, Wren?'

'Another question. What was his message all about? What did he take from the back of the van and leave on the footpath?'

'A dead woman.'

'Can I see a picture, please?'

Cole looked at Wren's father.

'It could stress you out, Wren,' warned his father.

'I want to see.'

Cole took out his iPhone and found an image of Amanda Winton's body. He turned it towards Wren, whose face remained deadpan.

'He's very good at skinning dead females,' said Wren. He looked at his father. 'Don't you just wish Mum was here? She'd make this all right. Of course she would, wouldn't she?'

111

7.33 am

'Would you describe yourself as a truthful person, Norma?' asked DCI Clay.

Norma looked up at the CCTV camera pointing at her from the corner of two connecting walls and said, 'Yes.'

'Are you a liar, Norma?' asked Clay, across the desk in Interview Suite 1.

'What kind of a question's that?' asked the woman sitting next to Norma Maguire. Clay looked at the visitor badge hanging from her neck. Rowena Rice. Norma Maguire's solicitor.

'It's an essential question in a serious criminal investigation that needs addressing promptly,' replied Clay. 'I had a visit from Lydia Ball in the early hours of the morning. She told me that her husband, Daniel, left for work yesterday morning but didn't return home in the evening. She called you and you informed her that Daniel hadn't been in the office at all that day. I was there with Detective Sergeant Stone when Daniel opened the office yesterday morning. Why did you lie to Lydia Ball?'

'What I meant was this. He wasn't in the office for long.'

'Lydia had no idea that she was going away for a break with her husband. You told her it was happening.'

'Because that's exactly what Daniel Ball told me. Maybe it should be Daniel you're interviewing, DCI Clay? Not me.'

'Assuming Daniel did mislead you about going away for a break with his wife, why do you think he did it?'

'People do all manner of strange things. People say all manner of untruthful things. I'm not one of them. If you take one tiny lapse as a sure-fire sign that I'm a liar, then you're wrong.'

Rowena Rice leaned into her client's ear and shielded her lips with her hand. Norma listened and nodded.

'We asked Daniel Ball for a list of names of people who worked for or had worked for Maguire Holdings, including the ones who'd resigned. His response was to disappear, walking away from his wife, not telling her where he was or why he was hiding. Why?'

Clay watched Norma as the information percolated through her head.

'You were there with him after we left, Norma. What happened in your office yesterday after we went?'

'His last words to me were *See you on Monday*.'

'OK, Norma. OK. So, he informs you that the police want a list of names of your former employees and that was it? Nothing else was said on the matter?'

'I told him the list could wait until Monday. And if the police wanted it sooner, I'd sort it out.'

Hendricks slid a spiral-bound notebook and a pen across the table to Norma.

'I gather you have a maternal relationship with your employees,' said Hendricks. 'Would you say that's true?'

'I care for the people who work for me. Yes, maybe you could say I mother them.'

'I think you could reel out the names of everyone who's ever walked out on you.'

'Perhaps I could remember some of them.'

'Write down for me on the pad the names of the last six people to walk out on you from Maguire Holdings,' said Hendricks. 'Start with the most recent one. Francesca Christie.'

'Fran,' said Clay. 'Start with Fran.'

Clay watched Norma closely, saw how the sound of the name *Fran* made her blink rapidly for a couple of moments. Norma looked at Ms Rice.

'Norma,' said Ms Rice. 'Give them the names they've asked for and be done with it.'

Norma picked up the pen and, as she wrote, she covered her forehead with her left hand and lowered her eyes. To Clay, it looked as if she was making a mask for her face.

Upside down, Clay read Norma's words as they appeared on six separate lines on the same page.

Still looking down, Norma pushed the pad back across the table to Hendricks. Her eyes flicked towards Clay.

'What are you smiling at, DCI Clay?' asked Norma.

Hendricks turned the notebook around, 180 degrees, and Clay checked the names provided by Norma Maguire.

Francesca Christie
Max Rodgers
Peter Gould
Eric Smith
Richard Ezra
David Ellis

'These are the last six people to walk from Maguire Holdings?' confirmed Clay.

'Yes.'

'Absolute and final last answer?' Clay pushed.

'Yes,' replied Norma Maguire.

Clay turned the pad around, showed it to Norma.

'I'm going to suspend the interview now,' said Clay. 'Look at the list. The last six?'

'Yes. The last six to leave.'

'I'm asking you again – would you describe yourself as a truthful person, Norma?'

Norma looked at Clay with the beginnings of bush fires in her eyes.

'Yes.'

'You need to have a seriously candid talk with your solicitor, Norma.' Clay tapped the list of names. 'You're a liar,' said Clay. 'Watch this space. There's much, much more to come.'

112

7.51 am

As Sergeant Harris escorted Norma Maguire from the interview suite, Clay's iPhone beeped with an incoming message.

Mason sent you a picture.

She opened it. There were two pictures. One of a white nylon hairnet and one of a sheet of lint roller.

Clay counted. On the lint roller there were three distinct, long hairs, their ends hanging over the sides of the sticky rectangular sheet.

Her iPhone rang out.

'Eve, did you get the pictures?'

'I did, Terry, thank you. You got the hairs from McKee's hairnet, right?'

'Right. They're all covered in various shades of crap but they've each got a follicle. We can test them for DNA. Do you want us to go ahead or send them to the lab? Your call, Eve.'

She felt like a sword had descended from the sky, splitting her into two perfectly even halves.

'How long will the lab take?'

'Thirteen hours plus.'

'You?'

'I can do it a lot faster than the lab.'

'Can the lab retest the samples once you've had a go?'

'Of course they can, Eve.'

'I've known you for years, Terry, and I trust you to the limits. Send one of the samples to the lab and test the others yourself. Tell them to drop everything and fast-track it. We're hunting down The Ghoul, tell them.'

'Eve, don't get over-excited by this. It's possible the hairs could have come from one of McKee's co-workers or even one of the prostitutes he employs.'

'You've done it before and made a great job of it, Terry. Tell Pricey to be on standby in case anything crops up. I'd like you to stick to the DNA hunt to the exclusion of all other things.'

She hoped with all her spirit that the hairs belonged to Annie Boyd.

'If he's used his abattoir skills to scalp her, I think we've got a better than good chance that it may be hers.'

Clay saw the remains of Annie Boyd's face and head on the mud at the bottom of the Mersey and the indelible image electrified her.

'Edgar McKee, we're coming to get you.'

113

7.58 am

Waking up in darkness, Francesca Christie lay on her right-hand side, the pain from her shoulder down to her foot cranking up with each passing moment.

She tried to make out any shape in the darkness and, even though she guessed there was none, there was one thing she did know.

After she'd been drugged, she'd been moved from the basement.

As she progressed further into wakefulness, Francesca could hear her heart beating faster by the moment and the blood in her head pounding in her ears.

'Breathe deeply,' she said to herself. 'And listen to the noises outside your own skin. Yes, Francesca. That's good, Francesca. Calm down, Francesca.'

As Francesca listened, she became increasingly aware of her body. Her feet were tied tightly at the ankles with rope or cloth and her hands were tied behind her back at the wrists.

She couldn't make out any sound beyond the space.

'Hello.'

She spoke softly and, listening to her own voice, was certain she was no longer in the basement.

Beneath her was a blanket, and beneath the rough fabric there were indentations on the floor.

'Hello. Hello.'

From the acoustics, she knew she was in a confined space, a place much smaller than the basement.

She drew air in slowly through her nose and her senses of smell and taste picked up metal and rubber.

Francesca rocked herself on to her front and the relief down her side was instantaneous and intense. The space rocked, a tiny motion.

I'm in a vehicle, she thought.

In the distance outside the vehicle, she heard a sound but couldn't place the direction it came from. Der. Der.

It was a train, moving at speed, and she was filled with envy for every last person travelling away from the place where she was trapped.

Oil.

She smelled it close at hand, heard it slosh as it moved from left to right in what she guessed was a can centimetres away from where she lay.

'Jesus,' she whispered into the slackening darkness that still engulfed her vision. The blanket of murkiness grew grainy with dark particles of grey specks dancing in front of her.

I'm not in a car, she thought. *It's too big. I'm not squashed into a car boot. This space is big enough for me.* She sensed space above her head and beneath her feet. *The space is bigger than me.*

The smell of raw meat infiltrated the trinity of oil, rubber and metal.

A butcher's van. Lamb. Beef. Pork. Chicken. Meat from different animals with one thing in common: all dead, all skinned.

For the first time in captivity, she had a feeling that was stronger than the terror that had possessed her. Nostalgia. Thoughts of her past life, freedom, boredom, excitement, work and rest, family and home, sorrow, grief, joy, love and sex drowned the all-consuming sickness inspired by what the future held for her.

'My name is Francesca Christie.'

As she spoke, clarity swept through her brain and she put all the pieces together.

'I am in the back of a van. The van is not moving. The van is parked within hearing distance of a length of rail track. And I am alone.'

She fell silent at the throb of an aeroplane flying directly overhead.

Francesca closed her eyes against the immediate darkness and pictured the lights on the aeroplane and the people inside it travelling to their homes and loved ones or their holidays, and she was consumed with the width of the world beyond her captivity.

She pictured The Ghoul wearing the face and scalp of a woman who had died because of *it*. In her mind, she stared into The Ghoul's eyes, lurking beneath the stolen skin, and watched the mouth beneath the woman's lips.

'Annie,' she said, recalling a picture she had seen on the television news and the name of the missing primary school teacher that went with it. 'Annie, I'm so sorry.'

Annie's hair hung down on to The Ghoul's shoulders. It peered at her, close-up, and she felt its breath touching her skin from the flap of Annie's lips.

I am not going to die quietly. I am not going to go easily. I will fight you...

The words flooded into her like divine commandments.

'If I'm going to die, I will hurt you for taking my life.'
Silence.
'I will find a way. Have you got that...'
And a single word came from her mouth, a word she had heard many times down the years but had never once used in her life.
'...motherfucker!'

114
8.30 am

'When Daniel's not here, I open up,' said Carolyn Wilkes as she led Hendricks up the stairs to Norma Maguire's office. 'Norma should be here at some point this morning if you need to talk to her. She tends to come and go a bit on Saturdays.'

Carolyn opened the door to the office and Hendricks followed her inside. She closed the door and, although they were the only two people in the estate agency, she dropped the volume of her voice a couple of notches.

'Is this to do with Francesca Christie?' she asked.

'It is, yes.' Hendricks indicated the seat at the desk to Carolyn and, grabbing a nearby chair, sat in Norma Maguire's place.

'Norma won't be happy if she bowls in here and finds us sitting at her desk.'

'That won't be happening, Carolyn. Norma's currently in police custody.'

Carolyn looked as if she'd been hit on the head with a blunt object.

'What's she in police custody for?'

'I'm not at liberty to tell you.'

Hendricks gave her a few moments to absorb the information.

'There's an unmarked police car outside your office. As soon as we're done in here, the officers in that vehicle will start searching Norma's office and taking away evidence.'

'It's Francesca, isn't it? Has she done something to her?'

'I don't know. Is she capable of doing such a thing?'

'I don't know. She was furious with her.'

Hendricks took two pieces of paper from his pocket.

'I'd like you to look at these two lists for me, Carolyn.'

He passed her the first paper, a copy of the six names of former employees supplied by Norma Maguire.

'We asked Norma to give us the names of six people who had resigned from Maguire Holdings.'

He read his own writing, upside down on the desk.

Francesca Christie
Max Rodgers
Peter Gould
Eric Smith
Richard Ezra
David Ellis

As she looked at the list, the lines in her brow deepened.

'You recognise these people?'

'Yes.'

Hendricks passed her the second list and asked, 'How about this?'

Francesca Christie
Geoff Campbell

James Griffiths
Thomas Saddler
Richard Ezra
Michael Towers

'They all worked here in the past?'

'Yes.'

'What's the difference between the two lists, Carolyn?'

She turned the first list round and passed it back to Hendricks.

'With the exception of Francesca and Richard, these were temporary members of staff, agency workers covering short-term illnesses and maternity leave. Max, Pete, Eric and David didn't leave as such. Their time here came to a natural end. Norma didn't care about them leaving.'

She passed the second list back to Hendricks.

'These were all full-time, permanent members of the team. When they walked out, Norma felt betrayed by them. They all went on to better things with other estate agents and that really was the icing on the cake. There was a pattern in Norma's reaction. Anger and hurt were followed by barely concealed rage. The rage calmed down but didn't go away, it smouldered beneath the surface. And no one dared mention their names.'

'Why?'

'Just after he'd left, she overheard one of the juniors talking favourably about Richard Ezra. She went mad at him and fired him two days later on a trumped-up pretext.'

'She hated them that much?' Hendricks checked.

'Norma spends a lot of time on her own when she isn't here. Alone in that big old house with too much time on her hands. In my view, she festers there. In her head, she demonised them.' Tears welled up in Carolyn's eyes. 'She's done something to Francesca, hasn't she?'

'I hope not. But we don't know where Francesca is and that's worrying. How would you describe Norma Maguire's feelings towards Francesca Christie?'

She looked extremely uncomfortable.

'I need to know, Carolyn.'

'She was absolutely head over heels in love with Francesca from the moment she walked over the threshold. The way she acted around her was farcical and embarrassing. She was like a schoolgirl around a pop star.'

Hendricks said nothing but then asked, 'Are there places that are special to Norma Maguire? Places she goes to when she's sad or needs to think?'

'I'll think about it, DS Hendricks.'

'Please do.' He handed her his contact card. 'And ask around the office. Ask if Norma had any favourite haunts. Please keep our discussion absolutely to yourself and thank you for your co-operation. My colleagues will come in now to search the office.'

On the pavement outside Maguire Holdings, Hendricks' curiosity about Norma Maguire was spiked and he called Riley on his iPhone.

'How's it going, Gina?' asked Hendricks.

'So far we haven't found anything in the house to incriminate Norma Maguire. I don't know what Poppy's going to pull from the laptop and iPhone that Eve took from her. It's like an old lady's house. I can imagine a person dying of boredom between these walls.'

'Interesting. Anything in the loft?'

'A box with a couple of old scrapbooks. I haven't seen it myself, but I heard it's newspaper cuttings, reviews of plays her mother, Cecily Levin, was in. It's on its way to Trinity Road, along with boxes of receipts and bills. There's no evidence of her having relationships with anyone except the people she paid to work for her.'

'What about the basement?'

'Two rooms and a massive anomaly. One room's empty. The next room's got a huge mirror on the wall. I've been in every room in the house, including the bathroom, and that mirror in the basement is the only mirror in the house.'

Hendricks recalled the first time he saw Norma Maguire, when he knocked on her door. She had appeared painfully shy and had physically done everything she could so that he couldn't see her face.

'Keep me posted, Gina.'

Hendricks clicked on his Messages icon and picked out Clay on his list of contacts.

Eve, Norma Maguire has massive self-loathing issues. Catoptrophobia. I'll tell you when I see you.

115

8.35 am

Detective Chief Inspector Eve Clay noticed that as he watched her walk past, the contempt Edgar McKee had worn on his face on their first encounter had returned, but was bigger and deeper than ever.

She maintained eye contact with him as Winters formally opened the interview.

'Tell me about your mother.' asked Clay.

'Jesus, you really are clutching at straws.'

'Humour me, Mr McKee. I know where this is going.'

McKee looked at his solicitor, who smirked. *Go on. Humour her.*

'I never knew my mother. But I know things about her. She was a single mother when she gave birth to me in the 1970s. She had no way of keeping me. She was forced to sign me over for adoption. I was a sickly baby and I grew into a sickly child. So I didn't get adopted. Everyone wanted a healthy kid. The home I lived in literally couldn't give me away.'

'Where was this house?'

'Russell House. Near Wrexham, in Flintshire. I went looking for her when I was in my thirties but I was too late. She died in 2001.'

'When was she born?'

Edgar McKee rolled his sleeve up and showed Clay the tattoo on his wrist.

'She wasn't a kid when she had me but she was a single woman. It wasn't like nowadays when no one gives a fuck about anything much. Everyone had too much to say for themselves in the 1970s.'

'Where's her grave?'

'I don't know. The moment I found out she was dead, I got the tattoo and gave up on the job. What's your point?'

'Is it possible she's buried in Springwood Cemetery?'

'It's possible. Or Anfield Cemetery. Or she could be in Graceland with Elvis. Seriously, how the fuck do I know?'

Edgar McKee looked at his solicitor with an expression of extreme frustration that begged an essential question.

'Are you going to charge my client or let him go?'

'We will be charging you before the twenty-four-hour time window closes.'

Clay pulled up a series of images from her gallery.

'Our Scientific Support officers found something odd in your DVD collection. It was ninety-nine per cent hard-core pornography...'

'...Which is perfectly legal and advertised in national tabloid newspapers.'

Clay turned her iPhone towards McKee.

'They found some Hammer Horror films. Not that many but enough to stand out from the rest of your collection. Look!'

'What do you want me to say, Clay?'

'Why are they there?'

'Because I was into them when I hit puberty. I fancied the actresses in them, when I was becoming sexually aware. It's the only sentimental thing you'll find in my life, I'm telling you.'

'Who were the actresses in them?'

'I can't remember.'

'Cecily Levin was in *Twins of Evil, Lust For A Vampire, The Vampire Lovers, Dracula AD 1972*. Ring any bells?'

'No.'

'Really? Sex is clearly of great importance in your life. As you know, we've been talking to Marlene Black. She's one of three sex workers you go and visit on a regular basis. That's not cheap. How do you pay for it?'

'I live a frugal life. It's the only joy I get.'

'I went to Marlene's house,' said Winters. He turned his camera towards Edgar McKee. 'This is her in her kitchen at home.'

'So that's what she looks like without make-up,' observed Edgar McKee.

'How many women have you had sex with in your life?' asked Winters.

'Thousands.'

'You must be very proficient in the bedroom. Experienced. You have a powerful gym-honed body. You've been round the block and back many times.'

Clay saw a glint of pride and a sheen of machismo in McKee's eyes as Winters spoke.

'How do you think women perceive you?'

'Let's just say the women I pay for sex don't fake their orgasms. I'm better than good in bed. They tell me all the time. I know when people bullshit me. These women aren't bullshitting me.'

'Ever been in a permanent relationship with a woman?'

'You're kidding me. No. Of course not. What's the point?'

'After we're done here, Mr McKee,' said Winters. 'I'm going back to see Marlene. Do you want me to pass on a message to her?'

'Tell her I'll be calling her as soon as I get out of this swamp.'

'Mr McKee?' Clay drew his attention. 'Have you ever had sex with a woman called Norma Maguire?'

Clay showed him Norma Maguire's picture, a blown-up image from the most recent framed staff portrait.

'I wouldn't have sex with her if she was the last woman on earth.'

'Do you know Norma Maguire?' suggested Clay.

'Never seen or heard of her.'

She picked out the image on her iPhone of Cecily Levin as Jocasta in *Oedipus Rex* and showed it to Edgar McKee.

'Who's she?' asked Edgar McKee.

'Cecily Levin was Norma Maguire's mother. She was a successful actress. She was in the Hammer films I named that we found in your DVD collection.'

He scrutinised the screen of Clay's iPhone.

'She had all the good-looking genes in the world. I guess she didn't pass them on to her daughter.'

'You sure you don't know Norma Maguire?'

'Fucking certain!'

'It's just we've got Norma Maguire in custody on the same investigation that's keeping you here. Do you want to get ahead of the game and tell me exactly what's been going on between the two of you?'

'Sefton Park,' replied Edgar McKee, his face passive to the point of death.

'Why do you say that?' asked Clay.

'Because there's a lake there. If it's a fishing trip you're looking to go on, go there and leave me alone.'

'OK. Here comes the very bad news for you, Mr McKee. Wren's changed his story from *I don't know*. He's given us an in-depth description of what happened on the footpath. You were out of the van for four minutes and nine seconds exactly. He counted. We've got a witness whose dog found Amanda Winton's body and saw you running away with a torch in your hand. What do you say to that, Mr McKee?'

Edgar McKee turned to Detective Constable Clive Winters.

'I say, when you go and see Marlene, do yourself a favour and fuck her brains out. She's soooooo good!'

116

9.05 am

'Where's Terry Mason?' asked Stone as he looked around the shell of Norma Maguire's office and the evidence bags lined up at the door.

'He's back at the ranch, running DNA tests on hairs found on Edgar McKee's hairnets from the abattoir,' replied Sergeant Paul Price, taking photographs of the empty drawers of Norma Maguire's desk.

Riley looked at the three filing cabinets mounted on trolleys at the door to be transported back to Trinity Road police station.

Stone looked around the room at the Scientific Support officers drafted in from Admiral Street and was touched by the quiet confidence swelling in Sergeant Paul Price as he orchestrated his colleagues in the manner of his mentor, DS Mason.

Looking around Norma Maguire's office, he saw the last thing to be done. He snatched up a handful of evidence bags and walked to the line of framed staff portraits on the wall facing the door.

'I'll get this one, Pricey,' said Stone, as the filing cabinets were wheeled to the lift and evidence bags were piled on to trolleys.

He started with the oldest image, the first in line where Norma looked her youngest, and slipped it from the wall into a bag. Sticking the next frame into a bag, Stone noticed the clean rectangle where the picture had been beneath the four-cornered lines of grime on the wall.

Stone stopped at the third picture, his eyes drawn to the face of Richard Ezra, smiling at Norma's side. As he bagged the picture, the image of him that The Ghoul had falsely circulated to his victims danced through his mind.

Lifting the next picture from the wall, he saw a pattern of sorts emerging. The disappearance of individual men from the photographic timeline, and he realised that they were the ones who had resigned from Maguire Holdings, and whose names had been plundered by The Ghoul, hunting down women on the internet.

'Do you want me to take the bags from you?' asked Sergeant Price.

As Stone handed the bags to Price, he said, 'We can easily work out what the real James Griffiths and Geoff Campbell look like. It's a process of photographic elimination. They just disappear one by one on the photographic timeline.'

'There's only one part of Norma Maguire's body that's more fucked up than her legs. Her brain.'

Stone took down the last two portraits and noticed that the only person not looking directly at the camera in every shot was Norma Maguire.

He focused on the last portrait, his eyes drawn to Francesca Christie, seated centre front next to Norma, the smile bleeding from her lips, her eyes lost and bewildered, the back of Norma's hand drooping from the side of her wheelchair and resting against Francesca's thigh.

Taking it from the wall, the glass moved within the frame, unstable in the wood as it sank into the darkness of an evidence bag.

Stone handed the bag to Price, the look in Francesca Christie's eyes melting into his brain, and he wondered what the young woman was looking at now, if the act of looking was still a reality for her.

117

9.15 am

Norma Maguire gripped the metal hand rims of her wheelchair as she rolled herself towards the desk in Interview Suite 1.

Clay sat in front of two photographs face down on the table and two folded papers. She formally opened the interview, staring into Norma's eyes with each word.

'Have you had any thoughts since our last discussion?' asked Clay.

'When can I go home? The same thought, over and over.'

'You can't go home,' said Clay. 'Your house is being treated as a crime scene. Your personal laptop and phone are being explored by our IT specialist. Anything you've deleted can be easily undeleted and anything you've tried to hide will be found.'

Norma Maguire looked at her solicitor as if she'd woken from a nightmare.

'DCI Clay,' said Ms Rice. 'Would you describe Ms Maguire as a prime suspect in the abduction of Francesca Christie?'

'Yes.'

'On what grounds?'

'Look at me, Ms Maguire, not the backs of your hands.' She noticed the veins bulging beneath the skin of her hands and the power in her wrists. Her lower forearms were riddled with muscle and her fingers were thick and meaty.

Clay slid a piece of paper across the desk.

'Recognise the handwriting?'

'It's my handwriting.'

'And what's on it?'

'The names of the last six people to leave my employment.'

'Read it back to me.'

'Francesca Christie. Max Rodgers. Peter Gould. Eric Smith. Richard Ezra. David Ellis.'

Clay looked at the second list of names.

'So that's definitely the last six people who walked out on you?'

'Yes. I told you that earlier when I gave you the list.'

She presented Norma Maguire with the second list.

'Read that list to me.'

'Francesca Christie. Geoff Campbell.'

'Carry on, Norma.'

'James.' There was the catch of rising tears in her voice. 'James Griffiths. Thomas Saddler. Richard Ezra.'

Hendricks turned over a photograph of Richard Ezra staring lovingly into a doctored space.

'Is this the Richard Ezra you've just mentioned?' asked Clay.

'He used to work for me. What of it?'

'Keep going with the list,' said Clay. 'There's one more name on it. Read it to us.'

'Michael Towers. What are you driving at, DCI Clay?' asked Norma Maguire.

'All the people on the second list you've read have two specific things in common. They were all permanent members of staff at Maguire Holdings and they all walked away from you. With the exception of Francesca Christie and Richard Ezra, the list you provided was fallacious, a set of half-truths meant to misguide me. The other four names of the six you provided were agency staff, temps who came and went. Do I carry on or are you going to tell me about the list in my handwriting that I've just given you?'

Ms Rice glanced at Norma Maguire with a cloud in her eyes and a knot in her brow that told Clay the suspect had withheld information from her solicitor. Clay met the solicitor's gaze and guessed that Norma Maguire's untruthfulness had centred on the list of former employees.

'I find rejection very difficult to come to terms with.'

'All that statement gives you is something in common with billions of other people on this planet. Frankly, you're avoiding the question I've just asked you.'

Norma wheeled herself back from the table.

'You're going nowhere, Ms Maguire,' said Clay. 'Because there's nowhere for you to go.'

'If you're not happy, Norma, you can always go *no comment*,' said her solicitor.

'Are you aware of the name Sandra O'Day, Ms Maguire?' asked Hendricks.

She said nothing and as seconds ticked away, Clay said, 'I'll take your silence as a *yes*. Annie Boyd? Ring any bells?'

'I heard about her on the radio.'

'Was this after you'd been a party to her murder?' pressed Clay.

'We need to talk,' said Ms Rice. 'I'd like to suggest an adjournment to this interview. I need to speak with my client.'

'OK,' said Clay. 'But before we do that, I need to know. Are you aware of the existence of a person called The Ghoul?'

'Through the newspapers,' said Norma Maguire.

'The Ghoul has used an internet dating site called Pebbles On The Beach to track down his victims. Are you aware of the existence of Pebbles On The Beach?'

'No, no comment—, yes of course I am, I tried to warn Fran off going on it, for heaven's sake. I've told you already, the first time I met you.'

'The thing is, Ms Maguire,' said Clay, 'The Ghoul has been masquerading under a series of false names. The list in my handwriting, with the exception of Francesca Christie, they're all men, and the men on the list have three things in common. One and two. They all worked for you and resigned. Established fact. And three? The Ghoul assumed their names as *it* hunted down lonely women on the internet. I'm 100 per cent certain that The Ghoul isn't one person acting alone.'

Ms Rice looked hard and sideways to her right.

'Wait! The Ghoul could be anybody associated with Maguire Holdings with insider knowledge of the comings and goings of my firm. Just because I own Maguire Holdings doesn't automatically mean that I've got anything to do with these horrific crimes. It could be a lot of people.'

'Point taken, Miss Maguire,' said Clay. 'It's your job to convince us now that you haven't had anything to do with the abduction, murder and mutilation of Sandra O'Day, Annie Boyd and Amanda Winton. But there's something else I'm desperate to know about in the here and now. Something really pressing.'

'What?'

'Where's Francesca Christie?'

'Pardon?'

'You heard.'

'I don't know.'

'If you won't tell me, maybe someone else will.'

'What do you mean, DCI Clay?' asked Norma Maguire, her colour rising.

Clay looked to Hendricks and he turned over the second photograph on the table, pushed it towards Norma Maguire.

It was a copy of the mug shot Sergeant Harris had taken of Edgar McKee as he'd been taken into custody.

'Don't look away, Ms Maguire,' said Clay. 'Look at the picture.'

Norma Maguire lowered her eyes, looked at McKee's meaty face and cropped ginger-grey hair.

'Do you know him, Ms Maguire?'

'I have never seen this man before in my life.'

Norma pushed the photograph back to Clay as if it was an obscenity.

'We've got him in custody. His name's Edgar McKee. He's in custody for the same reason you are. Are you sure you don't know him?'

'No, I don't know him. You'll be telling me next that he used to work for me and that he left me and that he's now killing young women.'

'He's not exactly a Maguire Holdings kind of guy. But you do know him.'

'You have to prove that, DCI Clay.'

'I get that, Ms Maguire. Talk to Ms Rice, go to your cell and think things through. I'm offering you the same break I've offered him. So far, neither of you have cracked. He's in one cell. You're in another. Same crime. This is your chance to get in first and tell your side of the story before he does.'

'When I go back to my cell, DCI Clay, I'm going to try and work out how you think I'd even be capable of taking part in such murders. Look at me. Look at my wheelchair. I'm a cripple. How could I possibly take part in abduction or murder or mutilation? Why should I even want to do such horrific things to other women?'

Clay looked at Norma Maguire, locked her in with her eyes.

'That's an interesting slice of superficial logic. But you don't need legs to take part. You have Edgar McKee's legs at your disposal. Go back to your cell and think damage limitation. Your arrogance isn't helping you here, Ms Maguire.'

'What do you mean?'

Clay held up the list of names. 'Christie. Campbell. Griffiths. Saddler. Ezra. Towers. You couldn't help yourself, could you? You couldn't stand them leaving you. You couldn't help relegating these traitors to the level of low-life murdering scumbags.'

Clay waved the paper in the air.

'For your information, Carolyn Wilkes blew the whistle on you. She told us that four of the people on the list you provided were temps and you didn't care less when they stopped working for you.'

When Norma wheeled herself to the door of the interview suite, Clay said, 'Wait there for Sergeant Harris.'

Standing behind her, Ms Rice folded her arms and looked down on her client with the bitterness of a woman who had been treated like a prize fool by someone she had done her best to help.

'You need to tell me everything, Ms Maguire,' whispered Ms Rice. 'And when I say everything, I mean everything!'

'As I said the first time we were in the room together,' said Clay. 'You're a liar! And before you know it the truth will tie you in knots.'

118
9.30 am

Detective Constable Karl Stone sat at one of two tables specially set up in Interview Suite 3 and looked at two large scrapbooks taken from the loft of Norma Maguire's house in Grassendale Park. There was a thick layer of dust on the covers of the blue leather books and the condensed smell of decades rose from the pages.

At the second table, PC Ryan Marsh and WPC Dana Wallace sat in front of two folders of receipts, with DC Barney Cole between them.

'Show me everything you look at as we go through the receipts and invoices,' said Cole. 'When you've got the hang of it, I'll leave you in peace.'

The filing cabinets from Norma Maguire's office, which had housed the receipts, now lined the back wall of the interview suite.

'What are we looking for, DC Cole?' asked PC Marsh.

'Stick anything incongruous in one pile. In another pile, place anything that's been paid for between 1st July and 31st August this year. Make a third pile of any purchases relating to Warrington.'

'The Sandra O'Day set?' confirmed Wallace.

'Two piles for Sandra,' said Cole. 'Any receipts from the last month, stick into a fourth group. That'll cover anything that may relate to Annie Boyd, Amanda Winton and Francesca Christie. Anything outside those categories leave to one side and we'll sift through it when we've squeezed the lemon dry on the others. They're ordered chronologically. Norma Maguire's an OCD stickler and that's to our advantage.'

Stone looked at the staff portraits from the wall of Norma Maguire's office, set out in the same order. They were on the floor, propped against the wall, and there was something about them that caused an itch beneath his scalp.

He opened the first of the two scrapbooks and, when he did so, the mustiness intensified.

On the first page, there was a small black and white picture and two columns of newsprint. It was a review for a provincial theatre production of Seán O'Casey's *Juno and the Paycock*.

From the grainy picture, Stone picked out a very young-looking Cecily Levin and skimmed and scanned the newsprint. It was deemed to be a good production with a great performance from Cecily Levin as Mary Boyle: *a poignant hymn to a young woman's disillusionment in the narrowness of human nature.*

He flicked through the next few pages and saw more positive newspaper reviews for theatre productions up and down the land in which Cecily Levin was singled out for rich praise.

Turning to the back pages of the book, Stone saw that Cecily was still working prolifically in theatre at the tail end of 1967.

He pushed the first book away from himself and opened the next one at the first page, where he saw a monochrome shot for a TV drama, *Z Cars*, in which Cecily Levin was dressed and made up to look brassy.

Under the picture, Cecily had written: *First break into TV.*

Stone's instinct told him that the pickings were going to be richer in the second scrapbook.

While the pages of the first scrapbook sat level, the pages of the second were parted by bulk. He turned the pages over and over and saw publicity stills from a range of 1960s' TV shows, all featuring Cecily Levin.

Stone looked at the table next to him and saw that Cole and the constables were already constructing separate sets of receipts.

He looked at the clock on the wall and worked out that DS Terry Marsh was just over an hour and a half into his DNA testing of the hairs found in Edgar McKee's hairnets from the abattoir. At three o'clock or thereabouts, there would be a result, for better or worse.

With each turn of the page, Cecily Levin's star rose higher.

Oh my God, thought Stone, as he came to a colour publicity still from *The Vampire Lovers:* Cecily Levin with fake fangs and a plunging neckline.

In a pair of dusty scrapbooks, she'd walked on to the stage in a Sean O'Casey play as little more than a girl but had waltzed into the Hammer House of Horror as a fully grown woman and screen siren.

As he turned the pages of the scrapbook, the earliest days of his love affair with horror films were brought vividly to life.

In between the film stills were newspaper reviews for shows Cecily Levin had been in at the Liverpool Everyman Theatre, her bread and butter between her work on the big screen.

He smiled at a picture of Cecily Levin and Christopher Lee, a still from *Dracula AD 1972.*

As he turned the page, Stone realised he had come to the end of his whistle-stop journey into Cecily Levin's acting career and reached the point where real life had kicked in.

Cecily Levin was dressed in a white bridal gown. She stood next to a tall, muscular man in a dark suit on the steps of a church, an intimidating individual who looked at the camera as if he was staring down Satan.

'Terry Maguire,' said Stone to himself, turning the page and seeing bride and groom among their guests. *Marrying*

Terry Maguire was the end of your acting days, he thought, with a great degree of sadness. *He was loaded and called the shots, offered you the security and lifestyle that film, TV and theatre probably never would.*

He came to a picture of Cecily in a hospital bed on a private ward, holding a newborn baby. He guessed the baby was Norma Maguire. Cecily looked tired but enormously happy.

As he turned the pages, he saw the little girl growing up next to her mother and he looked at the pictures from Maguire Holdings propped against the wall. Norma Maguire in the different stages of her life.

He came to the end of the scrapbook and found two envelopes glued to the surface of the last page.

He opened the top envelope and saw Norma Maguire's birth certificate.

He opened the bottom envelope and saw a marriage certificate.

Stone looked at the boxes and the neat cursive print inside them. Bachelor – Terrance Maguire. Spinster –

He looked at the bride's name and muttered, 'Holy fuck!'

Stone picked up his iPhone as Cole, Marsh and Wallace stopped sorting through the receipts and looked directly at him.

'Found something?' asked Cole.

He nodded.

'Eve?' He picked up the marriage certificate and headed for the door. 'Where are you?'

'The incident room. You OK?'

'Better than OK. I've something to show you. I'll see you in a couple of minutes.'

119

10.05 am

Susan Hurst's mother snored in the armchair in the corner of her daughter's front room, buried alive in the deepest of sleeps.

In a playpen in the middle of the room, Susan's elder son, Charlie, played with a set of interconnecting bricks while her baby son, David, sat on her lap drinking formula milk from the bottle in her right hand.

'Thank you for agreeing to see me at such short notice,' said Winters. 'I can see you're busy.'

'On the phone you said it was about Edgar McKee. Is he still in police custody?' asked Susan.

'He is.'

'I told you last time. You've got the wrong man.'

'Time will tell, Susan, but for now he's a suspect in a pretty disturbing series of crimes.'

She plucked the empty bottle from her baby's lips and transferred him on to her shoulder, where she patted and rubbed his back with motherly love.

'How can I help you, DC Winters?'

'Mind if I film our conversation?' He took out his iPhone.

She looked around the room. Charlie peered over the side of the playpen and sank on to his bottom as Susan's mother descended even deeper into sleep.

'OK.'

Winters turned to video, pressed record and pointed his iPhone in Susan's direction.

'We need to learn everything we can about Edgar McKee, and as quickly as possible. We're trying to build a picture of who he is. He's a loner. Judging from the notes in his diary, you're the person he has most social contact with. He sees two other women from Dream Girls but not anything like the amount he sees you. What do you know about him?'

'He's polite, generous and works in an abattoir.' She fell silent. 'That's about it. He's not a great conversationalist. Some of my clients don't know when to shut up. But not Edgar. He's quiet.' Her baby brought up a volley of wind. 'Good boy.' Susan lay the baby down on the sofa next to her and, as she patted his chin and cheeks with his bib, she asked, 'Did you tell him you'd been to see me?'

'I did.'

She looked up, appeared interested.

'What did he say about me?'

'The relationship was straightforward. Sex for money.'

'Is that all?'

'No.'

'You've got to understand, DC Winters. I don't get to hear what my clients say about me when I'm not there. I'm helping you. You help me. Don't mince your words. I want to know. What did he say?'

'He recommended your services but he didn't put it so politely.' His voice dropped to a whisper. 'He suggested I should, quote, *fuck your brains out.*'

She looked astonished and sourly amused.

'Did he really say that?'

She pressed her face close to her baby's and he made a noise rich in contentment.

'You've got him marked down as a gentleman, Susan. I didn't find him particularly gentlemanly in the way he spoke about you. Quite the opposite, in fact.'

'Just for the sake of, we are on the same hymn sheet here? He indicated that you should have sexual intercourse with me.'

'He also said that he satisfied you and other women he paid for sex. That you had orgasms as a matter of course because he was so skilled at sex.'

She picked up her baby and, walking to the playpen, placed him inside with his older brother.

Susan turned. 'How would he know what sexual intercourse with me or any of the other girls is like?'

'Susan?'

'If you want further clarification, I can give you the mobile numbers for Chloe and Erica, his other regulars from my agency.'

'I'll take those numbers before I go but for now, tell me what you mean, Susan?'

'Edgar McKee's impotent. It's all in his head. He tried Viagra. Even that didn't work. The brain to penis highway's closed and bombed out. He simply can't get a hard on.'

'You wrote down that he performed anal sex on you.'

Susan shook her head as she sat down next to Winters.

'Wrong way round. I perform it on him.' Two images from Edgar McKee's phone sailed through Winters' mind. 'I use a range of phallic-like objects and insert them into his anus.'

'What about the other activity you mentioned?'

'He likes to go down on me. It goes on for ages. It's the best he can do. It's all he can do. It's boring beyond belief but I charge him top rate for it. He likes me to talk dirty while he's doing his thing, which I can do on automatic pilot. I'm usually thinking about the kids, or what's going to happen next with my mother, or what to buy for dinner when I go to Tesco.'

'That's an incredibly useful insight, Susan, thank you.'

'He actually said he satisfied me?'

'He told us he did satisfy you and he can tell when people bullshit him. You weren't bullshitting, according to Edgar.'

He watched the knowledge sink deeper inside Susan and noticed the annoyance it caused her, and he couldn't wait to get into his car and call Clay.

'The cheeky bastard.'

'In no uncertain terms, Susan. Is there anything else you can tell me about him?'

'No. Is there anything else Edgar said about me?'

'He said to tell you that when he got out of the swamp, meaning the police station, he was going to call you straight away.'

'Well, I've got a message for him. Tell him from me to keep his money and fuck right off, the impotent piece of shit. There isn't a man alive who can satisfy me on any level. Boasting about how good he is at my expense? Making himself look good at my expense? I'm just not having it. Edgar McKee? Give a man a good name, speak up for him when he's in the shit and he throws shit back in my direction. He's not making me look weak. Me and the girls are going to have a really good laugh about this.' Winters zoomed in on Susan laughing. 'You've cheered me up no end, DC Winters.'

'I'll pass your message to him directly. Can I have those numbers for Chloe and Erica, please?'

In his car, parked at the corner of Armitage Gardens, Winters called Clay and got her on the third ring.

'How did it go with Susan Hurst?'

'I'm going to send you a film of her. Edgar McKee's managed to piss her off and amuse her in the same breath. Wait for this, Eve, you're going to love Susan.'

'As in Edgar McKee, sexual action man?'

'Spot on. Do you need me, or are you happy for me to go down to the Royal to the medical records department?'

'Edgar McKee's records?'

'And Norma Maguire's while I'm at it.'

'That sounds like a very good plan, Clive. Get what you can on their medical backgrounds and get back to the farm.'

As he headed down Booker Avenue for Mather Avenue, the music of Susan Hurst's laughter rang in his ears. And he pictured Edgar McKee's face when that music was played back to him loud and clear.

120

10.33 am

As she approached the open doorway of Norma Maguire's kitchen, Detective Sergeant Gina Riley could tell by the look on the young constable's face that he had conquered something particularly difficult and had made a first-rate job of it.

'How did you get on with the plaster chips from the basement, Tom?'

'I think I've pieced it together, though it's not perfect.'

Riley looked at the dust in the bucket at his feet and at the assembled plaster on the table in front of him.

'Some of the letters aren't complete. I've been through the bucket looking for the chips to round them off but I reckon the missing black paint is on the dust particles. But you can tell what the words are.'

'Do you know what? You've got more than enough here, Tom. Very well done.'

Riley read the jagged and broken words out loud. 'And, so, off she floats to nowhere.'

She took a series of photographs on her iPhone and sent it directly to Clay with a message.

Eve - This puts Norma Maguire's basement in a totally new light. Where's she going to float to? The Irwell? The Mersey? A flooded sinkhole? OMFG Gina.

Riley raised the hatch and, torch in hand, stepped on to the wooden stairs leading into the basement.

Walking deeper into the room, she cast a beam of light around the walls. She picked out the wall-mounted light near the door to the adjoining room and turned it on.

Riley walked to the space in front of the hacked-out wall and, looking at the image on her iPhone, mentally transferred the words in front of her on to the wall.

'And, so, off she floats to nowhere.'

Images of Annie Boyd on the riverbed and Amanda Winton in a water-filled sinkhole flashed through her mind and the words took on a chilling significance that tightened the twisting knot in her guts.

She walked backwards, further from where the graffiti had been hacked away, but the words flew around the pathways of her brain.

Riley faced the wall to her right and saw a hole in the brickwork. She stooped to examine it closely and noticed there was something lurking under the small mound of dust in the hole. With her index finger she scooped out the dust and encountered metal within the brick.

She felt the outline of a semi-circle on a metal base buried in the fabric of the wall.

Turning 180 degrees, she saw an identical hole at the same height on the wall with the door.

Riley considered the dimensions of the space in relation to the position of the graffiti and a bleak picture formed in her mind.

She took pictures of both holes and of the metal links sunk into the bricks.

Projecting the picture in her head into the space around her, the image became almost real, its details harrowing enough to make her run up the stairs two at a time.

In the kitchen she shouted, 'Stop!' The movement and noise in the house ceased. 'Everyone in the hallway, ASAP. Now! Move! Please!'

As she called Clay on her iPhone, she noticed that her hand was shaking.

'Did you get the picture I sent you, Eve?'

'*And, so, off she floats to nowhere?* Have you been down in the basement?'

'With a brand-new pair of eyes. I'm speculating but I'd gamble on it big time, Maguire and whoever she's been collaborating with have had Annie Boyd and Amanda Winton captive together in the basement. Buried in the walls on the left- and right-hand side of the room are two metal links. They're the first links in a pair of chains. They've had the two of them chained to the walls, staring at a vision of what was going to become of them. And, so, off she floats to nowhere.'

Officers gathered in the hall but no one uttered a word.

'Norma Maguire knows if Francesca Christie's still alive,' said Clay. 'She also knows, dead or alive, where she can be found.'

Riley looked at the silent officers and all eyes were on her.

'Have we found anything of interest in the house?' asked Riley.

Silence.

'How many are we?'

She counted over a dozen bodies.

'I want three to conduct a fingertip search of the first room in the basement and the wooden stairs leading down into it, and another three to do the same in the adjoining room. We're combing the floor, walls and ceiling.'

Riley turned and walked back to the hatch, turning her iPhone on to video.

'Do you want me to glue this together, DS Riley?' asked the young constable as she passed his broken mosaic.

'I would love you to make that piece of wall as permanent as you can, Tom.'

She hurried down the wooden steps and decided she would start with the place where the graffiti had been and work her way round the room in an anticlockwise direction.

Above her head officers assembled and, as the picture of the two women chained to the walls of the squalid space meshed in with the rank smell of the basement, a storm gathered in Riley's heart.

121

10.43 am

'Where's Francesca Christie?' asked Clay.

'I don't know,' replied Norma Maguire, her hands flat down on the table in front of her in Interview Suite 1.

'Is she still alive?'

'How would I know?'

'Because you're responsible for her disappearance. Your accomplice is Edgar McKee.'

'I don't know Edgar McKee.'

Clay watched Norma Maguire closely, witnessed the mounting desolation in her eyes.

'I'll return to *Fran* later. Do you want the bad news or the bad news?'

'I want to go home.'

'The bad news is that information's coming in thick and fast about you. The bad news is that it implicates you heavily in these very serious crimes.'

In her hands, Clay held three photographs and a folded piece of paper.

Clay turned over a picture of Cecily Levin, a copy from the framed portrait on Norma Maguire's office desk.

'Who's this? Remind me?'

'Cecily Levin, my mother.'

Clay turned over a second photograph.

'Look at it, Ms Maguire. What you're refusing to look at, is a photograph of a grave in Springwood Crematorium,' said Clay. 'The headstone reads: Catriona West, 1940–2001, Wife and Mother, Stolen in an Instant.' Clay waited. 'Seeing as you're insisting on looking at the wall behind my head, I'll describe the picture to you.'

'Are you sure you don't want to look at the picture, Ms Maguire?' asked her solicitor.

'No.'

'The second picture. Does the name Catriona West mean anything to you? Catriona West, stolen in an instant by a hit and run driver in 2001.'

Clay turned over a close-up image of the dead woman from the table and presented it to Norma Maguire.

'This is a picture from the gravestone when Catriona was middle-aged.'

Norma Maguire's eyes dipped to the table. Clay pointed to the picture of Cecily Levin and said, 'Young.' She indicated the next picture on the table and said, 'Middle-aged. Anything to say on that one?'

Clay unfolded the green paper.

'Want to see what we found in your mother's scrapbook?'

She made a show of examining it closely before placing it in front of Norma Maguire. Clay looked up and saw beads of perspiration forming on her top lip and forehead.

'You're sweating, Ms Maguire. Please help yourself to the water on the table.'

Clay pointed to the name of the bride.

'Catriona West was your mother's maiden name, her real name. Cecily Levin was your mother's stage name. Why didn't you make that distinction clear to me?'

'You were in my office. You commented on a picture of my mother acting in a Greek tragedy and asked who she was. In the capacity you saw her, she was a stage actor so I told you her stage name.'

'You accept that Cecily Levin and Catriona West were one and the same woman, your mother. Catriona West? How come she wasn't named as Catriona Maguire on her gravestone?'

'Because my father was a bully and a brute. When he died, she reverted to her maiden name by deed poll. What's her grave got to do with this mess? Why can't you just let her rest in peace?'

'Because one of the aliases given to Annie Boyd on Pebbles On The Beach was Richard Ezra and his address was listed as 66 Springwood Avenue. Turns out there's only one house on Springwood Avenue so it wasn't 66. But I dug a bit deeper and found the cemetery's divided into plots. I visited Plot 66 and your mother's grave's there. Richard Ezra, Catriona West, Plot 66.'

Clay drilled her complete attention into Norma Maguire.

'Richard Ezra. Catriona West. I guess you hated both of them with the same vengeance. Link his name to her address in death. It must've felt like banging their skulls together.'

'How dare you say I equate Richard Ezra with my mother.'

'I said it because you did it.'

Norma Maguire pushed the pictures of her mother and the image of her grave away from herself but Clay pushed them back into the middle of the table.

'Please don't do anything in this room other than answer my questions, Ms Maguire.'

Clay scrolled on her iPhone to the images sent to her by DS Gina Riley. She found the reconstructed graffiti from the basement wall and turned her iPhone round so that Norma Maguire could see it.

'Read it to me, Norma, the words on the wall of *your* basement.'

'And, so, off she floats to nowhere?' She looked at Clay as if she was an alien.

Clay scrolled on and showed Norma Maguire the pile of dust and chippings.

'Careless, very careless. Maybe too many other things to do in a microscopic time window?'

Clay rested her elbows on the table and leaned forward.

'You're madly in love with Francesca Christie, aren't you? And she rejected you, didn't she? You stalked Francesca Christie on Pebbles On The Beach, masquerading as a human rights lawyer called James Griffiths, didn't you?'

Norma Maguire covered her face with both hands.

'If you love Fran, Norma, tell me where we can find her. If you really love her, tell me if she's dead or alive. And if she's still alive, give her a fighting chance of staying alive. Look at me, Ms Maguire.'

Her hands sank slowly away from her face.

Clay scrolled through the images on her iPhone until she found the last staff portrait from the wall of Norma's office. She made a close-image of Norma Maguire and Francesca Christie.

'What did you do to Francesca, Ms Maguire?' asked Hendricks.

She looked startled at the sound of a man who, up until that point, had been a silent spectre in the room. He looked at an image on his iPhone.

'What did I do?'

Hendricks turned his iPhone around, showed her an image of Annie Boyd, scalped and faceless on the mud of the River Mersey.

Clay took in her reaction, the way she turned to stone; horror consumed Ms Rice's face and she touched her forehead with both hands.

'What did you do with their faces and scalps?' asked Hendricks, pushing his iPhone a little closer to her.

There was a knock at the door.

'Come in,' said Clay.

The door opened and Sergeant Harris walked into the room, followed by Poppy Waters.

'Sorry to interrupt,' said Harris.

'No problem. Speak of the Devil. Come here please, Poppy.'

Poppy Waters walked slowly towards Clay, an open laptop in her hands. She placed it on the desk in front of Clay.

'That's my laptop,' said Norma Maguire to her solicitor, like a child reclaiming a lost ball.

'You've cracked it then, Poppy.'

'I think you need to look at Ms Maguire's activity on Pebbles On The Beach,' said the IT specialist.

'I'm closing the interview, Ms Maguire. I need to look at some things on your laptop. I'll talk to you shortly. But would you like to tell me where Francesca Christie is?'

Norma Maguire looked torn, like a firestorm of words was raging inside her brain.

'When this gets to court, this lack of co-operation is going to be translated into one thing by the judge and jury. You have no remorse. That lack of remorse will be reflected in the sentence you receive. Think about it.'

122

11.30 am

Clay looked at Norma Maguire's Pebbles On The Beach page and said, 'This is great work, Poppy. There's no way out for her now. Michael Towers aka Richard Ezra aka Thomas Saddler aka James Griffiths aka Geoff Campbell.'

She looked at Riley, Stone, Hendricks and Cole and saw quiet optimism in all their faces.

There was a hush in the incident room and, sitting next to Clay at her desk, Poppy Waters said, 'She tried to delete everything last night. Maybe she had a premonition that you were on to her. I called it all back up. It wasn't difficult.'

'I'm very pleased with the speed and thoroughness of your work. Thank you.'

Clay looked at the linguistic glue smeared across the internet, the slime of language that was posted in the name of love, hope and happiness, and had to bite down on the passing need to be sick.

'He's intelligent in his own way but there's no way Edgar McKee could have come up with language like this,' said Clay. 'Norma Maguire set the traps, Edgar McKee pounced on the ensnared victims.'

She looked at Hendricks and saw deep unease creep into his eyes.

'What is it, Bill?'

Hendricks said, 'A part of me's thinking we all want this to be Edgar McKee too much. Nothing's come off his laptop or phone. There was nothing in his flat to connect him to any of these women. He doesn't do internet dating sites. So as we're looking at it, Norma Maguire's been luring them in and Edgar McKee's been collecting them from near the places where the meet-ups were arranged. But he's got a cast-iron alibi for Francesca Christie.'

Clay considered the problem.

'I'm thinking Francesca Christie was the odd one out. I don't think Edgar met the victims until date night. But Norma knew Francesca. That alters the dynamic completely. While Edgar was with Susan Hurst in the hotel room, Francesca might have been approached by Norma. Norma could have talked her into coming with her, despite the fact that Francesca had just walked out on her. Francesca comes across as a sweetie. Maybe Norma played her out on a guilt trip. Anyone?'

'McKee's alibi doesn't rule him out for Annie Boyd or Amanda Winton, but Sandra O'Day? He's got a great alibi. He wasn't even in the country, he was in Amsterdam. We could be looking at a third party. What do you think, Eve?' said Riley.

'We can ask the question but as it stands right now we're not going to get the truth from either of them.'

'Daniel Ball?' suggested Stone.

'She's been blackmailing him for years over his homosexual love affair. I suppose it isn't a massive leap to embroiling him in murder. Maybe she had something on Francesca. Maybe that's how she managed to get her to go with her. We can get in touch with Lydia, Daniel's wife, check on where he was on the nights Annie Boyd and Amanda Winton went missing.'

'Want me to go and see her?' asked Stone.

'Yes, thank you. You've got her number in case she's not in.'

Stone stood up with his eyes fixed on the clock and Clay guessed they were all of one mind. Time was growing increasingly tight.

'Yes, Eve.'

As he walked towards the door, Clay said to Riley, 'I want you in on the next interview with Edgar McKee. Given what Winters sent to my phone from Susan Hurst, two female faces may prove twice as distressing as one. Bill, come in with us. Barney, stay here in case anything comes in.'

Clay looked at Norma Maguire laptop. 'Have you backed everything up, Poppy?'

'Everything's sorted.'

'Eve, shouldn't we be frying Norma Maguire first?' asked Cole.

'She's a dead duck, Barney. Edgar McKee's the biggest problem here. And if we don't get a result from Terry Mason's DNA hunt, we'll probably be releasing him this evening. We're going to expose him as a liar and destabilise his macho head. Let's show him what his lady friend makes of him and his oh-so-pumped-up masculinity.'

123

11.55 am

Edgar McKee looked at Riley and asked, 'Who's she?'

'This is DS Gina Riley. The officer standing behind us is DS Bill Hendricks. I'm going to play back some of the remarks you made in a previous interview, on audio. Are you ready?'

Clay pressed play at the selected place.

Let's just say the women I pay for sex don't fake their orgasms. I'm better than good in bed. They tell me all the time. I know when people bullshit me. These women aren't bullshitting me.

Clay turned the recording off.

'Is that correct, Mr McKee?'

He smiled at her and she was sure the words *wouldn't you like to find out* were running through his head. Edgar McKee glanced at Hendricks, smiling, seeking his affirmation and admiration but receiving absolutely nothing back.

She turned her iPhone round, paused at the place where Winters went in with the big money question.

'Watch and listen, Mr McKee,' said Riley. 'We've been watching this, all of us have. The *he* that DC Winters is referring to is *you.*'

Clay waited, watched his eyes settle on the still image of Susan Hurst in her front room. She pressed play and released Winters' voice into the interview suite.

'He also said that he satisfied you and other women that he paid for sex.'

A cloud passed over Edgar McKee's face.

'Why's she smiling?' asked Clay.

'She's smiling at the idea that they had orgasms as a matter of course because you were so skilled at sex.'

'Turn it off,' said Edgar McKee.

'You need to hear her response to this,' said Clay as, on screen, Susan Hurst put her baby in the playpen.

'How would he know what sexual intercourse with me or any of the other girls is like?' asked Susan Hurst.

'Turn it off!' He slammed a fist down on the table. 'Do you hear me?'

'If you want further clarification, I can give you the mobile numbers for Chloe and Erica, his other regulars from my agency.'

'I'll take those numbers before I go but for now, tell me what you mean, Susan?'

'Edgar McKee's impotent. It's all in his head. He tried Viagra. Even that didn't work. The brain to penis highway's closed and bombed out. He simply can't get a hard on.'

'Turn it off now!' He stood up and within half a second Hendricks was at his side.

'Sit down!' said Hendricks.

Edgar McKee sat down, his face bright red, his breathing heavy.

'She's a fucking whore, do you believe her?'

'Yes, I do.' Clay looked at Riley, addressing the answer directly to her colleague.

'Me too,' responded Riley.

'What are you bitches smirking at?'

'I'm not smirking,' said Clay. 'Are you, Gina?'

'Nooo...'

'She went on to explain that she stuck things up your anus, phallic objects, and that you used to perform oral sex on her because, I guess, there was no point in her performing it on you because your penis was flaccid.'

Edgar McKee looked at his solicitor. 'Say something. Do something.'

'DCI Clay, what are you establishing with this?'

'Two things.'

She pulled up the pictures McKee had taken of himself on her iPhone.

'There were a lot of selfies on your phone, Mr McKee, that support Susan Hurst's version of events.'

She showed him the images he'd made, penetrating himself with a rolling pin.

'There's a lot of naked selfies but there isn't a single image in which your penis is erect. You clearly enjoy having items inserted inside your body. So, you're a liar. You lied to Wren. We know that. Sandra O'Day, Annie Boyd and Amanda Winton. There was no sign of sexual trauma on any of them. That's because you're not capable. Your impotence ties you in even more closely with what happened to these poor women. You must hate women. You must hate men who push prams, men who can build relationships with women and perform adequately in the bedroom. But women? You must hate them with a vengeance. Talk about salt in the wound.'

'Do you hate women?' chipped in Riley.

Rage was printed deep inside his eyes and his head rocked from side to side as if his brain was about to start dribbling out from both ears.

'Are you impotent, Mr McKee?'

Clay tapped the screen of her iPhone.

'What are you doing?' he shouted.

'DC Winters gave me her number. You think her name's Candy.'

'Who?'

'Erica. I'm calling her.'

'Stop! Stop it now!'

'It's ringing out. I'm going for a second opinion. It's gone to answer machine. Hello, Erica. My name's DCI Eve Clay. You personally have nothing to worry about. I want to ask you...'

'Hello?' A woman spoke.

'Is that Erica?' asked Clay, staring at McKee, twisting on his seat.

'I'd like to talk to you about Edgar McKee.'

'Susan tipped me off. I was expecting a call from you. Edgar McKee's a limp dick. A perv who can't perform. Do you want the details?'

'Lying cunt!' screamed McKee.

'Fuck off, McKee,' retaliated Erica. 'I've got a nickname for you. Tic Tac Dick.'

'Thanks for that, Erica.'

'I'm coming for you next!' shouted McKee.

She disconnected and Clay looked across the table at McKee, Harris and Watson either side of him.

'You just threatened Erica, Mr McKee. You said, *I'm coming for you next*. Next? Who did you go for before?'

McKee covered his face with his hands.

'Norma Maguire. Edgar McKee. Was there a third person involved in this barbarity?'

There were tears in Edgar McKee's eyes.

'I'll ask again. Was there a third person involved? Give me a name.'

'No, there wasn't!' He screamed and jumped out of his seat. 'No! No! No! How do I know?'

Clay lay her hand on Riley's sleeve. 'Did you hear that? We aren't looking for a third party. Straight from the horse's mouth. It's just McKee and Maguire we're dealing with. We're going to close the interview there.'

'You tricked me into saying that. I'm not involved in murdering women.'

'I think we've now got a rather substantial motive for why these murders have been happening. You're threatened by women. Every woman on the planet is a living reminder of your inadequacy as a man. So what do you do to that threat? Snuff it out. The only good bitch is a dead bitch. Who is Norma Maguire to you? Maybe it's time to tell me, Mr McKee. She's your partner. You've stepped over the last line together. You've murdered together. Don't insult me. Don't tell me you don't know her.'

124
1.20 pm

As he walked away from the medical records office of the Royal Liverpool Hospital, Winters called Clay.

'How'd it go, Clive?'

'According to the records, Edgar McKee's had no treatment in his life for any physical illnesses but was briefly under the shrink for his sexual dysfunction. He went for cognitive behavioural therapy but he wasn't a model patient. In the end the hospital discharged him because he wouldn't do the work. He thought that Viagra was going to be the cure-all but as we've learned from Susan Hurst, it was a no-show.'

'What about Norma Maguire?'

'Thirty years ago, she was admitted to A & E with spinal injuries. 19th August, 1991. She'd been to Crosby Beach with her father, Terry Maguire. She'd been swimming. On the way back to Liverpool, a truck heading towards Hornby Dock went into Maguire's Bentley. Driver fell asleep at the wheel. Her father walked away without a scratch but Norma was admitted to the Royal with spinal injuries. A week after she'd been admitted, Norma's mother, Catriona West, signed her daughter out and transferred her to a private clinic. There the trail goes cold.'

'It didn't say which clinic?'

'No. The initial medical examinations said she'd never walk again. I'm on my way back.'

'By which time, I'll have charged Norma Maguire with conspiracy to murder. We'll build it up from there. She's been preying on women on Pebbles On The Beach. It's time for her to face up to the misery she's been spreading.'

125

1.23 pm

As Clay made her way towards Interview Suite 1, the swing door leading into reception opened and DC Barney Cole came on to the corridor.

'I've come straight to see you, Eve,' said Cole as he handed her four receipts. 'They're from Norma Maguire's office.'

The door leading into the cells opened and Norma Maguire appeared on the corridor with Sergeant Harris and Ms Rice behind her. She stopped and stared at the group ahead of her with a look of sour premonition.

Clay scrutinised the receipts. Eurostar Gare du Nord. Paris to London St Pancras. Then Virgin, London Euston to Liverpool Lime Street, all on 31st July, 2021.

'Come here, Ms Maguire,' said Clay.

Slowly and reluctantly, Norma Maguire wheeled herself down the corridor. Hendricks made his way through the automatic doors from reception towards the interview suite, carrying Norma Maguire's open laptop.

Clay showed the receipts to Norma Maguire.

'What are these, Ms Maguire?'

'I don't know.'

'Does your credit card end in the digits 3245?'

She was quiet, looked as if someone was sticking pins in her scalp. She nodded.

'From your office. Did you travel from Gare du Nord to London St Pancras on Eurostar on Saturday, 31st July this year? Whoever travelled on these tickets left Gare du Nord at 9.15 am. Was it you? If it wasn't you, who was it?'

'It could have been anyone.'

'Did you travel from London Euston to Liverpool Lime Street on the same day?'

'I can't remember.'

Clay held out a stamped train ticket, Liverpool Lime Street to London Euston, on Friday, 6th August, 2021, and a ticket from London St Pancras to Gare du Nord, Paris, 6th August, 2021. She showed Norma the receipts, pointed at the last four digits of the credit card used to pay for the trains.

'You bought these tickets with your credit card. You paid for them and saved the receipts in your office on Allerton Road. Who did you fund to travel back to Liverpool from Europe and back to Europe from Liverpool on these two dates?' Norma Maguire looked at the ground. 'I'm asking you now because I've got quite a few questions to ask you once we're behind that door. About your laptop and what was found on it. Want to tell me who the tickets were for?' Silence. 'No?'

Clay turned to DS Cole.

'Go to the incident room and ask DS Stone to send Edgar McKee's picture to passport control at Gare du Nord, Paris. He's to ask them to look at who passed through the border on Saturday, 31st July, heading for London, and find a match for Edgar McKee. Ask them if they could also look at CCTV footage from the same day. Once that's sorted, go with DS Stone to Lime Street Station. Ask to see the CCTV footage of passengers disembarking from all incoming trains from London Euston on the same day, Saturday, 31st July.'

Hendricks opened the door of Interview Suite 1.

'Do you want to confirm that you purchased the travel tickets for Edgar McKee or are you going to make us show you the truth, Ms Maguire?'

She looked at her solicitor and said, 'Help me.'

'Help yourself, Ms Maguire,' said Ms Rice. 'I've told you several times. Tell the truth.'

126

1.26 pm

As he prepared to leave the incident room to look at the contents of Norma Maguire's office in Interview Suite 3, the landline telephone on DC Barney Cole's desk rang out. He didn't recognise the number on display as he picked up the receiver.

'DC Cole speaking, how can I help you?'

'It's Carolyn Wilkes from Maguire Holdings. I was asked to find out if Norma had any favourite places she visited and to let you know.'

'Fire away.'

'I rang around everyone and it was strange. We all thought we knew Norma so well, but when it came to it, what we knew about her didn't add up to very much.'

Cole resisted the urge to laugh at the bitterness of the truth that had just slipped blithely from Carolyn's mouth.

'We know she likes classical music and sometimes goes to the Philharmonic Hall to listen to concerts. She loves her house in Grassendale Park.'

That's been torn to shreds, thought Cole, *and Francesca Christie wasn't there.*

'The restaurants on Allerton Road where she takes us when we hit our targets. And then, when we thought that's about it, my colleague Carly Cross reminded us all of the summer of 2018 when it was really hot. One Saturday she told us we had to dress down for work on Sunday because of the heatwave. We all showed up in our shorts and T-shirts and there was Norma with hampers of food and coolboxes full of bottles of wine and beer. It was a big surprise. Norma took us to Crosby Beach. She'd hired a bus and a driver so we could all have a drink if we wanted. I sat behind her on the bus and I asked *what's this for, Norma?* It turned out it was a very special anniversary for her, but she wouldn't give anything else away. Just that she loved Crosby Beach and it's a place she comes to every so often to look across the water, see what floats off to nowhere, and watch the comings and goings.'

'She used that expression, *see what floats off to nowhere?*' checked Cole.

'Yes.'

'What was the date?'

Carolyn considered the question for a few moments.

'Sunday, 19th August, 2018.'

'What kind of a day did you have?' asked Cole, pulling up a map of Crosby Beach on his laptop and looking at the relationship between the Irish Sea, the beach and the network of roads leading down to the sand.

'Strange. One minute she was really happy, the next she was withdrawn. By half eleven most people were muttering that they wanted to go home, but they couldn't because they were on office hours and we had to stay until four o'clock, Sunday closing time. It was unpleasantly hot and the beach was crowded.

'She had a couple of glasses of wine and started saying how much she loved swimming in the sea. I thought to myself, maybe she likes Crosby Beach because that's where she used to go before her accident. Then she started going on about her father, how he drowned in the Irish Sea. He'd gone out alone in a motor boat and his body was washed up on the shore. She said it was suicide but he never left a note. The bizarre thing was, she smiled as she told the whole story about her father.'

'That's very helpful, Carolyn,' said Cole.

'It was well meaning of her, but altogether it was a horrible day. Oh, yeah. She asked Des, one of the lads, to push her down to the water's edge so that she could get a closer look at the Iron Men. It nearly killed him getting her wheelchair across the sand and back.'

'Did she say anything to Des?'

'No. She got a bit weepy. Des thought it was a combination of too much sun and too much wine. That really is all, DC Cole.'

'Thank you, Carolyn. That could be incredibly helpful.'

He placed the receiver down and attached a map of Crosby Beach and the surrounding area to the email he composed to the whole team.

Norma Maguire's favourite place. Where are we looking for Francesca Christie?

127

1.37 pm

'I've got to hand it to you, Ms Maguire. You certainly know how to manipulate lonely women. Your tag team strategy was little short of masterly. Danny Guest dumps Annie Boyd and she goes running into the arms of Richard Ezra. It's all on your laptop. Why did you delete all these messages?'

Norma Maguire said nothing.

Clay turned Norma Maguire's laptop around and showed her the brief and hurried dialogue between Sally Haydn and Geoff Campbell.

'You went from being cool and patient to being in an awfully big hurry. You just couldn't wait to get talking on the phone with Sally Haydn. Only when DS Riley did speak with you, it wasn't you. DS Riley spoke with Edgar McKee. Posing as Sally Haydn, she told him something like *I love roaring log fires, drinking wine and making pictures in the coals.*'

'I don't know what the policewoman said. I didn't take the call. Edgar…'

'Go on. Edgar?'

'If Edgar took the call, whoever Edgar is, how do I know what was said?'

'I don't think there was any *if* in your mind just then, Ms Maguire. You were going to say, Edgar took the call. Edgar who I know. Edgar who murders lonely women with me. Edgar who abducted the women.'

'His Sandra O'Day alibi has just crashed and burned,' said Hendricks. 'You paid for him to come back into the country on the day before Sandra was reported missing and to go back to Europe on the day after she was killed.'

'That's right, isn't it?' pressed Clay.

'Tell the truth, Ms Maguire,' urged her solicitor. 'The evidence against you is compelling, and I'm pretty sure there's more evidence rolling in on the next wave.'

'I admit I talked to the women on the internet but that was because I was lonely and bored.'

'You admit to all the evidence on your laptop?' said Clay.

'Yes.'

'If it was company you were after, genuine company, why didn't you go on Pebbles On The Beach as yourself?' asked Hendricks.

'Because I'm hideous! I'm hideous! Hideous! Hideous!' She exploded, tears cascading down her face, which was one shade down from purple.

Norma Maguire leaned over the left-hand arm of her wheelchair and retched, but all that came up was a ball of wind and a string of phlegm.

Clay took out her iPhone and dialled.

'Sergeant Harris, can you come to Interview Suite 1, please.'

'Sit up, Ms Maguire,' said Hendricks.

'Do you mean, the evidence makes you hideous?' asked Clay.

'No, that's not what I meant at all.'

Norma Maguire took a series of short, shallow breaths.

'The only mirror in your house is in the basement,' said Hendricks. 'Would you say you had particularly low self-esteem?'

She wiped her eyes with the backs of her hands and looked down at her lap.

'I have a hideous face. I can't bear the sight of myself.'

'Your face isn't hideous,' said Clay.

'My face is twisted. I have the eyes of a dog. My nose is pig-like. My hair is like black straw. My ears stick out at odd angles. Both sides of my face are at war with each other and it's reflected in my whole being. My skin is riddled with deep pockmarks from the years of chronic acne I had when I was a girl. I am hideous. I am vile. I am an abomination.'

Her breath came and went in shallow waves, and her chin was wet with saliva.

Norma Maguire looked up at Clay as if she was waiting for her to say something else. After many silent moments, Norma Maguire asked, 'What are you thinking?'

'I'm thinking about your mother's picture, when she played Jocasta at the Everyman.'

'And?'

'Was it when you were a child?' Clay waited. 'When were you told you were hideous?'

'She told me I was hideous and she was the most beautiful woman in the world.'

'Your mother said that to you? Was it said to you over and over, a form of brainwashing?'

'Mother said it every day, but she had no need to. I've got eyes. I told me.'

'Right now, I want to talk about your victims, Ms Maguire. Was Sandra O'Day hideous? How would you describe her?'

'Young and beautiful.'

'How would you describe Annie Boyd from the pictures she sent to you?'

'Young and beautiful.'

'How would you describe Amanda Winton from the pictures she sent to you?'

'Young and beautiful. Why are you torturing me?'

'Just answer the questions, Ms Maguire. How would you describe Fran? Day in, day out, in your office for little chats. How would you describe Fran?'

'Young and... very... very beautiful.'

'Is she young and very, very beautiful and alive? Answer my question,' said Clay. 'Or is she young and very, very beautiful and dead?'

'Young and very, very beautiful and I don't know.'

'Do you love Fran?'

'Yes.'

'Then show that love. Have mercy on her.'

'She... She had no mercy on me. Walking out on me like she did.'

'You only claim to love her. If you really loved Francesca Christie, you'd tell us where she is,' said Clay. 'Or is it too late?'

128

1.59 pm

In Interview Suite 3, Cole looked at the row of framed photographs from the wall of Norma Maguire's office, and drank in the musty smell from the scrapbooks found in her loft.

Cole picked up the portrait in which Richard Ezra sat at Norma Maguire's side, smiling the smile of the coerced, and a thought that appeared from nowhere turned his marrow to frozen sleet. He picked up the portrait in which Francesca Christie was at Norma Maguire's side and noticed that the glass wasn't as firmly in the frame as the picture in which Richard Ezra featured.

He carried them to the table, placed the portraits on either side of the scrapbooks, took out his iPhone and called Mr Doherty's direct number.

On the third ring, Mr Doherty picked up.

'Brian Doherty, how can I help you?'

'Mr Doherty, it's DC Cole, Trinity Road police station.'

Cole could feel the energy rising in Mr Doherty, could see him sitting up straight in his seat as he asked, 'Is it true? Norma Maguire's in police custody?'

'Yes, it's true...'

'Francesca...'

'I can't comment.'

'Jesus. I saw the van taking all those things away from Maguire Holdings.'

Cole looked at the same things around him and counted quietly to three.

'Thank you for sending Richard Ezra's address book back to me so promptly.' Cole heard the sound of a man almost choking on his own curiosity.

'Why are you calling me?'

'Richard Ezra. Could you find out for me the date he travelled to Florence and the date his wife was murdered?'

'I don't have to find out. I know those dates.'

Cole took a pad and pen from his pocket and scribbled down the information as Mr Doherty said, 'They travelled to Florence on 4th July, 2019. Sarah was murdered on 8th July, 2019. Richard returned to England on 14th July, 2019, and Sarah's body was repatriated on 21st July, 2019.' There was a brief pause. 'Are those dates suddenly relevant, DC Cole?'

'I'm grateful for the information, Mr Doherty, but please don't attach any significance or make a connection between this phone call and the fact that Norma Maguire is in police custody at the moment.'

'Is there anything else, DC Cole?'

'No.'

The line went dead; the petulance of a man who didn't like being told what to do or not to do.

As Cole wrote the dates out legibly, he turned to PC Marsh and WPC Wallace as they ploughed through the receipts and invoices. 'Are they all ordered chronologically?'

'Yes,' replied PC Marsh.

'So it wouldn't be too hard to go back and find these dates.'

He passed the dates from July 2019 to WPC Wallace.

'What are we looking for?' she asked.

'Receipts for travel to Florence from any airport in England on and around those dates.'

'No problem.'

He turned over the latest staff portrait and counted eight small metal clips on the inside of the frame that kept the hardboard back and photograph in place. Cole unpicked the clips and lifted away the frame.

He looked down at the back of the group portrait and saw a smaller rectangle face down against it. The smaller photograph was older than the big portrait and bore the yellow discolouration of time.

Both photographs had the same single word written on their backs.

Family.

The word on the large picture was in an adult hand and the word on the smaller photograph was a child's handwriting.

Cole took a pair of latex gloves from the box and snapped them on to his hands.

He took the edges of the old photograph between his index fingers and thumbs and turned it over.

It was a picture of a mother and her newborn baby.

129

2.08 pm

Clay stood at the back wall of Interview Suite 1, staring at Edgar McKee as he fidgeted on the seat next to his solicitor.

Hendricks faced him across the table and slid two pieces of paper from an A4 envelope. He placed the top sheet in front of McKee and asked, 'Do you know what that is, Mr McKee?'

'I suggest you look at it, Mr McKee,' said his solicitor.

McKee looked down.

'Answer the question. What is it?' Clay served from the back line.

'It's a DNA profile, a series of broad and narrow bands.'

'Do you know whose DNA it is?' asked Hendricks.

'No.'

'It's Annie Boyd's. It was taken from a hair follicle found on a brush in her bedroom. It was found after her body had been dumped on the mud at the bottom of the River Mersey. It was found after her parents had been told that their daughter's corpse had been discovered. Look at that picture very closely, look at the bands, look at the narrow bands, look at the broad bands, look at the spacing between them. It's a genetic fingerprint. It's what Annie Boyd was made of.'

Clay watched Hendricks sitting back and Edgar McKee staring down at Annie Boyd's DNA profile. He placed the second sheet next to the first one.

'Compare and contrast, Mr McKee. Not that there's anything to contrast.'

McKee's solicitor looked closely at the profiles and looked up at Hendricks. He whispered in McKee's ear and, after a few moments of deeply troubled thought, McKee nodded.

'Remember what we agreed, Mr McKee?'

Clay walked to the table and sat next to Hendricks.

'Mr McKee acknowledges that the DNA from the hair follicle found on his hairnet in the abattoir does belong to Annie Boyd. He believes he can explain how this came to be.

'Mr McKee would like an assurance that his co-operation will be taken into account when it comes to sentencing.'

'We can convey that to the judiciary,' said Clay. 'Look at me. Where is Francesca Christie?'

He looked as if there were a pair of wasps hovering close up to his face, their beating wings brushing against the pupils of his eyeballs.

'The last time I saw Francesca Christie she was chained up in the basement of Norma Maguire's house. If she's not there now, Norma must've moved her somewhere else because she was spooked. I haven't spoken to her since I've been in custody, so I don't fucking *know*.'

'When did you last speak to her?'

'Half an hour before I came in to Trinity Road police station.'

'Did you tell her you were coming here?'

'No.'

'Why not?'

'Because I was going to wash my hands of her, let her take the full rap for what she did. I was going to get away with my part. Wren was my way out of the shit. Along with the absolute lack of evidence pointing in my direction on the phone and laptop. All the evidence pointed her way. I was going to get away with it and drop Norma in the shit.'

'What was the content of your last conversation with Norma?'

'It was brief, very brief. I asked her why the money hadn't been paid into my bank account. She told me she wasn't happy with the quality of my work. Then she hung up on me.'

Clay took an envelope from her pocket and pulled a set of old photographs from it.

'Who is Norma to you?' asked Clay.

'She's fuck all to me.'

Clay turned the top photograph round.

'We found these from a search of Norma's office. They were behind framed portraits of her staff teams down the years. In the picture you're looking at, Norma's five years old or thereabouts. Who's the little boy in the picture with her?'

'No more pictures.'

'Who's the little boy in this picture?' She laid down a photograph of a little boy with red curly hair, on his own in a large garden. 'That looks like the back of Norma Maguire's house,' said Clay.

She placed a photograph of the same little boy, slightly older and with his hair cut short, smiling up at his mother.

'That's Catriona West,' said Clay. 'I recognise her from her publicity shots and stills from TV and films. Her stage name was Cecily Levin.'

She spread the photographs out. A boy's journey from a toddler to a young child.

'All of a sudden, when the boy turns five, the pictures stop. I want to know two things from you, Edgar. What was your part in these killings? And what happened when you were five?'

He pushed the pictures together and said, 'Take them away from me.'

Deeply buried pain surfaced in his eyes.

'If you want us to cut some slack with you, Edgar, you need to start talking now. Do you still want a reduced sentence? Or have you changed your mind in the last minute or so?'

He sat up and drew a huge breath.

'I swear I am not, not, not a murderer. Norma Maguire is my sister. I tracked her down when I tried to track down my mother. My sister has my inheritance. My sister is a murderer. Norma Maguire killed Sandra O'Day, Annie Boyd and Amanda Winton. Norma Maguire was going to kill Francesca Christie and Sally Haydn. I'll tell you everything straight but you've got to understand I'm not the killer, she is. After she killed them, strangled them... I...'

'Go on, Mr McKee.'

McKee looked into Clay's eyes.

'She paid me to skin them.'

'I don't think for one moment you did it just for money,' said Clay. 'Your relationship with women, it's bizarre. Why did you make yourself a party to your sister's crimes?'

After a deep silence, he muttered.

'I caught the word *living* and *dead*,' said Clay. 'Could you repeat what you've just said so that your meaning is completely clear.'

He turned his chair at an angle, spoke into the empty spaces in the room.

'I have no power over living women. The only power I have is over dead females. It's the only way I have of

A DATE WITH DEATH

asserting myself. When I was a child... I saw... things that have stayed with me. Now. And forever. In her bedroom, my mother made me watch her with men. Fucking her as she stared at her own reflection in the mirror. Every time I become aroused, I see those pictures and it makes me useless. I knew what it was like to skin cows. I wanted to know what it was like to skin a dead woman. It felt... it made me feel powerful.'

He turned his chair round and faced Clay.

'That's very interesting, Mr McKee. If you know enough to understand that she killed these women, then surely you must know why she did these terrible things?'

Edgar McKee looked at his solicitor, who poured a glass of water for him. As he drank down the water, his Adam's apple bulged and his hands shook.

'It goes back a long way. She was five, younger maybe. She made me watch her.'

'She made you watch her do what?'

'She found a cat in the back garden. It couldn't move. It'd broken its leg. Its leg was sticking out at a weird angle. She told me she was being kind and putting it out of its misery. She told me to watch the cat and not to move or else. She went to the kitchen. She came back. She had a carving knife in her hand.'

130

2.32 pm

Walking up the stairs to the incident room, Clay felt her iPhone ring out in her jacket pocket.

She saw MARGARET CHRISTIE on display as she connected and took a deep breath as she stopped on a turn in the staircase.

'Margaret?' Clay hung her name in mid-air.

'Norma Maguire, DCI Clay.'

'Yes?'

'She called to the house when it was established that Francesca had gone missing. When she arrived, my sister walked into the kitchen holding Francesca's favourite childhood toy. A doll called Kizzy. I got upset...' Francesca's mother took in a string of short breaths, the battling down of tears.

'Take your time, Margaret.'

Clay heard Francesca's aunt speaking in the background but couldn't make out what she was saying. A moment passed and then another, and then Clay felt the transfer of the conversation from hand to hand.

'DCI Clay, I'm Francesca's auntie. I placed the doll down on the kitchen table while Norma Maguire was in the room. I followed my sister out of the room because she was upset and told Norma Maguire to let herself out of the house. When we returned to the kitchen, we didn't realise it at first but we both had the same feeling that something was horribly wrong. Francesca's Kizzy doll was gone. The bitch stole Francesca's doll.'

'Are you one hundred per cent certain about this?' asked Clay.

'We're certain. Please ask Norma Maguire about it. Shame on her.'

Clay waited.

'Have you a picture of Francesca as a child with the doll?'

Francesca's aunt relayed the question to her sister.

'Yes,' replied Francesca's aunt.

'Send it to my iPhone, please,' said Clay. 'Thank you for calling. And I'm sorry I couldn't give you positive news.'

She called Riley.

'Gina, I'm going to send you a photograph of a doll. Please go to Norma Maguire's house and find that doll. It's called Kizzy.'

131

3.01 pm

Clay looked at Edgar McKee and was reminded of a rapidly deflating, man-sized, man-shaped balloon.

'Where were you when Sandra O'Day was abducted and killed?'

'I was in Holland.'

'No you weren't. You flew out to Holland but on 31st July you came back to Liverpool via Gare du Nord in Paris to King's Cross and London Euston. You went back in the opposite direction on Friday 6th August. You were in England between 31st July and 6th August.'

McKee's eyes shifted and met Clay's.

She pulled up the images she had made of the receipts on her iPhone and showed him four pictures.

'All found in Norma Maguire's office.'

'If the receipts were in her filing cabinet, it stands to reason that she was the one who made the journeys.'

'I've just had a call from security in Gare du Nord. They confirmed it. They processed your passport on 31st July.'

Edgar McKee looked at his solicitor and whispered in his ear for what felt like a long time.

'Mr McKee, repeat to DCI Clay what you've just said to me.'

In the turn of a moment, Edgar McKee looked like his final thread of self had been snapped into two jagged pieces.

'I didn't commit the murders. I have never committed murder in my life.'

'Are you referring to the murders of Sandra O'Day, Annie Boyd and Amanda Winton, Mr McKee?'

He nodded.

'If you didn't kill those women, who did?'

'Ask Norma Maguire about it.'

'You know Norma Maguire?'

He looked at the clock and muttered, 'Christ.'

'You know her? Yes or no? It's not a hard question.'

'Yes, I know her.'

Edgar McKee looked up at the clock and smiled the smile of a man with a trump card tucked neatly into his sleeve.

132

3.05 pm

The sea.

The edges of waves pushed on to the shore and into the middle reaches of Francesca Christie's dream. She was in the basement and The Ghoul stood looking at her, wearing Annie Boyd's face and scalp.

Francesca looked into The Ghoul's eyes lurking beneath Annie's skin and she saw the two dots of light that she'd seen reflected in her rear-view mirror as she'd driven at knifepoint down Riverside Drive. The dots exploded into a hailstorm of light, falling from pitch darkness behind which lurked the faces of people she saw every day and the interiors of vendors' houses she walked around, measuring, describing, writing up, conducting viewings, selling, beneath a surface of white light that made the images dance.

The sound of the waves turned into a shushing noise and she knew she was listening to a sonic memory from before her earliest conscious recall: her mother shushed her as she jigged her on her shoulder, lulling her into sleep when she was little more than a newborn baby.

Tears streamed down her face, tears of happiness at the deep stamp of love that she had known all her life.

'Shush,' said the waves. 'Shush,' said her mother.

She saw her mother's face as she placed her down in the cot, the night light picking out her features, her mother yet not her mother, her mother as a much younger woman, her mother as a version of herself.

'I love you, Francesca Christie.' The words that followed her from wakefulness into the deep darkness of infant sleep.

Snap.

Francesca Christie woke up and had no idea of whether it was day or night, evening or morning.

'My mum. My poor mother.'

She speculated at the levels of anxiety her mother had been living through in the time that she had been missing, and her feelings rocketed from sorrow to heights of rage.

Francesca held on to the deepest of breaths, didn't feel the cold, the hunger or the thirst, just the rage that filled her from her scalp to her toenails.

Hold on to the breath! Hold on to the rage! Hold on, hold on, hold on...

The waves came and she knew she was near a beach.

Der. Der. A train.

The land and the sea.

The air was salty.

The sea.

Shush.

133

3.15 pm

Sergeant Harris opened the door to Norma Maguire's cell and Clay entered.

'Ms Maguire?'

She didn't move or respond.

'Your time's running out,' said Clay, standing over her, staring down at her. 'I know you can hear me.'

Norma Maguire's arms hung over the sides of her wheelchair, her head was down and her eyes were shut. Clay sat on the bench close to her.

'I saw your gun and I realised you weren't who you claimed to be. Alarm bells went off in my head. I looked in your bag. I saw your warrant card, and I knew I was totally out of my depth. I panicked. I left you where you were.'

Norma Maguire opened her eyes as she lifted her head.

'Are you sorry for Francesca Christie? Are you sorry that you abducted her?'

'I have remorse. She could kill me with a sideways glance.'

'One thing at a time, Ms Maguire. Why did you steal Francesca's doll?'

In her wheelchair, she started to turn a circle.

'I wanted to be close to her.'

'Edgar's told us everything.'

Something horrible shifted from Norma Maguire's brain and it cast shadows across her eyes.

'*Shut up, Norma. Shut up your fat, ugly mouth,*' said Norma Maguire, in a mean theatrical voice. '*Shut up your fat, ugly face. You look and sound like your fucking bastard father.*'

'Were these your mother's words?'

'Yes. *Keep your ugly face out of my sight and stop polluting my beauty.*'

Norma Maguire's wheelchair tipped forward and she spilled out of it on to the cell floor.

Clay stooped and extended her hands towards her.

'Keep your hands off me.'

Norma Maguire crawled away from the chair into the corner of the room. On its side, the right wheel spun to a halt as Norma came to a dead end.

'You're moving your lower limbs, Ms Maguire,' said Clay.

From the waist up, Norma raised her body, supporting her weight with her hands against the cell walls, her face buried in the corner.

Clay walked a few paces towards her and said, 'Stand up!'

Sobbing, Norma lifted her left knee, placing the weight on the sole of her foot. She did the same on her right side and, in a handful of moments, pulled herself up with her hands against the wall.

She turned.

'Walk with me, Ms Maguire.'

She began walking in a tight circle, her hands between her armpits, her eyes shut, her face knotted.

'I'll tell you where Fran is. I'll tell you everything but just leave me alone.'

134

3.53 pm

Clay looked in her wing mirror as she drove from Regent Road on to Crosby Road South, saw Riley, Hendricks and Stone in the three cars directly behind her.

Pulling up at a red light, Clay looked over her shoulder at the back seat, saw Kizzy next to a folded dressing gown. She felt the weight of a set of keys in her pocket as she pressed play on her iPhone on a recording she had made of her last conversation with Norma Maguire.

'We found the clothes Francesca was last seen in on CCTV. They were in your wardrobe. Did you give her alternative clothing?'

'No.'

Norma Maguire started humming.

'Where is Francesca Christie? You still haven't told me.'

'Oxford Drive, Liverpool 22.'

'In a house on Oxford Drive?'

'Oxford Drive.'

'Give me a post code?'

'L22 1BX.'

'What number?'

'Not a number. Not a house.'

Crosby. Close to the beach. Clay recalled the moment of mental clarity back in Interview Suite 1. She took the keys from her pocket.

She pressed stop on the recording and looked ahead as she listened to directions from her satnav.

Clay opened the window to let in the cold and let out the mounting claustrophobia.

Birds swooped over the sand and the sea crashed into the shore as she turned on to Oxford Drive.

In the distance, Clay saw a white van parked outside a semi-detached house.

She accelerated.

135
4.11 pm

As Clay and Riley hurried towards the white van, Clay said, 'They've swapped the licence plate.'

'That's how they've dodged the ANPRs and CCTV cameras.'

'Francesca Christie? Francesca? Police.' Clay banged gently on the back doors of the van. 'My name's DCI Eve Clay. It's the police. Speak to me.'

The silence that followed grew more worrying with each passing moment.

'Francesca?' said Clay. 'I'm a policewoman, talk to me.'

'Hello?'

'You're perfectly safe, Francesca. We've got the people who've been holding you captive. They're in our custody and no longer have any power to harm you.'

'Where? Where am I?'

'You're in a white Ford Transit van on Oxford Drive in Crosby. Can I open the door?'

'Yes.'

Clay turned the lock and pulled back the right-hand door, took a deep breath and focused on Francesca, tied up and naked on the floor.

'The woman coming into the van right now is my colleague, Detective Sergeant Gina Riley.'

'Francesca?' said Riley, stepping up and into the back of the van. 'I'm going to untie your hands and feet. I have your dressing gown with me. Once you're untied I'm going to help you into the dressing gown. Do you think you're able to stand on your feet?'

'My legs feel dead. I feel dead from the waist down. I can feel my fingers and hands. I've got sensation in my arms.'

'You're cold, you've been tied up. The feeling will come back to your legs and feet.'

Clay watched Francesca blinking rapidly in response to the street lights flickering into life against the darkening sky and wondered if she'd seen any natural light at all during the time she'd been in captivity.

As Riley untied Francesca's feet and hands, Clay flashed torchlight into the confined space and took in the things in the back of the van. She felt her pulse quicken as she realised that the contents of Norma Maguire's basement were stored in the back of a van on a quiet side street near Crosby Beach.

Two filthy mattresses were propped up either side of the van and the smell drifting from them was fetid.

Clay saw a metal table and on it a range of surgical implements. Coldness passed through her as she faced the table where the tools used to scalp and skin the faces of the dead women were gathered. On a shelf beneath the tabletop, chains were piled up.

A washing line ran from the doors of the van to the back of the driver's cab. In the middle of the line was a sheet draped evenly over either side.

On the floor of the van, Riley helped Francesca to sit up and slipped her arms into the dressing gown. Francesca looked over her shoulder at the metal table.

'Who abducted me?'

'A man called Edgar McKee and his sister, Norma Maguire.'

'Norma Maguire?' She spoke her name as if all the reason on the planet had vanished in an instant. 'Where are they?' asked Francesca.

'McKee and Maguire are in the cells in Trinity Road police station. Do you know Edgar McKee?'

'No,' said Francesca, looking deeply into the street light that broke up the mounting darkness.

Clay stepped up and into the back of the van.

'I've got something for you, something that Norma Maguire stole from you.'

'What did she steal from me?'

'Kizzy.'

'Kizzy? She went into my house and stole my doll? Why was I so surprised when you told me that Norma was involved in all this madness?'

Clay handed the rag doll to Francesca and she pressed her face against Kizzy's body.

'Take your time, Francesca,' said Riley. 'Wait for the feeling to come back into your limbs.'

Francesca rubbed her thighs with the palms of her hands.

'I can feel pins and needles in my feet,' she said.

Clay's torch bounced from the metal table for a split second.

'Are you thinking what I'm thinking, Eve?'

'Yes,' said Clay, quietly.

Wind screamed from the Irish Sea and, as the van rocked under its force, there was a noise in the confined space, metal against metal, as the surgical tools clattered on the table.

Riley stood up and nodded at the cover hanging over the washing line.

'I want some fresh air,' said Francesca.

Clay and Riley positioned themselves either side of Francesca and moved her to the open door at the back of the van.

'Drop your legs, Francesca. Give your circulation a boost.'

Francesca's feet touched the tarmac.

Clay moved back into the van, lifted the cloth that hung on the washing line and inspected the eyeless faces and scalps of the dead women. She felt as if she'd been hit in the core by an iron fist as, one by one, images of their scalped and faceless corpses prepared to haunt her.

A cocktail of formaldehyde, glutaraldehyde and phenol rose from the soft skins under Clay's nose and she worked out that Maguire and McKee had used the chemicals to preserve and soften the stolen flesh of their victims.

Inside her head, she counted, *one, two, three*, and the names Sandra O'Day, Annie Boyd and Amanda Winton screamed through her mind.

'Are you looking at the masks, DCI Clay?' asked Francesca.

'Yes.'

'The Ghoul used to come down to see me wearing the masks. The Ghoul preferred Annie Boyd over the other two. I recognised Annie from her picture in the paper. The light wasn't great in the basement but I'm thinking about the shape of The Ghoul, from the neck down. I thought it was a man but I was wrong. The Ghoul was Norma Maguire.'

'Francesca, I'm dialling your mother on my iPhone. Talk to her.'

Clay handed her iPhone to Francesca.

'It's ringing out, Francesca.'

'Mum, it's me. I'm OK. DCI Clay and DS Riley have rescued me.'

Clay heard Margaret Christie cry out in joy.

Margaret spoke and Francesca replied, 'I've got some bumps and bruises but I'm OK. I'm OK! Don't worry...'

Clay lifted the cover off the washing line, hung it near the faces and scalps, and took pictures on her iPhone.

'Mum, I'll be home as soon as I can.'

She recognised the three women from photographs she had seen and her mind went spinning into Annie Boyd's home and imagined the agony her parents were living through.

'And, Mum, I love you. And I'm so, so sorry for what I've put you through. I'm OK, I swear. See you soon. Love you too.'

She handed the iPhone back to Clay.

'Margaret,' said Clay, but the line was dead.

'She was going to kill me, wasn't she?'

'Yes.'

'And scalp me?'

'Yes.'

'The feeling's coming back into my legs,' said Francesca.

The sea lapped against the shore and an ambulance turned the corner on to Oxford Drive.

'Don't move, Francesca,' said Clay. 'The paramedics are here.'

Francesca turned her head.

'Don't look back, Francesca!'

She turned her head, eyed the things in the back of the van, half-lit by the sodium street lights.

'Look away, Francesca!'

She looked away and took a deep breath.

Francesca Christie's scream cut through the darkness of advancing night.

136

6.30 pm

In Interview Suite 1, Clay and Hendricks faced Norma Maguire. She looked at each of them in turn.

'Your brother has made a serious allegation against you, Ms Maguire,' said Clay. 'Edgar told me that you drove your mother to visit her friend on Mather Avenue on the night she died. Is that true?'

'Yes.'

'When you were on Mather Avenue that night, did you pretend that the car had broken down and ask your mother to check if the headlights were working?'

She nodded.

'As she stood in the road, did you reverse backwards suddenly and drive at her at speed?'

'Yes.'

'Did you ever have any feelings of remorse because you'd murdered your mother?'

'No. I hated her.'

Clay looked at Norma Maguire and said nothing, sustaining the silence in the room.

'What is it?' asked Norma Maguire.

'Did your mother write Edgar out of her will?'

'Yes.'

'Why did she do that, Norma?'

'I don't know.'

'You were the executor of your mother's will. In the last years of her life she had dementia. Edgar told us. His mother didn't write him out of that will. You did. You changed the will so that everything went to you. You got your demented mother to sign that amended will so that you got the lot. What do you say to that? Answer the question about your mother's will,' insisted Clay.

Silence.

'Who was the sole beneficiary of your mother's will?'

'I was.'

'Look at me, Ms Maguire. I'd like to go a little further down the timeline with you.'

Clay placed a set of travel receipts on the table and spread them out.

'Read them back to me, Ms Maguire. Where to, where exactly, and when? Can I translate your silence into an admission of guilt?'

'No, you can't.'

'Liverpool John Lennon Airport to Pisa Airport.' Clay pushed the receipt closer to Norma Maguire. 'Then, by train from Pisa to Florence. Date. 4th July, 2019. Shall I outline the date and destination of the return journey? OK, it was the first train out of Florence to Pisa on the morning of 9th July and then a flight back to Liverpool from Pisa, the day after Sarah Ezra was stabbed to death in the toilet of a pizzeria near The Fountain Of Neptune. Why did you kill Sarah Ezra? It was Richard who walked out on you.'

'Revenge. He loved her. I wanted him to suffer,' said Norma Maguire.

'Let's move further down that timeline. This year. This month and the summer beforehand. According to Edgar, and I'd have to say I agree with him one hundred per cent, you had a lot of financial clout and you used that power over him. Did he groom your victims over the phone?'

'Yes.'

'Did he abduct them for you?'

'Yes.'

'And when you'd strangled them, did Edgar skin their faces and scalp them for you?'

She held up a hand, showed the flat of it to Clay. 'Stop it.'

'Did he treat their skins with formaldehyde, glutaraldehyde and phenol to preserve them and make their skins ultra-soft to the touch, lifelike? £10,000 a time. You paid him for grooming the women over the phone, the women he went on to scalp. We're checking details of his bank account right now, all those transfers of money from your account to his. We've got all the travel receipts when you paid for him to come back from Holland. True or false?'

'True.'

'But you didn't want him to put his hands on Francesca Christie, did you? You didn't want anyone else touching her, only you. Have you got anything to say about Francesca Christie? Because you can walk. You could abduct her. You've lived as an elective cripple for years.'

Norma Maguire's hairline became a physical seam where beads of sweat started pouring down her forehead.

'When you were admitted to the Royal all those years ago with spinal injuries, the first doctors to see you didn't call it right. Edgar told us that your mother threw money at the problem and sent you to America for treatment and that it worked. You came back to England but refused to walk, refused to get out of your wheelchair in public. Why?'

'I don't remember.'

'Did you love the attention you got when you were in a wheelchair?'

'I – I don't remember.'

'Did you want people to feel sorry for you?'

'No.'

'Or was it just another layer of disguise?'

'No. One moment I could walk. One moment I couldn't walk. Life has fine lines.'

Norma Maguire looked up at Clay and she was reminded of a crab peering from the shadows of its shell.

'There's a psychiatrist coming to see you. To make an initial assessment of your mental state. The psychiatrist you see tonight will be the first of many to talk to you in the months leading up to your trial.'

'I'm not mad.'

'I know you're not mad. You're a cold, calculating killer who knew exactly what was going on and exactly what you were doing. You were envious of those young women and took their skins because you couldn't bear their beauty in the middle of your view of your own ugliness.

'You paraded around in their skins so you could drive your hostages into mental collapse. Another layer of disguise. You're evil. You're sadistic. But you're not mad, and that's the message I'll hammer home to every shrink who asks me.'

'Say something?' said Norma Maguire to her solicitor.

'Continue being as open and honest as you can be.'

The silence was as deep as it was dark.

'Can you hear that?' asked Norma Maguire.

'The wind?' asked Clay.

'The water beneath the wind. The waters where the women went. The lost and lonely women with no faces. The water women. And, so, off she floats to nowhere.'

Norma Maguire looked at Clay and there was a new air about her: she looked like she had left a precious heirloom in a public bathroom and had just returned to find it gone.

'What are you thinking, Norma?' asked Clay.

'I see it now. I see it all,' said Norma Maguire, fixing her gaze on Clay. 'I am lost, aren't I?'

'You've got a lot to face and much to go through in the next year. You need to take full responsibility for your part in the terrible crimes you've committed. This involves telling the truth.'

'Where do you want me to start?'

'Start at the beginning and don't leave out anything,' said Clay.

Norma Maguire nodded and whispered, 'The truth, the brutal, ugly truth?'

'Yes,' said Clay.

'Look at me!'

Clay looked at her and was convinced of one thing: if Death had a face, it would certainly look like the woman facing her.

'My name is Norma Maguire and I am a killer.' She smiled at Clay. 'I have felt the urge to kill since I was three years old.'

A nostalgic smile formed on her face.

'It was a compulsion I never tried to resist. Three years old, yes. What a happy summer's day it was when I found a sparrow with a broken wing in my mother's back garden.'

The rain picked up a gear and hammered the building.

'I remember. I folded it in my little hands. I could see its eyes peeping between my fingers. I could feel its heart beating against the palms of my hands. I went looking for a stone.'

137
8.29 pm

'I liked the way your hair used to be,' said Philip. 'Why did you change it to blonde?'

Over her son's shoulder, Eve Clay caught sight of herself in the tall mirror in the hallway of her home. She looked at the blonde hair that hung down from the woollen hat she wore, concealing her bandages from her son.

'Do you remember when you started putting gel on your hair, Philip? You were curious to see what you'd look like. It was a bit of that...' She hugged him a little bit tighter. 'But guess what? Don't tell anyone. I did it to trick a baddie.'

'Did it work?'

'It helped, I think.'

Eve Clay realised that the last time she'd seen her son, she'd had her own natural colour, brunette.

Philip stepped out of the embrace and looked closely at his mother's face and hair.

'It is you. But it isn't you, Mum.'

'Don't worry, Philip. When you wake up in the morning, I'll have dyed it back to my own colour and be one hundred per cent me.'

The rattle of glasses came their way from the kitchen.

'What's going on?' asked Eve Clay.

Philip smiled at her.

'A bit of a late night, Mum.'

Philip wandered into the front room, chuckling.

'Thomas?' she asked, as her husband walked into the hall carrying a tray with a bottle of red wine, two glasses and a can of Vimto.

'Welcome home, Eve,' said Thomas.

'You've read my mind. Again!'

Eve Clay sat on the end of the sofa and watched Philip crouch by the gas fire.

'What are you doing?' she asked.

He stuck his hand into the mechanism at the base of the fire. 'Putting the fire on.'

She looked at her husband as he poured wine into two glasses and dropped a straw into the can of Vimto.

Philip turned his hand and after a series of clicks, flames shot up from the artificial coals.

'How long's this been going on for?' asked Eve.

Philip looked at his father.

'A week ago, Dad?'

'Yeah, about then,' replied Thomas.

'You'll be telling me you're doing online banking next!'

'Don't be silly, Mum. I haven't got a bank account. Yet. Unless you want to open one for me?'

Philip sat on the sofa in the space between his parents and Eve took his hand.

'So, how was your day, Mum?'

A thousand pictures flashed through her in a second as she looked into the flames.

'Well… it most certainly was a day.'

She dismissed most of the images that had invaded her head and seized on the picture of Margaret Christie's face when she saw her daughter in Trinity Road police station.

Eve raised a glass of wine and said, 'Cheers.'

She clinked against Philip's can of Vimto and her husband's glass.

Tiredness came over her in a sudden wave. She sipped her wine, placed it down on the tray and looked at her son. She wrapped her arms around him and was glad to be alive.

In her mind, Eve Clay stepped back and grabbed the moment with all her being. She looked at her husband and son and made an indelible memory to store in her heart against the harsh things that lay around the next crooked corner.

She felt the weight of Philip as he sat on her lap, his arms wrapped around her neck, and wished that the world would be kind to him.

Thomas shifted along the sofa and sealed the three of them in a single embrace.

'Whatever happens next,' said Eve, 'we've already won, boys. We've won big time.'

Acknowledgements

I'd like to thank Peter, Rosie and Jessica Buckman, Laura Palmer and all at Head of Zeus, Steve Le Comber, Martin McKenns, Arlene Cresswell, Frank & Ben Rooney, Linda & Eleanor Roberts, Paul Goetzee, John Gunning, Barbara Heath and Alexander Naden.

About the Author

MARK ROBERTS was born and raised in Liverpool, and was educated at St Francis Xavier's College and Liverpool Hope University. He was a teacher for twenty years and for the past seventeen years has worked with children with severe learning difficulties. He is the author of *What She Saw*, which was longlisted for a CWA Gold Dagger.